T0283299

BY REGINA PORTER

The Rich People Have Gone Away

The Travelers

THE RICH PEOPLE

HAVE GONE AWAY

THE RICH PEOPLE HAVE GONE AWAY

A Novel

REGINA PORTER

HOGARTH

LONDON / NEW YORK

Published in the United States by Hogarth, an imprint of Random House, a division of Penguin Random House LLC, New York.

HOGARTH is a trademark of the Random House Group Limited, and the H colophon is a trademark of Penguin Random House LLC.

Photography credits can be found on page 341.

LIBRARY OF CONGRESS CATALOGING-IN-PUBLICATION DATA
Names: Porter, Regina, author.
Title: The rich people have gone away : a novel / By Regina Porter.
Description: First Edition. | London; New York : Hogarth, 2024.
Identifiers: LCCN 2023045536 (print) | LCCN 2023045537 (ebook) |
ISBN 9780593241868 (hardback) | ISBN 9780593241875 (ebook)
Subjects: LCSH: COVID-19 (Disease)—Fiction. |
Missing persons—Fiction. | New York (N.Y.)—Fiction. |
LCGFT: Detective and mystery fiction. | Novels.
Classification: LCC PS3616.O7855 R53 2024 (print) |
LCC PS3616.O7855 (ebook) | DDC 813/.6—dc23/eng/20231005
LC record available at https://lccn.loc.gov/2023045536
LC ebook record available at https://lccn.loc.gov/2023045537

Printed in the United States of America on acid-free paper

randomhousebooks.com

2 4 6 8 9 7 5 3 1

First Edition

Book design by Fritz Metsch

For my grandmother,
Dorothy Booker

PART ONE

Door: barrier of wood, stone, metal, glass, paper, leaves, hides, or a combination of materials, installed to swing, fold, slide, or roll in order to close an opening to a room or building. Early doors, used throughout Mesopotamia and the ancient world, were merely hides or textiles. Doors of rigid, permanent materials appeared simultaneously with monumental architecture. Doors for important chambers were often made of stone or bronze.

—ENCYCLOPAEDIA BRITANNICA

UNION SQUARE RAMBLE

Come daisy chain round Gandhi's statue

Come cheeses, raw, pasteurized, cow, sheep, goat

Come bread, whole wheat, challah, pumpernickel, rye, sourdough

Come sausage sweet hot turkey with/without casings

Come plain sugar apple cider donuts, salted/unsalted pretzels

Come scallops, mussels, squid, oysters, clams

Black sea bass, swordfish, cod, hake, fluke, mackerel, tuna, sushi
  grade

Come rosemary, thyme, sage, oregano, basil, cilantro, parsley,
  tarragon, dill, mint

Beefsteak tomatoes, heirloom, plum, cherry, green, tomatillos

Come field garden sugar snaps snow peas

Cranberry, string, lima, fava, and broad beans too

Stalks of celery, Brussels sprouts, Jerusalem artichokes, turnips,
  radishes, kohlrabi

Arugula, spinach, lettuces, mesclun, green leaf, Boston, romaine

Come farm fresh eggs, chick, duck, ostrich

Yogurt and milk in recycled glass bottles

Come catnip, fresh lavender, eucalyptus, wool, yarn

Finger Lakes wine, honey, ale, maple syrup. Cold apple cider/
  grape juice poured from a tin spigot

Come pears, apples, raspberries, blueberries, blackberries,
    strawberries, peaches, figs, and plums

Thick slabs of uncured smoked bacon, bison, free-range chickens,
    lamb chops, pork loin, ground beef patties, chuck roast,
    kielbasa, rib eye steak

Come onions, yellow, Spanish, white and pearl, fennel, garlic
    snapes, leeks

Broccolini and broccoli spears

Come okra, eggplant, zucchini, pumpkin, butternut squash

Come mushrooms, shiitake, oyster, cremini, chestnut, lion's mane

Sweet potatoes, yams, russet, fingerlings, Yukon Gold, Idaho

Come collards, turnips, mustard greens, Swiss chard, kale, Russian
    curly dinosaur

Mondays, Wednesdays, Fridays, Saturdays

Come chef with early morning recipes swirling in her head

Union Square jaunt before the afternoon crowd appears

Sideswiping puddles and eyeing golden beets on scale

A grocery list completed; tonight's menu unveiled

Mizu to Yama Restaurant Is Temporarily Closed for Business
Ruby Black and Katsumi Fujihara, Chef and Executive Chef,
March 16, 2020

DAILY CLEANSE

MR. HARPER takes sex in doorways. Halts new lovers at the threshold of his front door. Left hand on shoulder. Right hand on hip. He searches the ninth-floor hallway for furtive eyes before pressing the whole of himself in the tender nook of his lover's ass.

"Here," he says. There is gravel in Mr. Harper's voice. He understands the implications of force. Social distancing was in place before the March lockdown, gloves and masks. He waits for a greeting, a slight rearing back, a double-cheeked sway, the perfect balance of ass to cock and cock to ass. He will undo his pants in a matter of seconds and let left hand descend, down, down, down the slender side of his lover's body, bringing disorder and chaos. He has done this deed a thousand times where he now stands: gripping the doorknob to his front door. If you asked him, he would tell you with gravelly certainty that his profession as an aesthetic advisor helps. Geometric shapes on beveled glass door, volute, chrome handles, ornate gold bell. Fixtures that have stood the test of time. Inanimate objects are immune to pandemics and viruses, though the wrong touch, in this environment, could make a well man sick. He knows the right cleansing agents to refinish, to buff, and to restore. *Tournez à gauche*—left is for opening doors. *Tournez à droite*—right is for closing them.

If a woman is wearing pants, he waits for her to unzip while he unbuckles. "Pants are so damn cumbersome," he says, mouth working the curving nape of her neck or the armpit of a shirt he's just pulled off. And if she wears a skirt or a dress—God's gifts, he thinks, for the ease with which they allow him to peel away under-wear, cotton, spandex, polyester, or silk. Perhaps it's his midwestern upbringing, but Mr. Harper is always a little disappointed when he finds women riding bare beneath their clothes. Exposed private parts make the public part of sex less private. To rip, to tear. He's never worn nor does he sniff/collect underwear as souvenirs. But he has annihilated a fair share. Hers. His. And theirs. Why grapple with social constructs or the contradictions within himself? Every-thing is an opening onto something else.

But the stores are closed.

And the city's shut, shut, shutting down.

Hard to believe—rock bottom, rock-bottom hard—that not even a month ago he helped a real estate agent sell three houses in one week. Walked into a 1900s Victorian in Ditmas Park where West Indian families, intent on suburbia and white picket fences, will never be able to return upon sale. *May Florida and Long Is-land keep them*, he thought, turning to Simon Pratt, the real estate broker, and the eager young buyers.

"Let me tell you a thing or two about doorways. The Egyptians built them as portals to the afterlife, a means of transcendence, their version of somewhere over the rainbow via waterways . . ."

What he wanted to say was, *The trick to sex in doorways is to see if you can begin and complete the act—slam bodies together tight as clams. The sex is for you, never for intruder, voyeur, happenstance, other, her, him, them, though the anticipation comes with its own frills, thrills, and expletives. When the sex plays right, your throat con-vulses, oh, yes it does, and the air threatens to leave your body. When the sex plays right, you stare at the ones who beg for a change of scenery—wanting to finish fucking on the Persian carpet or the hard-wood floor or the sofa, bed, desk. Whinny whoop. Whinny whoop whoop. "Next time, darling . . ." you tell them. But that honor is saved for women or men you want to see again. There is sex and there is meaning.*

The hidden door you point out to the eager young couple—right behind the fireplace—lands the sale. As soon as they leave—calling their real estate attorney on the way home—you fuck Simon Pratt to celebrate. The outing is better than cognac or Veuve Clicquot. But Simon's experience rates altogether different. He confesses later to his husband, Felix Ramirez, with whom he shares an open marriage and hides nothing, that fucking you made him grateful he isn't straight.

"We have our anger," Simon said. "But straight anger's a human rake."

Now, if you live in the wrong neighborhood or the right neighborhood—Mr. Harper lives in Park Slope—toilet tissue is in short supply. He goes to Glory Groceries on Seventh Avenue on the way home from work and you would think a colony of ants had usurped humanity. The shelves are depleted and the manager—what is he? Maybe he's Hispanic? Latino?—the manager has worked in Glory Groceries over a decade and Mr. Harper, who has shopped in the store for just as long, has never thought to ask his name. The manager is frazzled and lugs two twenty-pound bags of Canilla rice on his back. Every aisle in the store—one through eight—is jam-packed with customers. The rice, like the beans and the cooking oil, jars of tomato sauce, pasta, all things canned, are going, going, gone.

The manager assaults Mr. Harper with unexpected civility. "How's your wife?"

Mr. Harper smiles and says, "She's coming along. We're pregnant."

"Congratulations," the manager says. He waves his ungloved hand. "Never thought I'd see this."

This is the early days, the eve of the lockdown. Mr. Harper doesn't know how to respond or what to say. "Welcome to the zombie apocalypse." Is it his imagination or when he blurts out "zombie apocalypse," does the manager step away from him? Do the anxiety-ridden shoppers quicken their pace?

The manager says, "My wife thinks the world is ending. I don't know. Maybe the world *is* ending."

There are too many people in the store. There are too many people on the planet. There are too many people invading his space and being frantic. Mr. Harper prefers his frantic coital, carnal, strings undone but not attached. Surrender. Hands up. It is Mr. Harper's turn to back away. He'll find a better day, another store. "Mother Nature's acting out. Population overload."

A senior citizen, wire glasses, gray beard, pushing a buggy piled sky-high with Gorton's Fish Sticks, Stouffer's family-sized lasagna, Amy's Pizza, and Green Giant frozen vegetables, does a U-turn.

"You hush your mouth. People said that shit during the AIDS epidemic. Hotspot. New York City. Hotspot. Pandemic, fucking politicians. Where's the lard? So stupid."

He walks away, leaning on his buggy like it's a walking cane, black-and-white shirt a moving chessboard.

Mr. Harper retreats through the store's double glass doors.

Theodore Harper brought the art deco door with him when he closed on his Park Slope apartment. He had scoured antique stores around the city in search of the perfect door. The one that would set the entrance to his home above the rest. That was over twelve years ago. And that shopping spree, that splurge, marked a shift to a successful career as an aesthetic advisor after selling furniture to rich people at ABC Carpet & Home for close to a decade. He never shares with lovers that his co-op was once rent stabilized—a third of the renters second- and third-generation African American and Puerto Rican families. Or that his neighborhood was considered part of Prospect Heights before the real estate agents rechristened it the North Slope, creating an imaginary zoning line that synced with his new career. From the South Slope to Fort Greene to Bedford-Stuyvesant to Manhattan and Williamsburg, real estate agents now came equipped with aesthetic experts like himself.

Most of them, in his opinion, shams. Mr. Harper made peace years ago with his midwestern architecture degree and background. Frank Lloyd Wright country, he barks/smiles whenever there's the need to put down East Coast comeuppance.

Possibility.

Probability.

Personality.

He wears a mask and plastic gloves when he leaves the apartment now or ventures down to the lobby to retrieve his mail or pick up takeout. Only residents are permitted to enter their co-op building. The board's decision—Mr. Harper is on the board—resulted in half the residents' fleeing Park Slope for country homes. Other residents have hunkered down—he and Darla among them—in their apartments. A handful of fledgling couples consisting of girlfriends, boyfriends, and others are betting that love will endure the quarantine.

In the lobby, a subletter—*must be a subletter*—holds the elevator, waiting for Mr. Harper to join him. Mr. Harper does not recognize the young man. Only three families of color reside in his building. The skinny African American teenager seems dwarfed by an oversized Cardi B T-shirt with "Diamond District in the Jag" splayed across Cardi B's authentically fake breasts. The teenager wears a red bandanna over a disposable mask. Mr. Harper is certain he is neither resident nor resident's kid, but the teenager pushes the close button before Mr. Harper can confront him.

"Fuck it," the teenager says as the door closes. "Be that way then."

Hell nor high water could get Mr. Harper on an elevator right now. He walks up the nine flights of stairs to survive. He sings Darla's favorite song. Coldplay's "The Scientist."

He does not like Coldplay, but Darla plays the song at night on her bassoon. She paces up and down the barren hallway. No need to worry about disturbing their neighbors. One plus one equals two. He and Darla are all the ninth floor's got, not including baby boy or girl on the way. Mr. Harper inserts the key into the front door and then removes his gloves. Retrospection is a slippery thing. And plastic irritates his skin. Is it retrospection or the plastic gloves that irks him?

"Gloves give you a false sense of security," Darla likes to say.

She uses hand sanitizer in between each mask she makes for friends and family. She has made over twenty from leftover cotton and flannel fabric in her arts and crafts kit following a tutorial on YouTube.

Like many Americans, Theo and Darla share daily rituals. Theo is an early riser, so in the morning when he wakes up and before he makes coffee, he moves about the apartment wiping down everything: tabletops and counters and knobs and the handle to the refrigerator, the economy washing machine and dryer, the dishwasher, faucets, toilet. Darla takes over the task in the afternoon—after lunch. She is not nearly as thorough as Theo and prefers eco-friendly cleansers with lemon, baking soda, vinegar, and lavender. He does not trust the eco-friendly cleansers to get the job done. When Theo takes over the daily cleanse in the evening (after Darla has gone to bed), he unleashes the industrial-strength cleansers developed in U.S. factories during the Second World War. His wife constructs her day, as much as humanly possible, with menial tasks followed by hours experimenting with original digital compositions that seldom hold up to her personal standards. Composing music was never Darla's strongpoint. But with so much spare time on her hands, she's determined that her ebb succumb to her flow.

When Darla sleeps, Theo has the apartment to himself and rewinds his bachelor years with insufficient sadness. Chance encounters are scarce during a pandemic. No one wants to get it, catch it, give it, chance it. On the news, the governor and mayor say there are not enough ventilators. Theo has never had to think about being sick. He has never had to think about ventilators. He and Darla are in optimal health. They are not wealthy, but they have wealth.

Theo does not understand how there cannot be enough ventilators. The five W's drop off the shelf: who what why when where. And how? The lack lacks sense. Sometimes he sits on their private balcony and stares down at Prospect Park. The Soldiers' and Sailors' Memorial Arch at Grand Army Plaza. The main branch of the Brooklyn Public Library. The entrance to the park with its sprinkling of people. Everything looks almost the same, almost normal, but then he remembers the masks. The world has changed in more than air.

Darla's mother, a retired dermatologist living in Paris with her boyfriend Pierre, calls on Sunday morning for a breakfast Zoom.

Darla is a professional musician. She plays the bassoon. A classical musician's career is feast or famine. Darla lucked into a two-year gig playing in the orchestra of a cheesy Broadway musical. The musical was running when the virus hit the city, forcing the Great White Way to lower its curtains.

"Mom, look at my hands." Darla's hands are covered with puckered dry spots around the cuticles and between the fingers.

"Cut back on the hand soap and sanitizers," Maureen says. "Everyone's going overboard. We need some bad bacteria in our bodies." Maureen is blond and pretty. A youthful sixty-four. Darla is blond and pretty and a youthful thirty-two. Maureen peers into the screen. Pierre Bernard sits in a chair beside her.

"Theo," Maureen says, "let me see your hands."

"My hands are fine."

Darla tries to get Theo to hold up his hands. "No they're not. Your hands are more irritated than mine."

Theo peers into the screen too. "I absolutely refuse to hold up my hands. Is this really how you want to spend your precious Zoom time?"

Maureen sighs. She does not like the way Theo is speaking to her daughter. But she is on the other side of the Atlantic. "You two look awful. Why don't you go up to the summer cottage until the pandemic blows over?"

"Blows over?" Theodore frowns. He does not appreciate his mother-in-law's suggesting they flee to the country. He likes the city. How could he not love a city with so many entrances and exits, places to be seen or hidden, remembered or forgotten? Every evening he pours a glass of bourbon and grabs a skillet for the seven P.M. clanging of pots and pans.

"Maureen," he says, "what's the death rate in Paris?"

"High enough for me not to want to know."

Pierre waves a naughty finger at Theodore. "Paris is a red zone."

Theodore waves a naughty finger at the Zoom camera. "New York is a hotspot."

Maureen shrugs and says, "You sound like the president. Why so divisive?"

"Here, the rich people—like you—have gone away."

"Don't worry. We always come back," Maureen says. "And Theodore, you're not exactly poor. The last time I checked, your apartment was close to two million dollars."

Theodore stands up. "Thirty percent."

"What's wrong with him?" Darla's mother asks when Theodore disengages from Zoom.

"I don't know," Darla admits.

"Well, he certainly was rude."

Darla adds, "We're together all the time. Twenty-four seven."

"Which is why I think you two should get away. You need breathing room and fresh air when you're pregnant."

In the Zoom background, Theodore pours himself a noon cocktail. Holidays and vacations and pandemics warrant nourishment. The liquor stores are categorized as essential businesses. Standing in line—six feet apart in a liquor store on Seventh Avenue—a hipster and her boyfriend were stuffing pints of gin and bitters and vodka in a recyclable NPR bag. Theo had two bottles of wine: a French Sancerre and an Italian ripasso. The hipsters looked at him and grinned, then said, "Hey, you gotta keep your priorities straight. Some people need toilet paper. Others require gin and cigarettes."

Later Darla tells Theo, "Zoom reminds me my mom's not here."

Theo says, "Well, sweetie, that's because she isn't."

"I wish she was here. She's not even married to Pierre."

"You just don't like the idea of a stepfather."

"No, I just always thought she'd be closer to home when I had my first baby."

"*Your* first baby?"

"You know what I mean . . . our baby—with Mom around to dote and annoy us. Share advice we didn't ask for. Babysit on our first new parents' date."

"Maybe you should write her a letter. Say the things you've always wanted to say, but don't mail it. Say those things in snippets next time we talk to them. So the conversation won't seem so strained."

"Theo," Darla sunbeams. "That's an excellent idea."

Theo is always ready with some clever statement to ease the crow's feet that have begun to creep up on Darla's delicate pinched face. Darla who is three months pregnant. Darla who sleeps with a body-length pillow at night. Darla who tosses and turns and just when the two of them at last surrender to sleep, even the baby inside her dozing happily, shoots up in search of the passing siren. "Someone's dying, Theo. That's someone's life."

He is Greek on his mother's side, Theodore Thanos Harper. His maternal family owns one of the best Greek restaurants in Des Moines, Iowa. His mother still runs the family business with the help of his uncles and two of Theodore's siblings. Famous Greek celebrities and politicians, from Jennifer Aniston to Kitty and Mike Dukakis to Frank Zappa, grace the walls. He is German, Native American, and African American on his father's side, his paternal great-great-grandfather having been a fugitive slave who confused North with South and ended up in Florida among the Seminoles.

The trajectory that led his namesake, the First Theo, and his Seminole wife and daughter to Des Moines, Iowa, remains loose and
gravelly. Theirs is an origin tale with a beginning, but the middle
keeps shifting. As a boy, Theo never grasped how the black side of
his family washed into whiteness. For a time, he asked—until he
didn't. He only knows that now, generations later, his father, Alfred
Harper, is a medical equipment executive. Alfred is socially liberal
but fiscally conservative. He abhors debt and has raised his six adult
children (three boys and three girls) to be model citizens. Whenever Alfred veers off the path—drinking binges that result in the
occasional court date or brawl or excommunication from the Lu-
theran Church—he has been known to say, "It's that thirty percent." Thirty percent being the random percentage of African and
Native American blood he regularly assigns to himself and his off-
spring. "No getting around it, kids. We've got this thing in us. Temper yourselves. It'll lead you to heaven. Or hell in a handbasket."

"I like to fuck people in doorways. Don't ask me why. Is this going
to be a problem?" Theo whispered to Darla in his hallway on their
first nondate. Less than an hour after attending a Broadway performance of *Hamilton*. Not even a quarter mile from his first apartment in New York City, which was now a luxury building. Theo
and Darla had climbed into the same taxi, each descending from
opposite sides of the street. Darla with her bassoon and umbrella-
less. Theo with a Strand umbrella that was doing more harm than
good, getting bested by a torrential downpour.

"I'm sorry," he said, fumbling with the umbrella and hurrying
to get out of the taxi when he realized she had beaten him to it.
"Ladies first."

Her hair was wet-plastered against her face. The musical instrument was in the middle of the seat.

"Brooklyn," she told the taxi driver. "Dumbo."

"I'm going to Park Slope," Theo said. "Maybe we could share?"

She scrutinized him and Theo wondered if she saw what he saw: Jim Morrison thirty-eight-ish with a Mediterranean tan.

"Okay, me first," she said, "you second." She smiled, full of cheek and cheekbones. Theodore Harper took Darla Jacobson and her smile home. Their age difference melted to nothing as the taxi carried them over the Brooklyn Bridge to the threshold of Theodore's front door. Nature girl. Runner. Family cottage in the Catskills that she escaped to when she wasn't working. She wore neither skirt nor dress, but when he turned the gilded knob to his art deco door, she stepped through the threshold and placed her bassoon on a high-back chair, removing her black sweater, which he caught midair, a tapered white blouse, which he let fall to the floor, and slim-fitting black trousers, which revealed no underwear underneath and a beseeching tangle of pubic hair.

"Darla," he said, "you've got quite the bush on you. That's a yeast infection waiting to happen." She sat on the sofa with her runner's legs crossed and lit a cigarette.

"This is a nice apartment."

Theo laughed and said, "Well, I'm glad you like it."

"Take off my bra, Theo."

"If you insist."

Darla massaged Theo's neck while he undid her bra strap.

"There's something you should know about me, too: I don't want to fuck around forever. It feels great in the moment, but after a while, there's this Groundhog Day effect. Give me sex that lands somewhere."

That was two years ago. Technically they are still newlyweds. Newlywed and pregnant.

He lived in a railroad flat in the Theater District his first month in New York. Theodore found the two-bedroom apartment on Craigslist and paid the first month's rent and security deposit based on photographs his landlord had posted online. Eight hundred bucks for his own room in the bustling hub of Manhattan was a risk worth taking. But the two-bedroom apartment was, in truth, a two-room apartment, not including the kitchen. Theodore's room was situated in the rear of the apartment and looked out onto a fire escape. The room was large enough for a twin-sized bed, pirate's chest, and wooden chair. When he cracked open the window, the smell of food from every restaurant on Restaurant Row penetrated the air. To get to his bedroom, Theodore had to walk through his landlord's room, which was purple and only moderately larger than his own. She was a middle-aged white woman, but to a boy fresh out of college who took care of his mind and body, middle age was relative. She might have been a hard-living thirty, for all he knew. He thought she might be lonely, but she never showed it. A pack a day of Marlboro cigarettes seemed to fill that void. When he left for work in the morning, she would sit on her daybed watching *Jeopardy*, and when he returned eight hours later, she would still be watching *Jeopardy*. Only the food in front of her changed. Chinese. Italian. Mexican. Indian. She did not own a single pan or pot. The overall effect was ascetic, slovenly, and claustrophobic. In his parents' home, a pot of fasolada, Greek bean soup, was always simmering.

Theo longed to tell his landlord the photos she had posted on Craigslist constituted false advertising. Where was the common area? Where was the living room? But he had not yet secured a new living arrangement.

"What time does *Jeopardy* come on?"

She turned and stared at him. "Depends on the time zone. There's Eastern. Central. Pacific. Some others that don't matter."

"Huh." His *huh* dripped with sarcasm.

She lit a cigarette. It was seven-thirty in the morning. Her hair was red but her roots screamed brunette. "Where did you say you were from again?"

"Iowa."

She chuckled. Theodore didn't bother to ask her what was so

funny. People had ideas about Iowa. They confused Iowa with Kansas. People had ideas about Kansas.

"Okay, Mr. Iowa. What do you do?"

Something in the way she asked the question made him want to withhold. "I'm a recent college graduate."

"I've been at this share business for a while. Trust me. Go home."

It was true: Theo hated his job. He hated the subway, the bus, the pollution, and crowds. He would stroll down Ninth Avenue and cut over to Sixth Avenue every morning so he would have time to compose his thoughts, to compose himself. He worked in the sales department of an expensive hardware store in Chelsea. They sold tony reproductions of antique fixtures and faucets and lamps. Theo couldn't believe the money people would pay for knockoffs.

"I wouldn't be satisfied with anything but the original," he told the one coworker, also a recent graduate, that he could halfway stand. She was a skinny girl from Fishkill, New York, working overtime to pay for reconstructive surgery for a class 2 overbite. The overbite made her self-conscious. When her colleagues told a joke, she would cover her lips and stifle her laugh.

"Don't do that," Theo would tell her. "Why do you give a fuck about these people?"

He thought most of his coworkers were snooty and arrogant. They could afford to eat out for lunch every day. Theodore ate out once a week—usually at Famiglia's pizza parlor, where he could get two plain slices and a can of soda for five bucks. Otherwise, he worked through lunch or he brought spanakopita. His parents shipped a box of his favorite foods packed in dry ice every month: beans gigantes, pistachios, grape leaves, moussaka, tzatziki, and figs—Middle Eastern dishes Theo occasionally substituted with Kraft macaroni and cheese because he could buy two boxes for sixty-nine cents at the convenience store on Ninth Avenue on Wednesdays.

His landlord stopped Theo one morning on his way out the door.

They lived in a tomb of silence. He could not even bring himself to utter salutations.

"What do you do for a living?" she inquired.

"I'm an architect," he said.

She shrugged. "Every architect I ever knew had a trust fund."

Nowadays people would say the woman brought the hate out in him. Back then, Theodore reckoned with what his father called their inherent thirty percent.

"Aren't you agoraphobic? You don't seem to get out much. Land-lady."

He resented that she had him pegged. His architecture degree in interior design from Purdue University meant absolutely nothing in New York City. The previous week, he had scored an invite to a house party in Williamsburg where every other architect was a Yale graduate who had interned in Barcelona or Rome. There was talk of windmills in Africa and temples in China. Theo's under-graduate degree started out as agricultural architecture, but he had switched to interior landscaping and design his junior year when it was time to declare a major. Iowa was prone to sudden thunder-storms and blizzards that could leave you homeless. Theodore cared more about where people lived and how they resided in their homes than the havoc wreaked on them by the elements.

"The architecture in this area is schizophrenic," he said quietly. "The terra-cotta façade on this building could be exquisite if you took some time to renovate the place, but like everything else in this dump, it's going to hell in a handbasket. You see the roughness reflected in the uneven scale of the neighborhood. Al Smith had some logic about him when he erected the Empire State Building to give this side of town something to look up to. If I owned this building, my guess is you don't, you rent, but I'd sell the air rights. Then your fat ass can walk away with a lot of money and maybe, if you play it right, an apartment in the high-rise or luxury condo-minium that's going to occupy the space where you're currently sitting. But not if you stall, not if you sit on that daybed and wait. The brownstone next door has already corrupted the foundation of your property, and the first one to sell leaves the other to shoulder the financial hit—so that the new management company or real estate firm can declare eminent domain and buy you out cheap."

His landlord turned the television off. Once she had been a looker. Not really.

"Well, this is better than *Jeopardy*."

Theo could not resist the sudden urge to mark territory. "Come here."

She unglued herself from the daybed and Theo thought, *There is beauty in there somewhere. Maybe underneath the brunette roots trying to escape the hair color that had sailed a long time ago.* She wore a green dress that could have been a tent or loose robe from the indifferent way the fabric dangled from her body. Theo flung the front door open and turned her around and proceeded with intense concentration to fuck her.

"Are you mad?" she shrieked.

"We can stop this anytime," he groaned.

But she clutched the door frame. And the sex he had intended to put on her worked twice as much on him. Flecks of chipped yellow paint coated her hands like pixie dust. Her nails were much cleaner than he had expected, manicured in the French style. Theodore looped his hands through hers and engaged her from behind, a favorite position because someone had told him during a middle school bonfire party that it was a good way to give a girl pleasure without getting her pregnant. "There is no way this doorway isn't full of lead," he told her. "The entire building is full of lead. I am fucking you in lead."

There were three apartments on their floor. Three doors (with peepholes) that a tenant could open at any time, but no one did.

Theodore would arrive to work an hour later and receive a blistering reprimand. During his lunch break he would jog to the

School of Visual Arts on Fifth Avenue and pretend he was a graduate student in desperate need of off-campus housing. It would take
two weeks before he found his next apartment, but when he saw his
landlady that same night, he set clear boundaries.

"Pretend this never happened."

Without missing a beat, she said, "Something happened?"

She returned his security deposit no questions asked. And Theodore took it as a good omen for his future that she turned off *Jeopardy* while he packed his duffel bag.

*

Six weeks into the pandemic, Darla says, "I can feel our baby kicking, Theo. Our baby wants out."

They are packing for the summer cottage. They will leave early
and stop for a day hike on one of the quieter stretches of the Devil's
Path. Theo is concerned the trails might be treacherous, muddy.
But that's what decent hiking boots are for: to tread and maneuver,
provide traction and support when you climb or scale. Darla was
raised on six-mile treks during family getaways. Darla is undaunted
by the perils of spring. The only thing that daunts Darla is the
virus. The virus came out of nowhere and now it has several names.
For their child, Darla and Theo have not yet settled on a name. Nor
do they know the baby's gender.

"Does a baby kick in the first trimester?" Theo asks. "Unlikely."

Darla shrugs. There has been coercive give and take. Theo has
begrudgingly agreed to one week at the cottage. Darla's two-week
request he has ignored, put down with brittle silence and longer
outings for groceries and provisions.

"I hope we have enough food," Darla says with a smile. But she
thinks, *Let Theo be angry. Months from now, he will be a father. And
I will be a mother.*

"We have enough food to feed an army. We'll only be there one
week."

"Don't forget the cleansers."

"You bet. Done."

Theo packs the cleansers. His. Not hers. Darla searches for her cell phone and calls her best friend, Ruby Tabitha Black. The "Tabitha" in Ruby Tabitha Black's name is inspired by the daughter on the TV show *Bewitched*. Her parents are Brooklyn eccentrics and founders of a black-owned bookstore. And Ruby is the head chef at Mizu to Yama, a two-star Michelin restaurant in a boutique hotel in the Bowery with her partner, Katsumi Fujihara. But no one's eating in restaurants and it's not the best time to be Asian.

"I wish you could come up, Ruby."

"And hurt my godbaby? What if I have the virus?"

"What if *I* have the virus."

Theo is packing zucchinis. He appreciates their heft. Aim a bag of zucchinis the right way and they would make one helluva weapon. To harm someone or to defend yourself. Theo packs the zucchinis in a red-and-white beach cooler.

"Eventually we're all going to get the virus," Theo says.

Darla covers the phone. "Some of us are at higher risk."

"My hands are full with the restaurant right now. And I promised my mom I'd help her upgrade her website at the bookstore this weekend."

"Well, we'll be there if you change your mind."

The two women have been friends since a middle school sleepaway in the Adirondacks sponsored by their private school. To hear Darla tell it, the Jacobson and Black families both took an egalitarian approach to playdates and sleepovers early on, alternating between Manhattan and Brooklyn in a way that facilitated their daughters' becoming best friends. No geographic micro aggressions or chaperones or nannies every visit. No pretense.

The only positive aspect of COVID is that Ruby Black is supposed to be in the delivery room when the baby comes. Not likely to happen at this rate! Theo has never seen Ruby's thirty percent, but he knows it's there. Then again, he's wobbly about his thirty percent. He's wobbly about race and politics and food cooperatives, which is ironic, given where he lives. He's wobbly about marriage. And he's wobbly about kids.

"Son." His father rang Theo the evening of the 2008 presidential election. Theo was at an election-night party hosted by the owners of a real estate firm he worked with regularly. "I filled in the wrong goddamn bubble."

"I don't follow you, Dad." Alfred Harper seldom called. Theo was the youngest of the six T's: Tamara, Thalia, Troy, Thaddeus, Toni, and Theodore. "T" being the symbol of the Trinity. Father. Son. And Holy Ghost. It was understood that Theo was the favorite. A swan in a flock of average to ugly ducklings.

"I wanted to see if a black man can make president. . . ."

"You voted for Obama?"

"Pretty much," his father said.

Theo had his buzz on and was drinking his third beer. He wondered if his father had a buzz on too. Theo already knew the woman he would take home. She lived in a brownstone two doors down and reminded him of his first landlord. He would Jim Morrison Mama Cass her. Shame. Shame. Shameful.

Theo thought his dad might be crying. "Listen, I think Obama's going to win."

His father mumbled, "Thirty percent."

Theo could hear cheers in the background of his family's split-level bungalow. Paved front and backyard for efficiency—so his hardworking parents never had to worry about weeds or grass. Hanging flowerpots and herbs and mint for Sideritis tea enough to suffice. His mother and siblings are fierce Greeks who never forgave the Republicans for what they did to Mike and Kitty Dukakis: Ourwimpwillbeatyourshrimp. Thirty Percent. Ourwimpwillbeatyourshrimp. Thirty percent. Ourwimpwillbeatyourshrimp.

"Perhaps," Theo said, slipping into his coworkers' landscaped backyard, "it's time to make peace with that thirty percent?" The Harpers kept their thirty percent within the family. Better to let their Mediterranean flow.

Theo's father laughed. "This country will never forgive us for voting for a black president. But son, I did. And it is what it is."

*

Darla charges her cell phone. "Ruby said she'll drive up to the cottage with food if we need it."

"Great."

"Theo, are you okay?"

"Sounds like a plan."

"You know, I love you, but lately you've been a real asshole." When necessary, Darla stands her ground. "I hope it's not me."

"You read too much into things."

"If you say so," Darla says, considering him. "But a baby can shift dynamics in an open marriage."

"Only if expectations change."

Theo wants to tell his wife that the pandemic is making her neurotic. That the pandemic is making him extra horny and crazy. That his favorite app, Tinder, is about as active for his needs as the fucking Broadway Theater District. He wants to tell his wife that Ruby Tabitha Black should keep her ass in the Bowery and respect social distancing. That he is not now and never will be cut out for lockdowns or quarantines, especially with another human being. That there can be such a thing as too much time together and too much intimacy and a swell of fucking memories. Instead, he skims around the immaculate kitchen counter and lifts her off the ground and carries her toward the threshold of their beautiful front door.

THE TEENAGER IN
THE CARDI B T-SHIRT

ACHOO. The doorman/super in Mr. Harper's building sneezed on a resident the first week of April and was sent home without a fever. No one has seen or heard from him since. Nor has the board found a replacement. Due to the executive order/lockdown/building mandate, only immediate family or designated family members may enter the co-op beyond the vestibule. The Teenager in the Cardi B T-shirt is new to the premises. Yet tenants zip past him in the hallway or lobby, drop a five or ten note in his hand and say, *Buzz me when the pizza comes. How's your dad? We miss him.*

His name is Xavier Curtis. He is not the son of the doorman/super, nor does he live in Mr. Harper's building. Home is a high-rise condominium near Myrtle Avenue that his parents were initially reluctant to buy because the massive apartment complex reminded them of housing projects. Sometimes you get what you can take. Sometimes you take what you can get. They took a neighborhood that was on the upswing where they could own instead of rent.

His parents call their son "Xayxay." One day Xavier will say to his mother and father, "Drop the Xayxay," but given the current state of the world with the coronavirus disrupting shit all over the place, the nickname is a term of endearment he doesn't want to quit. He and his folks have lost a lot already—an aunty in Los Angeles to the virus on his father's side of the family. Aunty Pat gave up the fight early on, before they were flagging the virus, but now they all agree the signs and symptoms were there. They just thought Aunty Pat had succumbed to asthma. She had been asthmatic most of her life. Xavier and his parents flew out to Leimert Park for the funeral and there was no social distancing, no masks, no gloves. Later, information began to come out about this novel coronavirus. And Aunty Pat's husband died within three weeks of her funeral. Xavier's parents could not afford a second trip but sent a bleeding-heart coffin spray with their sincere regrets.

Xavier is a junior at Stuyvesant High School in Manhattan, where he was one of ten African American students who tested in his freshman year. The rate of African American students in specialized schools has been on the decline for decades. Theodore Harper does not remember that he once shared an elevator with Xavier when the boy was in the eighth grade. But that's cool copacetic. Most days Xavier can barely recall his eighth-grade self. Only that he wanted to erase middle school for high school and style-shift away from baby boy clean-shavenness, trade the traditional fade that his daddy's barber on Fulton gave him for something else.

When Xavier's hair first took to locs, his mother Nadine said, "Xayxay, is this a fashion statement or spiritual quest in homage to the Nazarenes?"

Xavier tried to tell his mother that he was loosening his inhibitions, but she heard loosening his belt. Her first boyfriend had locs she admired with her chin held high and on both knees. Nadine left a box of condoms on Xavier's chest of drawers and when she found them exactly as she had left them, Nadine turned to her husband, proffering the box of Trojan condoms and a green plantain: "Talk to Xayxay."

Irvin Curtis was a Correctional Treatment Specialist at a federal prison in central Brooklyn. For years Irvin had sworn he would stop bringing his work home with him, but if he was home in time for dinner, he always reserved thirty or forty minutes to tie up the "loose day ends" before relaxing into dinner with his wife and son.

The following morning while Xavier was wrestling his text-books into a JanSport backpack, Irvin stirred Honey Nut Cheerios around in a bowl. Irvin didn't know why he even messed with Honey Nut Cheerios. He would be hungry an hour from now.

"Xavier," Irvin said. "Do you know the score?"

"Yes, Dad," Xavier said proudly. "I tested in the ninety-ninth percentile."

"That's one score. There are many others."

His father had grown up in Virginia but rooted for the Lakers, Magic and Old Kareem and then later Kobe.

"I don't think it's basketball season," Xavier said, checking out his reflection in the mirror, twisting a loc that was coming undone. He had not foreseen the care needed to manage great locs or the different philosophies about the pros and cons of freeform versus manicured locs. Beeswax versus styling gel. Who were the first people to let their hair mat? Egyptians? Ethiopians? The Hindi holy men. Everybody had an opinion these days. Bob Marley and the Rastas, Xavier would say, stepping back when a curious classmate asked to touch his hair—*Bro, do you want to feel the dread part of locs?*—had made wearing locs essential, natural, mainstream.

Irvin watched Xavier twisting his hair. When Irvin was in high school, he had grown out a belated Afro only to be teased merci-lessly. *I'm sanctifying my kitchen and decolonizing my naps*, he had said to his mother and stepfather. *Honey child, that's all right but you better massage some Pink lotion into that sucker.*

"Maybe score is the wrong metaphor. Your mother wants me to confirm you know what time it is." He retrieved the box of condoms and the green plantain from a kitchen drawer next to the dishwasher.

Just to mess with his father, Xavier squinted and said, "Seven A.M.?"

"No, son, you're not dense."

Xavier smiled. "Oh, you're trying to talk to me about sex? Dad, come on. We've been having sex ed since like fifth grade."

Irvin shrugged and said, "That's too young."

"Some parts of the world, they marry girls off at ten. In our history textbook, we read about this fifteen-year-old boy and ten-year-old girl in Sudan who were arranged to be married—"

"X, you can let your locs flow, but think twice about how you dip into the history of marital customs from other cultures and countries when you haven't been there."

"Well, I'm just giving an example—about the present reality of child brides. I don't approve."

"Neither do I. I don't think anyone in this zip code does. Of course, one can never be too sure. Listen, just cover your dick," his father said. "Don't let anyone do it for you. There's more than one way to be a child bride. Handling your arsenal shows respect for you and your woman."

"I don't have a woman."

"We are in the now stage of yet."

Xavier was beginning to turn a corner in the looks department. Growing from just a notch below average to a potentially handsome young man. Dark brows that inquired and black eyes that answered and skin that reflected the healthy diet Nadine, a former dancer, maintained for her family.

"You have my word: I will protect my dick, Dad."

Irvin nodded his approval. He had worked in the state and federal prison system for over twenty years. It filled him with ambivalence, the things his son could afford to be both pithy and flip about. Xavier's excellence, the distance from here to there, made Irvin proud, cautious, and sometimes inexplicably sad when navigating young brothers through the prison system.

"What am I supposed to do with this plantain?" Irvin asked.

Their eyes both fell on the trash can. Irvin tossed the plantain into the trash can. He opened the box of Trojans, took two out and slipped them into the sleeve of his son's backpack.

"Don't go getting any ideas. But it's smart to always have some on hand."

*

Four years ago, the day after Christmas, on what the Europeans called Boxing Day, Xavier and his parents had gone over to celebrate with Julian, Irvin's first cousin. Julian had not been permitted to eat animals' intestines and castoffs as a child, but whenever his southern nana came to Brooklyn she would invariably get a taste for tripe and fix the dish while Julian's parents were at work. Irvin was the grandbaby she would bring north with her for two weeks in the summer, sealing a bond and a love of tripe, chitlins, liver, gizzards, pig and chicken feet between the cousins that stood the test of time.

"Well, something smells delish," Theodore Harper said, stepping into the elevator, holding the door for thirteen-year-old Xavier and his parents. Nadine carried a poinsettia plant. Xavier carried two six-packs of original Coca-Cola in glass bottles. And Irvin carried a covered dish on a baking sheet. Outside, the sky was nonstick metal-clad Calphalon. Like the pots and pans whose prices spiked before the holidays and went on sale after.

"Thank you," Nadine smiled.

"Happy holidays," Irvin added.

"Happy holidays," Theodore said, nodding, pushing the button to his floor and then turning to ask, "Which floor?"

"Eighth floor," said Irvin.

"You're here to see?"

"Julian Curtis," Irvin said.

"Oh, I know the Curtises. They are good people," Theo said, tapping his feet. When the building turned co-op, Julian's partner, an intellectual property lawyer, had served as legal counsel along with a real estate attorney for the handful of black and Hispanic families determined not to be bought out of the building.

"None better," said Irvin. "Julian's my cousin."

They reached the eighth floor; Theo waved goodbye as Xavier and his parents stepped out. "Please give Julian my regards."

"You live in the building. Give him your regards yourself," Irvin said.

"Irvin," Nadine said. "Why do you have to be that way. He was a nice man." She lifted the earbuds from Xavier's ears. "And you, you're missing life on that iPhone."

But Xavier had missed nothing.

"Nadine," Irvin said, and shrugged. "Sometimes I think we've been up north too long. Was a time when I wouldn't have to point out the obvious. That white-ass nigga was taking our temperature."

Now there is another kind of temperature taking going on. In the morning when Xavier wakes up and in the evening before he goes to bed, he checks his temperature with a cheap under-tongue thermometer and a digital one (made in China) that he places on his forehead or the palm of his inner wrist. Xavier can hear his mother's voice when the thermometer beeps what seems to be his consistent body temperature: 98.7. "That's good, baby. Keep at it. You can never be too diligent." He has been housesitting for two weeks running, changing the litter box for cousin Julian's tabby cat, Cornhusk, who seems to have some confusion about whether she is a cat or a dog. Her meow is a bark in the universal language of "Where's my person? Why is my person not here?"

"I could ask you the same question," Xavier says as the cat purrs and rubs against his legs.

*

First the inmates at Irvin's prison began to come down with the virus. The nurses tried to make their own COVID tests because COVID tests were not yet readily available. That didn't work. Then the staff began to come down with the virus. Protocols were in place, taking temperatures, masks, social distancing—as much as one can social distance in prison.

Irvin came home one day and said, "To be on the safe side, I think we had better take precautions and assume that I am asymptomatic."

A week after Irvin tested negative for the virus, Nadine woke up with a fever and the sound of rain pelting against the bedroom window.

"Why," Nadine said to Irvin as he checked her temperature with a mask and gloves on, "I haven't heard rain like that since our honeymoon in Granada, Spain. Wasn't the Alhambra just beautiful?"

When Nadine's fever spiked and she began to have difficulty breathing, Irvin called his cousin Julian in Yonkers.

"The hospitals are getting full, but I hear there's room at Methodist," Julian said. "Just don't take her to that one with the bodies piling up in the halls and parking lot. That's a tragedy and a travesty."

Julian's mother lived in a retirement facility in Yonkers about an hour from the Victorian he and his partner were renovating. He had gone up on Sunday, March 15, for the usual Sunday outing with his mother and could not bring himself to return her to the nursing home.

"After much consideration, I've decided to keep my mother here at home for the time being." The nursing home supervisor protested, reminding Julian of the contract his mother had signed.

"I'm sorry," Julian said. His mother took his cue and coughed loudly in the background. "*I don't think I quite hear you?* The past few days, I've not been feeling one hundred percent. And Mother's cough is starting to scare me." Julian, his mother, and his partner, Gary, had been up in Yonkers ever since, but his mother was allergic to cats.

Irvin took Julian's advice and checked Nadine into Methodist—a crisp ten-minute walk from Julian's apartment. It was decided that Xavier would stay at Julian's apartment until his mother was released from Methodist, ensuring social distancing and proximity to the hospital.

*

"Mom, don't throw that away!" Xavier and his mother were in the apartment hallway halfway between Xavier's bedroom and a little nook where they kept the stacked energy-efficient washer-dryer. Nadine was holding up a T-shirt she had just run through the wash. More blood orange than red and more red than blood orange, the shirt had Cardi B in a multicolored halter top and pants. Nadine had come upon Wendell, one of her chemistry students, peddling T-shirts before assembly. Ten dollars for a small, medium, or large T-shirt for the school trip to Montreal—which would later be canceled.

"Shouldn't you be in assembly? Wendell, I know for a fact you should be in assembly."

Wendell was Xavier's age. His people were also from the South. She wanted to extend Wendell goodwill, but then she saw his mouth frame itself into what was about to be a lie.

"Thank you very much," she said, relieving Wendell of the box of T-shirts and heading down the hall without looking back. She had Mrs. Curtis pep in her step. The pep she shared liberally with students during chemistry class and college prep pep talks. These young people were something else. It took a lot of energy to win their attention and not to lose them.

On the Friday before school went online, Wendell would find Nadine during her office hours and ask after the Cardi B T-shirts. She would return the box of T-shirts to Wendell and tell him to be good and keep safe.

"Look after your folks," Nadine said. She and Irvin had had four miscarriages. They loved Xavier four times over. Once for himself, and three times for the babies they couldn't have.

"You aw'right, Mrs. Curtis," Wendell said.

Wendell left a large Cardi B T-shirt folded into a ball on her desk. The same shirt Xavier coveted.

Nadine tossed the shirt to her son.

"Cardi B is too vulgar for me," Nadine said. "Her tongue hangs dead dog out her mouth."

"Cardi B is a good rapper. And 'bout the music and the money."

Nadine loaded the dishwasher. "Money comes and money goes. . . ."

"Naw, Mom. Not for everyone. Not in the same way."

Nadine caught the judgment in her voice and lowered it a notch. Judgment is how you lose them, she thought. And shaming. Wasn't she a young woman once? In love with her body? "I suppose there's always been more than one way to be a woman. Maybe she's found a way that works for her."

Xavier waved the shirt in front of Nadine. "You sure you don't want it now?"

"Boy, get out of my face," she said.

At first, Xavier rallied against housesitting at Julian's apartment. His mother was in the hospital and he wanted to stick close to his dad, but Irvin wasn't having it.

"I'm the king of this high-rise castle."

"What happens if the king gets sick?"

"He'll rest easy knowing he didn't pass the virus on to his son and take his ass to Methodist to mend alongside your mother."

Monday through Friday, his father leaves work an hour early and orders glazed donuts to go from 7th Avenue Donuts and then they go and sit, six feet apart, on a metal bench across the street from Methodist. They sit across the street from the hospital blowing on their hands to warm them up, watching the steam rise from Irvin's coffee or Xavier's Lipton tea, and without sharing what they are doing, they pep talk the hospital, the doctors, the ventilators, the air, and then they get rice and beans or Thai or Turkish food or burgers from Purity Diner or whatever takeout is available. And then his father drives Xavier back to Julian's apartment. Xavier always wears the Cardi B T-shirt his mother gave him. He knows he and his mother had other conversations before she got COVID—but for some reason the Cardi B conversation is the one that sticks. If she were there, she would grief him for wearing the Cardi B T-shirt in Cousin Julian's building. "Why couldn't you wear Bey or Drake or Kendrick Lamar or Missy Elliott?"

Xavier is an older wiser taller sixteen. His locs cascade past his oversized bomber jacket. This Teenager in the Cardi B T-shirt looks about as menacing at sixteen as he did when he was thirteen and in the eighth grade. Book smart (invited during his junior year to attend summer programs at Caltech, Stanford, and Reed) but also street savvy (leaves his backpack in the locker, goes to lunch, and puts on a Stuyvesant cap so no one assumes he's trying to steal anything), Xavier understands that for boys like him sometimes a hello is just a hello and other times a how are you is a clocking of sentences to gauge where you come from, where you're going, and how long you intend to stay.

IN THE WOOD

WHERE I AM BLACK

THEO LOWERED the top on his aqua-blue convertible but raised it somewhere along Route 17 in Bergen County when a particularly sour memory of an ugly breakup in New Jersey assailed him. The drive had been sublime until that point, with the crisp April wind tussling Darla's and Theo's hair hither thither and the occasional driver giving a thumbs-up sign or a fervent honking horn in admiration of his 1967 Cadillac Eldorado, a vintage car that would fetch a hefty sum on the collector's market. Wonderful, thought Theo. It was pretty fucking wonderful to be out of the apartment and on a car trip for a change. Almost as soon as he had picked up the Eldorado from the garage and climbed behind the steering wheel, a lightness had befriended him, a willingness and a readiness to shift gears and relax into the promise of the Hudson Valley.

"I always forget how big this thing is," Darla said, pressing her tight back into the plush leather upholstery. "Large enough for an afternoon swim. All that's missing is the ocean."

Theo listened for a hint of reproach, but his beautiful wife was happy as a kitten on catnip. "Nice to see you smile," he said, reaching over to adjust her side of the passenger's seat. A midmorning nap for a pregnant lady might not be a bad thing.

Darla gave a final wave toward their apartment building—in the direction of the Teenager in the Cardi B T-shirt whom Theo had seen only a few days earlier.

"Poor kid must only own one shirt." Theo took Darla's lead and offered up a slant smile and a quick wave to the black teenager. "You know him? He's everywhere these days."

"Nope. I thought you did," Darla said, freeing her ponytail from a pink scrunchie and accepting Theo's kiss. It was Darla's nature to wave or go out of her way to be nice to people of color when she saw them. As a child in private school during open houses and tours, Darla Jacobson had been the girl on the greeting committee, the blond goodwill ambassador who invited the new students to her house for play-dates or sleepovers and birthday parties. The student who was willing to leave the security of her Upper West Side home and travel to her classmates' apartments in Brooklyn or Queens in a show of solidarity.

"I love you, babe," Theo said, peeling off.

"Feeling's mutual," said Darla, turning off her cell phone, which would remain off until it was found in the woods a month later.

Darla dozed off and did not startle until the tail end of their trip. She slept through the gridlock and traffic they had hoped to avoid leaving Brooklyn on a Sunday morning. Theo packed apple butter sandwiches. A favorite from his childhood on Harper family trips. But Darla had a craving for an herbed chicken sandwich from her favorite deli café on the town's village green. The deli café was known for incredible chicken sandwiches. In fact, the menu was limited to three varieties of chicken sandwiches: barbecue, herb, and a mango curried chicken salad on sourdough bread for lunch, or eggs, bacon, corned beef hash for breakfast. And homemade donuts, all day long. The deli café served coffee all day long too and an assortment of herbal and black teas, fancy soda pop and imported mineral water. In the summer, locals and tourists sought out the homemade ginger ale, root beer, and raspberry lime rickeys to take the heat off.

Theo and Darla arrived at the village green around half past two.

"In and out, okay?" Theo said, looking at his watch, secretly wishing they could stick with his apple butter sandwiches. But Darla's hormones were a changing and her taste buds were explosive and her hunger pangs were for two. Theo wanted to keep his woman happy. Considering some of the claustrophobic thoughts that had clutched his head lately, keeping Darla happy was the least he could do.

Outside the café, there was a line that curved around the block. No standing six feet apart, much less social distancing. Most of the customers seemed unaware masks should cover their noses. A plump clerk stood at the takeout window taking an order from a woman in her mid- to late twenties. The woman sported a buzz cut, skinny jeans, and a corduroy jacket with a faux fur collar that stopped at her midriff.

"Well, I don't know if I want a cinnamon donut or lunch."

Theo and Darla were toward the back of the line. Darla was still a little sleep groggy and COVID shy of crowds. Theo could feel Darla's body tense up, so he massaged the inside of her hand, along the lifeline. She had been told her lifeline was too short or too long, depending on who was doing the reading. The last tarot card reading was at a party on the Lower East Side, where she (prepregnancy) had knocked back mezcal Negronis with fellow musicians from her Broadway musical.

"I just don't see why we need this . . . ?" said the Corduroyed Girl, gesturing toward the *Keep Looking* disposable mask that she had yanked under her chin.

The clerk cocked her head to one side and pulled her own mask farther up her nose. "You know why we have to wear these masks, honey," the clerk said.

"But they don't stop you from getting the virus."

"Honey, you know that's not what the CDC says."

The Corduroyed Girl spun around. She knew she had an audience. She knew some of the people waiting in line were on her side. "The government tells us we got to hide our faces. What about our souls? They need to think about how this virus got here. They need to gather up the people who brought this damn virus here and send them packing."

"*Honey.*" The clerk was also in her mid- to late twenties. Bing cherries floated on her navy-blue mask. "You know why we need these masks. You think I want to wear a mask? You know why . . ."

Theo had the sense the clerk was on autopilot. He let go of Darla's hand and made his way toward the front of the line. They were never going to get on the trail at this rate.

"I'm sorry, but in case you hadn't noticed, there's a line. A lot of people are waiting."

The Corduroyed Girl looked Theo up and down. "I'm just about done here." She took out her wallet and motioned toward a blueberry donut. "Notice how they don't talk about the flu anymore," she said loudly enough for everyone to hear. "Whatever happened to the good old-fashioned flu and all the other stuff that kills people?"

As the clerk packaged a blueberry donut, Theo said solemnly, "So many people have died from COVID. It would be a shame . . . if you got sick. Wouldn't people miss you?"

The Corduroyed Girl could feel saliva gathering at the back of her throat. Growing up, she had an awful habit of spitting in people's faces or behind their backs or in their food or on their floors or at their cars when they offended her. Spitting never won her any friends, but the hell if she cared—until she sprayed spit on a new boyfriend who told her: *That's some serious goodbye bullshit right there. Lose the spit or me.*

The Corduroyed Girl didn't understand why this stranger was butting in on her business. "Spare me," she said. "I should be dead already."

"So," Theo said, "in my building, there was this young woman. Not much older than you. She died from COVID. Five days gone, in her bedroom, before someone caught wind of the smell. Sometimes we just don't know. And we live in a friendly building. If you got sick, wouldn't someone miss you?"

The Corduroyed Girl's fiancé was now the love of her life. They were engaged and had saved up to buy a little nothing of a house in the town of Saugerties. She had been working double shifts at Target for the past two years to pay for her wedding when the pandemic hit and then the rich came flooding into what seemed like every corner of the Hudson Valley in search of bargains, a $150,000 shack of a house that no one would have looked at twice now went for $350,000 and climbing. Her wedding dress was still hanging in the closet and the date on their wedding invitations had passed. The Corduroyed Girl put on her mask and let the saliva slide down her throat. She accepted her blueberry donut and change from the clerk, who said, "Thank you, honey."

"You're welcome," the Corduroyed Girl said, and walked away.

Theo found Darla leaning against the Eldorado. She had walked away during his exchange with the Corduroyed Girl. The village green was people popping for April. Theo held up the brown paper bag of sandwiches. The clerk had thrown in two complimentary bags of Hal's kettle chips.

"How about we go straight to the house and hike fresh tomorrow?" Theo suggested.

Darla was quiet. A beat to consider and a beat to dismiss. "What do you suppose was in her head?"

It was true: the girl had put him, Darla, and everyone in the deli café who wore masks at risk, but his wife's question struck him as disingenuous.

"Darla," he said, "she's got her own take on the First Amendment."

"Well, I don't like what's happening to our town."

"I wasn't born here. And neither were you," Theo said.

"I've been coming to this town since I could hold a toy shovel and bucket."

The trail could be entered through the parking lot or a more remote and hard-to-find entrance that she knew well. They drove thirty minutes out of town, past the main trail entrance with its crowded parking lot. Darla directed Theo to park along the shoulder of a dirt road.

"We'll have the wood to ourselves," Darla said, using the old terminology.

Theo popped open the Eldorado, which accommodated their luggage, groceries, and staples like candles, matches, light bulbs, batteries, rock salt, and a spear-head shovel.

"Where'd you get the shovel?" Darla asked.

"Home Depot." Theo had borrowed the shovel on an impulse from the community garden shed. There was not much snow upstate this year, but you could never rule out ice packed into the driveway. Darla and her mother still owned the shovels that came with the purchase of the cottage house. Theo thought perhaps this was a sentimental WASP thing. His first cottage winter, after a particularly laborious afternoon shoveling snow, he had driven into Kingston and bought a snowblower for Darla and her mother. The two women smiled and thanked Theo with polite disappointment. Realizing that he had compromised something for them and wanting Darla's mother to like him—Theo sensed Maureen didn't—he manufactured a nick on the snowblower and returned it to Walmart the following morning. "I think I could get a better deal somewhere else," he said.

Later, over hot cocoa and toasted marshmallows, Darla explained that since her father's death, the lazy-eyed neighborhood hermit shoveled their driveway on a whim and as a courtesy.

"That fancy snowblower would hurt his feelings. We keep things simple here."

They started up a steep slope that was paved but gave way to gravel and then a hill and a boreal forest of fir, spruce, and pines. They climbed quartz conglomerates and crossed rock paths and wooden bridges, leaving behind a valley with running brooks and shallow creeks and pausing for drinks of water and for Darla to serenade a bevy of *Aleuria aurantia,* orange peel fungus mushrooms, with yellow pregnant piss.

An hour and forty minutes into their hike, the trail blazes on the trees disappeared altogether. Theo and Darla were no longer on anyone's marked path. They could taste, see, touch, hear, and smell nature. The damp aroma of wood and lichen and sphagnum moss and the slight mush of composted leaves, twigs, branches, breaking silence with a crinkle, crinkle, crunch, crunch against the heels of their hiking boots.

"You never told me that story about the woman dying in our apartment building," Darla said out of the blue.

"I made it up." A dangling branch caught Theo's forehead and scratched blood. "Shit," he cursed. Theo hated hiking. Even as a kid.

"Why would you make up such a thing?" Darla was glad he could not see the expression on her face.

"Convenience," Theo said. "It got her over herself and us hiking, didn't it?"

"Sometimes . . ." Darla shook her head and quickened her pace. "What?"

"Never mind, Theo," she said.

"No, *what?*" He worked to keep pace with Darla. She was on the shorter side and could duck branches that might blind him. He was also feeling their age gap and the early phase of a pandemic-shifting body.

"Hey, Darla, maybe we should stop and eat?"

"I know the view I want. We stop now and we won't get much of a view."

"You're carrying." Theo was out of breath.

"It was a lousy thing to lie about," Darla added, but she paused until Theo was on the trail beside her. They both took sips of water. She had chosen a relatively short hike—under four miles—that intersected with rougher parts of the Devil's Path. If he couldn't handle a few rock scrambles, well, that was his bad.

"Not a total lie. More half-truth. Something I read in the paper. This Asian exchange student was found dead in the shower of one of those international dorms in Manhattan. They think he caught a COVID fever and was trying to cool himself down."

"Theo, that's even worse. . . ."

Sometimes Theo thought Darla was a budding hypochondriac. "Well, Darla, add it to your list of grievances. Nothing I say or do is ever good enough these days."

"That's not true," she said. "I just want both of us to be our authentic selves."

Theo considered his wife. "Whatever that means . . ."

Darla did not speak to Theo until they reached the summit. She shouted out "Sunday" and listened as the day of the week traveled into the pewter sky and the spring valley far below. She let her troubles drift away. The view was spectacular; a bubbling waterfall gushed sprightly to keep them company. They unwrapped their sandwiches and sat on the outcrop of rocks with their legs dangling from the precipice.

Darla found contentment again. She turned to her husband. "Thank you for indulging me, Theo. I know you don't like hiking."

"Baby, you're welcome. And you shouldn't have to thank me. It gives me pleasure to please you, Darla."

"Yeah?"

Theo tapped his wedding ring. Then hers. "One hundred percent."

Darla bit into her sandwich. "I've been thinking," she said. "We could easily sell my apartment and your apartment and buy ourselves a Slope brownstone."

Theo had already wolfed down half of his chicken sandwich. He felt his stomach churn.

"Why would we want to do that?"

"For space."

"How much space does one child need?"

"A backyard."

"But we have the cottage."

"Mom's cottage house."

"You're an only child. One day your mother's cottage will be yours. She's practically committed to living in France. You said so yourself."

"I'm talking about a new home that would be *ours*."

Theo liked that they both owned separate properties. That he had bought his apartment before marriage and that Darla owned an apartment, which she sublet for twice the mortgage.

"Darla, I will never give up my apartment. It's a great investment. Something I worked hard for that I will always enjoy knowing is there. A legacy for our kids."

"Kids?" Darla stared at Theo, well pleased.

Theo could not backtrack. That would be an avalanche. A tempest. A storm. "Well, of course. In time. Three or four. God willing."

Darla began to cry. "I really don't get you." Hers were nose-driven tears, though not of sadness. Theo wiped her pink wet nose with a paper napkin.

"Look, Darla," he said, finishing his chicken sandwich, which was otherworldly in its goodness, before starting in on the kettle chips. "We live in Park Slope. Park Slope is wonderful, but I see a lot of inconsiderate kids. I don't want to raise inconsiderate fucking little shits. I grew up sharing a bedroom with my brothers and sisters. Less really was more."

Darla heard selfishness. The implication put her only-child self on defense. "You're considerate?"

"Fifty percent of the time."

Darla began to giggle. Theo didn't know why but the giggling infuriated him. He could see her giggling as a little girl. A little girl on the school welcoming committee. He had never sat well with teasing. Charging toward a third-grade classmate with scissors had resulted in expulsion from his neighborhood school and attendance at a subpar lower school a forty-minute drive away from his childhood home. Theo longed to inflict pain on Darla for the briefest second, but he reached for his water bottle and drank a huge gulp of water instead.

"Darla, I'm reckoning with my thirty percent," he said.

"So what?"

"How come you never ask me what I mean by my thirty percent?"

"Because sometimes you just talk to talk. And you talk nonsense," she said.

Theo leaned back on the rocks and ferreted out an apple butter sandwich. One bite in and he was convinced the deli café's chicken sandwiches were overpriced and overrated. He studied his wife. "My great-great-grandfather was black. Maybe you would call him colored or Negro. Some people would undoubtedly call him nigger. So, I'm technically black and Indian."

Darla did not know this. Not that it mattered. So, she laughed.

Theo told the story, as best he could, of that other Theo: his namesake. The fugitive slave, the Seminoles, the quest for gold, the settlement in Iowa. Theo told Darla and he clutched his water bottle so tightly that his hands took to tremoring. Darla noticed and stood up. She began to gather her things, the backpack, stained brown paper bag, and wrappings for the sandwiches carefully. She did not want to litter or attract black bears or other wildlife. She had brought a small thermos full of London fog tea, a mix of Earl Grey and milk and honey, a personal favorite. Another ritual. The tea was still miraculously piping hot.

Theo stood up and it seemed to Darla that he took the height of every tree in the forest and filled the sky with shadow and shade. Only they were in an outcrop where there should be sun. The trees were behind them. Theo drank the last of his water. He always drank too much on a hike. Darla had packed extra for them. Theo turned his water bottle over to dispel the last droplets so they wouldn't sop his backpack. He shook the flask in a way that struck Darla as borderline violent. He had been so erratic lately. She had been so erratic lately. The whole goddamn world was erratic lately.

"Why did you wait until we were in the wood to tell me you're black?"

"Well, I'm only a *fraction* black. One drop. And Indian. Let's not forget the Indian," Theo said, giving the water bottle one final shake before turning it right side up and sealing the lid.

"You could have told me this story any place and a long time ago."

"I didn't think it would matter, Darla. The one-drop rule doesn't really apply anymore."

"It *doesn't* matter. Except if you're saying it to fuck with me."

"I suppose," Theo said slowly, "it's conceivable that our baby boy or girl could come into this world with a hint of color on her skin."

Darla rested her hand on her stomach. She never polished her nails, but she kept them clean and clipped. Round, not square. Square was for older, more mature women—like her mother.

"Theo, do you want me to perceive blackness as a threat?"

"How can I make you perceive anything?"

"Just so you know," Darla said, squinting at her husband, "I don't have a prejudiced bone in my body."

Theo blinked. "Well, I have several. I calibrate them all the time. Every day. And sometimes the calibrating is exhausting."

Darla shook her head. "See, you admitted it, you did tell me you have black lineage to be fucking passive aggressive. You want to ruin this pregnancy for me because deep down you resent the impending loss of freedom. Soon, you won't be able to roam at length anymore."

"Your Positive, My Negative," Theo says. "That's what I resent. How will you explain, hypochondriac that you are, to a two-year-old that they have tested positive for COVID? What the fuck does it even mean? How do you say, 'We will not go to the playground. The playgrounds are closed.' 'Who closed the playground?' 'They were closed to keep us safe—from the virus.' 'What's a virus?' 'A thing that spreads and spreads and spreads.' 'Why does it spread?' 'Because of germs.' 'Are germs like cooties?' 'Kind of.' 'Mama, Dada, are cooties like germs?' 'You bet.' 'So *I* have cooties?' Meltdown. 'Waa.' "

Darla frowned. "I won't let you darken what should be a great first-time experience for us."

"Darken. Interesting choice of words. It's happening already."

"Theo Harper, you'll have to do better than that. Gaslighting won't work on me."

"Gaslight?" he said with a whistle. "Emotionally you're a roller coaster. And I'm a zip line."

"Fuck you, Theo." Without thinking, Darla hurled the thermos of hot London fog tea in Theo's face and Theo screamed. She was immediately sorry, and as Theo wiped at his eyes, she dropped her thermos and stepped toward him. He reached out, whether in momentary shock, blindness, or with some more malevolent intent, who can say, but he snagged the right strap of Darla's backpack, and there were Theo and Darla, Darla and Theo, Theo and Theo—hugging, a push, a tug, shoving—with the ground giving way and his darling Darla hanging precariously from the edge of the cliff.

"Don't let go!" Darla was the one screaming now at the top of her lungs and using her rock-climbing experience to angle and kick and find solid ground as Theo pulled her onto the rock outcrop with what felt like the flick of his strong wrist. Why do women always underestimate the strength of men? "Something is seriously wrong with you," Darla said, panting, adrenaline high, out of breath.

Theo knew he shouldn't say certain words, but here he stood in Darla's wood, and Darla's wood to Theo was a hostile environment. His tongue could not resist the urge to fork, hiss. "Why do you have to be such a sanctimonious little bitch?"

No more, thought Darla. There will be no more fighting. Or risks. She darted off, the backpack ululating as she disappeared into the wood and past the trees and behind rock formations on the un-marked trail, leaving Theo—Mother Nature had never been an ally or friend—to search for blazes, even though he was well off the beaten path.

"Darla?" he called, trying not to let his voice register menace or alarm. But the alarm gave his voice a distinctive tinge of menace, and the menace gave depth to Theo's and Darla's doubts, fears, alarm.

"Where are you?" Theo called his wife's name again and again, but Darla had fled in one direction and Theo, unwittingly, instead of moving toward her voice, had misjudged at first and turned in another, but the wind and its echo made Theo seem nearer to Darla than he was. As Darla ran and tumbled, losing her balance in a thicket of trees that were sometimes home to spring deer and bears and one particularly mean wild boar, she fell with her knapsack like a sled beneath her back. Hill down, hill down, hill down. Her body gathered errant leaves as she attempted to brace her fall and cover herself. *Goddammit, Darla,* was the last thing Darla heard as a rock slammed against her head.

KATSUMI AND I used to cook in the wee hours of the morning and play the "I Can't Believe Prince Is Dead" game. Katsumi would chop and I would simmer stir, and he would pucker his lips and I would wink and say, "Oh no you don't . . . *Kiss?* Come here with your fine, fine self. Time to spice things up and raise the temperature a notch. What's in your hot pot?"

Smack-dab down memory lane we'd roll in our penthouse kitchen accompanied by our personalized Prince playlist. Every year when the Artist Formerly Known as Prince went on tour, Katsumi and I swooped down on a city that doubled as a foodie destination and booked ourselves there. Our ritual started in 2010: luckily we didn't have to venture far. His Royal Highness, feathered fedora, platform shoes and all, gyrated to us for the Welcome 2 America concert in Madison Square Garden. We bargained with the devil for front-row seats (a complimentary weekend in our hotel, meals included). June 2011, there was the Prince Welcome 2 America Euro tour in Cologne, Rotterdam, and Budapest: cities with friends and colleagues who owned or worked in restaurants (Taku, Amarone, and Babel Budapest). Should I blush at the built-in tax write-offs? Inspiration is the caviar of life. I believe that music finds its way into the best dishes. So hell no.

In April 2013, Prince Live Out Loud came to the DNA Lounge in San Francisco, and in June 2014, we took the express train from London to Paris for HITnRUN Phase Two. Finally—*goddamn me, I loathe the word finally*—in 2016, our staff gifted us tickets to Montreal for Prince's Piano and a Microphone concert not knowing that we had already booked tickets for his concert in Atlanta a month later. Shoulda? Coulda? Woulda? And look back with regret? Katsumi and I did not cancel the Atlanta trip. I don't believe in God, but I will be forever grateful to the universe that we didn't. We own Mizu to Yama. Water and Mountain. A Japanese-Afro fusion restaurant in a boutique hotel on a cobbled street in the Bowery. The unique tasting menu and two Michelin stars have classed us as one of the most popular restaurants downtown, which makes for early mornings and late nights. When you own a restaurant, your life is not your own, so to take time off and travel when the margin of long-term success is precarious and paper-thin should put in perspective what Prince's death did to us. He flayed us, baby. Pan-style.

"I can't believe Prince is dead," Katsumi says to me some nights, throwing his arms over my hips in bed.

"I can't believe Prince is dead," I say sometimes to Katsumi after shopping at the farmers' market in Union Square where I see something—fresh lavender, a purple eggplant that, heaven knows why, makes me think of *Purple Rain*. But with so many people dying recently from COVID-19, the "I Can't Believe Prince Is Dead" game, part homage, part acknowledging the pain of losing an artist whose music played in tune with our first date at a night club in Ginza and set the ambiance in our restaurant, seems tone-deaf now. The Artist Formerly Known as Prince died in 2017. We're in the year of the novel coronavirus, April 2020, and bodies are piling up in hospitals and mortuaries throughout the city. How will we account for the unknowns, the sick who have died in bed, the silence and privacy and isolation of their apartments? Katsumi and I set firm limitations on our intake of news: a never-ending horror story most days with its charts and global tracking of a virus with the desire and stealth to outwit scientists and politicians and nurses and doctors and patients—mostly brown, poor patients. We already have our hands full strategizing reopening and retaining our stressed staff of twelve (including but not limited to two cooks for dinner service, a sous chef, our two lunchtime line cooks and lunchtime sous chef, and a three-person prep/porter team). It's a challenge making sure their bodies and ours won't rebel. Cooks are creatures of habit, and our bodies don't know what to do on unassigned days. Our bodies and minds are programmed to dice, slice, carve, and sauté. What's a normal hour? We don't keep normal days or hours, but we suddenly have a surplus of time on our hands. Katsumi and I were fortunate enough to give our staff four weeks' paid leave, a temporary bridge until unemployment kicks in or we receive (knock knock on wood) a Paycheck Protection loan. Everything right now is in flux and temporary. After that, most of our staff will be on their own and unable to stay in the city. Some have asked if they can come to work without pay. Their bodies need the kitchen stations to prep, knead, chop, flambé. We are like military people. Discipline is the foundation of what makes us creative. This month Katsumi has assumed responsibility for what we call mental health hygiene. We're hemorrhaging money and acquiring debt. I am short on positive things to say. Give me a plan of action, the Small Business Administration application to complete for the Restaurant Revitalization Fund, time on the phone arguing with the government to make sure the dominoes fall our way, and I am good for something outside of the kitchen. I leave it to Katsumi to engage our frazzled staff.

When the restaurant lights are off and the kitchen light in our home is on, my lover makes fun of people who tell him, usually white people, with arrogant admiration, "You are so very Japanese."

"Tabitha Ruby," he says. "What does 'You are so very Japanese' mean?"

"I think it means you're calm, Katsumi."

"Inside, Tabitha Ruby, I'm seething. Western conversations about anime or the beauty of Eastern civilizations do nothing for me."

The so Japanese that people think about my lover of fifteen years—we will never marry, nor do we need a piece of paper to validate that something-something we feel when we brush against each other in the restaurant or at home—is Katsumi's ability to make people think that he is hanging on their every word. When Katsumi says, "You're fired," the bartender who arrives late when he should have arrived early and doesn't flow with our staff or the routine will often leave feeling like he has been given a promotion. The next morning he calls to ask, "Wait, was I just fired?"

Katsumi passes the phone to me. Sometimes I think about the crazy black homeless woman in the subway who yells at the riders who insult her insanity by looking away. "Of course your tardy ass was fired," I say. "You *do not* show up at our restaurant at leisure or late."

We have sunk everything into our business. We have kept Mizu to Yama small in scale, thinking of overhead and the way some restaurants expand too fast or too large and how finicky New York restaurant-goers trend, always on the lookout for the next hot restaurant, the next new thing. That our restaurant is housed in a boutique hotel financed in large part by Katsumi's family has afforded us some autonomy. Prior to COVID, vacant rooms in our hotel were unheard of.

*

"How are Katsumi's people doing in Japan?" my mother asked earlier that day when I finally made it to Brooklyn to see her. We sat on the floor of Duke of Bedford Bookstore wrapping books in plastic to keep them safe from COVID, reshelve for pickup, or deliver to customers. I had been so caught up with my restaurant's survival, I hadn't made time until now, a month into the pandemic, to help Mom out at the bookstore.

"The Japanese shut things down early. They were a step ahead of us."

"Well, they always wear masks over there," Frida Black said tentatively.

"Not always, but Japan is a densely populated country." Conversations about Katsumi's family could go left or right. My parents had not expected me to partner with an Asian man.

"Maybe," Frida said, "I should reach out, put in a call. I only met them once, but just to say—"

"I think they would really appreciate that," I said. "And a little extra assurance that Katsumi's okay too."

One of the pleasures of owning the Duke of Bedford Bookstore for my mother was the persistence of discovery. A potential customer walked in off the street and found that first edition of Charles Chesnutt's *The Wife of His Youth* he had been looking for in the rare-books section of her shop. Or another customer popped in with no expectations, just a desperate need to hover in the fresh pages of a new book. Hungry for Frida's recommendations. "I've seen customers cry after coming to Danticat late or the messiness of Baldwin's *Another Country* early," my mother would say. "I sometimes pair Audre Lorde with Countee Cullen and Joy Harjo and tell readers to come back and talk to me." For Frida Black, owning a bookstore was a way to share an intense love of literature and live in the aroma, the smell of books. A smell stronger than perfume that wafted home with her at the end of the day. But to wrap her babies in plastic? I understood that the act of wrapping broke my mother's heart. A book was a thing its reader should live in, explore, plunder. She had wrapped over seven hundred books since March 18 and counting.

"I thought for sure we'd get funding," Mom said, staring at the remaining books to be plastic-wrapped, thinking for some reason of the tackiness of lamination.

"We'll get you funding the next round," I said. "Let's focus on what's in front of us."

Larger, well-established businesses had received the lion's share of government funding during the first round.

"Honey, all I know is a loan would be a gift from God," Mom added. "Owning this bookstore is nothing but a vanity project."

"And why shouldn't you get to have a vanity project?" I asked with a raised brow. "Anyway, you're focusing on the wrong things. Focus on what's in front of you. Keep present."

The Duke of Bedford was a community bookstore, which meant customers ordered books and the staff put them on hold based on foot traffic or word of mouth or book clubs. Before COVID, my mother gave discounts on punched cards for purchases of ten books. Ten percent off or a freebie, like coffee shops gave coffee cards. This old-fashioned approach to running a bookstore cost Mom most of her revenue the first month into the lockdown because neither she nor her employees were especially tech savvy and she had not been able to transition to requests for online orders fluidly. The current website had a picture in the window of the Duke of Bedford and a timeline of the history of the neighborhood, the former home to Canarsie Indians before Dutch settlers took the land in 1776.

My mother had two full-time employees. Bonnie, a third-year college student at Pratt with a side game as a dog walker (secondary income down forty percent, because her clients were working from home or leaving the city with their pets), and Herb, an avid forty-year-old career surfer whose adventures made him a font of book knowledge. Mom had reduced their pay. To boost sales, she was now offering home delivery once a week. Herb would come with his surfboard on top of his Saab, deliver books, and then drive out to Far Rockaway and surf in the frigid waters of the Atlantic, even though the beach was officially closed. "Only the ocean makes sense," Herb would say to the stray surfers wading into the water, comfortable with risk.

My mother had also lowered the membership rate from $25 to $20 and created a list called Soothing COVID Reads with Literature by African American Writers, trying to maintain the community vibe that had won her a loyal neighborhood following. The reality, however, was that while her neighborhood was trending hipper, wealthier, and whiter, most residents were hurting and feeling the financial pinch of COVID. Books were a luxury. Were it not for the income from the two rental apartments above her bookstore, the Duke of Bedford would already have gone out of business. Bookstore closings were averaging at least one a week, which was why I pressed Mom to hire a professional website company to update her web page, including but not limited to updates on Facebook and Instagram.

We worked until lunchtime, stopping to massage and stretch our fingers.

The full impact of COVID in the neighborhood hit when Mom and I came across a queue of men, women, and children—not all of them homeless—standing in a food drive line in front of a Baptist church near Lafayette and Fulton. Masked men and women handed bagged lunches to the needy from behind a gate.

"I haven't seen this since the eighties, when the government handed out generic cheese," my mother said. We would not encounter such long lines again until November 4, 2020, when America came out to vote for the next president of the United States.

I watched the line with interest. Katsumi and I had divvied up food with our staff the day Mizu to Yama closed and donated the rest to a food shelter, but eyeing the queue, I thought of a way to cover the expenses for a loan, if we received one, and to also make a difference. We could apply for a grant to lease the hotel short-term to the homeless. Why hadn't this occurred to me before?

"Mom," I said on the way to get Sicilian pizza. "You should give twenty percent off every book to the food drive at that church. Advertise that online. But you need a better web page." I shared my idea about making our hotel available to the homeless.

"No one will want to come to your hotel again," Mom said. "How exclusive will it be after the homeless are done with it?"

"You gain goodwill by extending goodwill," I said. Yes, I had acquired my mother's business acumen right down to understanding the importance of having rental income (the hotel) to support the restaurant, but my mother had always been tighter-fisted, even when family was involved.

After we returned to the bookshop and ate our pizza, my mother asked a question I could feel coming. "How come the two of you never had children?" This was the one thing perhaps missing from our lives. What would Katsumi and I have if our business failed? What was our glue?

"Are you asking me that because Darla is pregnant?" For the longest time, it was assumed that if I played a sport, Darla would too. Or if Darla practiced her bassoon for an hour, I would play my clarinet fifteen minutes more. Our GPAs were neck and neck and we even attended colleges within an hour of each other, though there were periods when one of us pulled ahead or one of us struggled—but we would always turn the bend together. So why wouldn't we have kids at the same time?

"No, I just think children are such a joy. They wear you out, but they are a joy. You were a joy to me."

"I'm not completely out of time, you know. We're just not quite there yet." I deflected and lied. Katsumi and I had tried and given up two years ago. It had been hard at first to hear that Darla was pregnant, but I was learning to let that tinge of whatever jealousy go.

"Well," Mom said, finishing her pizza. "I wouldn't want you to be holding back because of something I did or didn't do."

I stood up and climbed the bookshelf ladder behind the register.

Mom kept a bottle of vodka on the top shelf. I poured shots for both of us. I could drink and stop. Drugs, no.

Why did it take so much out of me to tell Mom that we couldn't have kids? In the same way that she tiptoed around me, I tiptoed around her, casually noting the spread of the patches of white on her dark-brown skin. Vitiligo. Mom had walked out of the first twin tower without a scratch. And parts of her body had turned white in the weeks and months that followed. A condition exacerbated by stress that exercise, diet, meditation, LED treatment, and steroids slowed down, but there was no cure. The best she could do was manage.

"Come on, Mom," I said. "A COVID cocktail. One shot won't kill you."

Mom took the shot of vodka, and we sat down to resume wrapping her books.

*

Katsumi rinses off a bowl of raspberries and touches his hair as if donning a hat. I almost miss the cue: "Raspberry Beret."

Tonight we are having okonomiyaki for dinner, a Japanese omelet with cabbage and oysters and pork. We have a grill in the center of our small kitchen island to prepare the dish like his grandmother, who was born in Hiroshima, taught him. I mix. He stirs.

"How long do you think we'll last at this point?"

"Oh, I don't know. Nine, twelve months."

"Twelve months seems a stretch."

"I don't know, Ruby." I notice the slip from Tabitha Ruby to Ruby. Katsumi wants to change the subject.

He cracks open two bottles of Kirin lager. Outside, rain teems and teases. We live on the penthouse floor of our hotel. Separation from work is important. Boundaries are vital. Most partnerships don't survive the strain. We do not check messages or answer calls when we cook together at home.

I remember that I have forgotten to turn off my cell phone, and when I move back to the kitchen counter, I notice a text from Darla with an attachment.

"It's Darla," I say, automatically hitting the voice recording, and a musical rendition of "When Doves Cry" fills our kitchen played on Darla's bassoon.

"Ruby, I know how awful you are with texts, but I'm sending this to you and Katsumi, as, um, an appetizer," Darla says, giggling, "with future efforts to come. Please join us at the summer cottage and I'll play for you in person, a serenade. I'll get better at this."

We were certain that Darla and Theo would ask both of us to be their baby's godparents. But Darla asked me and continues to remain mum on Katsumi. Resulting in a shuffling of expectations and disappointments.

"Each parent should have a choice," Katsumi said when I shared the godmother news. But I know my lover. Even though the two of us are a couple, not wedded, godmother and godfather come as one.

"Not Prince," Katsumi says, and nods with appreciation. "But not shabby, either."

"Darla's such a perfectionist," I say, shaking my head. I return to the table to join my Not Husband. "She knows we won't be able to save her recording. Once it's played, that's it. Beauty, warts, and all."

We drink our beer and listen as the instrumental version of "When Doves Cry" fades away.

"Lovely," I text Darla and shut off my cell phone, shifting my attention onto Katsumi. These nights are ours and ours alone.

ROAD TRIPS,

PAST AND PRESENT

THERE ARE Hansel and Gretel breadcrumbs that tell the tale of relationships Theo lost on the road. Women and men who warmed some part of him he would rather forget. Donatella, the pretty Mexican antique dealer who traveled with Theo from Baton Rouge to New Orleans on an *Antiques Roadshow* trip only to be ditched during her afternoon nap at the Columns Hotel. During happy hour the night before, she had taken a sip from Theo's Bellini and said, "Look, we're almost the same color."

"No we're not," Theo replied.

"*Yes,* we are." Donatella touched his face lightly with her bronze triple-ringed fingers. The Louisiana sun was hot, but even back in Iowa, during May end-of-year school days, Theo had always worn a duskier hue to rival the handful of black students. And suffered dearly for it.

"Maybe so. Heat down here will burn you," he said. "In New York, everyone's vitamin D deficient."

Donatella was curvaceous and picked at her food so the curves wouldn't turn into worrisome roundness. She preferred brightly colored textured dresses that did something radical to her skin, a Day-Glo natural luster supple, not the same as sweat. Later people would pay for spritz bottles of tonic to achieve Donatella's (and Theo's) brand of sunshine. How they gorged—like heathens on crawfish—in fist-hot Cajun seasonings, and then reached for lemon-soaked wipes to dispel the crawfish smell from their hands. The smell lingered and gave them the excuse they did not need to suck at each other's pinkies, thumbs, and forefingers and inner palms trying to lick the odor away but then rubbing it all over their night-time bodies.

When Donatella asked casually, "Do you believe in past lives?" she gave Theo the excuse he needed to peer up at the ceiling in the four-poster bed and pivot inward. The life they were living at that moment might have been a past life as far as Theo was concerned.

"It's difficult enough," he had said, "to live in the present. Most people don't know how. Sometimes I think this moment right here is best."

Donatella agreed, her head pressed in the hollow of his chest. "This feels so right." She listened to his heartbeat.

Lord it did. Lord it had. But Theo barely knew her. The raw rightness of cushy feelings scared the shit out of him. Theo watched Donatella sleep for over an hour and left a brief note on the zinc nightstand. "Donatella," the note said, "it's not you. It's me."

He picked up the tab for the room at the front desk on the way out of the hotel. A bicoastal relationship would never work anyway. Donatella lived in Los Angeles, home to five-lane highways, wild-fires, and water shortages. The past-lives bit, he told himself, could tip from New Age eccentric to New Age fanatic. Sophistication not-withstanding, she identified too strongly as Mexican, trading En-glish and Spanish during a conversation at record speed, expecting *him* to keep pace and acclimate to her linguistics. He preferred simple English phrases and declarative sentences.

Once or twice during sex with his then girlfriend now wife Darla, he had called Donatella's name out, grateful for the D and A in both names and the guttural nature of sex that made Darla not notice.

There was Wade, a pilot who lived in Austin and worked for Southwestern. Theo met Wade during a layover in Chicago's

O'Hare Airport. They had noticed each other in the line for Garrett Mix popcorn—each bought a ten-ounce bucket—and then sat side by side for ten-minute back massages at one of the airport massage stations, where they made small talk while two women they did not look at once or twice pummeled their backs. Theo did not think redheaded people were especially attractive, and Wade was the only redheaded man he had ever encountered to make him rethink what he took as fact. As they parted ways, phone numbers were exchanged and, in the weeks that followed, a plan emerged for Theo to pick Wade up in Boston and drive together to Acadia National Park in Maine. They stayed in a B&B on Mount Desert Island, where the desk clerk asked, "Are you brothers?"

Wade, who had come out two years before, said, "More."

Wade was an avid birdwatcher and taught Theo *twitchity-witchity-witch* goes the common yellowthroat; *zzzzzzz* sings the black-throated green warbler; *teacher, teacher, teacher* trills the ovenbird. Bird calls Theo later sang to his young wife, who replicated them with precision on her bassoon. One morning, after observing bald eagles stoop out of the sky and talon prey, Theo and Wade found a watering hole to sex and swim in. Unbeknownst to them, the lake was full of leeches.

"I like this East Coast weather," Wade said, picking leeches from Theo's back. "We don't have real seasons in Austin."

"That means you'll have to come back for a longer visit."

Wade hugged Theo close to him. "Maybe I'll never leave."

"Don't you like Austin?"

"Austin's great," Wade said. "I preserved a lot of friendships after my divorce. Sometimes the best you can do is preserve. And cut your losses."

Theo dipped into the lake for one last swim.

"Hey," Wade said, checking his watch as time wore on. "Aren't you getting cold out there?"

Theo climbed out of the lake shivering, and when Wade reached out to check for leeches, Theo slapped his hand away. "I can handle the bloodsuckers myself."

Wade was nobody's fool. The drive from Acadia National Park to the Boston airport might as well have been a barefoot walk across Siberia. There were chills and frost and a spilled mocha Frappuccino on the passenger's seat just as Wade said goodbye to Theo. Theo was relieved there was no curbside parking for departures.

"Did you fuck up this rental car intentionally?" Theo said.

Wade took out a crisp one-hundred-dollar bill. "Truly," he said. "I did not."

In Connecticut, Theo found a drive-in car wash. As he watched the liquid soap bubble all over the rental car, he heard himself say, "No more road trips with strangers."

There was Victoria, a Trinidadian ESL tutor with a political science degree from the Sorbonne. She kept her hair pressed Condoleezza Rice style and beelined to the bathroom to manage her tresses after sex. Theo loved the gyrations Victoria made when he reached out to touch her hair, which he understood was strictly off-limits. The off-limits part filled him with curiosity. One Sunday while on the jitney to Sag Harbor for a cookout with friends, Victoria became nostalgic for her halcyon days at the Sorbonne. Theo looked up from his *Architectural Digest* magazine. Victoria had graduated near the top of her class. Theo was a B-average student at best. He closed his magazine and ran his fingers through Victoria's hair like he was plowing a field of cabbage.

"Stop it! What the hell are you doing?" Victoria shouted, patting her hair down as he rushed his fingers through her hair from a different angle.

"Searching for knowledge and reassurance."

Victoria attended the cookout solo. Theo toured the Whaling Museum on Sag Harbor's Main Street while he waited for a return jitney to Manhattan.

Chris Beam was older by fifteen years with a mustache that made it seem like he possessed no upper lip. He strolled into the ABC Carpet & Home store one evening and selected four modern kitchen chairs to go. He needed them for a garden party in Chelsea that same evening. "It's a get-together for gentlemen," Chris Beam said, offering Theo a hefty tip to see to it that the chairs were delivered same day on time without a nick or flaw. His house was across the street from a park. A three-level on Sixteenth Street. Theo did not stay long but moved from room to room running his hands along the furniture, blind to the servers in black shorts and black matching shirts and black socks, and uninterested in the appetizers and cocktails. Beam watched Theo salivating over his house.

"My friends think you're a thief."

"No," Theo said, "but right now I have some serious fucking house envy."

"I'm going to a car show this weekend in Pennsylvania. With a pit stop in Philly. My hometown. Care to join?"

Theo shook his head. "I don't do so well on trips. With boys or girls."

Theo still shared a flat with two other roommates, who went to frat boy–style parties five years after graduating from NYU. He was determined to rent cheaply until he could buy. Aside from breakfast at Veselka, he had little in common with his roommates. But with nothing to do that weekend, he accepted Chris Beam's invitation. What soon followed were regular weekend getaways—Chris Beam sold vintage cars throughout New England and the tristate area. During a vintage car show in Hershey, Pennsylvania, Chris Beam noticed Theo admiring the aqua-blue Eldorado. He purchased the car on the spot and handed Theo the keys.

"You can't just go giving people things," Theo said. "Don't you know they'll hate you for it?"

"Theo, you could never hate me." And it was true, this was

Theo's longest and most intense relationship. Theo had been exclusively a topper, but Chris Beam bottomed him. He had begun to pick out items of furniture for Chris Beam's friends, who raved about the additions Theo made to the Chelsea town house—and the Jersey Shore apartment. Theo still hooked up with women on the side when Chris Beam was working or out with friends or seeing his family or just not looking.

Even so, Chris Beam was genuinely confused a year into their relationship when he invited Theo to move in with him and leave the frat boys to debase themselves.

"No," Theo said, and began to pack the handful of things that were his in the town house.

"What's the problem?"

"It's not you, Chris. It's me."

Chris Beam wasn't letting him off that easy. "Is it because I'm older?"

Theo smiled and said, "One day I'll be old myself."

Chris Beam poured a drink. "Theo, you've struck me as many things. Superficial is not one of them."

"Meaning what, exactly?"

"For some of us, the receiving end of pleasure is too much."

"I'm human," Theo said, ghosting Chris Beam on his phone while he stood talking to him. "A human being can get used to anything."

"Get the fuck out of my house, you ungrateful piece of shit."

Theo thought Chris Beam would use his connections to get him fired from ABC. He waited for the Eldorado, which had not yet been signed over to him, to be repossessed. The roster of clients, straight and gay, that Theo had begun to build, thanks to Chris Beam, he thought would wither on the vine, but they continued to contact Theo even after he set up camp in Brooklyn.

The week before Theo was scheduled to move, Chris Beam showed up at his apartment in the East Village on Eleventh Street and Avenue A. Theo came to meet him on the sidewalk, prepared to return the car keys.

"Is it because I'm older?" he asked again.

"I would rather not say . . ." Theo offered him the keys to the Eldorado.

"Keep the goddamn car," Chris Beam snapped. "I thought we had something going here."

"Chris," Theo said, pocketing the keys. "When you look at me, you see yourself. When I look at you, I see everyone else."

*

Theo's raw knuckled bloody hands fumbled in the dark for the light on his cell phone. He used the light as a beacon to guide him along the lip of the night road. He tucked the car keys into the driver's door of the Eldorado Chris Beam had gifted him years ago and found there was no need. Someone had broken into his car. The passenger-side window was cracked, and the passenger seat glistened with triangular shards of glass, the glove compartment left rummaged and wide-mouthed. A quick scan of the back seat revealed a blanket but no bassoon. Theo was tired and he wanted to go to sleep. Theo was sleepy and he wanted to go to bed. But sleep was not an option now. Several hours passed before he had given up looking for Darla. Was it possible that he was humbled by the yip-howls of coyotes and hadn't looked hard enough? He let himself drop inside the car and rested his head on the steering wheel, where he received a staccato honk that hit him like a verbal reprimand. Jesus, son of Mary, beneath the dashboard and around the steering wheel—what's this now?—Theo spied one or two screws loosened, wires exposed, a failed attempt—Darla?—to jump-start the car. Of course, it made perfect sense that Darla might beat him back here. And if Darla beat him here, it made perfect sense that she would go to the cottage. Theo cranked the engine with a fresh burst of vigor and hope. No need to get anyone involved just yet. And what would he tell them, anyway? *My pregnant wife and I had a bad argument and I lost her in the woods.* No, the best bet was to head to the cottage, where he would, crisscross apple sauce fingers crossed, find Darla, sort things out, take a shared hot shower and cuddle chuck the experience as a moment that wound them together for the long haul; a cautionary tale to revisit over vino with their adult children from the sweet spot of old age.

The Jacobsons had wanted a cottage—not to be confused with a summer house—away from the city crowd. And so, they chose carefully and frugally a cottage in a nondescript rural Hudson Valley town that could not be accessed by public transportation and where their Manhattan friends or associates were less likely to follow. All the better, the side glances or nose snubbing, when Daniel Jacobson said in mock lament at board meetings in his twin tower office on the ninety-eighth floor, *Would you believe there's not a decent sit-down restaurant in town to take friends to when they visit?* The Jacobsons could have afforded a chalet on a mountaintop with his finance salary, but vacation meant time to themselves and being unseen and doing what they could to be inconspicuous to the locals. Occasionally they would explore the Hudson Valley or join friends in New Paltz or Hudson for dinner on Warren Street with its renovated Federal-era buildings and antique shops and burgeoning artistic vibe, secretly bemused by the moniker "Brooklyn North."

The cottage was sequestered in a valley on seven acres of verdant land. It was unpretentious and made of cedar, about seventeen hundred square feet, with a wall of forested bluestone that Daniel, Maureen, and Darla Jacobson erected over the course of three years with bluestone found on their own property or gifted to them by the Lazy-Eyed Hermit, or from one of the local abandoned quarries.

Theo did not have to worry about being seen by anything or anyone outside the cottage. But if he had hoped to find the lights on there or his wife, he was sorely disappointed. Once again, he fumbled with his cell phone flashlight, which he had recharged on the way up the swerving road and back into the valley, and called his wife again. He had called Darla one, two, three times. All of his calls went to voicemail.

He lifted the spare key to the cottage from behind the black metal mailbox where Maureen kept it. Theo's nostrils picked up the remnants of winter. The cottage looked exactly as he last remembered it: chunks of wood in the fireplace, a rocking chair, a checkered afghan, an orange fleece blanket thrown over the tweedy couch, and a massive leather ottoman with an oversized silver tray holding a preponderance of magazines. A shelf with secondhand books and board games: Clue, Life, Monopoly, Parcheesi and, from when Darla was little, Twister. A wicker basket full of wool slippers and socks. And on the kitchen counter, an assortment of whiskey, gin, bourbon, wine, sherry, port, vodka, and other spirits. Darla and Theo had eaten Thanksgiving here last year—and Maureen's new man, Pierre, had prepared ballotine de dinde, a deboned French take on turkey with roasted pistachio dressing. The dish passed inspection from Ruby and Katsumi, who were relieved to have a night away from their restaurant and came bearing tapas.

 The first room past the kitchen was the master bedroom, where Maureen usually slept. Theo turned on the light and felt an invisible force field repel him. He left that bedroom alone and went to the room opposite it, a small office with a roll-out queen-sized sofa bed made so friends would visit and not get too comfortable. A night or two and then upwards and onwards.

Darla's room still had the stuff of childhood but not in a sad way. There were pictures of her with her parents on her pony Polly and riding along some bridled path overlooking the Hudson River. There was a purple sequined jewelry box with rings and friendship bracelets and a bucket of different types of lipstick and sheet music and old boots that she outgrew but kept. Theo fell on the bed with the Middle Eastern damask comforter he and Darla had bought at a garage sale the summer Theo had come to help Darla take the cottage front door off its hinges and varnish the door with almond furniture oil. They had reinstalled the door together and Darla had shown him the hand marks on the bluestone made from wild black-berries Mama, Papa, and baby bear Darla had forested. Theo touched Darla's side of the bed, which felt lived in and warm. He closed his eyes, thinking what to do next, maybe this trajectory was wrong, maybe Darla headed back to their apartment or to the near-est police precinct, maybe he should go back and look for her now instead of waiting until morning. Theo knew he ought to pick up the phone and call Ruby or Maureen to ask if they had heard from Darla. But instead, he went into the kitchen and poured himself a double shot of whiskey and soda and returned to Darla's bed and nodded off.

Bang.

Bang.

Bang.

My wife was Theo's first thought when he heard the banging on the front door. He sat up and stared at the analog wall clock with its curving numbers: five-thirty A.M. *My wife.* He had overslept. *Bang. Bang. Bang.* Not a dream state, but Theo's reality. Darla was pound-ing on the front door. Theo started in Darla's direction. If he had looked through the peephole first, he would have seen the Lazy-Eyed Hermit staring back at him. But the impulse to open the door overtook him.

"Morning," Roland Paige said.

"What?" Theo looked confused. The Lazy-Eyed Hermit spoke of morning in the dead of night. Of course Theo knew from the clock it was morning, but this morning felt . . . different. And it had begun to rain, icy and slick.

Roland Paige wore a heavy yellow raincoat, the kind that crossing guards wear. Despite being known as the town hermit, he had worked as a crossing guard for the past three decades at the local elementary school. He was sinewy in build and manner. "You left your car running and the door open. I thought I had better make sure everything is okay."

Theo took the keys, ran his bruised, thicket-scratched hands through his hair. He was aware of the Lazy-Eyed Hermit's watching him and regretted falling to sleep without taking a shower.

"Yes, we got in late. . . . The traffic coming up here last minute like we did was not anticipated." He was lying. Stupid. Fucking. Mind. Why was he lying?

Roland Paige didn't really have a lazy eye. It was a kind of droopy on one side of his face like Bell's palsy that had never gone away. A flash flood in the Finger Lakes. The family minivan overturned in the water. His mother, father, and four siblings drowned. His family had pushed Roland through the window first because he was sinewy and thin.

"Lady Wander asleep?" Lady Wander was the nickname the Lazy-Eyed Hermit had given to Darla, who during fits of temper would wander around his family's property until her parents collected her.

"Sound asleep," Theo lied again, feeling like Peter waiting for the third lie to come.

The Lazy-Eyed Hermit patted his stomach and was joined by a long-legged Irish wolfhound that rushed past him and greeted Theo by licking his hands. The dog had the unmistakable smell of wet dog, which, now that Theo thought of it, so did the Lazy-Eyed Hermit.

"Best get your rest now—with a bunny in the oven."

Theo looked at Roland, surprised he would know about Darla's pregnancy. Had this fool seen his wife?

"Mrs. Jacobson told me," the Lazy-Eyed Hermit said. "What a blessing."

A thousand thoughts competed for front-page status in Theo's head as Roland Paige turned around with his massive Irish wolf-hound in tow and blended into the frigid landscape, which looked for all the world like a Christmas postcard.

Alfred Harper had just sat down with a bowl of Jiffy Pop popcorn to watch *Bonanza* because he was feeling sentimental and didn't want to watch anything that reminded him of the pandemic. He listened to his son, who sounded like he was having a panic attack.

"The first thing you need to do is calm down. The second thing you need to do is get your ass up in those woods pronto for recognizance. Recognizance meaning find your wife. Don't come out of those woods without your woman."

"Dad, it's not my fault."

"Spare me the details. It's always someone's fault. Though I'd keep that to myself for now and let your feet do the talking. Go back. Find Darla."

"And if I don't?"

"Then you go to the local precinct. And we'll see what-is-the-what when I get there."

"I don't think you should come."

"It's a fourteen-hour drive from Iowa to New York City. Longer if I stop in Ohio."

"Don't come."

"Son, now you sound ridiculous."

There was a crackling noise in Theo's ear. It sounded like his father was chewing on popcorn kernels. "Please don't tell Mom yet."

"Your mom just got up to get salt for the popcorn. I warn her about the salt and blood pressure. How's that going to work? Me not telling your mom about your predicament. You know we don't keep secrets."

"Shit."

"Listen, you're not a kid. And you damn sure aren't ten. Man up and get yourself back out there."

Click.

When he was a little boy, Theo's parents would sit through parent-teacher conferences after a bloody nose or a scrap that teachers often couldn't explain. Fights that materialized out of nowhere. He would sit slack-shouldered between his mother and father, one tall and pale, and the other, his mother, Elena, small with a dark Mediterranean face, while the teachers gave assessments. He was that kid who liked to topple the building blocks in kindergarten that half the class had spent assembling. *We must work on his destructive tendencies,* the teachers said. Theo loved counting how many blocks fell or remained standing before gravity pulled everything down. If someone asked Theo, he might say: *My early interest in architecture came from blocks and jungle gyms.* But he didn't believe in being overly analytical. He hated head talk and head thought and people who might link collapsing blocks as a child to a collapsed self. What could be worse than a collapsed self? Sure, he had his run-ins with kids who pointed out that his mother looked different. And maybe his mother had dark skin like the First Theo and a Greek accent, but she was a U.S. citizen. The Harpers were Iowans through and through. In one textbook on Greek myths, the history teacher had read aloud how the ancient Greeks believed blacks were once white until they ventured too close to Apollo's sun and the sun had burnt them crisp. He remembered that moment just like yesterday. Or did she say the sun boiled their skin? He caught hell during recess from the white boys who lumped him up with the one or two black kids in his grade, because even young, the girls liked Theo, and from the black kids who wanted to know why the ancient Greeks were racist. But Theo had never let those incidents burn into bitterness. Instead, he moved to New York and created a sparkling life largely void of the misery or regret that affected most people.

He took a hot shower and cleaned the glass from the car window and passenger seat, patched the car window up, and made himself coffee infused with bourbon before driving to the hiking trail a second time. He was calm now but full of strange thoughts, like the importance of being cognizant enough to pass a field sobriety test if pulled over, staying just within the speed limit to avoid being ticketed by a ranger. Driving on the graveled road, he felt like a twice-turned fool because the weather was god-awful and he knew that despite his father's warning, he was not venturing into "the wood" again. And that was when Theo put the pedal to the metal. That was when he decided to seek out his element: home. Theo resolved to call the police upon his return to Brooklyn, if Darla wasn't in their apartment, because he refused to be questioned by the local county police, who sometimes resented the Liberal Elite. Not that he was a member of the Liberal Elite, not that he was a liberal or a conservative or a libertarian. He was an independent in body and spirit and he was taking an independent drive home so he wouldn't be dependently interrogated at an upstate police precinct. Everything was foreign to Theo that wasn't New York City. He couldn't stop thinking about Darla. Was his wife out there in the cold? Were her last thoughts the awful things he had said? He attempted to create a daisy chain of more pleasant meanderings. But he had strong opinions. Oh yes, he had strong opinions about all this bullshit. The day had been night and the night was now day and so Theo wondered as he escaped the Hudson Valley what the rich people would do when they realized the school districts in many of the towns they were now fleeing to were full of the kind of people they wouldn't want their kids to socialize with. Only with different skin. He thought about his father and his father before him and the First Theo, whom they never talked about other than as a random percentage point, and he thought about what had happened to his sense of equilibrium and he wished he could go down to the lake in Prospect Park near his favorite birch tree and wait for someone to come along and pretend his dog was lost and he wished he could go to the park and fuck to forget. He wished for this and that and that and this and something to make him feel better today than he did yesterday or even a minute ago from now, but all this wishing was neither here nor there and he knew that finding or not finding his wife would determine everything about his future and he knew that he had better call Darla's mother and come up with an alibi that was not a lie. What was he trying to tell Darla up in those woods? Why had what he said become twisted? He tried to imagine a different conversation with Darla. Maybe suggesting that he was black or their baby might be born with darker skin was insulting and preposterous to Darla because, by all accounts, he wasn't black and didn't identify or present as black, although in some states the one-drop rule still existed. Theo thought he was trying to tell Darla about the hypocrisy of white flight. People weren't simply running from the coronavirus. They were running from what a city becomes when most of the people who live there are nonwhite and the economy goes crazy. And they can no longer flit around and pretend those people didn't exist. But Darla had accused him of making blackness a threat. When was blackness ever not a threat for white people like himself, except as a piece of clothing? Then black was a fashion statement. Black made you look slim and elegant, except when it was the color of your skin or maybe if you were an athlete with natural talent or a singer with a gift or a person of exceptional intellect. Man, was he speeding, *slow down, slow down,* back to the city, which was dead as Darla might be. He was faced with the real possibility that some harm had come to his wife because of him, but what about the bassoon. No one would steal a bassoon. Some local hick might steal a bassoon.

Two and a half hours later, there he was, the skyline taking his breath away, tranquility settling over him as he coasted down the West Side Highway and went east toward Chinatown, which was like so much of the city, quiet and still but still there. It took no time at all to get home once he crossed the Brooklyn Bridge, and when he arrived home, he made a point of parking the car, leaving it out front, putting the phone to his ear. He dialed Darla and left a voicemail. *Baby, baby, would you please pick up?* And this time Theo took the elevator, and it didn't even occur to him that he was mask-less. And he would have welcomed the face of the Teenager in the Cardi B T-shirt, but the hallway and elevator were empty. When Theo entered his apartment, he went around touching his things. He left an exasperated message for Maureen. *I was hoping you had heard from Darla. She just ran off in the woods and I came back to the apartment. I'm here waiting.*

The next call was to the local precinct. A terse-sounding officer told Theo to come in and file a missing persons report.

ROLAND PAIGE AND

THE IRISH WOLFHOUND

ROLAND PAIGE went back to the cottage that afternoon on a hunch. He didn't own a cell phone. He did not trust a device that could track him like hunters track deer. The idea that a small cellular phone not much bigger than a deck of cards could pinpoint his whereabouts on a map made Roland feel minuscule and less than human. As a crossing guard, he was often puzzled by how the elementary students and their teachers and their parents went around with their faces being eaten up by an inanimate device and their hands following suit. No, he didn't want an inanimate thing to eat up his energy or his affection. This afternoon was the first time he had regretted not owning a cell phone, because after looking through the windows in the Jacobson house and feeling like the pervert that some of the townspeople thought he was, Roland trekked back to his cottage with his Irish wolfhound (who went by the name of Irish Wolfhound) to the red rotary land phone that was attached to a wall in the kitchen. He called the local precinct and informed them of potential foul play at the Jacobson cottage.

"What makes you think something's amiss?"

"Well, they just got in last night and now they're gone," Roland said.

"People change their minds about staying upstate all the time. City dwellers can't hack the quiet."

"Not during COVID or this weather. Seems to me like they would want to stay put." He stopped short of mentioning the baby. That was Lady Wander's business, and he didn't know how far along she was and did not want to speak its name for fear of jinxing.

"You shouldn't have been out there on their property so early in the morning anyway," the officer said. It was a cold afternoon and the officer sat behind a warm desk. He was content to keep sedentary. Roland described the broken car window and glass on the car seat. "I'm a morning person. Not just a morning person but a *morning* morning person. I like to see the sun come up in the east and set in the west. I never knew it to rise the same way twice."

"Well, we'll swing by and check things out later."

"Maybe you should come and check things out now. Mrs. Jacobson's put good money into the town. And Daniel Jacobson died in the twin towers. So some might say he's a hero."

The hero portion, as Roland had hoped, struck a nerve with the officer. And this might be the same Mrs. Jacobson who had paid for the paving of several private roads in the county, his included. "Give me the address again."

"I'll meet you there," Roland said, peering over his shoulder. He was accustomed to encountering his dead family members throughout the house, and he was in the habit of conversing with them, though they paid him no attention. In fact, they walked through him, which never failed to set his tit hairs on end and, were it not for the isolation of his cottage, the acreage, neighbors would hear Roland asking his mother, father, brothers, and sisters what he could do to make their home more comfortable. A slice of cheddar cheese or a puffed pillow or some country white bread or wild mushrooms he had forested. His deceased relatives never answered, but they took the offerings Roland set out for them. His cousin Estelle had raised him until he hit eighteen and insisted on returning to his childhood home. The return was met with gossip and the interest of one or two women who noted that Roland was different but not altogether strange. You could joke with him and dress him and you could get him to share opinions and he was willing to take work in town and he restored in moderation the family cottage, which had fallen into disrepair, so that parts were habitable, even nice enough for a large family. Why not have a large family? Roland's relationships with women would seem to be going the women's way, which is to say well, until Roland stood up to toast bread for family members who had died long ago. Not just talking to them but expecting his girlfriends to engage his unseen relatives too. Invariably, the women decided they could not abide a home of invisible guests for the sum total of their lives.

*

The officers entered the Jacobson house and found a half-made bed and a towel folded neatly in the hamper and a washed whiskey glass left upside down in the sink and a mug with some dregs of coffee. There were marks from the car and broken glass in the trash can and a little dried blood on the sheets in the bedroom where Theo had slept. The officers reviewed the list of emergency contacts thumbtacked on the kitchen wall. Maureen Jacobson, Darla Jacobson, Roland Paige, followed by the local fire department, precinct, and pharmacy.

"You said Mrs. Jacobson was up here with her husband?"

"Mrs. Jacobson is in France. Her daughter, Darla," Roland touched Darla's name, "was here with her husband."

"But you didn't see her?"

"No. Mr. Harper said she was sleeping." Seeing his name on the tack board touched Roland, put him on the inside of the outside circle that had kept him removed from most of the living since the flash flood. Neighbors still brought food to him every now and again, but he was like a terminally ill patient who had been battling sickness for a long time. People empathized but they didn't want his bad luck to become their bad luck. What do you say to a man who loses his entire family in an afternoon? And yet, here his name was in the Jacobsons' kitchen as a contact. A reminder that he didn't just belong to himself. Roland Paige belonged to them. And in the best possible way.

The officers called Darla's cell phone number. The call went straight to voicemail.

The officers called Maureen Jacobson, who was just sitting down for an aperitif with Pierre. Maureen had been trying for days to reach her daughter. She listened to the officers, piecing together what they were saying from the other side of the Atlantic. "This connection is horrible. Now, what exactly is the matter?"

Roland asked if he could ride with the officers to look for Darla. But the officers told the crossing guard to head home. Maureen had given them Theodore Harper's number; they called and were directed to voicemail. The next step was to contact the local hospitals to see if there were any reports of accidents.

"Aren't you going to drive around and look for them?"

"Mr. Paige," the officer said. "Please let us do our job and go home." They had sent out two young officers. Roland recognized them as former students from the elementary school where he worked. Roland nodded, but as soon as they left the Jacobson house, he let the wolfhound sniff around the cottage again until the dog picked up a scent. Roland was not one to sit and wait, weather notwithstanding. He would go looking for himself. He knew the woods better than anybody, having grown up in them. And the Jacobsons, when they purchased the summer cottage, had made a point of asking him about the best places to hike. It was part of their ritual to go for hikes on their way to and from the cottage. An old green ribbon Darla had given him dangled from the rearview mirror of Roland's car. He kept a small cigar box full of Darla's childhood ribbons back at the house. Roland couldn't say why he saved them. With the wolfhound in the passenger's seat of his Jeep Wrangler, he roamed the back roads of the town with the window down despite the burst of cold air blowing in. The wolfhound was an emotional support dog he had adopted from a pound near Rhinebeck. The dog was trained to sniff out stress and had belonged to a wealthy couple and their teenage twins, one of whom was prone to epileptic fits, but the Irish wolfhound, still young and in training, would sniff out the parents' stress instead. On one occasion, when the epileptic twin, boy or girl, Roland couldn't say, had fallen into a seizure, the dog had become confused and distraught, circling around the panicked parents like a border collie, unable to determine whether the frothing child or the parents needed his help more. And so, the wolfhound froze and was of no use to either. It had surprised Roland how easily the wolfhound had adjusted to his family, who never acknowledged the dog but seemed to realize Roland needed one real breathing thing at home.

The Irish wolfhound eventually picked up a scent and whined and all but jumped out the window for the trail that Darla and Theo had traversed.

"Hold up," Roland yelled. "Heel. It's slippery out here."

*

Roland and the Irish wolfhound were coming out of the woods three hours later when a ranger pulled up alongside them. The icy snow had turned into sleet and Roland and the wolfhound were drenched; Roland held a silver thermos in one hand and Darla's green ribbon in the other.

"Are you trying to catch pneumonia?" said the ranger.

Roland went to the ranger's car and explained how he had found the thermos and how he had called the precinct earlier, but the ranger looked at him, lazy-eyed and soaking wet, and then fixated on the green ribbon and the imperious dog, who was whimpering in the icy rain.

"Tell that dog to stand down," the ranger said.

The wolfhound, conditioned to pick up stress, growled at the stress that was coming off the ranger. Roland petted the long-legged dog on the head. "Sit. And *leave* it," Roland demanded.

The ranger called the precinct and escorted Roland back to his cottage, tailing him and then asking politely if he might come inside and look around. They were soon joined by the two officers who had come out to the Jacobson house earlier that day. The officers came with warrants to search the premises. They took into their possession the cigar box full of ribbons and whatnots that Roland had kept of Darla's over the years, the library books he had never returned about celestial beings and the human anatomy after death. They took the silver thermos Roland claimed to have come upon in the woods. And last but not least, they took Roland, who cried like a baby because for the first time since the flash flood had claimed them, his relatives intervened on his behalf. They petted and restrained the Irish wolfhound so that no harm would come to the beast or their last living relative.

Oh, Daddy
Thank you for the eight new homes
The devil don't like it
But we don't care
The devil don't like it cause he ain't here
Oh, Daddy
Thank you for the eight new homes

THE CLOSER we are to death, the more we dream. In those uncertain days when the fluid made a soap mop of Nadine Curtis's chest, filled her lungs up so the doctors weighed the ethical merit of keeping her on the ventilator when there were patients younger and with more years ahead of them who stood a better chance of surviving the coronavirus, they prepared to code the fifty-year-old chemistry teacher (time, date, cause of death) and to share the news with her family. Nadine did not know she was dying, of course, only that she was somewhere else—away from her only son, Xavier, and husband, Irvin. Home, home, now where was home? She could not, in this dream state, put a pin on an address, a zip code, a street name, even a city or a borough. Brain fog was her enemy, but some gut-level survival mechanism kicked in and told Nadine to cling to her fragmented memories. Wasn't it just yesterday that she had turned to Irvin and said, "You've bothered me enough about going back home, Irvin. And now I'm here. Where are you?" She was on the ninth floor, alone save for the doctors and nurses and attendants, in the COVID ward.

Nadine Curtis had grown up in the United House of Prayer for All People on Ogeechee Road. Sweet Daddy Grace founded the church, to which her parents remained devoted. When she was a young girl, her mother volunteered once a week to cook in the kitchen and serve food buffet-style: red rice and cornbread stuffing and fried or baked chicken and smothered turkey wings or meat-loaf and shrimp gumbo, potato salad, macaroni and cheese, and candied yams. On the days she volunteered, Geraldine Spaulding would bring home leftovers in Styrofoam dinner plates for Nadine and her two brothers, Lawrence and Willy, and her husband, Skip Spaulding, who owned the Avis car rental franchise at the Savan-nah airport. *Daddy Grace. Bishop C. M. Sweet Daddy Grace. Charles Emmanuel to you. He come from across the water somewhere. Cape Verde,* they say. He dabbled in this profession and that profession, but nothing stuck until God reached out and touched him. Yes God did. And God's touch brought a flock to his calling.

Nadine was born eight years after Charles Emmanuel Grace had died. She grew up hearing with pride how their local United Prayer Church for All People had expanded from a modest holiness church with a sawdust floor to the modern building she entered every Sunday. By the time she was a teenager, the United House of Prayer still had churches all over the world, for whenever one door dwindled or closed, others opened. Nadine knew the lore. And the impromptu call-and-response. They intruded and filled her lungs with dream-like oxygen.

> *Ain' y'all my fools?*
> *Yes sir, Daddy, we your fools*
> *Thank you for the eight new homes*

Geraldine and Skip Spaulding were among the first blacks to buy a three-bedroom brick house with a two-door garage in Sylvan Ter-race when the wealthier Jewish families began to sell and move

south side to Habersham Woods. Skip converted part of the garage
into a hair salon for Geraldine, who worked Tuesdays through Saturdays, stopping on the weekend promptly at four P.M. She could do
a pretty Whitney Houston, box braids, finger waves, Mohawks, flat-
tops, mullets, a traditional press or curly perm, vertical bangs, extensions of every kind. Geraldine often took Nadine on weekend
trips with her to trade shows so her daughter could pick up skills
and possibly, when the time came, take over her business.

But Nadine showed little interest in being a beautician, and on
the occasions when she was required to apply the pre-perm conditioner to a client's hair or to set up the washing station or to heat the
big mouth of the hot comb or to run up to DeRenne to the hair supply shop and get a tub of pink or black Eco or Let's Jam styling gel,
she would cartwheel and dance all the way there and back like there
was a big body in her little body waiting to burst out, a volcano on the
verge of erupting, and every once in a while, like the afternoon when
she shimmied past her mother and caused the hot comb to kiss and
burn Helena Posey's temple so bad the woman shrieked and left in
such a huff, Geraldine wondered if a lawsuit was next.

"You know Helena's a first-class drama queen. That 'He' in Helena should be a D for too much damn drama." Nadine was grounded
for a week. She could not watch television. She could not join her
Savannah High friends after school for pizza at Pizza Inn or a mati-
nee at the Oglethorpe Mall or on Victory Drive. She could not stroll
the mall with friends and share the Savannah Pralines or go watch
the tourists getting drunk as skunks on River Street, and when she
came home from school she had to do her homework and chores
until bedtime, including but not limited to washing the towels and
wraps for her mother's salon, heating up the tuna casserole or macaroni her mother had made for dinner, tossing the carrot and raisin
salad, and setting the dinner table. Willy and Lawrence teased Nadine without mercy: *Come maid, go maid. We didn't know we could
afford a maid named Nadine.*

———

Helena Posey strolled into Geraldine's shop on a Saturday afternoon when the shop was full: two women under the dryers, a third
on the tail end of a steam treatment, a fourth enjoying a shampoo
from Nadine (who gave a nice shampoo when she focused), and a
fifth receiving a Chaka Khan weave from Geraldine.

"Why you want to do that mess to yourself?" Helena Posey
frowned at Geraldine's customer. "There's so much hair on your
head, just looking at you makes me sweat."

"Excuse me," the customer said. "Do I know you?"

Helena clutched her purse to her chest, incendiary style.

Geraldine continued to apply her customer's weave. "Helena, I
don't think you have an appointment today."

"An appointment?" Helena laughed. "Hush, I will never give
you my business again."

"Then why are you here?"

"My crown has been compromised." Helena touched her temple
where there was a dime-sized mark two shades darker than the rest
of her temple, but Geraldine knew the burn would heal.

"You and your husband got good jobs. Some of us out here catching hell," Helena said.

"My husband owns a car rental company. And I do hair. Your
savings account might outstretch ours by a Jesus mile. But I would
never imply or inquire."

"Hear this: you have scarred my temple for life."

Geraldine remained calm. She had discerned a week before that
Helena Posey had herself a boyfriend who lived on the same block
catty-corner from Helena and her husband's house.

"The best I can offer you is two free visits to my shop, two complimentary washes, two complimentary trims, and deep condition-
ers, too."

"Well, I'm not biting," Helena said.

Geraldine laid the 1B Afro Kinky Bulk hair on her workstation and took Helena aside. "Take it. I have nothing else for you except gossip to share with your husband. Neighborly gossip, which I normally hate, because if your beautician can't keep your secrets, tell me who can?"

Nadine's parents enrolled her in ballet as well as modern and tap. Skip installed a bar alongside a wall in Nadine's bedroom, but they soon began to wonder if they had two children instead of three, because their daughter sequestered away in her room for hours at a time practicing. Schubert and Bach and Rachmaninoff and Tchaikovsky spilled out of the room, and Lawrence and Willy sometimes, just to be mean and because that noise upset their equilibriums, responded by blasting Public Enemy's "Fight the Power" and Run DMC's "You Be Illin'."

During the Magnolia spring recital, her pirouettes and fouettés and grand jeté stole the show. She was one of four black girls in the recital and the only one given a solo.

Does she sing?
I do not.
If only she could sing.

Geraldine and Skip were amazed by Nadine's flexibility and grace. Their daughter was like a doe who had found its legs and its speed and rebuffed gravity. Even when Nadine touched ground she soared.

"She is my star pupil, you know?" said the dance teacher, who was thin. The slim frame had served her well in her youth, but in her late fifties, the thinness gave what was in actuality an attractive face a Broom Hilda witchiness.

"Why do you say 'star pupil' so sad?" Skip asked.

"Most of my students dance for posture and to pass the time. Or to manage their weight. But Nadine has the passion. She'll outgrow you. She'll soon outgrow me. I could teach her to be a perfectly fine dancer, but without proper training or, specifically, studying with dancers at her level, she will never become a great ballerina."

"She can't make a living dancing anyway," Skip said.

"Shouldn't Nadine be given the chance to prove us wrong?"

The dance teacher was a former prima ballerina for the San Francisco Ballet. She had given up her career and moved to Savannah with her husband, one of the partners at Gulfstream, opening the studio when her children entered kindergarten.

Geraldine and Skip Spaulding were not standard-issue Pentecostals. Owning the car rental afforded Nadine's father introductions to all kinds of people, domestic and foreign tourists, with philosophies that challenged his religious beliefs. And since a beautician—like a masseuse—is intimate with her clients, Geraldine had heard and witnessed enough to quietly question the ideologies of her religion as much as she embraced them in the pews on Sunday. And so, they debated among themselves and eyed their daughter's every move in the weeks following the recital. If she was gifted, did they not bear some responsibility to lend fuel to said gifts?

Nadine took matters into her own hands and, one evening after helping her mother dry the dishes, joined her parents in the living room, where they often played the card game I Declare War together while drinking Barefoot Bubbly pink champagne. Nadine placed a brochure and application for the Dance Theatre of Harlem on her mother's queen of hearts and her father's jack of spades.

"Mama, don't you have a cousin in Harlem?"

"All black people have a cousin in Harlem," said Geraldine, who took a prodigious sip of her pink Champagne. "That's what the Great Migration was. A cousin in Harlem. Or Philadelphia. Or Chicago. Or L.A."

Skip picked up the application. He knew of Katherine Dunham and Carmen McRae and the Nicholas Brothers and Mr. Bojangles, whom Fred Astaire and Gene Kelly acknowledged as the greatest tap dancer of all time. Tap tap tapping along with Shirley Temple, her blond curls shaking. Skip knew the smooth moves of the Temptations and the O'Jays and James Brown, who came down to Savannah every now and again and ate at the House of Prayer cafeteria. All the women fussing and calling relatives to come and meet Mr. Brown, who was good people and happy to say hello after he had eaten. And, of course, there was Michael Jackson moonwalking all over the place. Like Geraldine, Nadine's father might not be able to articulate how these forms were all linked, but if pressed, he could recall a popular dance like the jitterbug or the Charleston or the old man or the crawl from his parents' generation. Or their parents' generation. What Geraldine and Skip Spaulding could not recall was a black ballerina; nor could they imagine how Nadine would sustain a career as one.

"Why Harlem?" Skip asked, having been kicked on the shin under the table by Geraldine, a warning not to say no just yet.

"I don't want to be anything but a ballerina. I'm coming to dance late, Daddy, compared to some people. Arthur Mitchell was the first black ballet dancer at the New York City Ballet. He cofounded the Dance Theatre of Harlem for boys and girls who look like me. He even thought of flesh-colored tights, which I know seems like a small thing, but those tights say *make room.* I want to go dance and not hold back or second-guess anything."

Sometimes to amuse herself, Nadine would intercept one of Willy's or Lawrence's football punts. Already her brothers talked of college in terms of homecoming games and the positions they would play on college football teams. *Catch me if you can,* Nadine would taunt, and her two younger brothers would chase her around the block and back to the front lawn of their brick house, where she would beat them to the finish line and score a touchdown plié. She walked on her tiptoes. Her world was limber and pointy.

There, I am better than the best running back.

Who's the best running back?

How would I know?

Lawrence and Willy rolled their eyes and walked away, panting and out of breath but triumphant over Nadine's lack of knowledge about football. "This is a man's game."

"Let her go," Lawrence and Willy said. Their sister's going away to college constituted a family decision, and the younger brothers would not be left out.

"If you don't let her go," Willy said, "we won't get any peace. She will miserable up this house."

Geraldine's second cousin on her father's side lived in a Harlem brownstone on 138th Street. It took some working up to reach out to the cousin, all but a stranger for a big ask. But blood was blood, thick and thin. And people had been showing up or making such calls since the Great Migration, for better or worse.

"Well," her second cousin said, "I'm inclined to agree with Nadine's father. With grades like that she could get into a good school up here. It's not enough to dance. To stay with me, she'll have to do both."

For the audition, Nadine donned one of her mother's old fringe vests, for her mother had been a western girl in the United House of Prayer parades and her mother before her, and Nadine would have been a western girl too, except that her first love was ballet. Nadine danced like a girl who had been raised in the United House of Prayer for All People. She held her neck and chin high and lifted her legs and threw her fringed vest on the ground and leaped across it with a House of Prayer shout and twirled around and walked across the vest like Jesus Christ walking across water.

> *Look at all the people come out to see me in the rain*
> *This much people didn't come out to see Jesusssss*
> *Don't make me mad cause Daddy coming tonight*
> *Ain' y'all my fools?*
> *Yes sir, Daddy, we your fools*
> *Thank you for the eight new homes*

The performance was earnest and profane. Geraldine and Skip watched Nadine practicing and saw that the House of Prayer was in her, even if she would not always be in the House of Prayer. When they received notice that Nadine had been accepted to the Dance Theatre of Harlem, Nadine's parents and brothers helped her set up her bedroom in Geraldine's cousin's brownstone, signing a contract of Rules and Conditions, including monthly rent. The cousin, working in human resources at Sloan Kettering, had been married three times and brooked no foolishness. She declined their invitation to join them for a parting meal at the United House of Prayer on 125th Street. Nadine's mother, with tears in her eyes, told the sisters working in the cafeteria to look after her daughter and pray for her to do well. They assured Geraldine and Skip that Nadine would always have a home there, so that her mother and father and brothers left taking some solace that Daddy Grace's church was less than a ten-minute walk away from where their daughter now lived. Nadine was accepted into Bronx Science. Between the regimen of dance and the requirements of school, she would need God's intervention and have little time for mischief.

Don't your parents know that man was nothing but a con artist?

her second cousin asked with a raised brow after Nadine's family had left. *They look to have good sense.*

Let's not talk about Daddy Grace. Daddy Grace got me here, Nadine retorted, defending both Daddy Grace and her parents.

The contract was harder to abide. Written into it was a promise not to entertain young men in her mother's cousin's house and not to fall below a B+ average, like that was any of her old cousin's business. Nadine's second year in New York, she met and was often partnered with a dancer named Julian Curtis. When she told Julian that she was from the South, he asked her if she liked castoffs and intestines.

"What kind of castoffs are you talking about?"

"Hog cheese, ham hocks, chitterlings, tripe, pigs' feet."

"No," she said, "and I don't sing either. I am a ballerina."

Nadine hated assumptions and was prepared to put him on her No Time For list until he explained that his favorite cousin was from Virginia and when his Nanna came north she would always feed them slave soul food when his parents weren't around.

"I meant no offense."

Julian and Nadine became fast friends and her junior year— Nadine loved boys almost as much as Julian did—they rented an apartment on St. Nicholas Avenue across the street from Famous Fish Market.

Nadine danced well. She danced so well (along with Julian) that they were invited to tour in England and in France and Belgium. Julian's parents lived in Park Slope, but aside from monthly visits from his mother, he only traveled to Brooklyn on the holidays. "My father took my coming out harder than my mom" was all Julian said. Nadine understood that family was like stickleberry bushes of hurt and didn't press Julian further.

"Are you keeping up your grades?" Dance was still a stepping stone to being an adult for Nadine's parents, but Geraldine and Skip Spaulding supported her. They came to Europe and were awed at the company's performance. Nadine had graduated and told them college was on the horizon. After dance.

It was October 2003, the year the cops came to subdue a 425-year-old cat named Ming from the Drew Hamilton apartments in Harlem, that Nadine met Irvin, Julian Curtis's favorite cousin. Irvin had moved to New York City to attend New York University, politely declining his uncle's offer to reside in Julian's old bedroom and renting a studio apartment that was too small for him. Irvin joined them for breakfast at Sylvia's, where he ate a preponderance of biscuits and ham at the counter before going to watch the tiger being rappelled from the apartment building with other spectators. He was touched by how Ms. Sylvia welcomed everyone at the front door, and she reminded Irvin of his grandmother, whom he had lost to a stroke earlier in the summer.

"He must be grief eating," Nadine whispered.

As they stood in the crowd with Nadine's arm inadvertently brushing up against Irvin's arm and Irvin's thinking that New Yorkers were strange and why in God's name would anybody want to keep a Siberian tiger as a pet and who would be crazy enough to want to rent from the owner.

"I think he rented the room for a bargain," Julian said.

A group of kids in a youth camp paused with their camp counselors to watch the spectacle. Irvin overheard a thick little boy ask one of the counselors, who was busy trying to subdue the kids, already fired with impromptu field trip excitement, "Where's the tiger's owner?"

"In prison. Or if he's not in prison, he's soon going to be."

The little thick boy blinked. "What's prison?"

And this question resulted in its own questions, a titanic of laughter, and scorn, and the counselor stared at the thick boy like his parents had done something very wrong in the fundamentals of his education.

"Prison is Bloody Mary, the Bogey Man, the Bride of Chucky,

Count Dracula, Frankenstein, it's the thing lurking in the shadows, waiting."

The boy burst out crying. Later the counselor would be written up, but in that moment, Irvin Curtis, who had come up to Harlem with three disposable cameras purchased on the spur of the moment at Duane Reade to document the adventures of Ming, handed one of the cameras to the counselor.

"It should have enough exposures for every kid to take a picture." But then he turned to his cousin Julian as the tiger was being rappelled down the side of the building to oohs and aahs and stunned amazement. "What kind of shit is that to say to kids? Who does that bitch think she is?" he snapped. A moment of shyness caught him. Nadine didn't know him well. "Pardon my French."

"No problemo. I speak Spanish," Nadine said. What she wanted to say was, *You remind me of my mama and daddy and Willy and Lawrence, and I've given up a lot to be here. Sometimes I don't let myself miss them.* Around Irvin that day, she missed them less. And noting his prodigious appetite, she suggested they go to the House of Prayer for lunch.

"Huh," he said as the women fussed over Nadine in his presence. "This food tastes like home."

She beamed and said, "Doesn't it, though?"

Nadine Spaulding slipped and broke her ankle on black ice ten months later. Afterward, every leap and jump racked her legs with pain, but Nadine jumped and leaped and she leaped and she limped.

Are you keeping up your grades? her parents asked. They knew she wasn't enrolled in college. She had graduated from high school. She was a company dancer with a damaged ankle that would not heal.

"Nadine," Julian said, for he loved Nadine like a sister, "you would make a great choreographer. Choreography is in most dancers' future. It's certainly in mine."

"Yes," she said, "but that decision won't be forced on you prematurely."

If she could not dance, she would not choreograph. After nursing a period of distinct bitterness and spite, during which even Julian avoided her and slept over at his boyfriend's, Nadine enrolled at NYU. She ran into Irvin standing on the line in the bursar's office because she had forgotten to deposit her tuition check and had to come in to set matters straight.

"Something's different," Irvin said, regarding Nadine.

"I'm an adult," Nadine said, smiling.

That was twenty-something years ago. She was a chemistry teacher now, known for the pep in her step. Plié, fouetté, pirouette, grand jeté.

> *Ain' y'all my fools?*
> *Yes sir, Daddy, we your fools*
> *Thank you for my eight new homes*

DARLA'S MOM

MAUREEN JACOBSON sits with unhappy feelings about Darla, whom she loves but finds impossible to look at without being reminded there is no more husband Daniel. Their lovely daughter born after five in vitro fertilization procedures before Maureen was forty. Fun trying, but not easy to conceive. The difficulties of conceiving, another secret, like breastfeeding, that women, mothers, are reluctant to share until after the fact, when the nursing doesn't take or the nipples chafe and bleed. When the milk refuses to flow or comes in so scanty skim baby Darla screams. But you, Maureen, are a woman, and God help you, Maureen Jacobson, you are a professional woman. The feelings of inadequacy set you at war with fatigue and yourself. How you want this darling child, so much a part of you, your placenta, to drink to sip to nip, but when the elderly maternity nurse coaxes you gently, suggests with years of experience and concern, *Just a wee bit of formula for a wee thing,* and your wee girl gobbles the formula, you relax into the land of nod and your breast milk forms that evening, wets the hospital sheets and pillows, but Darla has taken the bottle and your breasts entice but neither match nor latch. Daniel paces the hospital room and wants you and the baby out of the hospital yesterday. His mother is a Christian Scientist. He has never been sick a day in his life and doctors, hospitals, are anathema to him. Daniel rockabyes your wee baby Darla, blessed thing, counting her fingers and toes, kissing her curled pink feet, pacing, saddlebags beneath his clear blue eyes. He will lose his man belly faster than you will lose your stretch marks. But you are a dermatologist and there are creams and lotions for stretch marks. Oh, but Darla is all Daniel, all blond. You are a natural brunette who peroxides blond, like Marilyn. Darla will forever be the spitting image of her dad, on her first day and even more so now in the hole that gapes in his absence like a cold sore you would Abreva so it disappears before blistering into a new sting.

Maureen loves a new man in an old city: Paris, the City of Light. She has reset slowly to love but rather well. Pierre Bernard, a dentist she met after a filling gave but the pain in her tooth roared. An emergency appointment Maureen's only option. In Pierre's office, alongside diagrams of human teeth, Pierre keeps a bicycle rack with a Bombtrack touring bike mounted to the wall. He is an avid cyclist. When Maureen tells Pierre that she could not imagine cycling around Paris, he says, "I could see you on a bike." Pierre resides in the 12th arrondissement on the way out of the city, close to the airport, and takes frequent cycling vacations.

Maureen shakes her head: no. While he drills, her numb gums bleed. She is out of shape in the years since Daniel's death, not fat but miserly toned. Chocolate, stored in the fridge, a nibble here, a nibble there, a weakness. An indulgence Darla inherits. Maureen plays tennis at the New York Sports Club on social outings with friends. But exercise in general gives her no joy. She is past the age when men or friends' husbands pinch her thigh or caress her back unnoticed. And relieved to have the elevator eyes and groping hands gone. After her husband's death, married friends kept their distance, which core struck her soft center, for Maureen is no gender trader. Feminist solidarity would not have her take a friend's husband. In his office, Maureen says to Pierre, "This body hasn't been on a bike in years."

Pierre responds, "But there are bike paths all over New York City."

"Well, I'm not in New York City, am I?" She shrugs off the temptation to tell Pierre that she used to ice-skate regularly in Bryant Park with her late husband. Their first encounter, a head-on collision during her lunch break. "Pardon you!" Maureen had said, as they tumbled and stood up again like proud *Homo sapiens.* "I think it's the other way around," Daniel Jacobson said. "But a disaster averted is always a relief."

Daniel was twenty-four and fresh from a year in Gambia. He had volunteered for a reforestation project with the Peace Corps upon graduating from Wharton Business School and Princeton undergrad. Community service time-out before accepting the financial analyst position that awaited him on Wall Street. Maureen learned this as she unlaced her cheap white rental skates on a bench. (He had come to the rink equipped with well-worn Riedells.) Between sips of Nestlé hot cocoa Daniel bought from the kiosk, Maureen apologized twice: first for bumping into Daniel and trying to play it off on him, and also for having to cut their conversation short. She was in the second year of her residency and ice-skated during lunch breaks to decompress. At the time, Maureen thought she would practice psychoanalysis, but around the time she began dating Daniel Jacobson, she audited a dermatology course and decided she liked the profession much more. Skin was the human body's largest organ. An object of beauty but also its first layer of defense against disease and contaminants.

Pierre Bernard snaps his magician's fingers. "You can come to the Bois de Vincennes this weekend. We'll rent you a bike and it will all come back to you." Maureen does not believe in magic. Still, she has a new filling and her mouth feels rational. Maybe she could learn to ride a bike again.

He takes Maureen to his neighborhood bike shop, and she tests various beginners' bikes before they come upon one that cushions her derriere. When she suggests a helmet, Pierre laughs and says, "Come, how old are you, two?"

They cycle around the Bois de Vincennes and the workout on her legs makes Maureen feel she has discovered a new life source when she clutches the handlebars.

"Something's not right with Darla," Maureen says to Pierre on the balcony of his apartment. She rents a long-term Airbnb where she seldom sleeps. A waste of money but for the military-style curfews and cards that track people's whereabouts. They have sex in her apartment sometimes just to have a change of scenery, a second place to go. In the evening, Maureen and Pierre enjoy across-balcony dinners with Pierre's neighbors. COVID neighbors he had not known or thought to know prior but now waves or shouts out or gesticulates to at night. Comforting to see strange familiar faces on a dinner schedule. Will they walk past one another when COVID is over? Their balcony dinners remind Maureen of the cottage house.

"We have our rituals," Maureen says to Pierre.

"You are feeling guilty," Pierre says while pouring a second glass of Petit Chenin.

"I should have left Paris when there was still time."

"Your daughter looked perfectly healthy on our last Zoom."

After their first bike ride, Maureen and Pierre dated cautiously. They were inseparable now. Winter was to be their trial period co-habiting before Maureen settled permanently in Paris. News she had not shared with her daughter. News she had held back upon learning Darla was pregnant.

"Easy for you to say, Pierre. The virus and the president have robbed me of my right to board a plane."

"For the time being."

Maureen shakes her head. "There is only now."

In truth, Maureen does not know how she will handle seeing Darla with child or, when the time comes, how she will hold a grandchild and not compare herself to Daniel/what Daniel would say if he were there to fill up the room with his bon vivant. But she heard the open disappointment in Darla's voice during their last conversation and Darla canceled their Sunday morning Zoom. The last message from her daughter came via text: *Can't talk, Mom, driving upstate.* So, Darla and Theo had taken her advice and gone off to the cottage for rest and relaxation. And Darla was giving Maureen the silent treatment—as Darla had routinely done, even as a little girl of five storming off into the wood with her plastic shovel and pail, stopping to stomp in puddles or creeks along the way or gather wild mushrooms and berries, which she had been taught not to eat until an adult tried them first, knowing that the Lazy-Eyed Hermit's door was never locked and that her mother or father would follow in her wake.

Which one of us will fetch her today? Maureen would ask her husband, thinking, as an only child herself, *If only we'd been able to give her a little brother or sister to play with.* When Darla was young, they loved to steal away to their cottage in the autumn months to catch the fall foliage. They were nearly three-quarters into building a stone wall that Daniel hoped to complete before the first frost came and the soil became inhospitable to building or digging.

Get the hot chocolate and marshmallows ready, Daniel would say, grabbing his favorite green vest on the way out the cottage door. *We'll be back within the hour.*

ALL THE ANSWERS

ARE AT HOME

THE SKY had three moods and Darla chose sunset to keep her warm. She had wakened, awoke, *God help me, I am woke*—Darla, wake up! Finally, with a sliver of grayish-white smoke clouds against a sky that was like sunburst pumpkin whoopie pie candy corns. The day was fading and Darla stirred and disengaged herself from the muddle puddle wet and thick and slippery on the forest leaves that made her snow-white bed. She knew instantly where she was in the wood and which direction she must go. She also knew, though vaguely, that Theo had abandoned her. Chased her, yelled after her—at one point *pushed* her—then beseeched her to stay. But she was angry. Her anger fled away from him and whatever he had to say, lies, lies, lies, all of it, most of it, with maybe a smidgen of truth, but *smidgen* wasn't a real word anyway. Smidgen was a dandelion blown to nothing stem stalk left to toss. Hadn't her husband tried to toss her over the edge of the mountain and away? Let her hang there with a slight smile on his face? Oh, the spinning in her head and the tricks the mind played on itself. She had run like Lola in *Run Lola Run,* that movie her parents used to watch. Intuited over rock paths and bridges, aware that the wilderness belonged to wild creatures once the sun went down, trusting that wild creatures mostly shunned the unknown, random unpredictability of men. For Darla, Theo constituted an unknown too. How long had he been unknown and how long had she pretended he wasn't? *We always know.* Deep down, we always know.

The quickest way out of the forest revealed itself along a creek that was dry but in the direction of civilization, the graveled road. She saw two of everything, double vision that could have been worse, deadly, from the blow she had taken to her head, the full impact of the errant rock thwarted by a raised left hand, leaving her with a gash that bled but a mostly superficial graze that she stymied with gauze and ointment from the mini first aid kit in her backpack, all the while moving. No time to lament her cell phone, lost on the trail, fallen from the side pocket of her backpack. Darla paused and undid her backpack again with her right hand. The left hand hurt too much and was missing a fingernail, swollen, possibly broken. *I am a musician. Don't let my finger please God be broken.* She pulled out a thermal fleece, slipped it on her right side, and used her shoulders, head and torso, and right hand to get the fleece on. She filled the underside of the thermal fleece with leaves, careful to avoid another slip or twist her ankle, determined to keep warm and insulated in case she fainted and the temperatures dipped. All the while shortening her distance to the road. The denseness of the clouds told her a cold front was coming.

Darla used the backpack to break into the Eldorado. And plundered the glove compartment for a spare key. She thought Theo had mentioned keeping one there, but her hands fell on extra chewing gum, lubricant, and Durex Mutual Climax condoms. Steadying her body again, she ferreted out a switchblade and shimmed into the driver's seat, where she sequestered behind the wheel and began testing her blades out on the ignition, a trick from Aimsley, the townie boyfriend whose infatuation had gained such momentum she and her mother had skipped a summer at the cottage house, but not before Aimsley taught Darla the fine art of petty thievery, the joys of oral and anal sex, and how to roll a joint and reuse it. Darla experimented with the full range of switchblades, inserting them into the Eldorado's ignition slowly, methodically, noticing the double vision was becoming less pronounced and the world around her taking on its normal cast. She could see straight again. She heard the engine hum, but it refused to roar. She heard the engine sing, but one short verse. She cooed to the engine, but Darla was really talking to her unborn child. *We can do this, baby. We can do this, baby. My heart is racing, baby.* Darla continued to pump the gas and undo wires and the frustration mounted so that she burst out in tears, and that's when she saw the headlights of an approaching vehicle in the rearview mirror. She sprang out of the Eldorado and held her thumb up hitchhiker-style and elevated her stomach so that the driver could see she had a baby bump going. A woman with a salt-and-pepper Art Garfunkel afro poked her head out of a Toyota Corolla. She wore a blue trilevel surgical mask. Darla burst out in tears again. Grateful the driver wasn't a man.

"Jesus, what happened to you?" the woman asked.

Instead of answering, Darla backtracked to the Eldorado and retrieved her bassoon from the back seat of the car. The woman climbed out to help Darla.

"Put this on," she said, giving Darla a surgical mask and taking the bassoon and knapsack from Darla and placing them in the back seat of the Toyota alongside a worn leather medical bag.

"Thank you."

"Thank me once we know you're okay."

The woman, whose name was Jennifer Klein, stopped short of telling Darla she was one shit-in-luck lady. She guided Darla into the Toyota and lit a Virginia Slims cigarette as she rounded back to the car, enjoying a few quick intakes, surveying the Eldorado, the road, the scene, putting pieces together so she would know what to ask the pregnant young woman she had nearly run down on the road.

"So, my name's Jenny Klein. And I'd say our first stop is the local hospital."

Darla looked out the window. She could see her reflection in the passenger-seat mirror. She looked like someone's mutt, a battered,

fragile thing, hair glued to her face, blood stains on her hastily bandaged forehead, eyes swollen and bloodshot and dilated. She looked
nothing like herself. She felt nothing like herself.

"No hospital," Darla said finally.

"What's your name?"

Darla was quiet.

"Give it a moment," Jennifer said, for she was a general practitioner. She did house calls. And COVID was keeping her busy.

Darla continued to say nothing for the longest time. "Why aren't
we moving?"

"Before we go anywhere—"

"Anywhere is better than here," Darla muttered.

"Before we go anywhere," Jennifer said, "I have to ask you: was
this an accident or did someone hurt you?"

Darla shrugged, shutting her eyes, listening to her stomach
growl and realizing she was hungry, ravenous. Imagining food and
poison on a silver tray. Should I tell the truth or should I misre-
member it. Once you told the truth, it was not like a lie. A lie you
could modify, adjust, compartmentalize. But the truth, once you set
it free, was impossible to reclaim. And she was still uncertain
whether the rock had contacted her head as she fell or been thrown
at her by Theo deliberately. When Darla shut her eyes, she saw the
wood or Theo screaming.

"Everything's a bit fuzzy," she said. "Please, no hospital."

Jennifer was sure the woman in her passenger seat had a concussion.

"Got a first or last name?" Jennifer asked.

Darla blinked but kept mum.

An examination in Jennifer Klein's home office confirmed that
Darla had a mild concussion but her left hand and finger were not
broken. The doctor brewed her new patient a cup of tulsi tea and
gave her Valium. While Darla washed up, Jennifer defrosted one of

the plastic containers of chicken soup she and her partner kept in the freezer in case one of them came down with COVID.

"After the day you've had, one pill won't hurt the baby. But this high anxiety can do damage," Jennifer said, spoon-feeding Darla the last bit of the soup and then offering the pills with bread.

"I left him," Darla said.

"Who?" Jennifer asked.

"Please, we need to go back." The Valium was taking effect.

"I'll go and see if the car is there. You should rest. But it would sure help matters if you tell me your name."

Darla glanced at the clock on the kitchen stove and thought of Ruby. Calling her own mother right now was out of the question. What would Ruby do in her shoes? Hadn't Ruby run away once? There was a time shortly after her father had died when Darla would go to H&M in Herald Square or any store where she wouldn't be recognized and pretend she was Ruby. They were teenagers, fifteen, far too old for dress-up or make-believe, but the fickle game of luck and chance made Darla wish for the impossible. Especially when she spent time at Ruby's house. A welcome participant in their rituals of daily living. Back then, she did not yet grasp the concept of survivor's guilt, not that it would have mattered. Darla only knew that forces beyond her control had left one of them inexplicably fatherless.

She took a deep breath and let the words spring from her mouth. "Ruby Black," she said to Jennifer Klein. "My name is Ruby Black."

Darla fell asleep on the sofa while Jennifer was changing the linens in the guestroom. Two years before the pandemic, during several visits to restaurants and hotels on the LGBTQ+ list of Hudson Valley destinations, Jennifer and her partner had bought a fixer-upper as a retreat from their stressful jobs in the city. The couple had earned ire recently among some of their city friends, who did not understand why they couldn't make an exception and let them live with them during COVID. Neither Jennifer nor her partner, Ivy Reynolds, were from the East Coast. Jennifer was an Evanston girl, descended from one of the first Jewish families to buy a home in the Midwest, but she had started out as an English major, joining the protests in the 1960s during the Chicago Democratic National Convention and dating a good-looking agitator who would later turn informant, after which she followed a roommate to New York City and enrolled at Barnard. Darla could not know this, but in the crazy world where there were always six degrees of separation, Jennifer had sat in on a graduate psychology class with Maureen Jacobson, both considering becoming psychologists. Jennifer became a general practitioner instead and worked in several clinics throughout New York, the longest being a clinic near the Henry Street Settlement. Somewhere along the line she realized that she preferred the company of women to men, though she preferred work most of all. Then a pipe burst at the clinic and she met Ivy Reynolds, the owner of Om Lady Plumbing, when Ivy came to repair the clinic's boiler.

Jennifer tossed some blankets over Darla, debated rummaging through her backpack but decided against it, left the night-light on, and went back to the site, a good fifty minutes from her house near Rhinecliff. If the car was still there, she would call the cops and explain the situation.

Darla awakened disoriented by a cascade of lights on the sofa where she lay under a mound of covers. She sat up, trying to recognize the items that made up her and Theo's home, their space. Everything around her was Pottery Barn–esque and unfamiliar. It took a moment to assess where she was, but Darla lacked the agility or the will to move. A statuesque woman stood in the front doorway, stomping her snow boots on the welcome mat, before entering the house.

Jennifer Klein descended the stairs in a flannel nightgown and welcomed her wife. Jennifer lowered the lights until she and—Darla heard the name, "Ivy"—were silhouettes.

"We have a guest."

"I noticed," Ivy said. Jennifer helped Ivy out of her coat, their voice whispers. "I suppose introductions can wait until morning."

"I wasn't expecting you tonight," Jennifer said.

"I wasn't expecting me either, but I finished early. And thought rather than sleeping somewhere else, I want to be in my own bed."

Darla lowered herself on the sofa.

"Go back to sleep," Jennifer told Darla, checking her pulse. Darla was still groggy. She nodded and listened to the movement and shuffling of feet on the floor above her as Ivy and Jennifer made their way up the stairs. The gentle closing of doors, the soft folds of laughter, the last light gone off, and a hush as warm as the covers she raised to her chin and over her nose and over her head.

The next morning, there were short stacks of pancakes and frozen raspberries and a side dish of porridge that Ivy Reynolds made on the hottest and coldest of days. Ivy now worked as a plumbing contractor for big-box grocery stores upstate. She was the same age as her prematurely gray wife and, perhaps because of her uniform and her height, accustomed to people thinking she was a man at first glance until they looked at her face and saw the dimples and soft curves. She was African American, from St. Louis, Missouri. "When you can't afford a plumber, you do it yourself. First couple of times you get it wrong, but you still learn." The learning had become Ivy's trade.

"I drove by the lot last night and the Eldorado wasn't there," Jennifer said.

"Are you sure?" Darla asked, thanking them for the breakfast and finishing it almost as soon as she had started, thanking them for the spare clothes, too, and, as Jennifer Klein knew she would, expressing the need to go back to the trail.

"Even when you go back, you can never go back the same way," Ivy said.

"It was just a lovers' quarrel," Darla said softly. They did not believe her. Abused women were known to recant. Ivy Reynolds asked Darla the same question Jennifer had asked her the night before. "Do you have anyone you want to call? Let them know all is well?"

"No, I'll call them when I get home."

At the site, Darla was relieved and sad and pissed. She had come back for Theo, who had not waited for her. Her husband had left her and their baby in the wood, and it occurred to Darla that Theo had intended to do so all along. Darla's bruised head could see clearly into his devious mind. She recalled the shovel in the trunk. Theo had never brought a shovel with him before. And hadn't the argument been largely one-sided and fabricated? Why would she, of all people, care if their baby was brown or black or white? So much crap—*his* crap—had been projected onto her. Fresh salt began to settle on old wounds. How could Theo abandon her and their baby? Theo knew she had abandonment issues. Darla climbed out of Jennifer Klein's Toyota and stood where Theo's car had been parked. The missing Eldorado calcified something in her. A raw, renewed sense of the ugliness of being stranded.

Jennifer and Ivy dropped Darla off at the train station in Hudson, where she waited for the next available southbound train to New York City. The couple offered to stay at the station with Darla until the train arrived, but Darla told Jennifer and Ivy she had taken advantage of their hospitality enough already. There were other passengers waiting for the train, which made the two women less reluctant to leave her. Darla boarded the southbound Empire Service train, destination Penn Station, but at the last moment got off in Poughkeepsie. She did not yet know where or even how far she would go, only that if home is where the heart is, she felt uncertain, ashamed, heartless.

PART TWO

Doorframe: the jambs and upper transverse member enclosing the sides and top of a doorway and usually supporting a door.

—MERRIAM-WEBSTER

QUESTIONS TO A HUSBAND

REGARDING A DISAPPEARED WIFE

TWENTY-EIGHT HOURS after his wife went missing, Theodore Harper walked into the local precinct in Park Slope and filed a missing persons report.

"When was the last time and place you saw your wife?" Detective Felix Ramirez asked while typing the report.

"About four P.M. yesterday in Greene County."

"The Catskills."

"In that general area, yes."

Detective Ramirez made a face. "Why didn't you file a missing persons report upstate?"

"Well, I had reason to think Darla might come back here."

"Where's here?"

"It's on the handwritten form. The North Slope. Home. Where we live."

"Would you happen to have a recent picture?"

"Sure," Theo said. "On my cell phone." A tenseness crept up Theo's shoulder while he sorted through a gallery of photos. The most recent picture of Darla at the annual Broadway fundraiser for In God's Love We Deliver. She was playing her bassoon intently. Her face bore no lockdown lines.

Theo shared the picture with Detective Ramirez. "This is a good one. I can upload it. Of course, she's not pregnant here."

"Please do," Ramirez said, typing away. "How many months pregnant is your wife, Mr. Harper?"

"She's in her first trimester." Theo found another picture of Darla and him alongside her mother and Pierre and Ruby and Katsumi during Thanksgiving. "Look," he said, and held up the picture. "That's Thanksgiving. We were going up to the cottage this time to get away from COVID in the city."

"Have you filed any reports before? Domestic disputes? Orders of protection?"

"No."

Detective Ramirez rose from his desk with Theo's handwritten report. "Excuse me. I'll be right back."

Ramirez was new to the missing persons division. For seven years, he had worked as a beat cop in his neighborhood in Sunset Park before being promoted. He returned with another plain-clothed detective of medium height wearing a wrinkled white shirt and a narrow tie with flying saucers on it. The plain-clothed detective had gray sideburns and a gray beard. If Theo had to guess, the older detective was in his late fifties. He held a freshly printed copy of the report.

Detective Lutz started to offer his hand but then caught himself and held out hand sanitizer for Theo and himself and Ramirez.

Theo reached into his pocket and said, "I have my own."

"I'm Detective Lutz. You've already met my partner, Detective Ramirez, who was kind enough to brief me on your case."

Detective Lutz made an elaborate act of spritzing his own hands with Purell. He spoke casually. "Mr. Harper, we received a call from the local precinct near your wife's family cottage. Early this morning a Mr. Roland Paige, a neighbor of your wife's family, as I understand it, was apprehended coming out of the woods not far from where you say you and your wife had hiked. He had a silver bottle with traces of blood on it, and when they asked Mr. Paige what he was doing in the woods, he said he was looking for Darla. During a routine search of his house, the officers came upon artifacts—

ribbons and whatnots—that Mr. Paige has kept over the years that belonged to your wife."

Theo shut his eyes. "You don't think he did something to her?"

"The detectives in Greene County checked all the local hospitals, but no one fitting Mrs. Jacobson's description has been admitted or released to date. Mr. Paige is being held for further questioning and, given his mental disabilities, supervision. The plan right now is to send out a search party after the storm."

Theo stood up. "This can't be real."

Detective Lutz put a hand on Theo's shoulder. "Why don't you come on back to my office and we can review the report more thoroughly?"

Theo refrained from asking if he would need a lawyer. "Is this an interrogation?"

"No, we just want to corroborate your story, see what syncs with Mr. Paige's. They said he was pretty shaken up."

Theo leaned forward. "This is my wife we're talking about. *I'm shaken up.*"

"Felix," Detective Lutz said, "get Mr. Harper one of those little bottles of spring water. Unless you want some coffee? The coffee here is always middling to tepid in the afternoon, but it does the trick."

Detective Ramirez, it seemed to Theo, did not appreciate being addressed by his first name. He turned on his heel and left without waiting to hear if Theo wanted coffee or not.

These are the questions they ask when your wife disappears: *What was she wearing the last time you saw her? Was she happy? Was she sad? Did you have an argument? Did you do something to make her sad that day? Or yesterday? Or the day before? Had there been stress in the marriage that you were aware of or that flew under the radar? Did she suffer from depression or take prescription or recreational drugs? Is she an alcoholic? Are you an alcoholic or on prescription medication or recreational drugs? How much do both of you drink on average a week?*

"No, no, no, no, no," Theo answered to all the above. "As for drinks, I enjoy a glass or two or more."

"A day or a week?" Detective Lutz asked. He was the senior detective and tasked with asking most of the questions.

"Depends on the day or the week."

Detective Lutz drank the coffee. "Mr. Harper, you have a sense of humor? Does your wife have a sense of humor?"

"Yep."

"So you share a sense of humor?"

"Most of the time."

"Did she lose her sense of humor recently?"

Theo bit his lip and said, "You mean the sense of humor that we share?"

Detective Lutz looked at Ramirez, who was pacing. He wanted Ramirez to sit down and listen. He seemed preoccupied. "So, you admit at one time there was more humor in your marriage?"

"Well, technically we're newlyweds."

"How about your careers?" Detective Lutz started on the second cup of coffee.

"Our careers are somewhat on hold for now. COVID lockdown and all."

"Were you happy leading up to the demise of your careers?"

"What demise?"

"The halt halting delay break lockdown. Limbo."

"My wife's a first-rate musician. She plays the bassoon in a Broadway orchestra."

"So she has an artistic temperament?"

"She has a musical disposition."

"I see you're pregnant. Pregnancy brings up all kinds of hormonal emotions."

"I guess."

"Is it a happy pregnancy?"

"We are still an early pregnancy."

"Is your wife happy during her early pregnancy?"

"We're happy about our early pregnancy, but she is nervous about the situation with the world and COVID, naturally, bringing an innocent into a pandemic."

"Are you implying she has COVID sadness?"

"I am not familiar with the term, but we left the city so she would feel better."

"So, you are confirming you left the city because she might be depressed?"

"Everyone is a little depressed right now."

"But there were no medications?"

"Prenatal vitamins."

"No other pills in the medicine cabinet?"

"Tylenol. Benadryl, aspirin. Vitamin D. Zinc. And magnesium. For COVID, Theraflu," Theo said. "When I need to sleep, I take magnesium."

"Or the occasional drink?"

"Yes, the occasional drink."

"What's your preference?"

"My preference," Theo said, feeling like he was being toyed with, "is for this interrogation/non-interrogation to end."

"Oh, come on now, we're just making small talk," Detective Lutz said, and smiled.

"My preference varies. And what does my favorite drink have to do with my wife?"

This time Detective Ramirez interrupted and said, "Certain drinks prime us for violence."

Detective Lutz looked at Detective Ramirez. Whatever Detective Lutz was thinking he kept to himself. Detective Ramirez sat down for the first time. Theo preferred him walking and pacing. Theo didn't warm to the two detectives sitting across from him.

"You said this wasn't an interrogation," Theo reminded them.

"And it's not, Mr. Harper. You're not being recorded. We're simply trying to understand the context of your time together in the woods with your wife."

"We were hiking. It's all in the report."

"And then there was an argument?"

"Yes."

"Do you argue a lot lately?"

"No more than most people."

"How often do most people argue?"

"I wouldn't want to guess."

"But you would say you argue during COVID a bit more frequently."

"We disagree from time to time."

"How did you disagree in the woods?" Ramirez said.

The sparsity of speech was effective. Theo hesitated. "Darla wanted to keep going. I wanted to turn back. I am not a natural hiker. I am not inclined toward long treks in nature during spring or winter or summer or fall really, but the inclement weather, you'd think I'd be used to it, coming from Iowa, where the temperature often dips below zero. But no . . . ."

"So the two of you argued and she kept going?" Detective Lutz said.

"She stormed off."

"And you went after her?" Detective Lutz said, and gave Ramirez a definitive *no more interruptions* look.

"I gathered our things because we were at an overlook where we had stopped to eat lunch. And it felt like the perfect time to turn back."

"Did you attempt to stop her?"

"I tried to follow her. But then I lost her."

"So you think your wife is lost?"

"I don't know what to think after what you said about Mr. Paige. I would rather Darla be lost than someone hurting her."

"You want your wife to be lost?"

"No," Theo corrected himself. "I want her to be found. But you are spooking me with other alternatives."

"Am I spooking you or are you spooking yourself?" Detective Lutz asked. "After all, you did leave her in the woods."

"You know, I think if you don't have anything else to ask me, it really is time for me to leave now. Unless there's some reason I can't," Theo said.

"Why wouldn't you be able to leave, Mr. Harper?" Detective Lutz said.

"Then I will go."

"Is there something else you want to share?"

"Not that I can think of."

"We'd like you to put together a list of mutual friends. It might be nice also to have a list of some of your acquaintances."

"I work in real estate. My friends are all in the industry."

Detective Ramirez looked down at his shoes. Something registering that had not registered before.

"Maybe," Detective Lutz said, "you can put together a list for us."

"No problem. But why would Darla seek out my friends or work acquaintances? I mean there's not really anyone—"

"No one special?" Detective Lutz pressed.

"We have an open relationship if that's what you're getting at."

"How open is open?"

"Open enough."

"So you're both polyamorous?" Detective Ramirez interjected.

"I don't know what I am so much as how I am."

"How are you?" asked Detective Lutz, visibly annoyed with Detective Ramirez.

"Concerned. Afraid. Tired. Confused. Wishing Darla were here beside me. Wishing I had been more up for a fight."

"You know what they say," Detective Lutz added. "Mad sex is the best sex."

Theo pushed away from the desk and stood up. "Will you let me know if you hear anything?"

"More than that, Mr. Harper, we consider it our absolute duty to check in on you. We might also need you to return upstate and accompany the search party. There's a pandemic, so I don't need to remind you to stick close to home."

UNCLE FREDDIE'S PLATE

I AM unhappily acquainted with the 88th Precinct on Classon Avenue in Clinton Hill and the 79th on Tompkins Avenue in Bedford-Stuyvesant, and while sitting now at the 78th Precinct on Sixth Avenue in Park Slope, I have this distinctly déjà vu tingle where I feel the back of my thighs itch, the sense I have been here at least once before. Perhaps, at ten or eleven, tennis lessons aborted at the Prospect Park tennis court for an emergency trip to a precinct with Mom to pick up Uncle Freddie. I recall the metal chairs with fabric backs and pads—these ones are metal only—and me in a white tennis shirt and skort, crossing and uncrossing my legs while my mother talked to the local officer or social service worker or police lieutenant, always on the lookout for a childhood friend from the neighborhood who remembered Uncle Freddie fondly before his after.

Everybody's got an almost sometimes was been love you to death no good relative who breaks his mama daddy sister brother daughter lover's heart, and that was my uncle Freddie. Steady, solid, a red oak tree until everything in his life went up in smoke—poof—and he got on that stuff. Stuff being a holdover from our grandparents' vernacular passed down to us. Uncle Freddie, damn Uncle Freddie, what to say about Uncle Freddie? A mantelpiece of washed-out photographs accentuates his before. Five years senior to my mom, he doted on his little sister in the worst way, would sneak her and her friends into the movie theater on Broadway and Sixteenth Street in the city, where he worked the concession booth, or come home with "free" Chuck Taylors from Paragon Sporting Goods, where Freddie was one of the best sneaker salesmen. Or to the Strand Bookstore on Broadway, where Mom would read books and wait for him until his shift was over at Paragon. Then there were raggedy-ass arcades and games and rides on Coney Island, where Uncle Freddie would take Mom if she got a good report card and win oversized stuffed cartoon characters for her: Daffy Duck, Scooby-Doo, and Popeye the Sailor Man. Mom still held on to her stuffies, corneas milky now like a blind man's, but crystal clear when *whoosh* he nailed a shot through the hoop of the small-necked basketball net they rigged so the ball circled and circled and fell every direction but in. My mom, maiden name Knight, grew up loving her big brother Freddie Knight, which is not surprising, because their parents worked all the time. Work was their habit. If they stopped working the senior Knights would have to contend with their divergent lives, lovers, and friends and the cold reality that their children were the only thing that bound them together. Work was a good model for Freddie and Frida, albeit without a surplus of love or affection. Freddie received a basketball scholarship to Indiana State. He wasn't Kobe Bryant or Magic Johnson or Oscar Robertson great, but sixth-man-ready Philadelphia 76ers, Vinnie "the microwave" Johnson rising off the bench to make the shot in the crunch and help Isaiah Washington and his team snag the game, good. And my mom, boy, she loved him.

"What's new, big-headed Ruby?" Uncle Freddie would burst into our brownstone like he owned the place, wrap his arms around Mom, knuckle-greet Dad, and pick me up and pace while my mom told him to put me down because I was getting too old to carry.

"And don't you call Ruby big-headed. I don't need her having a complex."

"Well just look, Frida. Why wouldn't her head be big? She takes after her mama. You got a big head with too much sense in it. So much sense you always had to fill it up with books and numbers."

"All right now," Dad would say, "that's my wife you're talking about." But when Uncle Freddie visited, I noticed Dad always found errands to run that day. Dad worked for FedEx and Mom was a financial advisor at a UIT (unit investment trust) firm in the World Trade Center. During the fourth-grade parents' night dinner, Darla's parents struck up conversations with my mother and father, and when Maureen and Daniel Jacobson realized my mother also worked in Tower 1, they began scheduling playdates. Darla and I were in separate classes, but we had already bonded on a school trip. We got on so well that our parents did everything possible to make sure we would be in the same class the following year.

Uncle Freddie would come and pick me up after school sometimes or from Darla's house when I first started Trinity, and he would stand in their massive living room with its tin ceilings and wait while Erica Gonzalez helped me gather my shoes, backpack, books. Mrs. Gonzalez made sure we tidied up after playdates and put things back the way we found them. I would descend the maple stairs to find Uncle Freddie looking around and up and down, but if Uncle Freddie was impressed, he wouldn't show it, nor would he accept so much as a glass of water from Mrs. Gonzalez, or, on the rare occasions when Darla's mom or father were there, an offer for a glass of wine, cocktail, or beer.

"You got a nice house too, you know," Uncle Freddie would say sometimes on the A train back to Brooklyn and the Lafayette stop, where we always exited. "These brownstones were built for rich people. You're the new take on the landed gentry, Ruby. Don't forget it."

And when we'd get to Brooklyn, we'd make a snack detour to Ms. Ruthie's on DeKalb Avenue, where he'd flirt with Ms. Ruthie's daughters and ask them to fry the chicken hard. This was before Ms. Ruthie closed shop on DeKalb and after they opened up their second location in Clinton Hill and before you could find Carol's Daughter on the shelves of Target and after they started building the Long Island Railroad and before the tourists came to BAM and lingered to enjoy the neighborhood and after President Clinton visited the Cake Man's restaurant and said his red velvet cake was to die for and before you could peep through the windows of Mark Morris and see little brown girls in tights and tutus in class recitals for their parents and after our grandparents passed the deed of the house over to my mother and moved to a condo in Miami, with both of their lovers in condos within a quarter-mile radius, still pretending they were a couple when they were a quartet. And this was before 9/11 and, looking back on it now, I am amazed that Mom and Dad let Uncle Freddie pick me up from school on a semi-regular basis and that he showed up and I hadn't yet developed a private girl's snobbery and shame at seeing his round to thinning face. Maybe because he was still holding down a job as a manager at Modell's at the Fulton Street Mall, not as upscale as Paragon Sporting Goods in Manhattan, but still maintaining the family work ethic.

That stuff can take you down fast or that stuff can take you down slow. A lot depends on your habit or preference. Uncle Freddie was one person on pot and heroin but a different host altogether once crack took over his system.

By the time I reached sixth grade, he had the crack zigzag down, one body moving in two different directions. *Just say no*, Uncle Freddie would shout at the drug boys. An ironic nod to Ronald and Nancy Reagan's senseless "Just Say No" campaign, even as crack cocaine poured into major cities and impoverished neighborhoods throughout the States.

"No one wants to be an addict. I thought I could manage," Uncle Freddie would say. And then the drug boys would call him a hypocrite for proselytizing while he was negotiating his next fix. Our neighbors began going into their brownstones when they saw Uncle

Freddie coming. They had their own versions of Uncle Freddie to contend with and did not want to bear witness to the Knight family's public shame. Uncle Freddie still had his days and nights attached to the world, but his hygiene was reckless. Mom would spray him with Lysol before she let him in the house, and by that point, only on the ground floor. And if Uncle Freddie's clothes were filthy and he was especially strung out and rank, she'd keep the grated bar door closed and make him wait in the outside vestibule, and I would stand behind the grate and stare at him: the whites of his eyes yellow and jaundiced, his beloved red Chuck Taylors with a gaping hole in the left big toe that he had attempted to shut with Wite-Out and Krazy Glue, his hair most unhappy to be nappy.

"How're you doing in your Ivory Tower?" he would say to Mom, who could not make eye contact with him. She offered him a twenty and a plate of food, always a plate of food. Sometimes not the twenty but always food.

"I'm doing," she would say, closing the gate and slamming the door on Uncle Freddie midsentence. My grandparents had bought as an investment a building on Bedford Avenue for next to nothing before the neighborhood had become desirable. There was a storefront that housed a furniture store and three apartments on the floors above—one that Freddie stayed in free of charge as the quasi super. When his crack addiction spun out of control, Mom changed all the locks and gave a tenant a break on the rent to manage the building. The couple who leased the first floor for their furniture store threatened to sue Mom because their store kept being broken into and they were certain Freddie was behind it. Mom gave them three months' free rent, and when their business ultimately failed due to poor street traffic, she let them out of their lease early.

Before Union Market and Trader Joe's, there was Garden of Eden and Balducci's and D'Agostino's, and there was Fairway, Gristedes, and Gourmet Garage. Uncle Freddie would covet their steaks. He would ask a neighbor what they had in mind for Sunday dinner,

and he would secure the best cuts of meat in grocery stores throughout Brooklyn and Manhattan. He had a small top-ringed notepad
with a shopping list of orders, and he would come back with prime
rib and roast beef and leg of lamb and hanger steak. He would return with thick center-cut pork chops with the bone in. He became
known as the meat man. Weeks might go by when we wouldn't see
him and then Uncle Freddie would show up with ribeyes for four,
offering to cook for Mom and Dad and me, hoping to bribe his way
through the front door and into our affection.

"That funky steak belongs in someone's store," my father would
say. But then my uncle Freddie would shoot the finger at my father.
"Ain't no pussy in this meat. No man sausage, either. Don't you see
the plastic Saran Wrap?"

It was a well-known fact that professional shoplifters often put
their wares in their drawers and between their legs and walked out
of stores undetected.

"Get out of here you, with that filthy goddamn language," my
father would say.

"Do not take the Lord thy God's name in vain," Uncle Freddie
would say, laughing.

And even as he spoke, Mom would be guiding Freddie toward
the kitchen sink, making sure he double washed his hands—when
Uncle Freddie went shoplifting, he washed away the body odor and
dressed up for better access to nice grocery stores. Those were his
bathing days. And he was handsome then.

"Maybe you can get work as a short-line cook, Freddie?" Mom
nudged.

"You got to keep it real with Ruby, sis and brother-in-law. If
Mom and Dad didn't work so much and kept it real with us, where
might I be?"

"Oh, you're a drug addict because our parents worked hard?"
My mom shook her head, dismissing the idea as total bullshit self-
pity.

Chop, chop, dice, dice, peppers, onions, tomatoes, coffee. Rare. Me-dium. Medium well done. Rib-eye steak.

The drug dealers knew that if Uncle Freddie couldn't pay them, he was always good for steak. Sunday dinner and their people would have food, which could sometimes be more reliable than drug money as take-home pay. Uncle Freddie even honored debts when the dealers were in jail.

One night, a month before the towers fell, there was a knock on our front door and a drug boy, one of the runners, told Mom she needed to come say goodbye to her brother before EMS came and took his body away. We all dressed up fast and went down to the corner of Gates and Washington, a block from the Italian restaurant that Mom and Dad had gone to on their anniversary. Freddie was lying on the sidewalk with his eyelids turning ashen gray and no breath moving through his body. Mom kneeled over her brother, screaming, *What happened, Freddie, Freddie, get up, Freddie.*

The drug dealer shrugged and said, "He overdosed."

"What do you mean he overdosed?" There was anger in Mom's voice. "He didn't just overdose by himself. Someone gave him the drugs and the paraphernalia, despite whatever something in Fred-die that needed to kill himself." She shook Uncle Freddie and beat him like you beat a dummy.

The drug dealer looked askance at Mom, my father, and me. "Nigga barely had a taste."

And then two junkies ran out of a boarded-up building with a padded rectangular gym mat like the ones the PE teachers roll out during gym class, and they also carried a hose and buckets of ice, and they pushed Mom out of the way, lifted Uncle Freddie up like he was a target at an amusement park, pie in your face, but then they turned on the hose and sprayed him with water full tilt. His body writhed and shook like someone getting the Holy Ghost, and they beat the buckets against his chest, and it was horrible, just hor-rible, and Mom was crying and Dad said, "Frida, Frida, that is not your brother. That's not Freddie. Freddie hasn't been with us in a long time."

And suddenly Freddie was breathing and coughing and his heart that had stopped was revived. People were clapping, even the junkies and the dealers.

"All this love for me?" he said, coughing and spitting, and Mom hugged Uncle Freddie to her tight, though he was filthy and sopping wet and stunk. "Freddie, I promise to God I am never going to argue with you about money again."

"What's up, Frida?" he said, hugging her back and twirling her around. "Big-headed Ruby, let's play some Uno! Sis, that old white priest used to say, 'Don't fuss over money with your family.' Whatever you can spare, sis. You're not about to see this money again any time soon. But I will try. For you, I will try. . . ." Uncle Freddie held out his hand for money and my mom gave it to him, emptied her pockets and wallet.

And the drug dealer, decked out in North Face puffy jackets and Timberland boots, scoffed and motioned for one of his minions to take care of Freddie. "Yo, for real," he said. "Remind me to shoot my brains out right here on the spot if I ever get hooked on this shit." Then he strolled back to the corner and corralled his boys.

We were spared the inside of a police precinct that night and Uncle Freddie, at least for a little while, got a second lease on life.

I have only ever had one uncle. There are no more. And so, I try to hold the image in my mind of Uncle Freddie sitting on the shag rug in the den reading *Charlie and the Chocolate Factory* to me and how when he rolled up the sleeves to his Polar denim shirt and I reached over to trace the purple bruises along his veins, he stopped me.

"Don't you bother about that, Ruby," he said sternly. "Stay in your lane."

———

I met Theo outside the precinct after he texted me that Darla was missing. I did not yet understand all the details, but he looked like hell when he came over and hugged me with such force I felt conflicted about my sudden intense hatred for him. I didn't have any officers or friends or friends of friends in the 78th Precinct that I might have a word with like my mom used to for Uncle Freddie, and I resented having to revisit a time and place and space that brought up dirty family laundry. Katsumi and I had received the welcome news that we were awarded a generous Revitalization Fund loan for the restaurant. It was a great start to our day and an opportunity for me to run by Katsumi my strategy for paying back our loan, but Theo's text had turned our giddy relief and joy upside down. Darla was missing.

"Thank you for coming, Ruby."

"Theo, what happened? Where's Darla?"

"I wish I knew," he said. "We had a row."

"Explain yourself. When did you become British?" I said sarcastically.

"Darla's persistent. Especially when she sets her mind on something."

"And you're not?"

"She tempers," he said. "She just ran off and I couldn't find her."

I couldn't believe this asshole was telling me he had left my best friend in the fucking boondock woods. It was all I could do not to slap him.

He rubbed his cheek, which singed. Even though I had not touched him. "Of course, you don't really have to be here."

Was I being dismissed? I shrugged and said, "I promised Maureen I would be her stand-in until she gets this side of the Atlantic."

"Well, let's not argue. Help Darla. Help me. They want a list of friends and acquaintances. You know Darla better than anyone," he said. "I have to tell you—the detectives are pieces of shit and I'm not going back in there."

"A piece of shit calling out other pieces of shit. How rich," I said.

"Fine," Theo said. "Fair enough. But help us."

I hesitated. "Did you cut your hair?"

"A while ago," he said, turning away from me lickety-split and starting down the street.

I know when a person is lying. I grew up around an addict. Addiction gets under your skin. Addiction breaks your heart. I have also been an addict. They say once an addict always an addict. So I keep focused on what's in front of me. The present. Mostly.

"What if they only want to speak to next of kin?" I called after Theo, a pit growing in my stomach. I could not stop thinking of my uncle's face from so many years ago: less clear, muted like the Polaroid images on my mother's mantelpiece that had faded, blotted out by the sunlight that spilled into our living room. Or how the more Uncle Freddie drifted away, the more Darla Jacobson had stepped in to become my best friend.

XAVIER WANTED Mrs. Howard, the guidance counselor, to get to the point. She had asked for a Zoom meeting during what would have normally been his lunch hour if in-person classes were still in session. Lately, free period and lunch folded into a mini nap time so Xavier could concentrate on his afternoon AP Physics class. He had been nodding off during morning AP Lit and sometimes not bothering to turn on his video monitor at all.

Mrs. Howard was doing what any decent guidance counselor would: a mental health check-in, charting his coping mechanisms. Compensation for the hugs he could neither receive nor give. Global hug + less + ness = communal loneliness.

"You seem to be thriving academically in this current environment," Mrs. Howard said. Xavier sat in the living room looking at Mrs. Howard's Zoom backdrop of swimming fish. He had seen these fish swimming on fake Zoom backdrops before. Illusions. Not real. "Xavier, it's okay to give yourself permission to hit pause."

Xavier's backdrop was of wall-to-wall art books and photographs from Cousin Julian's performances when he was still a professional dancer. Looking at Mrs. Howard, he couldn't help but wonder how his moms would have come at him. Brevity. Levity. Mediocrity, as a temporary solution to stress? Xavier seriously doubted that.

"Are you telling me I don't have to do my work?"

"I'm acknowledging this is a challenging time for you. We're sorry about your mother."

Xavier hadn't told anyone, not even his crew, who sometimes went by the name the Five Amigos, that his moms was in the hospital. Why would he? In a school the size of Stuyvesant, three thousand strong, it was numerically impossible that he was the only student who had a relative down for the count with COVID. Besides, that kind of news fell under confidentiality. Other than what his dad told the school, Xavier wasn't talking about his moms and he wasn't exactly feeling school, either. Sometimes it was easier to tune out with Snapchat or TikTok escapist stupid hella alternative to Instagram, where people he didn't like kept showing him stuff he couldn't afford or didn't want. Nah dawg, he wasn't planning on withholding his moms's status for the long haul. For sure, he would tell his bestie Bayo and maybe the crew once his moms's condition improved. But things were wrong right now on so many levels. His dad hadn't taken any time off from work even when his moms went on the ventilator. And Xavier felt like he was being shoved out of both his parents' lives, by the virus on the mother's side and by his dad's unwillingness to "hit pause" when Xavier needed him. Maybe this solo quarantine time at Julian's was supposed to be a kind of tough love, man up, you got to be able to handle shit cause shit happens. Xavier only knew that when his moms got off the ventilator three days ago, he had thrown his belongings into a suitcase. That's how ready he was to roll on back home. But the following afternoon, the same doctors scheduled a telecom. His moms had relapsed with COVID complications. No one really understood what caused COVID complications or how long COVID complications lingered. His moms's once healthy heart was no longer functioning normally. "We're learning on our feet," the doctors said to

Xavier and his dad via telecom. *So, are we, bro. So are we,* Xavier thought.

"Look, I don't want to talk about my moms," Xavier said, shrugging at the monitor and Mrs. Howard. "But I'll apologize to the sub."

"Mrs. Volkert is her name," corrected Mrs. Howard. "And she's not going anywhere. So you had all better get used to her. As much as we all miss Dr. Foster, she would be the first one to give Mrs. Volkert her due. She's a wonderful English teacher who has stepped in at the last minute under less than ideal circumstances."

Xavier let his tongue roam the inside of his mouth. He already knew he would eat a Jamaican beef patty. His father had bought dozens of them from Kingston Bakery on Myrtle Avenue so Xavier could freeze them and nuke them for lunch. He had gobbled one down before the meeting and felt this sensation on the left side of his mouth next to his molar and thought he might be getting a cavity.

Four of Xavier's teachers had moved out of state shortly after the mayor announced classes would be going online. Dr. Foster relocated to Wisconsin to help her daughter look after her four grandkids, all under the age of ten. Dr. Foster was hippie-dippie and believed that even as adults it was a good practice to read aloud every day. In Dr. Foster's AP Lit class, students contended with the written word and the sound of their own voices engaging those words. Her students rolled their eyes and thought reading out loud was hokey at first—do we look like kindergarteners to you? But in a fiercely competitive school, reading out loud encouraged vulnerability and trust in her classroom because no two students engaged the written word in the same way. To mispronounce or stumble over a word you didn't know was presented as an opportunity to crack open its underlying definitions in various languages. This played out differently, of course, in person and on Zoom. Poor Mrs. Volkert, the new teacher, was simply trying to keep pace with Dr. Foster's approach and syllabus, but the sudden appearance of a fresh-faced sub and a virus that was upending senior trips and proms and science fairs and student government debates and tours to colleges and sports competitions and recitals and—

"*Mr. Curtis,*" said Mrs. Volkert. "Please turn on your video monitor and continue reading where the last student left off." It was first period.

Xavier hesitated, caught off guard. He turned on the monitor.

"I'm sorry," he said, "would you repeat that?"

"Page twenty-four," Mrs. Volkert said. "Scene two."

They were reading *A Raisin in the Sun,* which Dr. Foster had said was one of her favorite plays. Xavier had seen *A Raisin in the Sun* on Broadway at the Barrymore Theatre with Denzel Washington, LaTanya Richardson, Sophie Okonedo, and Anika Noni Rose in 2014. It had been the fiftieth anniversary of the play, and Nadine and Irvin Curtis had booked reservations at Sardi's before the show so they could be tourists for one night. They sat in the orchestra, staring up at Langston Hughes's poem "Harlem," white words, splayed against a blue scrim. Nadine had purchased their three tickets with her teacher's discount. It was a month into the production, but celebrities were still coming out strong to see Denzel and the cast. Xavier and Irvin were busy craning their necks for celebrities in the audience when the scrim rose on the set. An alarm clock went off and Ruth Younger appeared on stage in a robe and slippers. She ushered her sleeping son off the ugly plaid couch that doubled as his bed. The audience burst into applause, then fell silent. Xavier sat between his mother and father, suddenly aware that the black family onstage could be his own family. Tonight was special somehow.

He didn't have a hard copy of *A Raisin in the Sun* at his cousin Julian's apartment. His copy was on his desk at home. Xavier kept forgetting for one reason or another to remind his dad to bring him the play.

"I don't have it today," Xavier said.

"Why?" Mrs. Volkert asked.

"I left it in my dad's car." He hadn't even told people he was housesitting at his cousin Julian's place. One question led to two questions, two questions led to four.

"All right," said Mrs. Volkert. "Please be sure to bring your copy to class tomorrow. In the meantime, what do you think of the passage we just read? Mama's such an anchor in the world of the play. What do you think she represents, or Hansberry wants her to represent?"

If Dr. Foster were there, Xavier would have asked her why *A Raisin in the Sun* was her favorite play. Dr. Foster had regretted not joining the Freedom Riders. She had stayed north and raised money in Boston. But to Mrs. Volkert, Xavier said bluntly, "Look, I know *A Raisin in the Sun*'s a classic, but I respect Hansberry more than I like the play."

Mrs. Volkert leaned forward. Was he deflecting? "What do you admire about Ms. Hansberry?"

Xavier was in no mood to read, much less talk about *A Raisin in the Sun* with these people. He wanted to store the memory, that night when both his parents were at his side and well, in a safe place. He thought before he spoke and said, "I like that she and James Baldwin were friends. My moms told me he even had a nickname for her: Sweet Lorraine. Sometimes artists can be themselves with each other in ways they can't be with the rest of the world, you know. So they got this intellectual bond and this sense of social justice that they take to President Kennedy and his brother. She was kind of like Beneatha in the play. Or maybe Beneatha was like her? Forward-thinking."

"So, you like Ms. Hansberry's politics but don't see those politics reflected in her most famous play?"

"I didn't say that, but there were other moments," Xavier said, "when I saw—read—*A Raisin in the Sun* when I was like, forget these fucking white people in their neighborhoods. Mama, your son is riding around and he's a chauffeur. What does that do to Wal-ter Lee day in and day out to chauffeur? How does that blend with the scope of his consciousness? But then, after the money is stolen and the white folks come to do what they do—which is try to buy them out—I'm like, nah, nah, Mama get your garden—and Be-neatha should go to medical school and to Africa—and maybe, if they get out of the tiny dark apartment, Walter and his wife will get on better and their boy won't have to worry about getting shot or indoctrinated into a gang or some bullshit. Maybe Mama and her family will have a better chance of surviving COVID and not be out here dropping like flies left and right cause they'd be in a nice house with big windows instead of cramped up in a fucking housing project."

At that moment, Cornhusk, the tabby cat, jumped on Xavier's lap and brushed against the table meowing and purring loudly. Ev-eryone was silent. And then there were oohs and aahs for the cat.

"Thank you, Xavier," Mrs. Volkert said softly, "for your insight-ful comments. Anyone care to expand on Xavier's observations be-fore we part today?"

Silence.

Xavier thought of the Black History Month familiars: Sojourner Truth. Frederick Douglass. Harriet Tubman. Was it Lorraine Hans-berry's fault that *A Raisin in the Sun* felt like a Black History Month play? Would he have felt differently if his teacher looked a little like him? He wanted to say, *There are some times when you are a black student in a white classroom and you are expected to be the one to comment on the cultural relevance of everything black, like you are blessed with some special radar into every corner of the black experi-ence, and then there's most of the time when your peers don't give you a second look because it's easier to pretend you don't exist.*

After Xavier logged out of AP Lit, Cornhusk meowed and used her sandpaper tongue to catch his stray tears. She was still meowing when the phone rang. It was his cousin Julian.

"Xayxay, how's your mama doing?"

"They took her off the ventilator. She's not doing great but at least she's breathing on her own."

"What'd I tell you now?" Julian said. "Nadine's got a mean streak and she loves you too much to leave this world."

"Cousin Julian, I'm not going to even get into the science of that statement."

"See, that's the problem with your generation. You're too cerebral in all the wrong ways."

Xavier was glad to hear his cousin Julian's voice. Julian had always been easy to talk to. "We're cerebral because you guys were too passive. You dropped the ball on us. And now look."

Julian laughed. "Oh, throwing your cousin some shade. When you haven't been in this world five scores and six years yet."

It was Xavier's turn to laugh. "You hear your crazy cat? Talking about my mama's mean. The first couple of nights I slept here, I locked my bedroom door. So Cornhusk wouldn't suffocate me. She's kind of evil."

"Is she on your lap?"

"Yep."

"Then you're friends now for life," Julian said.

"And how's *your* mom?" Xavier asked.

"Fine," Julian said. "I'm fortunate to have a partner who understands that a good portion of senior citizens' lives are taken up talking about bodily functions, mainly the potty."

"I appreciate your checking in on me, Cousin Julian."

"No thanks necessary. You can't always share everything with your clan. But I could confide in your Dad. He was always there for me."

"Well, I wish he were here more for me."

"We don't all handle our loved ones' being sick in the same way. Try not to take his approach personally."

SHADY EFFERVESCENCE

YOU NEED to find your inner abolitionist seize the moment of this movement so you don't backstep and trip over your own heritage effervescence you one of us more than you one of them not that you have to choose or remember or forget people are tired of this shit what does it mean any of this how come we living and dying and catching hell and I think my moms's pep talk is extinguished and I think my dad can't stop from working because if he stopped he'd realize he has no one to come home to or to hang out with and I might get into Stanford, Princeton, Harvard, or Yale but who knows where the girls are prettiest and I know Moms wants to see herself in the face of the girl I choose and I know Dad would say don't ever forget your beginnings remember so your ass won't lead your head and any energy come sneaky lively like brush fire you can withstand dawg I remember that look I seen in my teacher's face and my classmates' gaze when I got the fucking A. You got the fucking A? And I say, Deal, yes, I always get the fucking A. Being smart means more to you than it means to me 'cause I work hard. And I was born that way.

FOR WEEKS Simon Pratt was convinced Theodore Harper had been flirting with him. During the prep period when they were renovating houses for future listings, Theo would make impromptu appearances. Simon thought Theo carried himself like a Golden Age movie star: Cary Grant or James Dean or Gregory Peck. Too damned handsome to blend into the scenery but happy to let the brokers do the talking, dropping in a well-timed comment only when necessary. The aesthetic advisor spoke of houses as interactive experiences and buyers as domestic explorers.

"Until you move in, you don't yet share a common language with your home. You are an adventurer seeking a fresh start. A new life."

Theo Harper would walk the rooms of a virgin property—one that had not yet gone on the market—pointing out the finders, keepers, losers, weepers: used and new furniture to weave into the staging, additions and details needed for renovations, decorative pieces in poor taste ripe for a dumpster or recycling bin.

"Weep now," Theo would tell an emotional seller. "And count your money later at closing."

They were in a former Episcopal church that had once held twelve pews, its minister an Eritrean priest forced into retirement as his congregation dwindled. For the open house, Theo suggested the two remaining pews be placed in the sanctuary, their centerpiece a long farmhouse table. Voilà! There it was, a formal dining area and, since the farmhouse table came with drawers, the dining area could also function as a workspace. Stained glass windows with pointed arches, three windows on each side, flooded the church with natural light and were architectural gems—keepers that the right buyers would love. Succulents adorned the windowsills in desert hues that played against the colorful stained glass with its lush reds and pinks and purples and golds and greens.

"Here's a story to tell," Theo said. "And we crave our stories. A former church turned into a modern town house is an investment a secular couple will love. So many stories here."

One afternoon, while balancing a medieval lamp on a marble coffee table, Theo asked Simon to polish a full-length gilded mirror behind an oversized chaise lounge. The forest-green chaise lounge, the coffee table, and a round Turkish rug were the only furniture in the nave with its twenty-foot ceilings under which parishioners once sang "Amazing Grace" and prayed.

"Why such a large mirror?" Simon asked.

"The vertical mirror will present a long, flattering angle for the buyers to imagine themselves lounging about or entertaining guests."

As Simon polished the mirror, he nicked his knuckle but was careful to stifle the blood before any spilled onto the Turkish rug. Theo offered Simon a mini first aid kit the size of a slim wallet with the softest leather Simon had ever touched. The first aid kit had everything inside like a toolbox. It was efficient, nifty, discreet.

"Go get cleaned up," Theo said.

When Simon returned to the living room, Theo had moved one of the pews back into the open living area. He was much stronger than he looked.

"You're good at this," Simon said.

"Well, I've been at it for a while now." Theo paused and stepped back, quite pleased with his decision. Simon opened his computer and showed Theo the virtual renderings of what the church laid out as a modern home with living room, kitchen, bedroom, and bathroom.

"Simon, how'd you get into real estate?" Theo asked, glancing with little interest at the virtual markups on Simon's MacBook. It was true that most clients could not visualize their way out of a shoebox, much less visualize a living space or room. The designer and real estate agent's job was to support their blurred vision. Sometimes, Theo thought, designers left clients with little room to fill the very spaces in which they would live.

"I dabbled with stand-up comedy for years."

Theo smiled and said, "I love a good joke."

"Then you should find a good comedian."

"That bad, eh?"

"Well, I'm here now. And let's just say I was very motivated to get my real estate license."

"We all have to grow up eventually," Theo said. "But you don't seem like you *need* the work."

Theo went into the modest parish kitchen, a 1970s addition to the church that also contained the retired priest's old bedroom. He lifted himself onto the counter, moving backward, opening doors and drawers. "Kitchen looks immaculate. Before the open house, percolate coffee to give the space a homey feel and aroma."

"Are you suggesting I pursue a different profession?" Simon was still stuck on Theo's last statement.

Theo jumped off the counter, slapped his nice pants. "I probably shouldn't tell you this because you're good-looking and young and might be future competition. Hunger has its advantages and disadvantages. Choose the right moment to feign indifference."

"How does that jibe with going the extra mile for your client? Or the customer always being right?"

"If you act like you don't need the sale, especially when there's a bidding war, the house will appeal more to buyers. People want what they can't have. They'll think someone else will make a better offer. And they'll look harder for reasons to justify buying, even as the price ticks up and a bidding war begins."

"Interesting."

"No, counterintuitive. My opinion only. But what do I know?"

Simon noticed that Theo never arrived empty-handed. There was always a container of Dunkin' Donuts coffee or a bag of peaches and, on the day the couple signed the contract for the Victorian in Ditmas Park, the celebratory Veuve Clicquot that set the mood for sex.

*

"Why didn't you tell him to stop if he was hurting you?" Felix asked, spitting into the sink and gargling with Listerine.

Much to his husband's chagrin, Simon replayed the events of his encounter with Theo in graphic detail months after the fact. Simon usually broached the subject in bed while Felix Ramirez was flossing his teeth.

"I thought I did," Simon said.

"And he didn't stop?" Felix watched as water, blood, tooth decay went down the drain.

"You know how these things go."

"No, Simon, I've paused on fucking other men."

"Have you really?" Simon said.

"Mostly," Felix said. "Are we going to pretend that sometimes you don't like it rough?"

"That's a scary statement coming from a cop. You wouldn't ask me that question if I was a woman."

"Yes, I would. To pinpoint when and where the line was crossed. If a line was crossed. Why do you always bring up my being a cop when we disagree about something?"

"Because your kind has not always been gentle to my demographic group."

"Your kind is my kind, Simon. Was the sex consensual or not?" Felix asked.

Simon looked at Felix. "Okay, okay. The sex was consensual." But deep down, Simon wanted Felix to say or do something to indicate he wasn't thrilled about his adventures with Theo Harper. "Sometimes I do. And sometimes I don't. Like roughness."

"At any point," Felix said, climbing in bed alongside his husband, "you can ask for a timeout and a reset. You should, if the sex doesn't feel right."

"Appreciate the advice. So-so on the judgment."

"And I'm so-so on the salaciousness. I'm tired of talking to you about this," Felix said. "It's hard to tell who's doing the fetishizing. Maybe you should talk to your therapist."

Simon's therapist, if he set up an appointment with her, would likely ask him why he would risk a perfectly good, no great, gratifying relationship for a married straight man who had left him feeling vulnerable and dirty and, here's the crazy thing, unfulfilled, and wanting to rush home to Felix and renew their wedding vows against some very bad juju. But he picked up his cell phone to call her anyway, but not before logging into his Tinder app and swiping left, left—possible right?—no, left. Until he saw Theo Harper's face. And there he was, Simon, simple Simon, swiping right on his cell phone.

Finders, keepers, losers, weepers.

Theodore Harper welcomed Simon into the apartment, past photos of his honeymoon with Darla, the newlyweds lounging poolside at the Hotel Bellevue Dubrovnik in Croatia. The Adriatic Sea, their backdrop. Too cold for the balcony, Theo said. It was a cold damp afternoon. So Theo and Simon drank tea in the kitchen. A brand

called Revitalize made with cinnamon and cloves and anise. Neither said much; small talk was not necessary. Theo looked tired but
younger with his Jim Morrison hair trimmed.

"Did you cut your hair?" Simon said.

"You're the second person to ask me that today," Theo said,
thinking of Ruby. He hadn't shorn off much hair. Just enough, he
had hoped, to detract from the good looks he feared might play
against him at the police precinct. But even with the trim, the interrogation had gone poorly.

After Simon finished his tea, Theo reached over the table and
whispered, "With your clothes on." Simon stood but stalled. "What
if I want them off?"

"Your prerogative," Theo said. "My preference."

Simon made his way into Theo and Darla's bedroom. "Of course
you'd have a real mid-century bed."

"If you'd like, I can pour you a drink," Theo said, "but I want
you sober."

Simon declined the drink. And then all bets were off and Theo
and Simon were on. Simon fell face forward onto the bed and Theo
lowered Simon's pants a quarter of an inch, kneading the small of
his back in little circles so that Simon felt himself harden against
the covers. Theo removed Simon's pants and rolled down his under-
wear, kneading his ass like it was dough, a cross between a shiatsu
and Thai massage, and then invading his ass with his tongue and
fingers and then removing his own clothes and sowing Simon like
a farmer sows a field but at such a pace and fury half the seeds
would be lost and Simon wanted to know what kind of seeds were
being planted and Theo kept saying, *You like this don't you, you like
this don't you, tell me how much you like this, Simon.* And when
Simon said he would like it more if Theo slowed down, Theo
turned Simon around and plowed-sowed him face forward, balls
bumping and thumping, and Theo wrapped Simon's hips around
his and tucked his arms around Simon, volunteering sloppy, messy

kisses without shifting his gaze, even when Simon hugged him clutched him rocked Theo, saying *more* until there was nothing to give or say and it was salty sweaty nasty sweet. A millisecond after both men came, Theo swooped down and swallowed Simon. Something Felix would never do. Simon sat back on the bed and looked at Theo. He waited for the beautiful monster to eviscerate intimacy with two words: *Get lost.*

But Theo smiled and said, "Where are you from, Simon?"

"Manhattan. I'm a native New Yorker."

"Huh," Theo said.

Simon had grown up in the West Village on Jane Street. His mother was a costume designer for the City Opera and his father a television casting agent. Raised in show business, he learned quickly that telling jokes or pulling gags was an effective way to get his parents' and stepsiblings' attention. He had met Felix while doing a set at one of the gay bars on Tenth Avenue in the West Forties, where he made a nice income as a bartender. More than he made as a comedian.

Theo rolled out of bed. "My wife's a native New Yorker."

Simon noticed that Theo did not say his wife's name. Simon noticed how much he disliked a wife's being mentioned at all while they were in bed. Again, he thought of Felix and the bad karma he would be taking home with him.

Theo started for the master bathroom. "There's a shower in the guest room, if you need one."

"No shared shower?" Simon asked. He felt oddly at home in the mid-century bed, though he knew he didn't belong there. Neither man nor furniture was his.

"My life's in shambles right now," Theo said.

"Shambles how?"

"In every way you could imagine. And then some," Theo said, backtracking just enough to steal one last kiss. "But thank you. This was kind of wonderful. While it lasted."

DARLA JACOBSON walked into a two-star hotel on Buffalo Avenue in Niagara Falls and requested a room. The front desk clerk gestured, held up his hand, and mouthed, *One moment, please.* He was overwhelmed with cancellations and was the sole clerk manning the reservations desk.

Darla smiled and waited patiently, listening as the front desk clerk attempted to pass the buck: *Due to the large volume of cancellations, we are offering a credit to guests for future stays at our hotel in lieu of refunds.* From the sudden color that appeared on his angular face, Darla ascertained that the clerk was having a miserable day.

He lowered the phone and apologized. "It's been insane with COVID."

"You're holding down the fort by yourself?" Darla asked with a raised, sympathetic brow.

"Everyone is sick. Or laid off."

"Here's hoping they give you a raise or something," Darla said.

The clerk was twenty-three and gangly, with his hair pulled up on top of his head in a bun.

"I need a room."

"Well, we sure got 'em," he said, laughing.

"A double," Darla smiled. "Standard. Nothing fancy. I'm on a budget."

"How about I give you an upgrade," he said, "for being so patient?"

"That's nice but not necessary." Darla smiled, reaching into her backpack. After a few seconds, she stopped and frowned. "Holy shit."

"What's the matter?

Darla resumed searching through the backpack with an air of fending off panic. "I think I must have left my wallet on the train. . . ."

"Oh man," the front desk clerk said. "That's the worst feeling in the world."

"No kidding," she agreed. "I was so bent on getting out of the city and away from my roommates."

"I'm so sorry. Did you come up on the Empire Express? I can put in a call to Amtrak for you."

"You've got your hands full already," Darla said, and shook her head. "How much is the room?"

"It's two hundred a night but I'll need to see some form of ID."

"Gosh," Darla said, reaching into the backpack once more, putting her bassoon on the counter for show, opening and closing the hand with the bandaged finger like she was squeezing a stress ball. "I'm a musician. I waitress and get by on tips. Glad to have some cash now."

Darla pulled out a wad of one hundred dollar bills rolled together with a thick red rubber band. She counted out enough money for seven nights, including the bed tax. "It's been one hellish day. I really need to get off my feet." She noticed his name tag. "Greer, work with me, please."

The front desk phone rang again. Greer handed Darla a guest form. Darla filled out the form quickly and signed in as Ruby Black. She wrote down Ruby's parents' Fort Greene address. After her mother and Erica Gonzalez, the Blacks' address was the emergency contact she gave even in college. Using Ruby's name, though perhaps no doubt a tad ethically iffy, was the additional bit of shelter Darla needed right now.

Greer gave Darla two room key cards.

"You're a mensch."

"Ms. Black, I would say dial down if you need anything, but you're likely to get a busy signal."

In Poughkeepsie, Darla found a gray 1990s Ford pickup, which was one of the easiest trucks to hotwire, and drove it as far as Buffalo. Even though the examination with Jennifer Klein had revealed only a mild concussion, there were moments during the drive when floaters invaded Darla's line of vision and she was forced to pull over until her eyes could focus on the road.

"I lost my virginity," she said aloud somewhere in Hartford near Glimmerglass State Park, merging the past with the present. Her brain spiraled to junior year and the tour of the Seven Sisters colleges (Wellesley, Radcliffe, Smith, Bryn Mawr, Mount Holyoke, Vassar, and Barnard) that Maureen Jacobson had taken Ruby and her on. Dexter Gordon's *Ballads* CD was playing in the rental car. For spite and to shut her mother up, Darla had blurted out, "No virgins here. Did you know I slept with Aimslee three times in the city while you were at work? Three times in your bedroom."

Maureen had turned around and looked over her shoulder at the girls, who were wearing matching Smith sweatshirts and taking selfies.

"Ruby, is that true?"

"Absolutely not," Ruby lied. Later, Ruby would tell Darla she could never speak to her own mother and father like that, much less tell them she had lost her virginity. "Awkward. I'd be flat on the floor."

"Your parents hit you? They don't look like the kind of people who would beat you."

"No, they don't beat me. I was exaggerating."

"You could tell me if they beat you."

"Darla, my mom and dad don't beat me. When you were little didn't you ever get a spanking?"

But in the rental car, Darla had challenged her mother. Challenging had become their norm. It was a little over a year after her father had died.

"Why are you asking Ruby who I slept with when you can ask me?"

"Because you two are as thick as thieves."

"Well, I just told you. And I'm here. Not that I want to be," Darla snapped. "Turn off that stupid song."

"What's that?" Maureen said calmly.

"Can I sleep over at Ruby's tonight?"

"No," Maureen said. "You have a home of your own. And I don't think Ruby's parents would appreciate your bad manners. I certainly don't." Neither Darla nor Ruby had temperaments suited to the Seven Sisters colleges, but Maureen felt it her duty as an alumna of Barnard to take them on this trip.

"You ruin everything, you know that, right, Mom?" Darla said, reclining in the seat and putting her feet up on the back of her mother's headrest. "If you'd been at the World Trade Center instead of Dad, my life would be easier."

Ruby had gasped. Darla loved Ruby but she hated when Ruby preened goody two-shoes. Of course Ruby could afford to be good. She still had a mother and a father at home.

"I miss him too," Maureen said, turning up Dexter Gordon's "Scared to Be Alone."

During COVID, Niagara Falls would lose sixty percent of its business revenue. Darla could not gamble at the Seneca Niagara Resort and Casino on the American side or the casinos in Canada. She could not tour the Cave of the Winds on Goat Island or experience the spray from the falls on the Maid of the Mist boat tours or explore the other water parks or the fashion outlet malls or cross the Rainbow Bridge into Ontario for the restaurants and shops and other waterfalls, but even under normal circumstances, Darla would not have done most of these things. In the hotel bedroom, she sorted through the items she bought at the local Walgreens. Darla normally shunned shiny lipstick, but she purchased hot-pink lip gloss and accessories (including raven Clairol hair color) and a pair of cheap gold hoop earrings, which she slipped in her ears, removing the antique diamond studs (gifts from Theo) and dropping them into a coffee cup with her engagement ring and wedding band. She rebelled against the heartbreak glam temptation to dye her pale locks Joan Jett black because when she looked in the mirror, she saw enough of what she remembered of her father to want to leave her hair unmolested. Staring at her reflection, she thought of Theo's brittle words as well. What if it was true that she expected, even wanted their child to look like her? Was it her fault that blondness was a rare commodity? A natural asset? For the hell of it, Darla took an eyebrow pencil and penciled in a Marilyn Monroe–style mole on the left side of her face, just above her mouth, thinking of her days at the New England Conservatory of Music when she and her roommates would crash parties with fake IDs or drive into Manhattan for the weekend and dance all night with older men who should have known better in the East Village.

It is true that you can hide in plain sight if you are clever. And it is true that Darla's backpack was stuffed with varietal junk food from Walgreens. Junk food she and her baby now craved. After her do-over, Darla sat on the edge of the bed, turned on the flat-screen

TV that hung on a wall above the dresser, and gorged like a kid at summer camp: nacho Doritos, Almond Joys, and Reese's Peanut Butter Cups, extra toasty Cheez-Its, and microwaveable cheeseburgers and pesto chicken panini sandwiches and double Oreos and a Kind Bar. She fell back on the bed, not even bothering to look out from the river-view room Greer had given her. We really don't need much to be happy, do we? There was a microwave, small refrigerator, coffee machine, ice tray, two rectangular glasses, and a complimentary bottle of water. She was regressing and the regression was liberating and wonderful.

In the days and weeks that followed, she would sleep a lot. Darla was uncertain if the sleep was depression, hormones, or the baby growing inside of her, but she was grateful to have been paranoid about the world possibly ending. The Jacobsons had survived several market crashes, including the stock market crash of 1929, which had wiped them out financially for a brief period. Their motto was to always have some dough in the mattress or a shoebox under the bed or behind a wall. She had never told Theo about this liquid money, because when COVID hit, no one knew how far the markets would dip or if they would always have access to cash. In addition to the money in her wallet, Darla carried two hundred $100 bills in her bassoon case, just to be on the safe side. Theo would have surely mocked her healthy skepticism. After a long nap, Darla showered up and took a short walk to the Niagara Falls State Park. She hoped the raw force of the falls would reveal answers, a clear trajectory for a better, if not altogether brighter, future.

QUESTIONS REGARDING

A DISAPPEARED FRIEND

"WHEN WAS the last time you saw Darla Jacobson?"

"It's been a few weeks with COVID, but I spoke to her the day before her trip."

"Did Mrs. Jacobson seem despondent or sad or display any behavior that seemed out of the ordinary?"

"No, she was excited and tried to talk me into coming too."

"Do you think she was concerned about being alone with her husband?"

"Why would Darla be concerned about being alone with Theo?"

Officer Lutz was taking notes on a yellow legal pad and asking most of the questions. His partner, Detective Ramirez, hadn't asked a single question so far. Ruby, as a person of color, didn't like that.

Detective Lutz continued, "Did Darla mention any diversions?"

Ruby sat back in her chair. She had compiled a list of Darla's contacts in the waiting area: old friends and boyfriends from college, the conductor and members from the orchestra pit. Musicians often riffed and drank with fellow musicians after-hours. In this, Darla was no different.

"Explain yourself," Ruby said. "What do you mean by diversions?"

Detective Ramirez noted something in Ruby's voice and assumed the lead in the conversation. He leaned forward, elbows on table. "Did she mention that she was going hiking?"

"That's what the Jacobsons do every time they go upstate."

Ramirez continued: "So you've gone up in the past?"

"Many times. Since middle school."

"How would you describe Mrs. Jacobson's relationship with her husband?" Detective Ramirez said, then turned to Detective Lutz, who nodded for him to continue.

Ruby answered, "She loves him."

"So," Ramirez said, "it's a loving relationship?"

"Yes, as far as I know. I've never had any reason until today to think otherwise."

"Then you admit, you now have suspicions?"

"Don't put words in my mouth. When did you hear me say that?" Ruby said. "I just want to know what happened to my friend. I don't like the idea of Darla being in the woods. Injured or worse."

"How would you describe your relationship with Mr. Harper?"

Ruby tried to read Detective Ramirez. "He's the husband of my best friend. Plain and simple."

"You said you've been to the summer house many times. Has Mr. Harper ever been inappropriate?"

"He's never come on to me, if that's what you're asking."

Detective Ramirez adjusted his surgical mask, which had begun to slip down his nose. "Did you know they have an open relationship?"

Ruby tried not to show her surprise. "Darla might have mentioned it, early on."

"Ms. Black," Ramirez said, "we know these questions aren't easy. . . . Assuming Mrs. Jacobson did make it out of the woods, who do you think she would call?"

Ruby had this image of someone apprehending Darla alongside the road. "After Theo, she would call me. Or her mother."

"Would she seek out anyone else on this list?"

"I don't think so."

"But you can't say for certain?" Lutz resumed questioning.

"I can't say anything for certain."

Detective Lutz rapped his fingers on the table. "Any ideas where she might go?"

"To the cottage," said Ruby. "It's her happy place. Or if she was injured, to a hospital."

"What about the neighbor in the house near the Jacobsons' cottage?" Detective Lutz asked.

"You mean Roland? He helped keep up the place after Mr. Jacobson died." Ruby smiled, but then her smile faded. She remembered that ninety percent of missing people were abducted by someone they knew. "Is Roland a suspect?"

"How would you describe Roland?"

Ruby thought. "He's Roland. He's different. Anything's possible, but if he really wanted to hurt or abduct Darla, he had so many other opportunities. Why now?"

"We're just fishing around, Ms. Black," Detective Lutz said finally, "trying to look at this from every possible angle. But trust me, you'd be surprised what people do when they think they can get away with it. And no one's looking."

WHEN MAUREEN first learned that Daniel was missing, she understood immediately but could not accept that missing meant dead. She had helped Daniel place potted plants from their upstate garden in his corner office situated in the upper tier of the World Trade Center's North Tower. He would often call her around noon, for they both took lunch early, and ask, "Good day or bad?" The impact from American Airlines Flight 11 ignited the flames and set off the blaze that melted the walls and sank the floors—and paper. Why, all these years later, did Maureen remember the random office papers drifting across an azure-blue sky? Papers New Yorkers (and New Jerseyans) would find for days, weeks, months after her husband had singed. Maureen looked at the footage of the towers collapsing only once, though the news looped repeatedly, for weeks and days and months. To look once was to look a lifetime. For that's what the two planes took: lifetimes with loved ones away.

Mondays were Botox mornings, easy procedures that Dr. Maureen Jacobson scheduled from eight in the morning until her noon lunch break. It was the receptionist, Sophie, who had rushed from office to office screaming, "The Twin Towers are on fire" as Maureen was injecting a syringe into her patient's forehead. Several months later, the patient, a sixty-year-old socialite determined to be forever thirty, would suffer a facial stroke and sue Dr. Maureen Jacobson for malpractice. Maureen, of course, would deny the mistake vehemently, but perhaps she had plunged sharper, deeper than normal? In any event, the malpractice suit was dismissed in civil court, the patient portrayed as a Botox digger, the equivalent of a dumpster digger, setting up appointments with dermatologists throughout the city and exceeding the recommended Botox treatments, and attempting to take advantage of a recent widow and single mother whose husband had perished in 9/11.

"I didn't appreciate your using Daniel's death to portray me as a victim," Maureen would snap at her attorney as they exited the courtroom.

But on September 11, 2001, she watched the footage with two fellow dermatologists and three of their patients in the waiting room of her practice, Park Avenue Dermatology, and then politely asked Sophie to settle her patient's bill, shook her patient's hand in parting, and stumbled to her office, where she sank to the floor. Repeatedly Maureen said, "How will I tell Darla?" She called her husband's number and whispered, "Daniel, Daniel?" Even when she went straight to voicemail, Maureen's query continued: "Daniel?"

Darla's high school was within walking distance of the Jacobsons' two-family limestone between Columbus and Central Park West on Eighty-Sixth Street. Erica Gonzalez, the Jacobsons' longtime housekeeper and sitter, had stopped escorting Darla to school in fifth grade, but Mrs. Gonzalez picked Darla and Ruby up from Trinity that blue morning. The imminent threat of losing a parent was one of many first experiences Ruby Black and Darla Jacobson would share, an agonizing window of uncertainty that rendered one of them fatherless.

"Mom?" Darla called her mother on the walk home from school. "What's going on? I can't reach Dad. Can you reach Dad?"

"I'm going to keep trying," Maureen said. "I'm going to go down there."

And Maureen had hailed a yellow southbound taxicab and directed the driver to take her to the World Trade Center like so many other desperate family members looking for relatives and finding chaos, roadblocks, smoke. But upon arriving within a twenty-block radius of the towers, Maureen understood that this was not where she was meant to be. And there was nothing for her to do. That her husband, whose office was on one of the top floors, would not be found and that she did not want to remember him as cinder, ashes. She asked the relieved taxi driver to U-turn and, by any means necessary, get her as close to Eighty-Sixth and Central Park West as he could manage.

Darla was in Garnet Hill peppermint candy pj's when her mother arrived home. Maureen abandoned the taxi and walked on foot the last ten blocks.

"You had better leave before they shut down everything. I paid for a driver," Maureen said, waving her employee of eighteen years away, not wanting to break down in front of Mrs. Gonzalez or Darla. "Go home to your family, Erica."

Darla sat watching the news. She did not get up to hug her mother. She held a fuzzy oversized pillow to her chest like armor. "The reporters are saying terrorists did this, Mom. Why would anyone want to hurt so many innocent people?" Darla's eyes were rimmed red around her blond lashes.

"I don't know."

The answering machine was full of messages and notes that Mrs. Gonzalez had scribbled down neatly. Daniel's brother Roy in New Jersey and his sister, Birdy, in Colorado; partners of coworkers of Daniel's, calling to see if by chance Daniel was home. Everyone wanted information about missing loved ones. Maureen poured herself a glass of wine, a Côtes du Rhône. She sat on the couch and offered Darla a sip of wine from the long-stemmed glass. Maureen had been a military brat. Her father a retired air force colonel. Both of her parents were old when she was born. Laughter evaded them. She had found in Daniel a mate who was spontaneous as well as practical.

"We have to prepare for the possibility that your dad might not be coming home, baby," Maureen heard herself say.

Darla let her head fall into Maureen's lap and she wailed, reminding Maureen of Sophie earlier that morning in the office. Maureen stifled some of her own tears with the overlong arms of Darla's flannel pj's from last Christmas. Comfort jammies.

"Cry, baby, just let it all out," she said.

"You looked for him?"

"As much as I could." Maureen wanted to say, *I prefer our memories.*

"I felt it, Mom, when we were coming home from school," Darla said. "We were running home like we were at the Trade Center, like we were downtown, but we were safe, here, uptown, and we got to our house and I felt it, I even told Ruby and Erica, *Oh no.* I looked down at my cell phone with the picture of the three of us on screensaver and my battery died on me. I don't know, but I thought, *What if that's Dad letting me know he didn't make it out?*"

The screensaver was an image of Darla, Maureen, and Daniel Jacobson on the Niagara Gorge Rim Trail in Niagara Falls State Park.

For Maureen Jacobson, COVID was 9/11 all over again. A foreign invasion manifesting inside the human body. She had thought she could avoid further unhappiness in Paris, but a pandemic did not know boundaries or borders or favorite nations. Four days after her daughter went missing, Maureen boarded a direct American Airlines flight to JFK. Roland Paige had been released two days earlier, and an initial search party had been sent to look for Darla, but they had come up empty. And after leaving Maureen a cryptic message about Darla's being lost in the woods, Theo was no longer returning Maureen's calls. And so, Maureen emailed her American colleagues and a handful of trusted friends for recommendations on private detectives. She received the names and numbers of two private investigators and went with the first one to return her call:

Yvonne Tender, a retired homicide detective with a stellar track record for finding "misplaced" people. The irony was not lost on Maureen that she would have to go straight home and quarantine for fourteen days once she cleared customs. Maureen's movements would be tracked while her only daughter's whereabouts remained a mystery.

MASKS

ALFRED HARPER graced his son's lobby with stubble on his chin and foul breath and hat hair, for he never went anywhere except work without his University of Iowa baseball cap. He had driven sixteen hours and fifty minutes from Des Moines, Iowa, to Brooklyn and looked exactly like Theo imagined someone would who sped solo across the country pissing into a gallon-sized plastic milk container, doing reverse Kegel exercises to fend off the need to shit because bathrooms were closed, lulling only for gas or to order a trio of McDonald's meals at the drive-in window and eating cold Big Macs, Quarter Pounders, and Filet-O-Fish along the way because he had driven off forgetting the care packages Theo's mother, Elena, had prepared that sat on the roof of his Ventura.

His father arrived on the same evening that Simon departed. Theo was stripping the sheets in his bedroom.

"I'll be right down," Theo said.

Theo hugged his father in the lobby.

"Last time there was barely room to move on the sidewalks. I had to elbow my way through the crosswalk. This go-round, coming in, sometimes I didn't see two people on a whole city block. Very Twilight Zoney, this Manhattan."

"It's good to see you, Dad."

Alfred shrugged. He wore white jeans and a black button-down shirt, both travel-grungy. He noticed Theo checking out his appearance. "My regular jeans don't fit."

"Neither do mine," Theo lied. "I'm just glad you're here."

"Any word on your woman?"

"Still waiting."

"And you went back the next morning and looked for her like I told you to?"

"The weather was bad."

His father shook his head. "I'm disappointed, son."

In the living room, Alfred walked around Theo's apartment picking up random objects. No one who knew Theo and wasn't his wife or father would have been permitted to handle his belongings so carelessly. His father did not know the value of the items he fondled: a leaf-shaped ashtray from Franklin Delano Roosevelt's Campobello estate (when Roosevelt could still walk), a whiskey flask that had belonged to George Harrison. After running his hands along the spines of books on the shelf, Alfred cleared his throat and asked, "Did you kill her?"

Theo's face reddened. He picked up his father's suitcase and carried it into the guest room. He returned and considered his father.

Theo spoke quietly. "How could you ask me such a thing?"

"I'm your father. I'm obliged to ask you what the cops likely think. What everyone will think until they find Darla."

"No, Dad. I didn't kill my wife."

"So there's no body upstate in the woods?"

"Not that I know of." Theo switched gears. "A lot of the restaurants close early now. I should order food. Are you hungry?"

Alfred sniffed himself and said, "After I shower." He was uncomfortable in his current state of funk, but the discomfort allowed Alfred to shoot straight.

Theo brought out an assortment of menus. "New York still has every kind of food you can imagine. Even during a pandemic. Tell me what you want. Tell me what you'd like."

"Something I can't get in Des Moines."

"I neither buried nor killed my wife," Theo repeated softly.

Alfred Harper seemed momentarily satisfied with his son's response, but said, "You are too calm for your own good."

That's because I fucked myself into a good mental space. "How is falling to pieces going to solve anything?" Theo said.

"This calmness makes you seem cold."

Theo ordered from a local Syrian restaurant. He ordered food that was similar to and different from the Greek dishes his mother made in part to get back at his dad and because he was surprised his mother hadn't sent a care package. To give his dad time to settle in, he went to pick up the food. He grabbed a pizza along the way to go with the Syrian takeout. By the time Theo returned to the apartment, his father was showered. Without the cap on his head, Alfred was almost completely bald. Theo wondered if similar baldness awaited him. His father wore his University of Iowa sweatshirt and sweatpants. He looked quite comfortable and pink. Instead of unpacking his luggage or taking a catnap as Theo thought he might, Alfred was opening and closing drawers and rummaging through the kitchen.

"Run by me what you told the cops and everything that happened with Darla again?" Alfred said.

Theo reached into the back of the Sub-Zero fridge and offered his father a cold beer. While they ate at the kitchen table, Theo's exchange with the detectives and his argument with Darla unfolded like dinner napkins.

"You pick a hellified time to claim your thirty percent," Alfred said, listening. "The blacks are dropping left and right because of COVID. You didn't think she'd find your confession provocative and disingenuous?"

Theo said, "Maybe I would have been more tactful if you hadn't raised us to be so damn ambivalent."

Alfred tipped the Brooklyn Brewery beer bottle upward and the malt poured into his throat. "Don't make me the scapegoat for what happened with your wife."

"I bear responsibility for Darla. I'm just saying, Dad . . . it might have been nice growing up if occasionally you had spoken of the man you named me after other than a joke or an example of all the ways life can go wrong."

"How would that have changed matters, son?"

"I don't know. I just have a lot more time to think about things I would rather avoid. Life's front and center and in my face and sometimes I don't like what I see in the mirror."

His father whistled. "Too much heady stuff. This COVID's getting a lot of people down. This COVID is messing with our heads. Going to be a lot of men, women, and children in the looney bin when all is said and done. *Ding. Ding. Ding.* Our job is to find Darla and make sure we aren't among the ones they strap down when the moon tilts full."

Alfred's appetite caught up with him and he ate the entire sausage and mushroom pizza in addition to half of the Syrian food. He had combed through Darla's work desk and craft table and discovered a stack of masks in two piles: complete and in progress.

"How well do you really know your wife?"

"You sound like the damn detectives."

"Son, what are her favorite places and things to do? Where does she eat? Where does she shop or buy clothes? Where does she hang out or get her hair done?"

"Most of Darla's favorite places are closed because of COVID."

"That doesn't stop you from writing them down to help yourself and the detectives."

After dinner, the two men sat at the kitchen table while Theo wrote down all of Darla's haunts and cross-referenced the names on the list Ruby had texted him. Theo called everyone on Ruby's list, which included two college roommates and musicians from past ensembles and music festivals. He noted that he didn't recognize most of their names. Half of the contacts were out of town or unreachable. No one Theo spoke to had seen or heard from Darla since lockdown. Alfred wiped his hands and went over to Darla's table and returned with the completed masks. Darla had handwritten labels with the names, addresses, and phone numbers attached to each mask with safety pins like one sees in upscale antique stores. Theo smiled at this little detail his wife had picked up from him. Alfred offered Theo a double-lined mask made with exceptional care. "This mask has two asterisks next to the name."

Theo had lived for two years on Eleventh Street and First Avenue in the East Village, where he shared a quad with three frat boys from NYU. The hardware supply store next door was now a check-cashing service. And wasn't that empty storefront the old Italian restaurant where he had taken his parents to the first time they had visited New York? They had only visited twice, the second being his wedding to Darla. Theo and his father found parking. The homeless were out in full force at ten in the morning.

Noah Pomerantz lived on a fifth-floor walk-up in a former tenement building on Tenth Street and First Avenue, right around the corner from Theo's old apartment. Theo had suggested meeting outdoors, but Noah said he wasn't coming out much. Noah had tried to press over the phone about the nature of his visit, but Theo had said only that it was about Darla.

"I'm autoimmune compromised and not really supposed to let

anyone in," Noah said, opening the door. The violinist was in his thirties and not at all the nebbish Theo had anticipated. He had sandy-brown hair and a mustache and what Theo thought might be the beginning of a man beard poking beneath an indigo mask with *Some Things Never Change* written in white letters.

"I'm Theo. This is my father," Theo said.

"Pleasure to meet you," Alfred said.

"I think we met once before," Noah said to Theo.

Theo frowned. "I don't remember."

"Okay. And so," Noah started, "since you called, I keep thinking about the last time I saw Darla. We were in rehearsal when management called an emergency meeting and announced this would be our last show until further notice. Just like that."

Theo said, "I'm reaching out to everyone, friends, family, co-workers, anyone who might have heard from her."

Noah crossed his arms. "How come you don't know where Darla is?"

"It's complicated."

Noah shook his head. "Darla's a pretty pragmatic woman."

"Meaning what?" Theo didn't appreciate the familiar way the violinist was speaking about his wife.

"Well, she's very talented and intense, but she knows her limits, you know?" Noah said. "She practices."

Alfred turned to Theo. "I think Mr. Pomerantz is saying Darla's not impulsive."

"Is that what I'm saying?" Noah mused. "Yeah. Maybe."

"A nice collection you got there," Alfred said, causing Noah to look over his shoulder and open the door a bit more, affording father and son a better view of his apartment. Noah lived in a large studio. The studio was sparsely furnished with a futon, a red chest with a Himalayan spread thrown over it, thick wax candles, the lingering smell of pot, and an old-school phonograph with floor-to-ceiling LPs lining a brick wall.

"Scrounging for old LPs is one of the things I miss most about the old world."

Theo recognized the song playing on the phonograph player and asked, "Is that Coldplay?"

"You know Coldplay?"

Theo bristled. "Who doesn't know Coldplay? Darla's into 'The Scientist.'"

A wide grin spread on Noah Pomerantz's face. "We'd warm up to 'The Scientist.' Our oboe and violin work well together."

"You taught her the song?" Alfred asked.

"We riffed and taught each other."

Theo was thinking, *That was* his *song with Darla.* He could see Darla now pacing up and down the sconced hallway, blowing notes sometimes with the phone crooked between her neck and her ear. Had she been talking to Noah Pomerantz? When Darla learned a new piece of music, she was obsessive and giddy and wouldn't quit until she had found her way inside the music.

"What have you been doing with yourself during COVID?" Theo asked, trying to sluice away the envy popping like bubble wrap inside him.

"I've mostly been staying in, ordering food, listening to Pitchfork," he said. "It's like a young people's Spotify."

"I lived in the East Village. Not even a block away, *before* it was like it is now, when people used to do more than sit in cafés all day and go out to restaurants and browse for LPs. My roommates and I would step over the drug addicts in our vestibule on the way into our apartment. Hell, we even had a tub in the kitchen that the landlord kept after he installed a shower. There was a hardware store next door and we were in there constantly getting steel wool to plug the holes the rats made."

Alfred looked at his son with eyes that said: *Where is this going?*

Noah Pomerantz pushed back. "You don't get to 'East Village after the fact' me. I am the East Village. This is my uncle's building.

We could stroll to the tenement building on Orchard Street, if it was open, and to the third floor, where my great-grandmother's fiddle is on display. She came to America in the early nineteenth century from Odessa."

"Did you sleep with my wife?" Theo blurted out.

"I'm sorry?" Noah said, blushing.

"You're sorry you did or you're sorry you didn't?" Theo persisted.

"Theo," Alfred intervened.

Noah began to usher Theo and Alfred into the hallway and out of his studio apartment, where they had insinuated themselves. "I need you both to leave."

"Why don't you just answer the fucking question?" Theo said.

"That's something you should know, man. That's something you should feel. I'd feel it if my wife was screwing someone."

"You are a forty-year-old man living in a studio."

"I'm not *that* old. And I'm intentionally keeping my carbon footprint small. Look at the planet we're living on. All this . . . chaos?" Noah said.

"Thank you for your time," Alfred said, keeping the two men separated. "Theo, let's go."

Noah slammed the door in their faces.

"Don't look at me that way," Theo mumbled after a beat.

"How am I looking at you, son?" Alfred said.

"He all but admitted to doing my wife."

"I missed that part." Alfred moved his University of Iowa cap around on his bald head. "Have you been monogamous during your marriage?"

"No," Theo admitted. He thought of Darla running, falling away from him like Alice through the looking glass. Or was it down the rabbit hole. He didn't know how real or deep her rabbit hole was. Maybe Darla had an openly secret life.

Alfred scribbled a note on an index card and slipped the note under Noah Pomerantz's apartment door. *If you hear from Darla, call us. During COVID, all things are forgiven.*

*

Detectives Ramirez and Lutz waited outside of Theo Harper's apartment building in a nondescript police vehicle. A background check on both Darla Jacobson and Theo Harper revealed six bank accounts between the couple. And that Darla Jacobson—or someone pretending to be Darla Jacobson—had withdrawn over twenty thousand dollars from Darla's Chase account. Husband and wife shared a single joint bank account through which mutual bills were split—utilities, monthly subscriptions, co-op maintenance fees. Theo owned the apartment they lived in outright and Darla owned her one-bedroom apartment in Dumbo outright, in addition to the bank accounts and a trust that would mature on her fortieth birthday. Theo Harper's portfolio exceeded Darla's, as did his savings. Monetary gain did not seem to be a motive.

"Do you think he killed her?" Detective Ramirez asked, studying the case file with Darla's face smiling beyond its celluloid image.

"I think she's dead as a doornail," Detective Lutz said, "and there's someone waiting in the wings."

"Any idea who?" Detective Ramirez asked.

"Does it matter, as long as they aren't an accomplice?" Lutz said. "This guy's sex life is all over the place."

"He's polyamorous."

"That's the catchphrase nowadays. Another generation called it free love."

Felix wrote something in a little black Rhodia notebook. "Free love wasn't about inflicting pain."

"What do you know about free love?" Detective Lutz laughed. "You were a nothing. A nada. Not even a blip on the landscape."

"Well, the blip's here now."

"And taking notes like Columbo."

Detective Ramirez and Detective Lutz disengaged from their vehicle as soon as Theo and his father parked Alfred's car. Detective Lutz cleared his throat and pointed at Detective Ramirez before accosting their suspect. "Keep the personal private."

"What?" Detective Ramirez froze.

Detective Lutz shrugged. "Do you think I don't know?"

"Fine," Ramirez said. He was married. He wore a wedding band. He had a husband. "You know my dirty little secret."

"The dirt on your secret is yours. I have no problem with your being gay, but you need to recuse yourself if this particular case hits too close to home."

"Have you been spying on me?"

"I'm four years from retirement. They give me a new partner. I want to make sure he doesn't come with unnecessary baggage."

"I'd like a go at this guy," Ramirez said. "And it's not personal. I think he's sadistic. And I think you're right. He probably killed his wife. Or hurt her something bad."

When Felix Ramirez announced that he was attending the police academy, his mother and father had turned away. Honest policemen did not always fare so well in Tamaulipas, where the Ramirez family was from. And police who fared well were often worse criminals than the outlaws who paid them to do heinous things. They knew Felix could do his job well but were not sure he could withstand corruption. But while his father had feared one kind of change for his son, another happened. Felix came into his own as a cop and a young man. For family gatherings, birthdays, funerals, weddings, celebrations, which Felix showed up to punctually and loved, he always arrived with buddies and never a female companion. He talked politely with the women who were introduced to him, flirted or danced with them and went on double dates, but nothing flourished.

"Felix is married to his work," his mother said.

"I was married to my work too," his father said, "and I still had time for a wife and children."

Felix exercised five days a week, Monday to Friday, at Planet Fitness before going home to Simon. COVID necessitated transforming a section of their living room into a home gym. That evening, after his workout and while Simon laid out the blueprint for a new town house that had gone on the market in Brooklyn Heights, Felix said, "What did you say the name was of the guy who attacked you again?" A visual image of Simon's description of Theodore Harper had flashed before Felix like lightning during the initial missing person intake.

"Attacked me?" Simon stopped, not registering that Felix meant Theo. Simon had not shared his most recent encounter with Theo with his husband. Nor did he intend to.

"Theodore Harper," Simon said. "Why do you ask?"

"No reason in particular," Felix said. "You haven't mentioned him recently."

When Felix took his post-exercise shower, Simon rifled through Felix's briefcase and speed-read Darla Jacobson's file. Simon thought she was a shoo-in for Marsha Brady, and a missing person report filed by her husband, Theodore Harper. So, Theo Harper was Darla Jacobson's husband! Simon had hooked up with him, and he hadn't bothered to mention that his wife was missing. The thought made Simon physically sick. He cut open a lemon and sucked on the inside to fend off nausea. And now Felix was no longer being forthright with Simon any more than Simon was being forthright with Felix. Each husband waited for the other to confess.

*

"What's this?" Theo asked as he was gifted by Detective Lutz with a search warrant.

"We need to confiscate the car," Detective Lutz said.

"My Eldorado's in the garage." The previous day, before going to the precinct, Theo had come out to find the Eldorado still parked in front of his apartment building. He had hoped it would be stolen overnight. When he found the car where he left it, Theo returned it to the garage before going to the precinct.

"Let's go get it then," Ramirez said with a smile. And handed Theo a second official document.

"Let me guess," Theo said, turning to his father. "Sorry, Dad, you have to witness this."

Alfred took his time climbing out of the car. His knees cracked and he did stretches. "Have you found my son's wife?" he asked accusatorially. As if Detectives Ramirez and Lutz had conspired to take Darla into the dark woods.

"You'd like to search our apartment?" Theo said, reading the second search warrant. This one for his apartment. The warrant included everything from medicine cabinets to closets. "My fingerprints are everywhere. Darla's fingerprints are everywhere." He looked at his father. "Dad's as well. Go for broke. Have at it."

Theo handed his father the keys to his apartment.

"I'm coming to the precinct with you," Alfred insisted.

"No, you should stay here, Dad. In case Darla comes home."

"Tomorrow," Detective Ramirez said, "we'll be transferring your son upstate to revisit the location where Mrs. Jacobson went missing, as a courtesy to the upstate precinct."

"That's lawyer language. I don't like the word *transfer* at all," Alfred said. "Did you read my son his Miranda rights? Is my son under arrest?"

"How about we'll be escorting your son upstate? Better?" said Ramirez.

Lutz took a gentler tone. "Mr. Harper could decline the trip upstate, though I wouldn't recommend it."

Theo smiled and said, "I'll continue to do everything possible to cooperate with your investigation."

"Tell them about the woods," Alfred said, and nudged Theo, who turned violently red.

"What about the woods?" Detective Ramirez perked up his ears. Detective Lutz leaned toward Alfred.

Alfred waved them back. "*I don't need COVID.*"

"Mr. Harper, do you know something that can help us find your daughter-in-law?" Detective Lutz said to Alfred. "If you are hiding pertinent information to protect your son, this is the time to come clean, because you will be charged with aiding and abetting a kidnapping or worse."

"Look, my father drove over sixteen hours to help me find my wife. He's a doddering old man rambling about the woods in Iowa, for Christ's sake."

"I'm not doddering," Alfred said.

"Dad," Theo said. "You really aren't helping here." He turned to the homicide detectives and thrust out his arms for arrest. "Let's do this."

"Such drama," Detective Ramirez said. "Kindly drop your arms, Mr. Harper. And move your legs toward the police vehicle."

QUARANTINE

noun

  1. a state, period, or place of isolation in which people or animals that have arrived from elsewhere or been exposed to infectious or contagious disease are placed.

  "many animals die in quarantine"

verb

  1. impose isolation on (a person, animal, or place); put in quarantine.

  "I quarantine all new fish for one month"

IRVIN CURTIS has noticed the change in his son's voice in the weeks since Nadine fell ill.

"I'm sorry, Dad, but I don't equate even one of those jailbirds' lives with moms." Xavier doesn't realize he is screaming into his cell phone.

"I brought your copy of *A Raisin in the Sun*."

"Well, you can keep it. Kimi let me borrow hers."

"Our neighbor's girl?"

"Yes," Xavier said. "She stopped by after school yesterday."

Irvin thought, *Two teenagers hanging out alone together in an apartment during a pandemic could be a problem.* But he said, "Okay, how about *Clybourne Park*? Your teacher says you'll need that play too for your next assignment."

So, his dad has spoken to his teacher(s). *So,* his dad is now up to speed on his homework. This registers with Xavier as a big fat not enough. Yet another so what.

"Do you love your maleness and blackness more, or my moms?"

"That question's like lava beneath the earth's surface, Xayxay. I love you both. And I don't really see my maleness or blackness competing with loving Mom. We've gotta have faith that Nadine will beat this."

"We don't even go to church."

"Faith," Irvin says, bypassing his son's adolescent sarcasm, "is independent of church or religion. Though maybe we should *go to church*. Just for the ritual . . ." Irvin's voice trails off. "It's been a tough day. I'd like to see you. At this moment, faith is you dropping the 'tude and eating with me. We can go and sit at the bus stop. You coming?"

"Nope."

"Well, I'll just drop both plays off downstairs in the lobby. I'll ring you when I'm close to Julian's apartment."

Irvin Curtis's son is mad with him and Irvin Curtis's mother in Los Angeles is mad with him and Irvin Curtis's two brothers-in-law are furious with him for telling their aged parents that Nadine is back on the ventilator. Xavier he can understand, because he is still a boy. And Xavier needs to be mad with somebody when his mother is sick. Irvin has lived and learned this firsthand: anger can't do jack shit without a target. A coworker, a family member, a friend, or a random stranger who happens to be at the wrong place at the wrong time. Jails and prisons were full of people on the inside or outside of some form of misdirected anger, blindsided by passion or greed or desperation or systemic misfortune. Sometimes all of the above, bundled up as a long-ass prison sentence. Irvin makes the mistake of calling his mother in Los Angeles while waiting for Xavier. She's living in Lincoln Park raising his late sister and brother-in-law's five kids. Casualties of COVID. And, maybe, some kind of poetic justice. Irvin feels a pang of guilt for not checking in more often, but now he remembers why he keeps conversations with his mother short and sweet.

You up in New York City helping these lowlifes who don't
    want to be

Nothing and who wouldn't if they could and okay so maybe
     they don't know how
You trying to be the dad to the world you never had
Just like your grandma was trying to be mom and dad to the
     world
Feed all the kids, a ready-made free foster care
Irvin, how many of those negroes turned into somebody you
     want to sit down next to in Barnes & Noble or the Olive
     Garden?

Irvin's grandmother looked after him, his late sister, and approximately nine other neighbors' kids who couldn't afford daycare or were struggling like she had back in the day.

Mama could have brought in some nice change from foster care.

Irvin hears himself mutter, though he knows it's far better to let her vent and get shit off her chest and live in her blitz of pain, "Grandma didn't believe in taking people's children away from them. Hasn't that been done to us enough?"

She's lucky none of those hood rats never sued her.

Irvin slips the cell phone into the pocket of his blazer and picks up a dozen pre-ordered glazed donuts from 7th Avenue Donuts. If Nadine were around, she would get on her husband for stress eating. That was something she had noticed about Irvin early on. *We stress eat down south 'cause we don't have fancy private country clubs to go to or lake houses. Or at least we didn't used to.* Maybe so, but sometimes Irvin just wanted a glazed donut, even if it couldn't hold up to down-south Krispy Kreme. And speaking of crispy. Popeyes chicken, breast and wing, spicy, would hit the spot right now. He could feel the heat coming from his cell phone and hear his mother prattling on. Irvin could also see his grandmother sitting out with him and the kids in the bungalow on her front porch with the bluegrass on the side. She hadn't gone past high school herself and had worked in the misses department at JCPenney. She would have the oldest teach the youngest, so that there was a kind of informal study hall in the screened-in back porch in the summer when the days were too hot. And she would let them pick figs from the tree and sort the good ones from the bad ones, reminding them to watch out for garter snakes and ignoring suggestions that she should cut a perfectly fine fig tree down because some folks claimed figs—not apples—were the cause of original sin. *Wasn't that quince?* She would tell the children as she picked through the figs for the good ones, *I'm not so sure about this Adam and Eve business, anyway. Maybe Adam was the one who ate the fig and Eve suffered the burden.* Even in the winter when the temperature was cold, his grandmother had the children sit on the porch for a spell, better always to do a portion of their work outside and by daylight. In this way, she also carved out quiet time for herself.

You know she could have remarried after my father died. She could have married a nice man, but she held out and some of the other kids with mamas and daddies, well, a two-parent household will always be the gold standard. I missed out on my gold standard so she could feed the multitudes. And look at you, neglecting yours and following in her footsteps. Charity begins at home.

And that is when Irvin loses it. "You brittle gray-haired old hussie heffa. You're closer to the grave than you are the nursery, but you're nursing wounds like no one ever did anything for you or you never got shit. Grandma willed me and you her house and you got to keep it. So do the world a favor and shut up."

Irvin Curtis has never handled sickness well. He was working part-time at the county jail and attending community college when his grandmother's cold turned into something worse. Irvin was disappointed at first not to go off to college but was pleasantly surprised by the number of foreign exchange students from Africa, the Middle East, and Southeast Asia that made his small pond full of big fish. But if community college was a sanctuary, the sicker his grandmother became and the more helpless he felt, the easier it was to tase the fuck out of two inmates when they were arguing rather than risk injury to himself; the easier it was to walk past or turn his back on a new prisoner getting his ass kicked. You got yourself here. Get yourself out. He moved up the ladder from corrections to contracts to probation officer and eventually, after social work and a post-graduate degree, he became a Correctional Treatment Specialist. He no longer wears a uniform, but he still wears the vestiges of anger. And what of Xavier? Irvin doesn't want that toxicity around his son.

Irvin Abraham Curtis, did you just call me a hussie heffa? His mother pretends to be stunned, but she likes hearing Irvin all riled up. It reminds her that her son lives far away but he hasn't completely gone away.

Now it's Irvin's turn to vent. "Look, I'm just doing what I can to keep it together right now. At the prison, a lot of these inmates aren't too mentally stable to begin with. A six-by-eight-feet cell will do that to you. We're understaffed and I'm hearing from clients that there's not enough soap or food. There's not enough masks. Instead of CDC protocols being enforced, mandatory social distancing, they're being crowded into cells, herded. The ones who are sick or high-risk that they say we have to release, we're releasing into a fucking dystopian society, with limited resources," Irvin tells his mother. He sometimes regrets that day up in Harlem when he went to see Julian and Nadine and encountered the camp counselor who put an imaginary cage in front of a boy for his ignorance and curiosity. The boy's face visits Irvin in his nightmares and melts into Xavier's face or Julian's or his own, and, of course, some of the boys and girls on his grandmother's porch who had not made it. Yes, there were others—a clerk, a teacher, a bank manager, a pediatrician, one lawyer—who had gone well. Sometimes, the porch children would DM Irvin on Facebook or Instagram or send an annual email Christmas card with updates on their lives and a thank-you note for the kindness his grandmother had shown them. How could someone who had so little give so much? In some ways she had been wealthy, but what did it mean to be spiritually wealthy anymore?

"Ma," Irvin says, reeling back his anger, "I'll drop a little something in the mail for you and Pat's kids. I'm sorry about the cussing."

"Well," his mother said, "I hope the next time you call me our conversation will be more pleasant. And Nadine is better."

On that note, Irvin ends the call. Xavier is standing on the curb waiting for Irvin when he pulls up and rolls down the window. "You want to climb in?"

"If you're so worried about me getting COVID, won't I get it in the car?"

But even as Xavier says this, he hops in alongside his father.

"How was your day?" Irvin asks.

"Are we really going to do the 'how was your day' thing? Did the docs telecom about Mom? What's the prognosis today?"

"The same," Irvin says.

"No, then my day wasn't good."

Irvin starts the car. "I'd rather drive closer to the hospital, if it's okay with you."

They park on a side street next to the Barnes & Noble, which is located across from the hospital. Irvin offers Xavier the bag of donuts. Xavier shrugs again but reaches into the bag and takes a glazed donut.

"Understand this: Your mother would want me to go to work. She would want you to stay in school and not lose your focus. She wouldn't want either of us sitting around worrying. Worry creates new problems."

"Tell me something I don't know." Xavier eats his donut in bits and pieces, breaking it up and putting it in his mouth underneath his mask. The window on his side is halfway down, but he rolls it down even more.

Xayxay talks plenty trash but he doesn't want COVID. Irvin thinks, *Good.*

"Did I ever tell you that my mom and I moved in with my grandma when I was nine? Mom could never keep a job. That's just the way she was wired. So life with Grandma was a game changer. Three square meals a day. And I'm talking *meals.* Nothing fancy, but homemade. She didn't go to church, but every night she made me recite the Lord's Prayer. She and her Lord's Prayer grew on me. The stability and all. But I had this terrible fear of losing her. Outside of you and Nadine, I have never feared losing anyone like that. So I'd pray after the Lord's Prayer quietly, *God, don't let anything happen to my grandma. If you take someone, God, take me.* And I meant it. With all my heart. But by the time I was ten or eleven, twelve, I don't know when exactly, it occurred to me that my prayer was selfish. That if my grandma knew I was praying for God to take me instead of her, she'd be outraged. I was asking God for something that was not in the right order of things. A parent—and she was the real parent in our household—always wants their kids to outlive them, to do better, thrive. If possible, excel."

Xavier opens the door and brushes the crumbs onto the curb. He stands for a moment and just stares at the hospital.

"You sure you don't want to walk around the block, Xayxay?"

"I don't care," Xavier says, turning to face his father. "Not like there's something else to do out here. We . . . might as well."

DETECTIVE TENDER laid out the guidelines Maureen Jacobson would need to adhere to before she could commit to taking on Darla Jacobson's case. First and foremost, Detective Tender assured Maureen Jacobson that she would do everything within reason to locate her daughter but could make no guarantees that Darla would be found, dead or alive. Second, Detective Tender stressed the pragmatics of private detecting in general and her methodology specifically. In the movies, private detectives and homicide units occasionally shared information or worked in tandem to close missing person cases, but in Detective Tender's experience, private investigators remained on the outside, the recipients of well-earned distrust, scorn, and derision for their ability to botch a good investigation with information that could not be used in court or misinformation that could overturn a case, resulting in a mistrial.

"Understand now," Detective Tender said, looking out her living room window from her 1960s ranch house in Milford, Pennsylvania, at a fawn eating up her spring lawn, "I got a sick man and I don't like to venture far from him these days. And with COVID, you can't just allow anyone in your home. But this sounds like a special case."

The contract Maureen Jacobson signed would include a per diem for travel, hotels, meals for two, and all incidental costs related to Detective Tender's search, including background checks, credit reports, access to phone records or calls Detective Tender would not normally be privy to, and all other digital or paper expenses.

"If you are at all skeptical," Detective Tender said, "I recommend a second call to my former clients. You have to want me as much as I want you." Detective Tender had a ninety-five percent approval rating. She was known as "the lady people finder."

"Is it true," Maureen had asked between packing her luggage for the States, "that most missing persons are found within the first twenty-four hours?"

Detective Tender did not want to further tax Maureen's nerves. She adjusted the phone to her ear and said, "A lot of things are true about missing person cases. Your daughter has been missing for forty-eight hours now. And time's a wasting."

"My son-in-law's not picking up the phone."

"Uh-huh. And you want me to contact his local precinct and get the what-about? Trust me, the less we interact with your son-in-law right now, the better. He is the number-one suspect, and the homicide detectives don't want or need me in their hair. Which frees me up to go upstate to where your daughter went missing. What's your son-in-law's name?"

"Theo Harper."

"Well, just like you don't know what's going on with Mr. Theo Harper, he doesn't know what's going on with you. These are advantages to consider."

Detective Tender had been told she had a soothing voice. And there were times when she milked her voice for dramatic effect. "Safe travels home, Mrs. Jacobson. Let's get the ball rolling, shall we now, with Mr. Roland Paige?"

The sheriff in the local county jail was relieved to have someone pick up Roland Paige. "I've heard of people not wanting to go to jail, but Mr. Paige doesn't seem to want to leave the premises."

"Mrs. Jacobson speaks very highly of you, Roland." Detective Tender smiled a greeting.

"I'd feel better if I could hear from Mrs. Jacobson myself if she thinks highly of me," Roland said when they were outside of the county jail and in the parking lot. Detective Tender unlocked the door to her Ford C-Max, where her husband, Ollie, sat waiting. She was in her late fifties, but she had gone prematurely gray in her twenties and couldn't be bothered with superficial alterations.

"Well, you might get your wish sooner than later," Detective Tender said, slipping a K-95 mask over Roland Paige's face. "This is Ollie. He's not much for words these days."

Roland shook Ollie Tender's hand, which trembled with the telltale sign of Parkinson's.

"You hungry?" Detective Tender asked, looking at Roland through the rearview mirror as she backed out of the parking lot.

"Listen, Mrs. Jacobson could tell them I didn't hurt Darla. I wouldn't murder her."

"Would you murder anyone?" Detective Tender said.

"All these trick questions you people keep asking me. Like I'm an idiot savant or something." He looked out the window. "They got good chicken sandwiches on Main Street."

At the deli window on Main Street, Detective Tender ordered six chicken sandwiches because Roland Paige swore they were the best he had ever tasted. She took out photographs of Darla and her husband, Theo, that Maureen Jacobson had emailed her.

"Hard to say with the masks and all," the girl in the store window said. "But I'm pretty sure he exchanged words with another customer a few days back."

"By *words* are you saying Mr. Harper seemed agitated?"

"He seemed like he was in a hurry," she said. "And the woman in the picture was with him but she didn't stand in line long."

Roland ate one of his two sandwiches on the way home and Detective Tender suggested that Roland recount (for what felt to him like the twentieth time) precisely what had happened on the night when he went to the Jacobsons' cottage as well as to the trail. She gave Roland a box of colored pencils and a sketchpad to draw, as accurately as possible, an outline of the trailhead with corresponding trail markers as he knew them.

When the wolfhound came through the dog door to greet his master, Detective Tender stayed in the car. She turned and almost cooed to her husband. The husband she had met when she wasn't looking. The man who sometimes couldn't make it to the bathroom and now relied on Depends. Parkinson's had not been part of the bargain. And yet here they were. "What do you think of Roland, Ollie?"

Ollie gave the thumbs-up sign. Detective Tender climbed out of the car and let the dog catch her scent, giving him a gentle scratch under the chin, where dogs liked to be massaged.

"Big pooch," she said. "Now, Roland, they're bringing Mr. Harper up for tomorrow's search of the trail. I think it would benefit us all if you could be present."

Roland Paige handed Detective Tender the paper. His rendering of the trails was very detailed with paths colored in like the Yellow Brick Road.

"I suppose you want to come in?" Roland asked. He was no longer in a hurry to be home. Since the dead don't sleep, Roland hadn't known how sleep-deprived he was among his deceased relatives until the first night in the county jail. Forensics tests had been done, including DNA and blood samples. His house and property gone through with a fine-tooth comb. And when the authorities suggested that Darla's body might be interred somewhere in the woods, Roland didn't want to return home more than ever. The dead did not come back as flesh-eating zombies, but they came back as unwanted guests.

A ten-minute walk through Roland Paige's four-bedroom house seemed to satisfy all Detective Tender needed to know. She turned to him before leaving and said, "I'll see you tomorrow. Seven A.M. sharp. Roland, it's none of my business, but this is too much house for one person."

If Roland Paige heard her, he didn't acknowledge what she had said.

Detective Tender climbed inside her car and gave Ollie the thumbs-up sign. She had booked a night in a hotel for them with access for the disabled. She knew Ollie sometimes felt useless. "I agree with you one hundred percent," Yvonne Tender said. "Roland's bred to be loyal. But loyalty's as much a weakness as it is a virtue."

*

Traces of Theo's and Darla's blood had been located throughout the Eldorado: the front passenger and driver's seats, the broken window, the driver's side door, the steering wheel, the trunk handle, where Darla Jacobson's luggage was found untouched. The search of the couple's apartment yielded only one piece of incriminating evidence: Theo's personal computer contained a list of divorce attorneys and profiles of clients whose cases they had won. Ramirez and Lutz now had a plausible motive.

At the Park Slope precinct, Detective Lutz watched Detective Ramirez interrogate Theo Harper from the observation room.

"Theo," Detective Ramirez asked. "You don't mind if I call you Theo?"

"Only if I can call you by your first name as well."

This dick is snugger than a cockroach in its exoskeleton, Detective Ramirez thought.

"Mr. Harper," Detective Ramirez continued, "were you planning on divorcing your wife?"

"No," Theo said. "I wasn't."

"Maybe after she had the baby?"

"Not after. Or before."

"You sure there's no one waiting in the wings?"

Theo glanced up at the walls. He was being recorded—this was an interrogation. Official. Unlike before. Without a lawyer present. Of course, if need be, if it ever came to it, he could say he was pressured to speak against his wishes. "Going to sound like a broken record here. But I really love Darla."

Ramirez slid a folder across the table to Theo. Theo opened the folder, scanned the list of names, confused at first. He looked at Detective Ramirez and smiled. Ramirez wanted to knock his perfect teeth out.

"You think this is about a divorce?" Theo wiped his eyes. He laughed. His was a tired laugh. "I'm an aesthetic advisor. Pre-COVID I went to the Brooklyn Supreme Courthouse every Tuesday morning. How do I break this down for you? Where there are divorces, there are houses that will need to be sold. Where there are exes or a separation, someone will need a new home or an apartment."

"Are you telling me these names are all work-related?"

"That's precisely what I'm telling you."

"So you troll divorce court for clients?"

"*Troll* is an ugly word," Theo said. "I go. I sit. I listen. I wait. Sometimes I initiate conversation, but most of the time I don't need to introduce myself. Divorced people want to vent about their divorces. Complain about their former partners, their attorneys— the egregious hourly legal fees. Custody. And, of course, how things will be divvied up in discovery. I can predict almost by rote how much their house will be appraised for by the court-appointed appraiser. Tell them which judge is on the take or which judge will appeal to them to settle, which judge favors women or is biased toward men, which lawyers will go into the little back room and work together to liquidate their house quickly, leaving them with next to nothing. I refer potential clients to real estate agents who will get them the most bang for their buck and who will keep the peace during a process that comes with temporary insanity. I give them a free consultation, tour their houses, and let them relive happy moments or bitter ones. And, if they listen—that's fifty-fifty, because emotions run high and the lawyers don't help—I encourage them not to wait until they're standing on the courtroom steps to settle."

Detective Ramirez shook his head. "That's pretty darn generous of you."

"Generous, no. Kind, sometimes. Lucrative, yes."

"And how many of your clients would you say you've slept with?"

"I don't mix business with pleasure," Theo said.

"Ever?"

"Never."

"How about pleasure with pain?" Detective Ramirez twirled his wedding band on his finger. In the winter months, the ring was loose. In the spring and summer, his fingers swelled and his wedding band did not budge.

"Sadomasochism isn't my first or second preference."

"Let's revisit Mrs. Jacobson's feelings about your open marriage."

Theo dug his hands into his pockets. Noah Pomerantz came to mind. "Darla wasn't unhappy."

"Usually," Ramirez said, "there comes a point when one partner wants the open relationship more."

Theodore bristled. "These questions are too personal. And since I haven't seen my wife, in what—three days?—I can't really speak to whether or not her views on open relationships have changed."

"Can you speak to the shovel in the trunk of your car? It seems a random item to have in the trunk of your car so close to spring."

Theo blinks. After a beat he says, "Weather is a precarious thing. Upstate winter can come early and stay late."

————

Four days after his wife goes missing, Theo Harper stands on the precipice of the mountain where his life went to hell in a handbasket. He is accompanied by sixty or so members of a search and rescue team, including New York State Police troopers, the county sheriff and one of his deputies, Detectives Lutz and Ramirez, the Lazy-Eyed Hermit, and an unknown woman. The morning trek up the mountain has been Theo's abject walk of shame. He feels the silent accusations and judgment from the entire group like hot daggers in his back. Nevertheless, he has held fast to his timeline and the series of events leading up to their domestic dispute, omitting that Darla threw hot tea in his face and that he had let his wife dangle, if only momentarily, over this very bluff. How easy it would have been to drop her.

In the parking lot the search team breaks up into five groups, A, B, C, D, and E, fanning out to form a containment circle with smaller groups working within segments of the larger grid from two preceding searches. The goal is to find clues, rule out possible exits Darla might have taken or been forced to take, and identify foot tracks. Theo does a double take when he sees the Lazy-Eyed Hermit. He has always found Roland Paige revolting. That lazy eye any decent man would cover with an eye patch, drooping and begging for pity.

"That's him," Theo says, and nudges Detective Lutz.

Detectives Lutz and Ramirez stare in Roland Paige's direction. "Who's the woman standing next to him?"

Detective Lutz chews on a piece of Wrigley's Spearmint chewing gum. He can spot a former officer anywhere.

"Private detective," Detective Lutz says.

"Who hired the private detective?" Detective Ramirez asks.

"My money is on my mother-in-law," Theo opines.

"That's him," Roland Paige says to Detective Tender, pointing at Theo from across the parking lot.

"Handsome. The photographs don't do him justice," Detective Tender offers. "It's rude to point. Don't point, Roland."

"Yes ma'am."

This morning Roland Paige woke up with an inclination not to venture off his property. His voluntary vacation in jail and Detective Tender's comments about the only home he has ever known being too big filled him with high anxiety. One day he will be old. Who will take care of him in his old age? He has always lived from moment to moment, but now the future weighs on him.

Detective Tender removes Roland's ready-made map from her brown bomber jacket. The map is as much for her to get acclimated to the forest as it is for Roland Paige to keep focused. She took her own leap of faith this morning and left Ollie at Roland's cottage in the care of the gentle wolfhound and the clumsy volunteer who sprained her ankle climbing out of a car.

"Listen up," she whispers to Roland. "Everyone will be watching you. And everyone will be watching him. Keep it together."

The trek up the mountain is steep and Detective Tender, and Detectives Lutz and Ramirez, all pause as they ascend the mountain toward the escarpment.

"A pregnant woman did this hike?" Detective Lutz whistles, out of breath. He smokes a pack a day and has been trying to quit. Nothing works. But he likes the flavor of Wrigley's Spearmint chewing gum.

Fifty minutes into the hike, the distance between Theo Harper and Roland Paige disintegrates and they are in a traditional line formation, then side by side on the trail. Their two groups, A and B, merge and Theo attempts to keep pace with Roland Paige, who is behind the official map holder.

"What did you do to Darla?" Theo asks the Lazy-Eyed Hermit. "Please tell me what you did to my wife."

It is one of Theo's rare displays of emotion or affection.

"Nothing," Roland says, turning to seek out Detective Tender, who had warned him to hang back and keep his distance.

"Well," Detective Ramirez whispers to Theo, thinking about the conversation he will have with his husband when he returns to Sunset Park. The conversation he has avoided. "At least we know you feel something."

"Let's keep it moving," Detective Lutz says.

Detective Tender notices that the farther the search team goes ahead of her, the closer their voices register. Like walking into a tunnel and hearing every echo.

"Are there any bears in this part of the country?" she asks Roland Paige.

"Yes," Roland says. "But they're more afraid of us than we are of them."

Theo's eyes are fixated on the valley below. The rescue team, of course, searched for Darla's body at the foot of the mountain. No one could have survived a drop that steep.

Detective Tender is among the last to make it up to the crest. She picks her moment to stand alongside the primary suspect. "Mr. Harper, I understand your wife is quite musical."

"Sorry, I don't think we caught your name?" Detective Lutz says.

"I didn't give it," Detective Tender says.

"My wife plays the bassoon," Theo says.

"Single or contrabassoon?"

"Standard."

Detective Tender's gaze remains focused on Theo. "These woods are musical. Like your wife."

Detective Ramirez leans in to Detective Lutz and asks, "Is she a PI or a poet?"

"Detectives, I heard that," Detective Tender says while waving a naughty finger. "I imagine the wind would have been something fierce given the storm that came later. Was it fierce, Mr. Harper?"

"I don't recall the wind."

Detective Tender persists, "You must have been really yelling at the top of your lungs. Must have been some argument. Perhaps volatile?"

Theo shouts back, "Did my mother-in-law hire you?"

"Yes, now that you ask. Name's Yvonne Tender. Pleasure to make your acquaintance. *All of you.*" She rubs her hands together. "Remind me again, Mr. Harper, where you were standing when Mrs. Jacobson ran off?"

"Right here," Theo said. "On this cliff."

"Exactly right there or approximately right there?"

"Well, damn," Detective Lutz says, clocking Detective Tender for the first time. "She's the cop who solved the kidnapping of Senator O'Connor's daughter eight years ago."

Detective Tender rubs her hands together faster. Theo finds the hand rubbing distracting. "I wish I could take all the credit. But I can't. And she wasn't a senator's daughter. She was a teacher's daughter. In my mind, same difference."

Detective Tender had been blindsided once. A decorated officer—now retired from the force—her claim to fame was the arrest of her third cousin in a high-profile kidnapping case. She and her partner had received a tip about a teenage girl and an older man on City Island fitting the description from a missing persons report. When they arrived at the condo, who should Detective Tender find but her own cousin, Nino, the one who dominated conversations at the annual family Thanksgiving dinners in Tarrytown. He kneeled on the floor duct-taping the bikini-clad teenager to a chair. The shower was running. And Nino had a carving knife. Detective Tender had seen some horrible things, but sometimes it was the sounds that stayed with you. Here, the sound of the water running mingled with the girl's whimpers. The proximity of the knife on the carpeted floor with the blood stains, new and old, and the terrified look in the girl's eyes, and the way the suspect, her cousin, turned around and picked up the knife, charging them, only to stop and say, "Vonney, is that you?"

"Who the fuck do you think it is? You stop right there. Nino, you're under arrest," Detective Yvonne Tender said.

And Nino had charged toward them, toward her brazenly, and she had pushed her partner out of the way and shot the culprit in the neck. During that time, as he lay bleeding out, her cousin would admit to two additional kidnappings, a sister and brother, some sixteen years before, who had gone missing on a playground in Ossining. "Where are they?" she had screamed. Their bodies were in the basement of the Tarrytown house where they all gathered for Thanksgiving, limed up under the floorboards. Detective Tender had read somewhere that most great scientific discoveries happen by accident. Pure accident and chance closing in on her cousin, who delivered refrigerators for an appliance company. Detective Tender and her partner made the evening news and graced local newspapers, though Detective Tender took center stage because of her years on the force and the personal angle to the story. After her fifteen minutes of fame, Detective Tender could never look at her job the same way again. She left the police force and decided to become a private investigator. She and Ollie Tender had three adult children: all sane and, as far as she knew, relatively healthy and happy. She no longer believed in coincidences or accidents, though she understood they were sometimes interchangeable.

"When your wife ran off," Detective Tender repeats herself, "*which* way did she go?"

Detective Lutz interjects again. "Detective Tender, I don't have to remind you that this case has been taken over by the New York State Police."

"And where's your state uniform?"

"We brought Mr. Harper here as a courtesy."

"Think he's going to jump?" she asks, and then turns to Theo. "Are you a flight risk?"

"I'm sorry?" Theo says. There is a swarm of activity around Theo. Theo can't quite follow the give-and-take between Detective Lutz and Detective Tender. Or the growing number of troopers and members of the search team as they converge on the cliff. The site where Darla was last seen. A helicopter flies overhead. He can see search dogs below and hear them barking in the distance. Theo points at the spot where Darla stood before she had turned away from him, her backpack and strong, taut body disappearing into the woods. He hears a search team member say PLS (place last seen) and LKP (last known position). There have been no sightings of his wife. No footprints. How to tell them that even if he held a compass in his hand with directives for north south east and west, the mental fog in his head, mental fog that predates COVID, would still unmoor him, render him lost. He is geographically challenged. And he came by it honestly. Yes, yes, he knows what it is to be lost in the woods, though not abandoned. Abandoned. Not left. Like he . . . *left* Darla. Coward. Coward. Goddamn coward. He is glad Detectives Ramirez and Lutz deterred his father from joining them on the search, though he recognizes that not all the members of the search team are professionals. "I left my wife," Theo says out loud. And everyone turns to look at him. "I left my wife." He begins walking back, then running like a wild man through the forest as his words echo back at him.

"Where's he going?" Detective Tender asks.

"What the fuck," Detective Ramirez says to Detective Lutz, who is content to let his rookie partner do the chasing.

"Maybe he's training for the New York marathon," Detective Lutz snaps. "Go after him, please. I'm not cut out for this shit."

They can hear Theo shouting, "I left my wife. Darla? I left my wife." The more the truth sinks in, the harder Theo runs, but he is outflanked on all sides by shadows and murmurs that fly at him like a witch's brew of happy sad happy sad memories.

A hurricane on the way home from a family vacation. His father determined to play chicken with Mother Nature, speeding along Highway 39 departing the Great Lakes for Aurora and Davenport and their hometown, Des Moines. The rain and the hail and the wind and a road that buckles before their eyes. The Harpers land in a ditch and his mother scurries into the back seat to confirm their six T's are all right. Once their children's good health is confirmed, Elena Harper pummels her husband about the face and neck. "I told you we should find shelter. Turn back around. Alfred, let's turn back!"

But Alfred Harper reaches over and kisses her small, dry lips. The six T's, ages nine to sixteen, step out of the station wagon into the pouring rain and work together to get the car out of the ditch and change the flat rear right tire. And off they go; the game of chicken resumes with Alfred shouting and telling the six T's to join his chorus. He outpaces funnel clouds that unfurl like dirty half-and-half. It is Theo who spots the motel.

The Harper family piles into a room with two double beds and lays sleeping bags on the floor. In some ways, this portion of the vacation is better than the time spent on Lake Michigan because the Mennonite owner lets them take what they want from the broken vending machine. There is a wooded area across the way from the northern-facing portion of the motel. While Theo's parents and siblings watch Grease—*the TV blipping on and off and everyone grateful to have any electricity at all—Theo peers out of the hotel window at the splintered sky. He cannot resist cracking open the door to make sure the storm, the inclement weather, which has done so much damage, will not harm them.*

"What do you see out there, Theo?" Elena asks.

"Close the door, son," Alfred demands.

In the middle of the night, rain pelts against the motel roof, and

Theo, unable to sleep, crawls from his sleeping bag and looks out the window. He sees something—no, someone—trampling into the woods with a lantern. Theo puts on his rain boots and raincoat and grabs the flashlight he used to read The Hardy Boys, *thinking he will be brave and play chicken like his father with Mother Nature. He is mesmerized by the quaking of the wind and the stranger gliding through the squall with a blanket thrown carelessly over his shoulder and a flickering lantern. Theo crosses into the woods and hears the wind speak. This way now. Not to him, but to that someone who continues to forge ahead, indifferent or unaware of Theo until Theo gives himself away and trips. And that is when the blanketed stranger spins around, holding up the lantern. His face, aged and cragged and black as night. The First Theo. The thirty percent the Harpers have inherited. For Theo, it is like peering into a mirror and seeing his reflection projected into old age. But this cannot be—how can this be—the 1800s are long gone. Then it dawns on Theo. I'm going to hell in a handbasket. The First Theo has come to take me there.*

The next morning when Alfred and Elena Harper count their six T's, they are missing their most beloved T. Their baby. The family and the Mennonite owner fan out and around the property and into the nearby woods in search of Young Theo. They find him hours later sitting beneath a green tarp. A half-eaten rabbit roasting on a handmade spit. A moldy blanket thrown over his shoulders. Alfred and Elena and Theo's siblings gather round him, pulling him close. "Theo, Theo, what happened?"

"I saw him."

His parents are alarmed. "Him? Who, son?" Alfred wants to know.

"The First Theo. The black one."

"Theo has always had a vivid imagination," his parents whisper among themselves.

"You don't believe me?" Theo says, stung by their doubt.

"Of course we believe you, son. We just—"

"You don't believe me."

In Des Moines, Alfred and Elena take Theo for a physical. "Hypothermia could have been a factor," the doctor says.

"I saw the First Theo," young Theo insists. "It was the First Theo."

"People go into the woods all the time and have visions. Some mushroom-induced," the doctor says.

Behind closed doors, Theo hears his parents argue with the doctor. "How do you explain the rabbit and the blanket and the tarp?" Alfred asks the doctor.

"Count yourself lucky that your boy did not perish in the woods. And no physical harm was done to him."

Theo halts, sobbing and out of breath. It is Roland Paige who catches up to him first. The Lazy-Eyed Hermit is the last person on earth Theo wants to let witness him falling to pieces. For if it is true that familiarity breeds contempt, then so do freakish encounters with the dead, be they real or hallucinatory. But Theo does *fall* when his hiking boots skid on a patch of mud and he goes sliding down the hill and scrambling to latch onto something, anything, only to land flat on his ass. Undeterred, Roland Paige moves gingerly through the spring thickets and helps Theo from the entanglement of branches, rocks, and leaves.

"Get away from me you, ding, ding, ding!" Theo stands up, kicking off the dirt and leaves—only for the heel of his left boot to crack something hard and plastic. When Theo looks down, he sees the shiny, broken rectangular surface of his wife's treble clef iPhone case and her dislodged iPhone mere inches away.

PART THREE

threshold /ˈθrɛʃˌhoʊld/ *noun*

  1: a piece of wood, metal, or stone that forms the bottom of a door and that you walk over as you enter a room or building

  2: the point or level at which something begins or changes

—THE BRITANNICA DICTIONARY

THE NEW YORK State Police Department takes into evidence Darla's cell phone and the cracked cell phone case. Messages retrieved from Theo's and Darla's phone carriers reveal multiple desperate calls he made to her. The investigation is further complicated by the discovery of a bloodstained rock at the precise spot where Theo slipped. His fall, unwittingly, provides a scenario for possible injuries Darla might have sustained during a similar fall or fight. But where is Darla? Or where is her body? Without a body—a skull—the forensics experts cannot determine anything conclusive. The newly discovered rock has Darla's DNA but does not have Theo's fingerprints at all.

False, the adage that murderers always return to the scene of the crime, but true, true, true that domestic arguments often erupt into deadly violence. Detective Tender stops by the Jacobson cottage, which has been turned over by the local and state cops so thoroughly that she has nothing to work with. She stares at the photographs around the quaint cottage and studies them up close, a timeline of happy Jacobson family memories: horseback riding, gardening, rock climbing, fishing. Mrs. Jacobson has been in Paris for the past three months and has only recently returned to the States. Detective Tender understands that the cops might interview her, but asking to see Darla's childhood bedroom would only come to them as an afterthought.

On the drive home, Detective Tender calls Maureen Jacobson.

Ollie's next to her in the passenger's seat. "It would be nice to meet you. OK, if I swing by?"

"Sure. Why?" Maureen is hoping for good news.

"I'd like to just have a quick peek at your daughter's old bed-room."

"Darla hasn't lived here in years," Maureen Jacobson says.

"Even when our kids go off to college," Detective Tender says, "a part of them lingers behind in their chest of drawers and on their dressers and in our photographs. I'd like you to put together a box of photographs for the video."

Maureen swallows emptiness. "Video?"

"Next steps, Mrs. Jacobson. *We* control the narrative here," Detective Tender says. "Once the press gets hold of Darla's story, that's a feeding frenzy. The kind that turns a headache into a full-fledged migraine."

"But don't you think," Maureen asks, "that since women go miss-ing every day, a story about a pregnant woman will draw more at-tention to the case?"

"Yes," Detective Tender says, finally. "But I like my attention with a loving spoonful of grace."

*

2020 was a watershed year to disappear. The pandemic provided precious cover for people who didn't want to be found or know how to be found: senior citizens suffering from dementia or Alzheimer's who strolled out of their apartment buildings and were unable to find their way back home, because with few people out and about or walking on the streets, especially in cities, the markers and faces of entire neighborhoods looked unfamiliar, altered; cousins or sib-lings who now had a legitimate excuse to estrange an overbearing brother or sister or relative who voted on the wrong side in the 2016 presidential election; husbands and wives who saw an opportunity to break away from tired or fractious marriages; adolescents who had tasted freedom in college and night clubs and could not permit themselves to return to their childhood bedrooms. Members of the LGBTQ communities, runaways, teenagers, mostly Latinx and blacks, whose reports routinely fell to the bottom of cold case piles. Darla Jacobson would be one of thirteen thousand people on New York State's Missing Persons list.

She had thought her husband would relish her baby bump, but it was acne-faced front-desk clerk Greer. Two days after Darla checked in to the two-star hotel that was really a one-star hotel, Greer knocked on the door to her room. Darla answered the door in a striped blue-and-white Yankees T-shirt and the one pair of pants she owned.

"You look different," Greer said, noticing that Darla had cut her hair into a French bob. She wore dark eyeliner to match dark penciled-in brows. And a beauty mark.

Darla rubbed her belly. There was no denying her status without an overcoat. "Everything about me is changing. Hair's the least of it," she said, but she thought, *I have the people I love all over my body.* The bob made her feel close to her mother. Her face and hair, well, hadn't she always been a dead ringer for her Dad? And the baby inside her was half Theo's. Her newly acquired name, Ruby's, for sure. So . . .

"I didn't know," Greer said, gesturing toward Darla's stomach.

"Neither did I," Darla said. "My girl kind of snuck up on me."

"How do you know it's a she?"

"There's no male energy in this belly."

"Maybe I should leave . . . with that tone," Greer said. But he was very slow about it.

"You can't take a joke? *Gen Z,* I'm joking." Darla wanted to tell Greer that her mother was a dermatologist. She could do wonders for his acne.

Greer stalled in the hallway, which was the color of yellow and brown mushrooms. "Just checking in to see if you needed anything."

"I need my ID and my wallet."

"No luck?"

"None at all."

Darla crossed over to her backpack on the unmade bed, a comforter with tourist destinations from the falls. She returned to the door with a stack of bills.

"Well, I went ahead and put my credit card number under your name," he said, and shrugged. "When you check out, you can settle in cash."

Darla considered Greer. "I'm not sure what I did to deserve such kindness, but I'd feel a lot better if you'd take this money."

Greer pocketed Darla's offering. He grinned. "Are you trying to bribe me, Ruby?"

"What makes you say that?" Darla smiled.

The bonding happened naturally: Greer dropped by to say hello before and after work, and soon there were runs to the grocery store or to pick up prenatal vitamins or takeout. Soon there were evening, fresh-air drives around Niagara Falls. She wasn't ready for Greer to accompany her on daily walks yet. She went to the falls and the state park with her bassoon. In this way, she was not alone or lonely. Their first together errand was to buy maternity clothes. Everything was picked over or out of stock, so Darla bought extra-large women's activewear for ease and comfort and men's shirts and pants with elastic waistbands that she could expand into. While shopping, she learned that Greer was two years out of the University of Toronto. He was a computer science major. Figuring out next steps post undergrad. He currently worked two jobs: the computer and security Geek Squad at Best Buy on Sundays and the front desk at the hotel four days a week.

"I was thinking about quitting just before you walked in," Greer said.

"I'm sure glad you didn't," Darla admitted.

Darla tried the new clothes on in the back seat of Greer's father's Chevy pickup truck. She liked that Greer drove a pickup truck and that the truck was gray like the one she had stolen in Poughkeepsie. She couldn't try on clothes in fitting rooms, which were closed because of COVID, but Darla made Greer take an oath that he broke not to watch her through the side or rearview mirrors. She enjoyed the way peeping made him blush. His curiosity was a shot of adrenaline to her bludgeoned self-esteem.

Gambling was illegal outside of the casinos in Niagara Falls, but Greer took Darla to a laundromat with three vintage slot machines. There was an honor system and, if you hit the jackpot, all the proceeds were donated to charities.

"Which charity?" Darla said, squinting distrustfully when she won the jackpot and had to deposit her earnings into a silver "Charity Box" next to the change booth.

"I'm not really sure," Greer said. "People on the front lines? Doctors? Nurses? Stuff like that."

"That's too vague and amorphous," Darla said. "Greer, I smell a scam."

"I'm thinking you might have serious trust issues."

"You think?" She raised her freshly arched black brows. "9/11 did it to me. After the towers fell, professional scammers came out of the woodwork like vultures to prey on vulnerable families."

"I was four when 9/11 happened."

"Of course you were, Gen Z."

"Did you know anyone who died there?"

Darla brushed lint from the dryer off Greer's sweater. Growing up she had never been allowed to wear polyester. Polyester was bad for the skin. She hesitated for a second. "I have a friend who lost her dad in the towers."

"No shit, Ruby?"

Darla winced at the mention of Ruby's name. Greer thought she was wincing because she was talking about something painful. "Real shit. Her name's Darla."

"Jesus," he said.

"Satan," Darla said.

Greer had never lost anyone. His mother was Canadian. He had an extended family in Ontario. Three brothers, parents, and great-grandparents. They were known for longevity. Of course, even though he had dual citizenship, they couldn't cross the Rainbow Bridge. "That must have been hell for your friend and her family."

"We never really talked about it then or now . . . but I sometimes feel like she resents me, you know. Our parents—my mother, her father—both worked in the North Tower."

Greer thought about it. "Ruby, I'd resent you too."

"Huh," Darla said. For a second, her chest heaved up and down as though she might cry.

"Not forever," Greer corrected himself. "Just sometimes. Until I got over it."

"You don't 'get over' losing a parent, Greer. Or a husband."

"Then maybe you should drop—what's her name again?—Darla. Like you dropped your roommates. Life's too short, especially after COVID, to go around feeling bad."

"You Gen Zs only care about yourselves," Darla said.

"What are you, a boomer?" Greer said.

"Gen X? I don't know where I fall. I guess that's half the problem. But I love my friend. If you hold everything to heart that people do, you'd have no friends at all. And old friends sweep best," she said.

Darla was sitting on the desk chair with her feet propped up on the bed. Greer was spread out across her bed putting away the wooden figurines from a chessboard that doubled as a checkers board. He had taken the chessboard from his parents' house along with Telepathy, backgammon, and other board games that could be played by two. He had not spent the night yet, but he had an electric toothbrush in the bathroom that he used to brush his teeth after meals.

"I don't know why I didn't think to buy new shoes," Darla said. Of course it made sense that the shape of her feet would begin to change. Hadn't she read that some pregnant women went up two shoe sizes?

"We can go shoe shopping tomorrow."

This was what she missed about being in her twenties, even a teenager, before her dad died, how you could spend the whole day with friends smoking pot and doing absolutely nothing. Darla pulled up her men's T-shirt to scratch her belly. The rounder she became the more her belly itched. She knew Greer wanted to touch her stomach. She could tell by the intense way he stared. She was losing her navel.

"Go ahead," Darla said, nodding. "She can't bite yet."

Greer placed his palms flat on Darla's belly and massaged her stomach in small circles, letting each circle increase in size. It felt so good to have someone touch her. She still wore a bandage over her finger, which was beginning to heal.

"This feels amazing," Greer said.

"This feels uncertain," Darla said, also staring at her stomach. "Like when I first started playing an instrument. I thought I'd play the flute or clarinet. But those instruments weren't right for me. Then I tried the bassoon. We were in the music room at school. It was musical instrument day. Music instructors were there encouraging us to explore the instruments tactilely. My friends all went first for the violins, clarinets, and cellos. But the bassoon sat there looking so human, so lonely. 'What is this?' I asked one of the music teachers. Mr. Garrison. I crushed on Mr. Garrison. 'Pick it up and it will tell you everything you need to know,' he said. And I did. I picked up that bassoon and didn't know what in the hell I was doing. I fumbled with it and nearly dropped it, but Mr. Garrison caught it and steered my hands in the right direction, like I'm steering yours now, and the sound that came out of that ugly instrument once I got the fingering right was otherworldly. Beautiful. Later, I would realize I didn't choose the bassoon. The bassoon chose me. First couple of years, I barely practiced. But then 9/11 happened. After that, I couldn't practice enough."

"Darla's dad?"

She nodded. "I couldn't stop thinking about the way he died or what he was thinking when he died or *how* he died. You can know what's happening, see something happening right in front of you, and still not know the how. But the how doesn't matter when you're playing your instrument and keeping time in the orchestra."

Greer leaned over and kissed Darla's bare belly.

"Hey baby," he whispered.

Darla whispered too. *"Hey, baby."*

Greer looked up at Darla. "Hey, sexy pregnant lady."

Darla's expression hardened. "Don't become attached to me, Greer. I don't need or want a puppy crush."

"Okay. How could I? Gen Zs are only attached to themselves."

"I'm serious."

"Scout's honor." He made the sign of a Scout.

"Good, because you don't know where I've been. And I'm not sure where I'm going. I only know this is a two-person journey."

CHAT ROOM

@Save Darla Jacobson

THIS CHAT ROOM is dedicated to sightings of Darla Jacobson. Mrs. Jacobson, 5'3", flaxen blond, and three months pregnant, last seen on a trail in Greene County in the Catskills. She has azure-blue eyes and wore tan hiking pants and an orange overcoat with a green fleece underneath. She might or might not have a black Osprey backpack and an instrument known as a bassoon.

We at The Church of the Holy Redeemer of Lives are deeply disturbed by the disappearance of Mrs. Jacobson and have set up a prayer circle in her name. We will not stop praying until Mrs. Jacobson and her bundle of joy return to their loved ones.

CHURCH OF THE HOLY REDEEMER OF LIFE PRAYER COMMITTEE

This Jacobson family doesn't need a church or hotline. They need a psychic

1-222-PSY-CHIC

We are prepared to fast, if necessary.

CHURCH OF THE HOLY REDEEMER OF LIFE PRAYER COMMITTEE

Spring is Girl Scout season and our local branch will donate a percentage of our proceeds to the @Save Darla Jacobson fund

GREENE COUNTY BRANCH, GIRL SCOUTS OF AMERICA

Call 222-Psy-Chic.

1-222-PSY-CHIC

Did you check the ditch near Goat Hill Road in Saugerties?

ANONYMOUS

Maureen and Daniel Jacobson were active members of the school board. We are putting up flyers throughout the Upper West Side and Manhattan to aid the @SaveDarlaJacobson Fund.

NEIGHBOR, PARENT, MOTHER, FRIEND

Who is this white bitch?   CONCERNED CITIZEN OF COLOR

I object strongly to the word 'bitch.'

CONCERNED CITIZEN IN GENERAL

What does race have to do with this?   POST-RACIAL CITIZEN

Look up Gwen Ifill. White Women Missing.   ANONYMOUS

I am certain I saw Mrs. Jacobson on the southbound Acela train from Poughkeepsie to New York City on the afternoon of Monday, April 25th. She was seated toward the back of the train. I came armed with M&Ms in case the food car was closed. Mrs. Jacobson stared covetously at my M&Ms with peanuts and when I offered to share, she shook her head vehemently. I assumed it was because of COVID. Now that I've read she is expecting, she might have had a peanut allergy?

M&M FAN (AS IN PEANUTS.
NOT M&M THE RAP SINGER. RAP MUSIC DISORIENTS ME.)

Is she pregnant? She doesn't look pregnant in the picture you posted.   ANONYMOUS

I concur. Darla Jacobson does not look pregnant at all.

ANONYMOUS DOULA

Skinny white woman.　　　　　　　　　　　ANONYMOUS

You can never be too thin.　　　　　　　　　ANONYMOUS

My little sister disappeared on the eve of her Sweet Sixteenth party. We had just come from getting our nails done at Belle Salon. Her nails were still wet so she sat in the car while Mom, Dad and I took decorations into the venue for the party. When we returned to the car, she was gone. That was seven years ago . . .

LOVING SISTER

Native American women disappear at more than ten times the national rate.　　　　　　　　　　　　　ANONYMOUS

I lost my brother. He ran away from home at fifteen . . .

ANONYMOUS

Darla Jacobson was my first girlfriend when I lived upstate. I live in Minnesota now and would come to help but for the lockdown. Save Darla Jacobson!

FIRST LOVE, SUMMER 2002

We played in the Boston Philharmonic together.

ANONYMOUS MUSICIAN

She fucked around in college.

EX-GIRLFRIEND OF A BOYFRIEND SHE STOLE

What does Darla Jacobson's sex life have to do with anything?! No shame. And no shaming.

Save Darla Jacobson! Save Darla Jacobson! Save Darla Jacobson!

MEMBER OF THE @SAVE DARLA JACOBSON FUND

90,000 black women will go missing this year.

ANONYMOUS AFRICAN AMERICAN WOMAN

Go back to Africa Go back to Africa Back to Africa!

ANONYMOUS

Can we use this platform to talk about gun control and missing women?　　WE THE PEOPLE FOR SOCIAL PEACE AND HARMONY

Every missing woman should carry a gun!

GUN-TOTING WANDA

Every red-blooded American should carry a gun.

WANDA'S RIGHT-HAND MAN

Red blooded Americans carried guns and killed Indians.

ANONYMOUS, MODERATE-TO-CONSERVATIVE REPUBLICAN

I think you mean 'Native Americans'?

ANONYMOUS, MODERATE-TO-LIBERAL DEMOCRAT

Who is Gwen Ifill again?　　　　　ANONYMOUS

She was an American journalist.　　ANONYMOUS BLACK WOMAN

Where's everyone finding these statistics?

ANONYMOUS ECONOMICS PROFESSOR, NEW YORK UNIVERSITY

I lost my cousin. He was nine. We still haven't gotten over him. You don't get over a family member going missing.

ANONYMOUS RELATIVE

1-222-Psy-Chic.　　　　　　　　　1-222-PSY-CHIC

My name is Sandy Bryant and Darla Jacobson read books to me her senior year of high school. She read THE MAN WHO WALKED BETWEEN THE TOWERS. I don't know why, but I feel the need to order the book on Amazon now.

SANDY BRYANT

When we were dating—this is Darla's old boyfriend again— we used to like to go mushroom hunting. We would get totally smashed.　　　FIRST LOVE, SUMMER 2002

Her husband did it.　　　ANONYMOUS

Someone should disappear him.　　　ANONYMOUS

He is hotter than Ted Bundy.　　　ANONYMOUS

The serial killer?　　　ANONYMOUS

I'd fuck him.　　　ANONYMOUS

Do you have any idea how many women Ted Bundy killed?

ALARMED FEMINIST

I. Do. Not. Care.　　　ANONYMOUS/HORNY DURING COVID

The devil is truly busy in the land.　　　ANONYMOUS CHRISTIAN

Down with Toxic Masculinity.　　　ANONYMOUS

Down with Feminism.　　　ANONYMOUS

I saw Darla Jacobson in the basement of Comet Ping Pong in Washington, D.C!!!!!　　　ANONYMOUS

I am not signing on this link again.

UNITED WE STAND, DIVIDED WE FALL

268,884 women will disappear in 2020.   FUCKUUP

Are Transwomen included on this list?

TRANS PEOPLE FOR INCLUSION AND EQUITY

How do you know these statistics?

ANONYMOUS ECONOMICS PROFESSOR, NEW YORK UNIVERSITY

I will be responsible for a percentage of those missing.

FUCKUUP

*No one's talking about how many men will go missing. I smell
a double standard.*   DON'T FORGET ABOUT ME

People, we are all in this together.   ANONYMOUS

Until we aren't.   ANONYMOUS, BUT KEEPING IT REAL

1-222-Psy-Chic . . .   1-222-PSY-CHIC

What's happening to this country?

UNITED WE STAND, DIVIDED WE FALL

COVID   ANONYMOUS AT REVELATIONS

I am still waiting for the numbers on missing men?

DON'T FORGET ABOUT ME

Have you people no sense of decency or consideration for what the Jacobson family must be going through at this time? What all families in similar situations must endure?

ANONYMOUS, OUTRAGED

I would like to help. I am in middle school, but my parents said they are never letting me leave the apartment again.

ANONYMOUS 5TH GRADER

Hi, we live in Brooklyn. And we don't want to give the impression that we are holding our son hostage. COVID has been a challenge, but for exercise we are circulating Save Darla Jacobson posters in our neighborhoods in Brooklyn Heights and neighboring Cobble Hill, Boerum Hill, Carroll Gardens.

PARENTS OF 5TH GRADER, BH

We have reported a sighting of Mrs. Jacobson. My wife picked Mrs. Jacobson up on Sunday evening the 24th in the parking lot near the trail. She spent the night at our house and we took her to the train station for New York the next morning. Mrs. Jacobson went by the name of Ruby Black.

IVY AND JENN, RESPECT OUR PRIVACY

Ruby Black?　　　　　　　　　　　　　　　　ANONYMOUS

Who is Ruby Black?　　　　　　ANONYMOUS BLACK WOMAN

Check the dumpster behind the Steve's Candy Store and you will find Ruby Black and Darla Jacobson.　　　　FUCKUUP

This means Darla Jacobson may yet be alive. Praise Jesus!
THE CHURCH OF THE HOLY REDEEMER OF LIFE PRAYER COMMITTEE

Hoax.   ANONYMOUS

Darla Jacobson is Ruby Black?   ANONYMOUS

I am SOOOO confused.   ANONYMOUS, BUT KEEPING IT REAL

1-222-Psy-Chic. One person. Two auras.   1-222-PSY-CHIC

SHUT THIS CHATROOM DOWN.   DON'T FORGET ABOUT ME

Will the real Ruby Black please stand up?

                     UNITED WE STAND, DIVIDED WE FALL

THE YEAR was 2005. And Ruby Black was about to jump off the ledge of the dorm building when she heard her uncle Freddie's voice. *BigheadedRubyBigheadedRubyBigheadedRuby.* There was rousing applause and a cacophony of chants from partygoers, residential college mates, friends, singing: *go, go, jump, jump,* but when Ruby peered over her shoulders into the sea of sweaty, amped-up faces, one voice shouted above the others: *Ruby, no.* Monty Bennett yanked Ruby off the ledge and clutched her tight: *Ruby, no.* What strong arms he had, Monty: the boyfriend who had dumped her two weeks earlier for a freshman.

Blackout.

They were sitting in Monty's car.

Blackout.

They were walking through the front door of a diner. The New Haven landscape behind them.

Blackout.

Monty was asking Ruby if she would prefer to go to her dorm.

"Not yet," she said. "I can't face my roommates." Candy and Jacintha were political science majors like Ruby and Monty. The

foursome had bonded sophomore year during one of the many af-
finity groups on campus, this one the Black Student Alliance at Yale.

Blackout.

Monty stopped short of asking the question Ruby really wanted
to hear. *Why don't you hang out in my dorm?*

Blackout.

The red leather booth seats sagged from the multitude of asses
that had sat on them. Ruby kept nodding off, her head sloppy side
down on the table. Every time she dared to open her eyes, faces
from the party swirled around her: kaleidoscopic close-ups like a
Chuck Close painting. Candy and Jacintha pushing their way
through the crowd. Monty saying, "She's fine. She's fine," over and
over again.

"They're going to kick us out of here if you don't sit up," Monty
said, looking around the diner.

Ruby corrected her posture and sat up straight on her side of the
booth. She used a teaspoon to stir the oily tea and told Monty to
drink his Sprite. When they were still a thing, she would buy extra
cans of Sprite for Monty at 7-Eleven.

"This is not even Lipton," she said, pushing the cup of tea away.
Some of it splashed on the table and Monty dabbed at it with a
paper napkin.

It was half past four in the morning. Monty was not a late-night
person. Senior year, their divergent circadian rhythms calcified the
gulf between them. Ruby liked to go to parties and stay into the
wee hours of the morning. Monty preferred to leave early and be in
bed by ten. He stopped at one beer and excused himself when joints
were passed around. Ruby was always one of the first in the group
to take a hit. Carpe diem. Carpe diem. When would they be under-
grads again? Never.

"Do you want me to ask after Lipton?" Monty offered.

Ruby thought, *Something is seriously wrong with me to care
about these things.*

"Please," she said, dropping sugar cubes in the tea she would not drink.

"In England, our Lipton is PG Tips. It is strong and, if you brew it too long, it's quite bitter. Between the two of us, I prefer Lipton," Monty said.

Ruby sometimes forgot that Monty was from England. He was a catch—this black Brit named Monty. She loved saying: *Monty, Monty.* And how proud she had been taking Monty home for the first time to meet her parents. Look, look what I've accomplished. I'm at Yale and I've landed a good official (black) boyfriend. And the thing was, she really liked him. And Monty liked to stay in America during Thanksgiving and Easter to save money and he liked to talk football, as in soccer, with Ruby's father. And she caught a new glimpse of her own taken-for-granted status, the two-family brownstone on a pretty tree-lined street in Fort Greene, the cozy but elegant bookstore on top of three rental properties her mother owned, not elaborate wealth, not old-school or new-school Yale wealth, but a level of comfort in a neighborhood that was changing every time she returned home.

Ruby moved Monty's can of Sprite around on the table.

"Are you going to spill that too?" he asked.

"Maybe," she said. The green seemed a happy color. She struggled to anchor her focus on the can. Green represented prosperity, or was that red?

"You are the first Brit I've met who is so-so on tea."

"I think tea should be enjoyed. The water temperature, the milk, the cups and saucers, a process, a ritual. There's the whole colonialism aspect of drinking tea, too, which I don't like, but at home, it's something I enjoy with my family. Something we still do together in the morning or at night. If I'm going to grab a drink on the run, give me Sprite."

"Go ahead," Ruby said suddenly. "Out with it."

"Were you going to hurt yourself back there?" Monty asked.

Ruby did not answer. There was a possibility that she had gotten a bad batch of something. She had smoked pot and swallowed a cocktail of pills, but when she stepped on the roof, she had felt such clarity. The chanting, singing, post-homecoming game, a rallying call that made her want to resist Monty's buff arms. The *go, go,* even if not directed at her, its own giant question mark. Go to what, she wondered, go to where? Her firsthand knowledge of the world was limited to a handful of cities and countries and random things, almost all of them trivial, even though she attended one of the best universities in the world.

A man and woman with a sleeping baby in a Maclaren umbrella stroller sat enjoying a couple's night out: split pea soup with croutons and saltine crackers. Along with Ruby and Monty, they were the holdouts in the diner.

"Let's eat!" she said, pot hungry.

Monty nodded. "Order whatever you want." He was polite and proper and had dumped her for a black Brit from his old neighborhood, Kensington. Ruby didn't know what hurt her more: that the girl was an underclassman or a fellow Brit. Monty and his new girlfriend had grown up total strangers within five blocks of each other.

"Spoken like someone ridden with guilt," Ruby said. She poked out her tongue at Monty.

Monty poked out his tongue back. They sat at the table making silly faces at each other until a waiter came over and Ruby ordered fries with melted cheese from the colossal menu. She wanted a burger with mushrooms or blue cheese, but she could eat a burger any day. This was a special occasion. She surveyed the entrée options: Reubens, turkey and mashed potatoes, spinach pies, spaghetti and meatballs, grilled chicken breasts, but she perked up when she saw the Romanian steak.

"What the hell is a Romanian steak?" she said.

"A steak from Romania?" Monty said, laughing, relieved that

Ruby was no longer nodding off on the table. Was it his dimples or the accent she loved? An English accent on American soil did wonders for the speaker.

Ruby scrutinized the owners of the diner. She had insisted they go somewhere off campus where they wouldn't run into anyone they knew. "They're not Romanian?"

"Ruby," Monty said, and shrugged. "You know it would be the world's loss if you hurt yourself?"

Twenty years later, while reviewing the night's reservations at Mizu to Yama, Ruby will notice Monty Bennett's name on the list and come over to his table. Monty will say over and over again, "You look so well," and introduce Ruby to his lovely wife and take out pictures of their three lovely children, ages six to nine. By then, the restaurant will have received its second Michelin Star and Ruby will take great care to personally oversee Monty's tasting menu.

"I'm proud of you," Monty will say. His words will reach into the depth of her, and Ruby will wonder how much of her story Monty's wife knows, if she knows anything, but Monty's wife is a class act and will reveal nothing other than honest appreciation for an exquisite meal prepared by an artisan.

"Kindness made me stay," Ruby will whisper to Monty, pocketing the bill, giving a belated answer to the question Monty had asked her nearly twenty years before in the diner. That answer on the tip of the metal fork holding the Romanian steak that Ruby put in her mouth. One bite and she could tell the steak had been frozen a long time, probably beyond its expiration date, and recently thawed out. But Ruby relished the tough meat. The eating, the consumption, made her shiver with such fury that Monty reached out for Ruby a second time that night thinking she was having an adverse reaction to the drugs she had taken or going into shock. Ruby was remembering the taste of her uncle Freddie's stolen steaks.

"I got to do something different," she said, offering Monty a bite, which he took so she would not feel bad about eating solo. "My approach isn't working, Monty."

"Is this about your uncle?"

Her uncle Freddie had died that summer. Not from crack. Irony, irony. He had tripped on wet tiles in his bathroom and cracked his skull. To Ruby's knowledge, limited, limited, Freddie had been sober going on three years. But, like former addicts who pull away from friends with whom they share addiction, Uncle Freddie had come to avoid the house he grew up in and all its inhabitants the way a vampire avoids garlic. Sober Freddie didn't come around at all. And why should he? Ruby was in college and preoccupied with her life and friends, and Frida was always busy running the bookstore. Everyone kept their fingers crossed and hoped that Uncle Freddie would keep sober. Fool you once, fool you twice. No drugs or alcohol were found in his system. A freak accident. Wicked, wicked. At the service, in the funeral home chapel, the guests celebrated youthful Freddie. Happy Freddie. *Freddie Then.* Candy, Jacintha, and Monty, who had flown back from London, all sat together. Darla was the last friend to arrive, standing at the back of the church, coming in from a summer music festival in Aspen with a sad, nervous smile and little wave. Ruby had waved and smiled back, though she didn't know why. And after, at the house, despite Frida Black's protests, Candy, Jacintha, Monty, and Darla had moved around the living and dining room picking up half-eaten plates of food and throwing them away. "I'm the landed gentry too," Ruby said. "To die alone like that is a horrible thing. Hush, hush. To die alone like that is a horrible thing."

Darla Jacobson was studying for an advanced musical theory exam when Monty Bennett called. He drove Ruby to Darla's apartment in Boston the next morning. Ruby packed only what she needed and told her stunned roommates that anything she didn't take was up for grabs. On the drive to Boston, Monty didn't try to convince

Ruby to stay. He understood that sometimes college was the last place one could feel, much less think.

Darla rented an apartment off campus. There was sheet music all around Darla's living room, her latest boyfriend's clothes, open cans of Café Au Lait coffee, and unfolded laundry. Darla let Monty and Ruby say their goodbyes and tidied up the dishes piled in the kitchen sink. When Monty left, Darla said, "What will Frida and Ulysses Black say?"

Ruby stared at Darla through bloodshot eyes that would take days to clear. "*We're* not going to tell them."

During college, the two friends sometimes went weeks, months without talking.

"Well," Darla said, not without empathy, "now you know how it feels to lose someone—out of the blue—who means everything."

"Now?" Ruby wanted to add, *Not just now.*

Darla watched as Ruby weighed the pros and cons of all the things she could do and places she could go as quickly as you turn the pages in a magazine. "Ruby, this isn't you. You *always* do the right thing."

"Sure. On the surface. But this surface is killing me."

Ruby arrived in Tokyo two weeks into the first semester of her senior year at Yale. She left behind a circulating rumor that she had contracted mono during the breakdown party, resulting in an uptick in senior visits to the nurse's office. Ruby was as healthy as the galloping horses on the covers of the Mane 'n Tail shampoo, conditioner, and hair dressing oil sequestered in her canvas duffel bag. She wasn't sure how easy or expensive it would be to find black haircare products in Japan, so she cleaned out the African American hair care section at the CVS in Darla's neighborhood the evening before her flight. Around the time Ruby cleared customs at Haneda International Airport and stood in line to purchase a Japan Rail Pass, her constitutional law professor was reviewing the class roster. The professor marked Ruby Black absent for the second time that week. Attendance and class participation would count for fifty percent of students' grades. "If you can't make class at four in the afternoon, when can you make it?" the professor said. It was six A.M. in Tokyo and Ruby, upon boarding the airport express train bound for Asakusa with her overstuffed duffel bag strapped to her back, looked around the crowded car to see if there might be another face like hers. Seeing none, the impact of her decision to quit college for an impromptu trip to a foreign country where she neither spoke the language nor knew anything non-textbook substantive about the culture made her clutch her eyes against the world. Ruby saw her mother and father in the darkness. 9/11 had upended international travel for Frida Black. She would not board a plane. And Ulysses Black would let the situation play out before reaching for his passport. Ruby opened her eyes. The names of the stations, like the faces that regarded her indifferently, were foreign, but *she* was the foreigner. A minority among other minorities composed of a majority. She perked her ears to the conductor's voice over the loudspeaker while her eyes kept track of the destination signs written in kanji. Later, Ruby would say she had not felt angst or fear or apprehension on the train but a prickling sense that she was still on a mission to eradicate herself. This prickling made her dig into the pocket of her denim jacket and clasp the note-sized piece of paper with names of two friends of Monty's now living in Tokyo. In seconds, Ruby obliterated the paper. She was still picking up stray specks of notebook confetti from her jeans, jacket, and suede ankle boots when the train rolled into Asakusa Station.

The hostel was situated in a narrow passageway within walking distance of Asakusa Station. Ruby scored a clean, small double room with twin beds—at least temporarily to herself. One of the twin beds was unmade with a preponderance of toiletries and clothes stacked on top of it. The plan was to stay up and adjust to Tokyo time. But even as Ruby's mind said yes, her body pulled rank and caterpillared beneath the covers in the spare twin.

At three in the morning, she woke up to the sound of a Slurpee being sipped through a thin straw. Someone, a girl, her hostel-mate, leaned over the bed directly opposite Ruby's snorting lines of coke on a double-sized LED makeup mirror. Ruby thought of the saying, "We take our problems with us wherever we go." With the bedspread still draped around her body, Ruby started toward the door. She would go down to the front desk and request a different room.

"Like some?" her hostel-mate said.

Ruby stared at the proffered blade and all it promised. Her hostel-mate, half an inch shorter than she was and around the same complexion, smiled. "I'm Fijian by way of Australia." Spencer Edwards bypassed the what-are-you and where-are-you-from questions in one fell swoop.

Amazing, the coke felt amazing funneling into Ruby's nostrils. Fatigue slipped away and returned as a surge of energy. Ruby called Monty on Spencer's cell phone. "Monty, Monty, Monty—I'm so lit. So lit up, Monty. The things I would do to you if you were here."

"Bloody hell, Ruby," Monty said, "is this your new approach?" He knew Ruby well enough to know she was soaring. Birds could not reach her.

"Do you want to hear what I did to that piece of paper with your friends' names on it? I don't need you. And I don't need them." The line went dead. Ruby didn't know if she hung up on Monty or Monty hung up on her. No matter no how. She dialed her parents next, pacing around the small room in a furious circle. Frida Black seldom answered numbers she didn't recognize.

"Earth to Frida Black," Ruby said.

"Ruby?" her mother asked.

"Hi Mom," Ruby exclaimed in a high-pitched voice.

Frida reached for the steroid cream on her nightstand and began applying ointment to the white patches on her bare arms. "Is everything okay?"

"Yes and no," Ruby said.

"Tell me about the no," her mother said, capping the ointment and looking in her husband's direction.

"Well," Ruby said with a sigh, "the good news is that I'll be all right. The bad news is that if I'd stayed at Yale, no guarantees, not so sure."

"*If* you'd stayed at Yale?" Frida Black said loudly. Ulysses Black sat up on cue in anticipation of some dreaded directive: Pack your bags. We're through. Before his wife mentioned Yale, he'd thought it was his girlfriend calling, despite having explained in no uncertain terms that what they had was only a fling thing.

"Where are you?" Frida Black asked. And mouthed to her husband: *It's Ruby.*

"I'm in Japan."

Frida let the phone rest on her lap. She took a few deep breaths. Ulysses reached for the phone. Frida shook her head no. And picked up the phone again. "And what're you using in Japan?"

"Oh, Mom," Ruby said, giggling, and realized she sounded like a two- or three-year-old. "Why is *that* the first place you went? Must we really go there? Although I suppose we should go there. We didn't do right by Uncle Freddie."

"Says the girl who's calling from a different continent," Frida hit back, thinking it was pointless to cite the medical bills from Freddie's dozen stints in rehab, the items and money stolen from their home, the African American rare book collection that disappeared from the shelves of her bookstore. Frida had to go around to independent and used bookstores enlisting booksellers' help in finding, sometimes buying, her own books back. It was a small community and she had tracked the bulk of the books down at the Strand. The humiliation of having to explain. Always having to explain. "Freddie didn't do right by himself. And you seem determined to follow in his footsteps."

In the background Spencer was singing "Don't Cha" by the Pussycat Dolls and Busta Rhymes and twirling around the room and looking through Ruby's clothes for a party dress.

"Who's that?" said Frida.

"Spencer."

"Put Monty on the phone. Is Monty there?"

"Maybe you should be Monty's parents," Ruby said.

Her mother was quiet. "Put Spencer on the phone."

Ruby motioned to Spencer to swipe the snow from her nose. Spencer, who could hear everything since Ruby was on speaker phone, cleared her throat. "I'm Spencer Savoaa Lai Edwards after my grandparents' brewery. I am adopted. My adopted parents are quite wonderful. They douse me with love, I think. Do you know there's quite a market for ginger beer and nonalcoholic beverages around the world? Not that I drink them. I shouldn't joke about nonalcoholic beverages really. Or the love my adopted parents douse on me."

Ruby wasn't sure how much Frida Black could understand. Ruby wasn't sure how much of Spencer's story she could understand or believe, either. Everything was happening so fast.

"Did you let the school know you were taking a leave of absence, or did you just leave?"

"Hmm . . ." said Ruby.

Frida sighed. "All right, so nothing here is beyond repair. There's time to backtrack and manage this. I'll pay for your return flight and contact the school."

"Mom, I'm almost twenty-one. Technically I'm already an adult."

"Then for Christ's sake, act like one. Adults don't quit so close to the finish line. This is your senior year. You're only two semesters away from graduating. I can't stand to see you sabotage yourself."

"I'm where I need to be."

"And high as a kite."

Ruby glanced up at the ceiling and could feel herself levitating. There was silence. "No, I'm in cotton slippers on a wood floor."

After a beat, Ulysses was trying to wrestle the phone away from his wife. Frida held sway. "Your dad and I will be closing the joint account."

The money news, even in Ruby's elevated state, was sobering. She had about four thousand dollars in her checking and savings accounts. The tab for the monthly bill for the American Express credit card she applied for in college was paid by her parents. Ruby didn't even know her credit card limit. She tried to reel back panic. "I don't want to be a fuck-up, Mom."

"Ruby," Frida said, "you're not a fuck-up. Don't you know how much we love you? You're all we've got."

"Don't cut me off then."

"We're not cutting you off." Frida gave Ulysses the phone.

"It's Dad. This is your call, Ruby. You want to be dependent or independent?" Ulysses Black said. "You can't be both."

He returned the phone to his wife. "Say the word and we will come and get you."

Spencer spoke five languages and had been globetrotting with a group of high school friends around Asia. This was her gap year before attending university in Berlin.

"We've been using Japan as our base, but in Thailand things unraveled," she said. "Either I became smarter or they were always idiots."

Ruby owned one party dress: reversible, black on one side and red on the other. She could play either side up with a sequined bolero jacket and pretty ankle-strap pumps. She showered, donned red. They were already too smashed to take the train, so the new friends strolled arm in arm down the tiny backstreets that cars could not enter and caught a taxi for Shibuya. The oversized billboards in the dusk hours flashed neon lights that made Times Square seemed antiquated, minuscule. The taxi dropped them off near Shibuya Crossing, the busiest street in the world. Nighttime. More people bustling about than Ruby had ever seen in her life, in varying directions.

Spencer paid the taxi driver, speaking in fluent Japanese. As they stepped out of the taxi, Ruby told her, "I'll cover the tip."

"Rule number one, in Japan we do not tip," Spencer said with a wink, and they watched the pedestrians, most of them young, striding about. Spencer flitted Ruby around Shibuya Crossing several times and in several directions. The effect was dizzying.

"Techno tonight," Spencer said finally.

"I'm fine with techno."

They went to the second-largest techno club in Asia and danced beneath the gargantuan mirror ball. Ruby felt completely free, swirling her arms around on the dance floor, moving like a robot up, down, left, right, beneath the laser lights, traversing the various rooms and surrendering to chaotic music, shutting her eyes and imagining balancing the universe on her eyelids. She could do it. She could bump, grind, gyrate, and keep the world suspended on its axis. But as quickly as it started, the party was over. And Ruby and Spencer were in another taxi zipping back to Asakusa. Ruby's eyelids were heavy now and her throat parched with thirst. Each step toward their room was slower than a 1970s slo-mo film. Spencer sat on the bed and kicked off her heels. She wore a mini dress and Prada pumps. Ruby was tanked, but Spencer looked like she could go out and do it all over again.

"How do you balance everything so well?" Ruby said.

"I have a short attention span when it's convenient," Spencer replied.

Frida and Ulysses Black froze the checking account the next day. Ruby was left with three thousand dollars to her name. Her parents mercifully paid off the credit card balance, which included her ticket and first week's stay at the hostel. They were giving her breathing room, time to come to her senses.

"I'll front you the money," Darla said when Ruby finally got around to calling her best friend. Darla shared the good news that she had aced the music history exam. And had already been invited to perform at a musical festival in Prague that summer.

"That's wonderful," Ruby said.

"Do you remember Mr. Garrison?"

"Our high school winds teacher."

"He's running the festival."

"Did you fuck Mr. Garrison?" Ruby asked.

"No, but I'm going to." There was a finality in the way Darla spoke. Once Darla made up her mind to do a thing, she could not be deterred.

"Maybe," Ruby said, something in her not wanting to accept Darla's money, "it's not so good for me to have your cushion."

Spencer and Ruby agreed that when Spencer left in six weeks, Ruby would take over her tutoring gig, teaching English to two very bratty Japanese twins.

"My Japanese doesn't exist," Ruby said.

"They're really not interested in your Japanese, only your English. Anyway, in six weeks you might surprise yourself. And them."

Ruby gave her dwindling bank account the side-eye. She could not wait six weeks. Tokyo was one of the most expensive cities in the world. She needed to find a job ASAP. The hostel was owned by European venture capitalists who had resided in Japan for thirty years and owned hostels throughout Asia. Asakusa Peace Hostel was a laid-back, barebones affair catering primarily to international backpackers. You could work under the table for room and board if you had the right connections. Spencer was the right connection.

"You're so fresh," Spencer told Ruby. "I've seen a few beached whales in my life."

"Why don't you just stay in tonight?" Ruby asked.

Spencer went dancing every day of the week. Sometimes the Australian bravado made Ruby wonder what was going on beneath the surface.

"I guess that means you're not coming."

Ruby had begun studying the maps of the various neighborhoods around Tokyo. She was determined to explore a new neighborhood each week, but five days there, outside of partying with Spencer, she had barely left Asakusa. There was so much to see. She was still jet-lagged. And still frightened that she might have made the wrong decision. She could not learn Japanese with a fucked-up brain.

Ruby said, "Maybe this weekend?"

"Have it your way."

Ruby went to bed early and dreamt of beached whales. Sometimes a dream can seem more real than life and you wake up expecting blue skies and white sand and the intense unruly smell of something rotting. Ruby woke and found Spencer's side of the bed empty, well-made. The preponderance of toiletries, which she opened, hid lipstick tubes with pills, compact cases with coke, a pharmacy on the go on which Ruby willed herself not to indulge. Fast money. Spencer didn't need money. She was loaded. There was no logical accounting for human needs.

"Have you ever really seen a beached whale?" Ruby asked Spencer later.

"Yes," Spencer said quietly. "My mother and father died on a return trip to Fiji when I was three. Caught in the cross fire during protests. The same unrest between Indo-Fijians and Fijian nationalists that had spurred them to go to Australia for college and graduate school. They shared the top floor of a town house with the couple who would later become my adoptive parents. I don't remember the shooting. But I remember being tangled up in a stroller. People running like mad. I remember that on the day of my mother's and father's burials they were buried side by side, very Romeo and Juliet. I remember my soon-to-be adoptive parents arguing with my mother's parents and my father's parents, neither of whom had been on speaking terms during much of my parents' lives. Beached whales washed ashore in the village on the day of their funeral. I remember the smell of the beached pilot whales. And on the one-year anniversary of my parents' death, when my adoptive parents returned to the village to get me, there were beached pilot whales on Taveuni Island again. For the first time, my grandparents on both sides agreed. I was homesick for my mother and father and the only life I had ever known. So, they let me go. And here I am."

"That's so fucking random," Ruby said. "I'll never get over how random shit happens."

Spencer waved her hand around the room and at her own body, even the eye glitter container in which she kept coffee grinds to ward off puffiness. "My people, my real people—and believe me, I know who my real people are—sometimes it's easier to pretend not to know. They believe in omens. But whales beach all over the world. Signs mean nothing. All of this, life, is just an experiment in a semi-controlled environment."

"Spencer," Ruby said, "we're not experiments."

"If you say so."

Spencer went to sleep in her party clothes. She would go on to study cultural anthropology at Humboldt University in Berlin. She would marry a graduate student from Azerbaijan and, after having two boys (Seru and Joeli), relocate to Sydney with her husband and adoptive parents to wait out COVID.

"How goes the experiment?" Ruby would ask Spencer on their annual phone call.

"Pretty fucking open-ended," Spencer would say, having sobered up by then like Ruby. "I miss the days when drugs made me feel invincible. But I did decide that when I die, I want to be buried alongside my birth parents in Fiji."

Ruby found a weekend (under the table) job at her hostel's sister hotel in Shinjuku. The hotel was known for its traditional (Japanese) and modern (Western) breakfast menus, especially the weekend buffet. The first two weeks on the job, Ruby lost five pounds moving heavy trays of food in and out of the kitchen. The heat and steam from the kitchen sweated out her natural curls, so Ruby braided her hair with extensions, using Spencer's LED makeup mirror to loop the extensions along the crown of her head and nape of her neck. The vibe in Asakusa was old-world and laid-back, but the Shinjuku Peace Hotel catered to tourists who liked their perks. It was a tightly run, fluid business on the front end with all the crazy energy of the best restaurants in the back. The Shinjuku Peace Hotel had more than 150 rooms and suites. Ruby was thrown into the hellfire of a large—she couldn't keep track—rotating staff overseen by four chefs, two American and two Japanese. She was required to wear a long-sleeve white shirt and gray slacks underneath a black apron. Weekend breakfast and brunch buffets were big in Japan, and the Shinjuku Peace Hotel's extensive menu was popular with guests and locals alike. The more the merrier, if you had the money and the appetite. As a server, she was expected to refill the trays of food and beverages on the banquet-style buffet tables. She knew she was getting good at the job when she could do so without spilling food on the white linen tablecloths. The American chefs only spoke to Ruby in Japanese, brooking no patience for a learning curve.

Hurry up.
Take it out.
Are you a snail with legs?
How did you get this job?

Not that they were much kinder with the other servers and sous chefs or kitchen staff, but at least the rest of the staff had the advantage of understanding them. The Japanese chefs discarded Ruby with a swimming-like motion that she wisely interpreted as *Keep your distance.* Servers could not be trusted in the kitchen.

Katsumi's hunger won Ruby's attention before the rest of him did. He moved between the Eastern and Western tables for second and third and fourth helpings of eggs and seaweed and soba noodles and pickled veggies. Ruby wondered where the man, not slight but lean, and taller than average, with a sweatshirt and sneakers and jeans and reddish-gold highlights in his otherwise black hair, stored the food on his lithe frame. She was filling a container with a taro pudding when she looked up and saw Katsumi eating the last of the little triangular fish cakes that she loved so much. She spoke to him in Japanese: *Mou sukoshi meshiagaritai desuka?*

Katsumi repeated her words in English: "Would you like more food?" But corrected her pronunciation in Japanese. She made a mental note that one could travel the world over and still run into assholes.

As Ruby went in and out of the kitchen, she passed the table where Katsumi was seated with a middle-aged European man who she would later learn was one of the partners at the Shinjuku Peace Hotel as well as the hostel where she resided. She heard one of them say "Rihanna" and saw them both glance her way.

A young singer named Rihanna's debut single, "Pon De Replay," had dropped on May 24, 2005, five months before Ruby arrived in Tokyo. The same year, a much beloved children's book, *Little Black Sambo,* was rereleased in Japan. Ruby stopped in her tracks, buffet tray in hand.

"Don't think I know her," Ruby said, trying to find the right balance of flipness and levity. "My name's Ruby Black." She made eye contact with Katsumi, wondering if she would be fired, thinking,

Oh well, her parents would be appalled that she had dropped out of Yale to work as a server anyway. But beneath her shirt, her body felt stronger. And she slept soundly at night. She didn't wait for a response.

At the buffet table, Ruby looked up between stirring eggs, and Katsumi was standing in front of her with a clean plate.

"We didn't mean any harm back there."

"None taken."

"You sure?"

"Positive."

"You stand out here," Katsumi said, stating the obvious. She looked around the room. Yes, she was the only black person in the room. The Japanese were very polite, but sometimes at clubs she found herself fielding questions about famous sports figures and movie stars and musicians. "Yes, I suppose Rihanna would stand out even more. What do you want me to say, truly?"

"I'm Katsumi Fujihara," he said.

Ruby moved down the serving line. Katsumi Fujihara moved down the line with her. There were people in front of him and behind him.

"What brings you to Japan, Ruby Black?"

"I wanted to see if life is worth living."

Katsumi smiled, only mildly thrown off by her comment.

"And I crave adventure," Ruby added.

"The first answer is far more original," he said.

"I think you need to leave this buffet table. Before you cause me to lose my job."

Ruby picked up an empty tray. She would end the conversation one way or another.

"If you traveled here to confirm that life is worth living, be sure to visit the places that are worth seeing for a richer perspective."

"No worries. I've got it covered," Ruby said. "I came armed with *Japan for Dummies.*"

Katsumi handed Ruby his business card and bowed. Ruby bowed, trying to remember the appropriate ojigi. Had she bowed too little? Had she bowed too much?

Ruby would return to the hostel after work and practice Japanese. She would roam different neighborhoods reading the signs and teaching herself kanji. She watched movies in Japanese and read children's books and manga. She walked the stalls near Tokyo's oldest Buddhist temple, Senso-ji, where the merchants sold red bean cakes and teas and kimonos and good-luck charms and every kind of souvenir imaginable, listening to the shifts from English to Japanese and back again. She sought out bookstores: Books Kinokuniya Tokyo, Kitazawa Bookstore, and Books Tokyodo Kanda. She began to speak Japanese to the American chefs, letting them know she understood at least some of what they were saying, and—when she caught a fellow server's tray that was about to hit the floor while still holding her own tray—the senior of the two Japanese chefs clapped: good job. *Practice*, Ruby said in Japanese. But she internalized the word in English, understanding now the work ethic of her mother and father, her grandparents. If you didn't pray, and Ruby didn't pray, then you had better practice. She practiced herself into healthier distractions and mostly away from addiction. But she still let herself be young.

She had sex with a botanist named Jack McIntyre from Edinburgh who was living in a quad on the coed floor of her hostel. They hooked up one evening when she came in from wandering the Yanaka district and Jack was in the cooperative kitchen reheating soba noodles. She often brought home leftovers from the buffet and made them last the first two days of the week. Ruby shopped at markets that reminded her of 7-Eleven but with far more variety and much healthier options, and she would get cheap spicy sushi or karaage chicken and onigiri. She could not remember how or why it happened, only that sometimes after walking, it was easier to stay in at night and Jack McIntyre had a thousand questions about New

York, which made Ruby homesick and lonely. And he was there. Sometimes people are just there. And so is a couch. There was a handsome African American soldier who took the train up from the navy base in Yokosuka. They hooked up at a club in, yes, Roppongi. Jack McIntyre from Scotland had wanted to know about America, but Neville, the American soldier from Tulsa, Oklahoma, kept asking Ruby, "How do I know if these Japanese girls like me for me or 'cause I'm American and a ticket somewhere else?"

Ruby had always wanted to have sex in a public bathroom with Monty, but they had never found the right opportunity. Now the opportunity presented itself in the men's room with Neville. A peculiar question on which to climax, Ruby thought, but told Neville, "I suppose you talk to her like you're talking to me."

After, Neville pulled out of Ruby, staring at the condom, checking for leakage. "You're pretty. And nice," he said.

"Fresh," Ruby said with a tilt of her head. "Some say."

"Yes," Neville said. And wrote his name on her hand with an ink pen. "Aren't you here for a taste of something different?"

"I guess."

It was Spencer's last weekend in Japan before meeting her friends in Singapore. Ruby celebrated with Spencer and a group of hostelmates at a dance club in Ginza. She had splurged on a new dress on Takeshita Street in Harajuku. Ruby was drinking a margarita and admiring the way the shishito peppers floated around in the bell-shaped glass while the music pounded and the floor tilted. The dress, which curved along her back into a suggestive V, started to feel clammy. She was drinking but sober, but that feeling of invisible walls crept in and beads of sweat ambushed her body. How far is too far to fall? You don't know until you know, do you?

She gulped the margarita and the shishito peppers too and escaped for fresh air. On her way out, Ruby noticed Katsumi dancing in the crowd. He wore a tie and suit and looked older. He was on the floor with a group of guys who were dancing with a group of girls. Everyone danced close, like runny Monterey Jack cheese.

"You're everywhere," she said. After a beat. Happy, thrilled really, when he stepped outside into the alleyway. She had looked for him the following weekend after their exchange, and the weekends after that. She cringed a little, thinking the "You're everywhere" bit didn't make any sense.

"Only if you've been looking for me," Katsumi said.

"I have to say this: you're such a fucking smart, smug-ass dude. Don't you ever, I don't know, come at people mellow?"

Katsumi lit a cigarette. He smiled at her mischievously. "What's mellow?"

"The opposite of hard."

He looked down. "I could go all over the place with that one. Think I'll just smoke my cigarette." He blew circles in the air. "See? I'm mellow."

He held out his cigarette for Ruby to share. Ruby shook her head no.

"How do you know Spencer?" Katsumi asked.

"How do *you* know Spencer?" Ruby retorted.

"Tokyo can feel like a jigsaw puzzle, but the club scenes tend to loop-de-loop. The faces too. I don't think there's a mood Spencer Edwards won't help you find. But I wouldn't risk her moods in Singapore. You might want to tell her that. Since that appears to be her next stop."

"I don't know what you're talking about," Ruby said. But she knew Katsumi's words were true. "How's your mood?" Ruby deflected.

"My mood's fine right here. Unless I'm bothering you?"

"No, I just needed . . . to come back to myself for a minute. It's loud in there."

They stood. Silent. "Back yet?" Katsumi said after a few minutes.

She nodded and said, "Only if you're asking me if I want to dance?"

Katsumi dropped his cigarette and ground it out with his heel. "Finally," he said, "something we can agree on."

Prince's "Erotic City" was playing on the turntable. As they moved toward the dance floor, Katsumi stopped to introduce Ruby to one of his friends. "Do you see this knucklehead?" Katsumi elbowed his friend. "This is Daisuku. He's thirty years old today. The senior among us." Daisuku was bigger than Katsumi. In America, he could be a quarterback. He said hi and held out his hand, but the music ramped high, and as more people piled onto the dance floor, Ruby and Katsumi were swept into its circle.

The sun was wafting over the river the next morning when Katsumi dropped Ruby off in front of the hostel. All conversation had come to a halt on the dance floor, followed by a quietness, a shyness as their bodies found each other: hips touching, hands on shoulders, wait, so close, so close, what next-ness?

Outside the hostel, Ruby turned to Katsumi and kissed him on the cheek. "I'd be up for doing this again."

"Same here," he said. "But it will have to wait a few weeks. I leave for Kyoto tomorrow."

She tried to ask casually. "Are you taken?"

"I could lie and say I'm not and you'd never know."

"You're wicked."

He kissed her on the lips. "That's what my parents said before they sent me to live with Buddhist monks for a year."

Ruby laughed. "Seriously?"

"I'm not taken, Ruby. My family's business is based in Kyoto. That's home. And where I run a restaurant."

"What kind of restaurant?"

"Good question. The kind that's on borrowed time. I'd say I have another year or two to make it work, this Peter Pan project. Then I'm to take over my father's company."

"Damn," Ruby said. "I'm sorry."

"Don't be sorry. Come to Kyoto."

"Well," she said, smiling. "Kyoto is on my list of places to visit that 'will give me a richer perspective.' "

"You're not going to let me live that down, are you?"

"Nope."

"Okay. But the invitation's there when you're ready."

The tutoring gig fell through. Before Spencer flew off to Singapore, Ruby tossed her the reversible party dress as a parting gift.

"Katsumi told me they execute drug traffickers in Singapore."

Spencer said, "They have to catch them first."

"Don't do anything stupid with your stupid friends, Spencer."

"How do you know my friends are stupid?"

"Your lips. Spoken."

"Hmm, they do like to have fun at the natives' expense."

"You're a native too."

"I am, aren't I?" Spencer winked. "Keep fresh. Stay in touch. I'm going to miss you."

Ruby's new hostel-mate was the kind of backpacker who did not bathe or shower. She was of an indeterminate age and from an indeterminate country. Ruby sensed that the woman had been on her own for a long time. She didn't engage in conversation. She was also waging a funk-out contest in their room. And so, Katsumi Fujihara did not have to wait two weeks to see Ruby Black again. They met in Kyoto Station five days later. Ruby took out the extensions and rocked her natural curls, curious to see if Katsumi could separate her from the waist-length synthetic Senegalese twists she had washed and repackaged for later use.

"Now I can see all of you," Katsumi said. She took his hand.

He lived in the Nakagyo Ward in central Kyoto, not far from

Nishiki Food Market and Pontocho Street, where he owned Fuji-hara Kitchen. The restaurant consisted of a bar with six stools and four tables and chairs. It was the size of an American living room, with LPs mounted on the walls like the autographed pictures of celebrities in touristy American restaurants. Katsumi abandoned his blazer and tie on a coatrack, rolled up his sleeves, and washed his hands. He seemed instantly younger, happier. Three cooks worked in the closet-sized kitchen. It was Tuesday afternoon at four o'clock and the cooks were busy preparing for dinner. Katsumi gestured for Ruby to take a seat at the bar, but Ruby knew enough to give the cooks space. She took off her coat and eyed the LPs, mostly Ameri-can and Japanese hip-hop: Nas's *N.Y. State of Mind,* Wu Tang Clan's *Triumph,* King Giddra's *Sora Kara No Chikara,* 2Pac's *Me Against the World,* Nujabes's *Metaphorical Music,* Foxy Brown's *Ill Na Na.* . . . There was a photograph of Katsumi in front of the Apollo Theater holding a trophy with a group of ten teenage boys and three girls dressed in nineties urban flair.

"Explain yourself," Ruby said.

"That's during my stint in boarding school in Connecticut. We placed second in the Apollo Double Dutch Contest. I went to the States and started doing the same stuff I did here in Japan."

"You ran away?"

"Not exactly. But when I was still living at home, every weekend I'd ditch Kyoto for the city. That's how I met Nam-gil, Christian, and Yuse. We'd hit the clubs and block parties. I learned to double Dutch in the parks hanging out with American military kids. They wanted to be off base. I wanted to be American."

"Oh, now I get what all this and this and this was about on the dance floor." Ruby mimicked trying to double Dutch.

"I hope I haven't dropped off that much."

She pushed him playfully and took a seat at one of the tables.

"The bar is better."

"I don't want to be in their way." She had read that Kyoto was famous for fancy multicourse dishes. When they had first turned onto the street, she noticed that every other business seemed to be a restaurant. "Is this a kaiseki restaurant?" she asked.

Katsumi said, "We prepare some kaiseki dishes. Kyo-ryori is a specialty. But mostly we're trying to do our own thing."

"I guess you could say I'm trying to do my own thing too."

"What's your own thing?"

"Who knows?"

"Kyoto's an old city. People cling to tradition. You can't go anywhere without bumping into a temple, and we're especially proud of our food. It's expected to be prepared a certain way. I want to hold on to the Obanzai tradition while bringing in a taste of something different."

Ruby looked at him. "I met a soldier from Oklahoma. He was stationed in Yokosuka. He said the same thing. He wanted a taste of something different. He said this while we were fucking in the bathroom, no less."

Katsumi lowered his head. "You don't need to tell me everything about yourself to be here."

"But I am here," Ruby said. And she pinched herself.

"And I was *there*. In your country. Dyeing my hair blond or blue, wearing mascara and channeling a hip-hop version of *Howl's Moving Castle*."

"Driving your parents crazy."

"Isn't that a rite of passage? Driving our parents crazy?"

"I like that."

"Anyway, when I finished boarding school, they looked at my grades and were too ashamed to have me come home. They sent me to apprentice with monks for a year. To cleanse my palate of American bad habits." He laughed.

"Did it work?" Ruby said.

"Well, the apprenticeship allowed them to believe they had

shifted my focus away from cultural influences they could not understand, but then I fell in love with the cultural interplay of food. Food rebels against colonialism and imperialism and capitalism, for the most part."

Katsumi lived in a wooden town house called a machiya. His machiya was traditional but the furniture was modern. He did not quiz Ruby about Fujihara Kitchen during her eight-course meal, but after, on the walk home, he wanted her opinion about each dish.

"You're asking the wrong person," she said. "My meal was free and yummy." However, Ruby could not, even soon after eating the various dishes, pinpoint what was outstanding about any of them, though she had liked the chefs, who warmed to her at once, and came over to make small talk when they were not cooking. Christian was Filipino and from the Yokosuka district in Tokyo; Nam-gil, Korean and from Osaka; and Yuse, Chinese and from Kobe. The three men, like Katsumi, seemed serious about cooking but also as much bros as chefs.

"What was yummy about it?" Katsumi persisted.

There had been vegetables prepared with adobo-style chicken, pickled fish with a combination of white beans and dried fruit from the region of China that Yuse's family had emigrated from; and bibimbap prepared with Wagyu steak by Nam-gil.

"I'm no chef," Ruby said.

"But you're a sentient being," Katsumi insisted.

"Says who? Anyway, I'd have to try similar dishes here in town to have something to compare your dishes to."

"Are you angling for free meals?"

"Hey, it's only funny when I say it," Ruby said. She hated the what-do-you-really-do-for-a-living question, but now she couldn't resist asking—even though she had referenced his business card.

"We've been in the construction business for over a century,"

Katsumi said. "Much, much smaller in scale than the oldest company in Japan, but family run."

"Your food is good, but I also think it's trying too hard. Like I was, I guess, when I overshared about the soldier," Ruby said.

"Thank you," Katsumi said, "for your honesty."

They made languid love until Katsumi whispered that he would have to work the following morning. They paused only to compare childhood scars—his stitches from a fall off a bike at ten, the chipped tooth after Ruby leapt off a swing in Lafayette Park, the freckles from the chicken pox Ruby had been vaccinated against, the broken arm from a ski trip that Katsumi noticed tingled when it rained. The windows in the machiya were open and air poured in. It was a perfect November evening but Katsumi warned Ruby not to be beguiled by the calm temperature. In the summer, heat and humidity staked claim on Kyoto and showed no mercy.

"So, your parents named you Ruby after the precious stone?"

Ruby shook her head and sang, "Bewitched. Bewitched. You got me in your spell. Bewitched. Bewitched. You know your craft so well . . ."

She tells him that her first name is really Tabitha, after the daughter on the television series *Bewitched*. She tells him how everyday after school her mother and uncle watched reruns of the show when they were babysitting themselves. That Ruby is a biblical derivative of Reuben from the Old Testament. Ruby is her middle name.

"Tabitha, when you're little, is a name that massacres itself. Or gets massacred by other kids," Ruby said. "I came home one day, before I started middle school, and told my parents, call me 'Ruby' or nothing else."

"Well," Katsumi said. "I'm calling you Tabitha Ruby from now on."

"Not without my permission."

The next morning, when Katsumi was headed off to work, Ruby

told him, "Your kitchen is missing a woman. Men and women eat differently. Just like they have sex differently."

He thought it over. "You have a JR pass. You can come and go as you please. Why not stay in Kyoto during the week and return to Tokyo for your weekend job?"

"That's a lot of back and forth. I've got to find more work."

"If you don't mind washing dishes, running errands, going to the market, sometimes waiting the tables, we could use the help at the restaurant. But the offer's only good if I get to call you Tabitha Ruby."

Ruby was soon washing dishes and chopping vegetables and tidying up the workstations in the kitchen. She soon knew where each chef's cooking utensils went and, more important, each utensil's purpose. She would go shopping at the market with Yuse for fresh vegetables and to get the knives sharpened. He taught her that a dull knife could do far more damage than a sharp one, as it was unpredictable, required more pressure, and thus, was much more likely to slip and cut off your finger. Nam-gil took Ruby with him to purchase fish, which he taught her how to fillet for sushi. Of the three of them, he had the most experience in a professional kitchen, having worked in a sushi restaurant for two years. Christian taught Ruby how to select the best cuts of meat. She refrained from telling Christian or, for that matter, Katsumi, that her uncle had been an excellent thief and procurer of choice cuts of meat.

She quit the hotel restaurant six months into her stay in Japan and began working weekends at Fujihara Kitchen. She and Katsumi squeezed in day trips to Nara and food expeditions to Osaka and visited his favorite temples in Kyoto. Ruby began to pick up Japanese more quickly, noting how Yuse, Christian, and Nam-gil adjusted their Japanese according to their environment. Sometimes they spoke in the patois of their youth, shuffling English and Japanese; other times, they were formal, precise.

In Hiroshima, where Katsumi's grandmother was born, over the okonomiyaki that was specific to the region, Ruby said, "I don't know what I was expecting."

There were modern buildings and hotels and people on bicycles. Hiroshima was more modern and popping than she had anticipated.

"We can go to the monument, of course," Katsumi said. Ruby sensed that he did not want to go. And she was learning the nuances of Japanese culture enough to know some things are better left alone.

"Have you been?" she asked nonetheless.

"No," he said. "My grandmother's family lived through it."

Ruby said, "Katsumi, am I going to meet your family at some point?"

Katsumi looked at Ruby. "You know the princess gave up her royal status this year so she could marry a commoner."

"I might cuss you out in a minute," Ruby said. "Are you saying you're a prince and I'm a commoner?" She laughed. "Though I suppose cussing you out would be proving some point."

"Do I treat you like a commoner?" Katsumi asked.

"No."

"Do I act like a prince?"

"You like Prince," Ruby said. And let the silence sit there.

In Fujihara Kitchen, Ruby had begun playing Prince LPs. She would always slip LPs on the turntable when Katsumi came to the restaurant after work. It was a cue, a reminder, that he could kick back and relax. "Sometimes you're prince-like. And I don't mean the artist."

He chose his words carefully and said, "Even though half my family is from here, we didn't talk about them. Or Hiroshima. My obaa-chan underwent a series of medical examinations before she could marry my grandfather."

"By 'examinations,' do you mean fertility tests?"

"After the A-bomb, many babies were born deformed. There was unnecessary stigma," he said. "Ruby, I hope you don't have to meet my family to love me."

"No, but when or *if* I meet them, I suppose I'll know how much I love you." Ruby smiled, a bit angrily. "We can tell them I went to Yale. That I'm the new take on the landed gentry."

"I know what you're thinking. It's not entirely a race thing. Yuse, Nam-gil, and Christian were born in Japan, but they'll always be gaijin. This is the reality we're facing as a couple."

In 2006, shortly after Ruby and Katsumi visited Hiroshima, Ruby and Katsumi began to argue. Ruby's decision to leave Japan coincided with a walk in Gion with Katsumi and Chie, his younger sister. Chie was the first member of his family whom Katsumi introduced to Ruby. Chie looked so much like her brother it was unsettling. The trio visited one of the oldest sweet shops in Kyoto, a building erected by the Fujihara family. Chie sent Katsumi in to choose their favorite sweets: ajari mochi, kyo baum, yokan, mitarashi dango, and konpeito.

"If you stay," Chie said, "you will owe Katsumi a debt. When his restaurant fails, it'll be a debt you can't repay."

"I don't think Katsumi's restaurant is going to fail."

Chie pinched Ruby, which came as a shock. Ruby was in the habit of pinching herself.

"Liar. Most restaurants fail the first try." Chie waved at Katsumi through the shop window. "He just might love you, you know? I can't say for sure. One can never say with boyfriends. I had a boyfriend at Dartmouth. We went to a party, and I looked down and there was a group of Asian women sitting on the floor in the hallway while their boyfriends partied inside. I watched my boyfriend step over them and thought, *Wow, we're finished.* I told them, 'Ladies, I don't know where you come from, but I didn't come here to sit in the hallway.'"

"Why are you telling me this?" Ruby said.

"You went to Yale?"

"I went to Yale."

"But didn't finish?"

"Not yet. I'm . . . figuring it out. I love cooking." Ruby thought of Monty and Candy and Jacintha. They were all going to be super-star attorneys and change the world. She was supposed to change the world with them.

"Then this has been a good apprenticeship," Chie said. "The minute I marry, I'll be expected to stop working. But I'm the one who should run the family business."

What a bitch, Ruby thought. But Chie's words stuck like carpenter's glue in Ruby's mind.

One evening, Ruby told Katsumi, "I am bored."

"Maybe we should go to Hokkaido."

"No," Ruby said. "I'm bored with Kyoto. I didn't come here to be a kept woman or take orders from you or your bros, as much as I like them."

"Chie got to you, didn't she?" Katsumi said.

"Your sister's just doing what sisters do," Ruby said. "It's me. I got to myself. Katsumi, I think I've outstayed my welcome."

Katsumi reached for his cigarettes. He was on the last cigarette the next morning when Ruby stepped out of the machiya with her duffel bag and climbed into a taxi. He would not see her again until a year later at the farmers' market in Union Square Park.

SHORTLY AFTER Darla's cell phone was recovered by Theo Harper, Maureen Jacobson unblocked her son-in-law's number.

"I don't know what to say," Theo said. He had avoided his mother-in-law like the plague. During a plague. But now here he was, making a gut-wrenching call.

"As much as you are loath to do it," Detective Tender advised, coaching Maureen while poring over boxes of photographs of Darla as a child and Darla in her teenage and adolescent years, with other personal family artifacts spread out on Maureen Jacobson's living room table, "it's time we put on a united front with your son-in-law for your daughter's sake."

"Theo," Maureen said, and cleared her throat. "There is nothing to say at this point. Only things we must do." She had feelings, of course. *As God was her witness, if her daughter was not found, she would find some way to exact revenge.* In the background of Theo's apartment, Maureen heard a cappella singing.

> *Lady, I'm your knight in shining armor*
> *And I love you*

"Is that Kenny Rogers?" Maureen asked.

"Excuse me," Theo said, covering the phone. "Dad, would you please go to your room." After a beat, the singing tapered off and

Theo uncovered his cell phone. "I am sorry, Maureen. My father has been staying with me. He sings to my mother every night."

"How sweet," Maureen said, bristling.

"Not really," Theo said. "Listen, you don't have to like me. I've never really cared all that much for you."

"Thank you for being honest on *that* front, Theo." And it was true, Maureen Jacobson had never liked Theo Harper. But she held fast to Detective Tender's directive. A local upstate paper had profiled the Jacobson family after someone, they believed a volunteer, leaked details from the investigation to the media. Over the years, several women had disappeared on roads and routes throughout the Hudson Valley, but Darla Jacobson, an only child, her father lost to 9/11, stirred something in the public. Detective Tender wasn't happy about the media circus and regarded Maureen suspiciously, but the media circus came with the benefit of keeping Darla human, if Darla was alive. A reminder that questions around her daughter's absence wouldn't go away anytime soon. Of course, if Maureen played devil's advocate, wouldn't the person who apprehended her daughter want to dispense with her body to avoid being caught? Or, if Darla was out there somewhere, alive and well and watching this monkey show, what was her girl thinking?

"I miss having my wife here in this apartment more than you know," Theo said.

"Ruby has offered to host a dinner for us at Mizu to Yama." Ruby Black had done no such thing, but Maureen would work that out later. "Perhaps we can sit down like civilized adults and come up with a joint statement."

"All in," Theo said. Since the search for Darla upstate, Theo was keeping a low profile in the apartment with his father. Sometimes he thought he heard Darla playing her bassoon in the hallway or splashing around in the guest bathroom with the walk-in shower and claw-foot tub she would soak in on Sunday evenings. Theo scribbled a reminder on a Post-it note, "Buy cream of tartar," to remove the ring of dirt that stuck no matter how hard he and his father scrubbed.

"More to come," Maureen said. And ended the call. At five o'clock every other night, Maureen ferreted out a joint from the baking soda canister where she and Daniel had always kept them. (The same canister preteen Darla and Ruby opened when Darla's parents weren't at home and Erica Gonzalez's workday was done.) Maureen fell back on the sofa and waited for Pierre's call from across the Atlantic.

*

Today, Felix Ramirez's niece will turn three. There will be no birthday gathering, but friends and family are welcome to drive by and sing happy birthday. They are welcome to leave gifts on the lawn. Felix Ramirez's sister and husband and his little niece will wave from the balcony of their apartment on Prospect Avenue. Simon has bought an international matching game and thick chalk crayons because summer is coming. He buys the gifts, as Felix is always working.

After they drive by and blow kisses at Felix's niece, they will return to their Sunset Park apartment. And Simon will turn on the television. Or turn on his computer and google @Save Darla Jacobson. On the drive back home from upstate, Felix Ramirez did some soul-searching. In the week since, he had recused himself from Darla Jacobson's case. Perhaps it was seeing Theo Harper lose his shit in the woods. Perhaps it was because he believed that damaged people damage. But mostly it was because Felix promised his mother and father that he would never become a corrupt cop. Nor did he want to be a corrupt detective. Withholding that his husband had a sexual relationship with Theo Harper compromised the Jacobson case. So, over donuts from 7th Avenue Donuts, Felix confessed to Detective Lutz what the phone records would soon reveal. "It's a good thing for you the case is officially out of our jurisdiction. You had better have a talk with your husband," Detective Lutz said quietly.

———

There are things you give up in a marriage as an interracial gay couple from divergent class backgrounds. If you are Simon, you don't go to Fire Island every summer. If you are Felix, you go to Fire Island every other summer to support your husband and tolerate his friends. If you are Simon and Felix, you note with happiness and relief during outings in the city how much the scene has relaxed and the younger gays mix. If you are Simon, the nieces and nephews you love, your husband's nieces and nephews, call you his best friend. But you are so much more. You have been so much more for a long time. If you are Felix, you don't understand why Simon chose to wear the pink hat and go to D.C. for the March on Washington when Trump was inaugurated. You don't understand why he's so comfortable accepting money from his parents, living off their income. If you are Simon, you don't understand why a gay Mexican man would want to be a cop, though you like his uniform. Uniforms are sexy. You like them more than the men who wear them. Except Felix. You love Felix. If you are Felix, you recused yourself from the case a week ago. You haven't told Simon any of this. You open the apartment door. And there Simon is at the computer. He looks up and says, "I made vegetarian chili."

"Simon, *fuck him*. When you love someone, you don't put their livelihood at risk."

And Simon says, "What?"

And Felix says, "Simon, I know."

And Simon says, "I'm so sorry, Felix, but if you couldn't be honest with me, why would you expect me to be honest with you?"

"Because my career means everything to me."

"*Everything?*" Simon repeats.

"We're married. My ring is on your finger. Everyone sees the ring. Even if they can't acknowledge it. They see it."

"That's not enough. This is 2020. We don't need to pretend we're something we're not to please other people. Especially when they already know what we are, who we are. Why should we be selfless so they can be selfish?"

"Fucking Theo Harper behind my back is pretty selfish," Felix says.

"I know," Simon says, rising from the computer.

"Tomorrow I want you to go to the police precinct. Tell them everything."

Simon understands the repercussions his confession might have on Felix's career. "What about your promotion? What about you?"

"What about me?" Felix said. "I'll sleep on the sofa. You take the bed for now."

When Felix and his family first came to New York, they lived in a two-story frame house in Williamsburg. The house was owned by a Polish woman who had broken it up into apartments with economy refrigerators and stoves. She rented to illegal immigrants and took payment in cash. It was a between-stages apartment, with a landlord who looked the other way so long as you paid your rent and kept quiet. As soon as one family moved out—sometimes six to a one-bedroom apartment—another moved in. And sometimes the families shared meals. There was a hen who always fled the house, and sometimes Felix and his sisters, Isabella and Carmella, returned from the neighborhood school his parents had enrolled them in to find the hen walking down the street like she owned it. She laid eggs that fed them, and they were scared that the hen would either get herself killed or get them deported. When his father started his own construction business and moved his family to Sunset Park, Felix's younger sisters tried to steal the hen, and his parents had to return it. Sometimes you must leave behind the things you love, their mother had told them. They had already left behind friends, family in Mexico, for the American Dream. Felix Ramirez sometimes wondered if the American Dream was a dream worth having.

"I hate that he hurt you, Simon," Felix said. "And I hate how much I wanted to hurt him for it. But then where would we be?"

*

Theo did not remember his father's ever singing at night to his mother and was convinced the singing was largely for show: a reminder of how Theo had failed as a husband and a man. He had been trying for days now to find the appropriate moment and the appropriate words to ask Alfred Harper to leave, but if the situation took a turn from bad to worse, he needed to have a close relative on standby.

"Did you know Dad sings to Mom every night?" Theo reached out to his siblings.

No, Tamara said.

Of course, said his sister Thalia.

Well, not every night, said Troy. *Every other night.*

Lady, you're my knight in shining armor, Thaddeus belted out hoarsely.

Did you ever try singing to your wife? asked his sister Toni.

In the police vehicle on the drive back into the city, Theo sat in the back seat and snored loudly so he wouldn't have to talk to Detectives Ramirez and Lutz, all the while remembering that Darla had slept most of their trip upstate. Had she been sleeping to avoid interacting with him, too? At one point, Detective Lutz said, "Marathon man, tell us about this First Theo?" And Theo realized that he must have dozed while playacting.

"The First Theo was my great-great-grandfather," he said. "I'm told I look like him, but who knows? He fled a Georgia plantation after his entire family, including his wife and two sons, were sold. We're not sure, but we think he was a carpenter and they leased him out, and when he returned home . . . Well, that was it. He had no people. So he ran away and lived in the swamps among the

Seminole holdouts before going west with his second wife and having a daughter who married a German immigrant named Harper."

Detective Ramirez looked at Lutz, whose eyes said, Yep, Darla
Jacobson's dead as a doornail. Only the guilty see the dead. And
they see them when they're close to a confession. He took out his
Rhodia notebook and wrote, "Suspect sees Magical Negroes."

*

Lasagna was in the oven when Theo came home to his apartment.
And Alfred Harper had stocked the refrigerator with food. This, of
course, reminded Theo of Darla. Those early days of the pandemic
when people carried on like hoarders. And scrubbed surfaces like
maniacs. His father had cleaned the entire apartment after the forensics team left. Only, with Darla's cleansers. So everything
smelled of lavender and lemons and vinegar. And, yes, Darla.

"Thattaboy," Alfred said as Theo described how he had come to
find his wife's cell phone, skipping the part about his meltdown.
The part that would later be leaked.

For the first time since Darla went missing, his mother, Elena,
came to the phone.

"Mom?" Theo said.

"I told Alfred, I know our son is not guilty," Elena cried.

But even as his father slapped him on the back and his mother
offered words of encouragement, Theo understood implicitly that
his family thought he was guilty. His father. His mother. And all
the other T's.

"Mom, I love you," Theo said, and grabbed his jacket. He left
the apartment, darting down the stairway two steps at a time. He
would not subject himself to his father's crooning tonight. Theo
needed some fresh air. For a second he thought he had the lobby to
himself. One of the perks of an empty building when you were
involved in a scandal was the absence of inquisitive board mem-

bers. Theo was not scot-free—for the Teenager in the Cardi B T-shirt and a pretty black girl in Levi's and a primrose-pattern fleece stood kissing each other goodbye in the lobby. The girl's backpack was on the leather chesterfield sofa that Theo had hand-picked himself. For the first time, Theo noticed that ferns and jade plants transplanted from the community garden were looking quite thirsty. Darla had been on the building's gardening committee. Theo made a mental note to water the plants.

"Nice to see you again. How are you doing?" Theo said.

Xavier and the girl separated.

"Better than you, bro," Xavier said.

Theo looked at them. "Vultures."

The girl's name was Kimi. She gave Xavier a "let's move around" look. She had seen pictures of Theo Harper in the paper and on the news.

"Not you," Theo said. "The fucking media. There's no such thing as privacy anymore."

"We're cool," Xavier said. "This is Kimi Whitaker. And I'm Xavier Curtis. *We met before.*"

"Yes," Theo said, filling in the blanks he had bypassed a month earlier as he dipped out of the building. "Recently, and when you were younger. Didn't I meet your parents too? You're Julian Curtis's people. . . ."

XAVIER AND KIMI

WHEN XAVIER was hip and Kimi was knee, Nadine and Irvin Curtis invited all the children on the floors above and below them to attend his ninth birthday party. Xavier's parents were new to Cobble Hill, recent owners in a building transitioning from rentals to condominiums. Kimi, short for Kimberly, sat on the stool in a corner of the Curtises' sunny two-bedroom apartment, a petite eight-year-old girl prone to shyness with a gap between her front teeth. She watched the older kids, ranging from nine to twelve, play games and eat pizza and crinkled french fries and Hebrew National hot dogs while the adults sipped homemade "punch." Xavier was a February birthday, so there was no frolicking about outdoors, and Nadine and Irvin sat back and let their new neighbors' kids get their ya-yas out. The invited parents were snap-happy to catch a break and do the bus stop until the kids barged in and interrupted their flow, trying to pick up the steps and then becoming bored with the oldness of it all and running around the apartment again. Irvin played Motown classics: Stevie Wonder, Diana Ross and the Supremes, the Commodores, and kid-friendly hip-hop beats like Kris Kross's "Jump."

"You're brave to let them run around your apartment," Katrina said.

"Well, you don't get to be a kid but once," Nadine said. "And these kids remind us of growing up down south. When everyone would just come on over."

Kimi was taken off the stool by an elderly neighbor with thick glasses. "We're going to put a stop to this right now. Don't be a wall-flower. Or when you're older, I'm here to tell you, the roses with the thorns will snatch the good men."

And the old lady danced with Kimi and showed her how to throw it out the window, which would later be called twerking, and how to do the old man with the walking cane. Everyone was shocked at how quickly Kimi caught the steps, especially Nadine, who knew a thing or two about dancing. The older children rushed in to see what all the fuss was about, and a boy named Pinkeye said, "No Jay-Z? No Biggie?" sparking an impromptu talent show. Kimi won.

At nine, Xavier studied capoeira, and Kimberly's mother would hear him dancing and playing the drums in his bedroom before bed. She and Kimi lived on the floor directly below the Curtis family. "I should say something about that damn drumming and noise."

But when Katrina met Nadine and Irvin Curtis, she was glad she hadn't. Irvin piled a generous portion of food on Katrina's plate. They had gone all out: pizza and such for the kids, and ribs, chicken, pasta, salad, even cold-weather gumbo for the grown-ups. Katrina was about to take a plate to go, but she saw how much fun Kimi was having. She decided to share some of the sunshine in her daughter's day. And wouldn't you know it, Katrina discovered she used to live in the same neighborhood in California as Irvin's sister. When

Nadine and Irvin asked how she had ended up on the East Coast, Katrina told them love. In truth, she was on a cross-country run with a boyfriend who was arrested for selling illegal guns. The Feds got him while they were in Philly and she had slipped into Jim's South Street to pick up his favorite cheese steaks. Katrina was afraid people back home would think she had put the pinch on her boyfriend, so she came to New York and took a job as a babysitter in Forest Hills. And then a job at FedEx, where she met Kimi's dad, UB, the man she would be waiting to divorce his wife long after Katrina graduated college.

Nadine and Irvin arranged for a tutor to come on Saturday afternoons to help Xavier and his friends prepare for the specialized entrance exams. Everyone had to "put a little something in the bucket" for the tutor, ranging from five to twenty dollars. Kimi was too young to take the exam, but she studied with the four remaining boys in Xavier's friend group still living in his building.

"I'm coming to Stuyvesant with you," Kimi said when she heard Xavier had tested into Stuyvesant. Xavier didn't really see Kimi the way she saw him and went to tell his friend Pinkeye the good news. Pinkeye's real name was Harrold but everyone called him Pinkeye because once a year he would come down with conjunctivitis, and Irvin would bring home medicine from the infirmary at the prison. Pinkeye had been Xavier's first friend in their new condo but his family had been one of several to move when the rents increased. Xavier found Pinkeye on the corner where he now hung out near Fulton. They slapped hands and Pinkeye slipped Xavier enough money for two pastrami sandwiches at Katz's on Jay Street.

"Congrats. My treat," Pinkeye said.

"Wait, you're not coming?"

Pinkeye shook his head. "Nah."

An hour later, Xavier returned with two pastrami sandwiches. Pinkeye looked left and looked right.

"What d'you see down on the ground, Xay?" Pinkeye asked.

"The sidewalk," Xavier answered.

And that's when Pinkeye punched Xavier in the stomach. "Fool," he said. "We can't be friends."

When Xavier asked his father why Pinkeye hit him, Irvin said, "That boy's not going where you're going, but he's been where you've been." What Irvin didn't tell Nadine or Xavier was that he pulled up on Pinkeye the next day and waved his Taser. "You think you're bad? I'm badder."

Kimi was smart, but she didn't test into Stuyvesant or Bard or Beacon, her coveted choices.

"They'll track my baby for a mediocre high school," Katrina said.

Nadine took a morning off and went with Katrina to the open house at a new progressive school. She listened to the principal and the teachers and the students. She read the essays on the wall. "Maybe ten years ago, but not this school, Katrina. It's for the culturally elite. You hire a tutor to make sure Kimi stays up to speed on the math. Have her take an acting class to boost her confidence."

The pre-COVID first semester of her sophomore year, Kimi wore nose rings and double-pierced ears and had a tattoo in the shape of her favorite flower, narcissus. Sometimes she would twist Xavier's locs while he talked to his Stuyvesant friends in exchange for help with her homework. She knew their names: Selim and Bayo and Veer and Lian. Kimi was hard on Xavier's locs when he talked to Lian.

"Ow," Xavier would say, "that hurts."

"Who's that?" Lian would ask.

"My sadistic cousin."

"I'm not your cousin," Kimi said, and frowned.

"Boys are so stupid in matters of the heart," her best friend, Taylor, said the summer she and Kimi bumped into Xavier at the Creamery in the Atlantic Avenue Mall.

"For real," Kimi agreed.

"You should tell him how you feel. If he a real nigga, he'll know you're gold."

Kimi rolled her eyes at Taylor, who code-switched at the drop of a hat. "Shut up," Kimi said. "You don't get to talk to me like that. Your family owns a house on Martha's Vineyard."

"Girl, are you sure?"

When Nadine caught COVID, Katrina began preparing plates and leaving them outside the Curtises' apartment. If Katrina went shopping for herself, she also went shopping for Nadine, Xavier, and Irvin, too. She still treasured the birthday parties in their apartment that had morphed into bowling nights and movies. Seeing Kimi tag along with Xavier and his friends to *The Avengers* and joining them and dressing up for the opening of *Black Panther* were rites of passage for her daughter that made it easier for Katrina as a single mother. Nadine and Irvin Curtis never pried or asked after Kimi's absent father, who wired money every month but believed Kimi was Katrina's failed attempt to get him to leave his wife.

The next thing Kimi and Katrina knew, Nadine was in the hospital. Kimi texted Xavier.

U ok
Yeah, Thxs.
Ur Moms?
Ventilator
Oh No. I'm sorry, Xay.
Dad has to work and doesn't want me to get sick. He didn't test
    positive for the antibodies. So he wants us to stay separated
    for now.

"He's staying at his cousin's?" Katrina said. "I don't know if I agree with that move. I mean Xavier is an old soul, but he's still a minor."

Kimi baked chocolate chip cookies with pecans while her mother was still at work and put her homework in her backpack. She would tell Xavier she needed help with algebra, but near Vanderbilt Avenue, she tripped on a pothole and had to dip into a corner store for Tate's cookies.

"Kimi?" Xavier said, buzzing Kimi into the building. "Hold up a minute."

She offered him the bag of store-bought cookies when he came down to the lobby, smiling.

"Yours are better."

"I'm not even gonna tell you what happened."

"You dropped them?"

"I dropped them."

"Lame."

In Julian's apartment, Kimi said, "Wow, you're living the fabulous life all by yourself."

"Yeah," Xavier agreed.

"It's so quiet . . ."

"Half the building is empty. Sometimes I step into the hallway and I hear an echo."

There were records and CDs and a yellow cat that came and sat and stared at Kimi.

"What's wrong with that cat?"

"You're like me, taking up space in her home. Cornhusk, she's good people."

Xavier washed his hands and put the cookies on a tray. He had vanilla ice cream in the fridge and held it up.

"Ice cream sandwiches?"

Kimi nodded.

He spread the ice cream on the cookies with a butter knife and laid the ice cream sandwiches on the counter between them. They ate their sandwiches quietly. And then had seconds.

"Kimi, does your moms know you're here?"

"Yes," she lied. "I told her you were going to help me with homework."

"Let's see what you got."

Kimi dumped out the contents of her backpack onto the coffee table. There was a copy of *A Raisin in the Sun*. Xavier picked it up. "You're reading this now?"

"We just finished it," Kimi said. "We had to act it out in class. Guess who I played?"

"Beneatha."

Kimi climbed onto the coffee table and shouted, "OCOMOGO-SIAY!"

"This isn't my house."

"Right." She climbed down.

"Do you mind if I borrow your copy?" This was the same day Xavier was called out for not bringing his copy of *A Raisin in the Sun* to class. Xavier helped Kimi with polynomial equations. As soon as they were done with her homework, he said, "I'll call you a Lyft."

"I'm so offended."

"Why?"

"Seems like you don't want me here."

Xavier was thinking more that Kimi smelled like mango butter and coconut oil and that there was this bit of static cling when she sat next to him. Yeah, he was thinking she had always been like a cousin. And now she was just a girl.

"I see things from every side."

Kimi didn't follow. "What things?"

"I overthink shit, you know."

She smiled. "What are you overthinking right now?"

"You."

"You've known me all my life."

"Exactly," he said. "Let's go downstairs and wait for your Lyft."

"Okay. So I shouldn't pop by again?"

After a beat, Xavier said, "We can hang."

And that was how Theo Harper came across Xavier and Kimi kissing in the lobby. Only by then, Kimi and Xavier were already their own island. What their parents didn't know wouldn't hurt them, but Xavier was glad his parents had given him prophylactics.

MAUREEN JACOBSON had no idea how close Detective Tender was to quitting her daughter's case and returning the retainer fee. There was no doubt in Detective Tender's mind that Maureen had dropped information to the press or orchestrated a leak via an acquaintance or friend. Like many active and retired homicide detectives, she kept a locked horizontal file cabinet in her home office. The cabinet contained hauntings: dozens of cold cases that had eluded her and would likely do so for the rest of her life. Yvonne Tender could not look in the cabinet's direction on the best of days without getting the shivers. She had seen well-intentioned family members unwittingly reveal to kidnappers a detective's next steps, turn a hot trail stone cold, and, in some cases, give a depraved killer the excuse he was looking for to kill again. Another trophy, another list, another mystery unsolved. Another restless night's sleep hunting the lost souls in her dreams who had outrun her during the day.

Detective Tender could not imagine losing a child—except that she could. Her brief visit to Mrs. Jacobson's town house was as unsettling as her walk-through of Roland Paige's cottage. Both homes felt weighed down by lives that were no longer there. If Darla Jacobson was not found, Detective Tender would give Maureen Jacobson the same advice she shared with Roland Paige: seek out the living and find little things to love until something or someone worth loving comes along. While the state troopers' and county sheriff's offices expanded their circles of potential suspects—looking at sex offenders in the immediate area, hapless encounters on the road, acquaintances Darla Jacobson might have visited or escaped *to, from, with*—Detective Tender made a timeline of the young woman's life on the gray carpet in her office. The Jacobsons were a small family. No siblings on the mother's side and only one uncle and aunt on Daniel Jacobson's side. The uncle, Roy Jacobson, had sired the biggest brood: five kids. There was enough of an age gap for Darla Jacobson not to have interacted with them after her father's death. And Birdy, a professor in Colorado, had one son employed at the American consulate in Dubai. Detective Tender reached out to her sources for access to Darla Jacobson's cell phone records dating back a decade. She did the same for Maureen Jacobson's landline and cell phone, as well as Roy's and Birdy Jacobson's cell phones and landlines. The pattern or thread she was looking for materialized in a series of phone calls from an area code in Brunswick, Georgia, made to Maureen, Darla, Roy, and Birdy Jacobson, respectively. It would have been easy to miss or mistake the phone numbers buried among the preponderance of calls from telemarketers, except these handful of calls all took place on or around Darla's, Maureen's, Roy's, and Birdy Jacobson's birthdays for the better part of a decade; and Christmas holidays, too, though never on the same day, suggesting a wrong number, misdial, or someone who wanted to check in without making their identity known. Detective Tender hired a short-term home care nurse for her husband and booked a flight to Brunswick, Georgia. She decided that what Maureen Jacobson didn't know wouldn't hurt her.

She had tracked the phone calls to a payphone in front of THIS & THAT, a souvenir shop in the downtown area on a pretty tree-lined street blooming all over with spring. Detective Tender thought Ollie would have liked to see summer come early as was its habit down south. She peeked into the gift shop window and a woman with frosted blond hair waved for her to come in.

"Afternoon," the shop owner said.

Immediately Detective Tender noticed the resemblance. The shop owner looked like a heavyset Maureen Jacobson. "Afternoon," Detective Tender said back. "Cute store."

The shop owner smiled, though Detective Tender could not see the smile because they were both masked. "Well, me and this cute store appreciate your business. Let me know if you need help with anything."

Detective Tender gave the store the walkabout: there were ceramics from local artists and candles and boxes of pralines and different sorts of savory and sweet nuts and jars of jam and relishes and handmade stationery and pens with quills, tourist-friendly mask-and-mini-hand-sanitizer kits and a 24/7 Christmas tree lavished with ornaments. Detective Tender's eyes gravitated toward an adorable ornament of a bearded farmer in red overalls on a green tractor. Ollie had been a landscaper. He had loved working outdoors, and that had been a godsend for Detective Tender and their three children, because so much of her work consisted of moving in and out of dark corners and creeping places.

She took the tractor ornament and a jar of pickled relish to the counter, along with stationery for Roland Paige.

The woman smiled as she wrapped the ornament in tissue paper. "I have this one at home. We put it up every Christmas. It's my husband's favorite, too."

Detective Tender looked toward the Christmas tree. "While I'm at it, I should grab a couple for the kids. They're all grown now but I give them ornaments every year."

"Well, we've got plenty to choose from."

"Do your kids have any favorites?" Detective Tender asked, cocking her head to one side. *What are the odds they will have a daughter?* she wondered.

"Oh, Danny and I married a little late for children. That train's left the station."

"Danny?" Detective Tender said. "Now, what a coincidence. I'm in town to see Daniel Jacobson."

"I don't know any Daniel Jacobson, and it's a small town. I know pretty much everyone here. My husband's name is Daniel Cast-away."

But even as she said this, Detective Tender, never one to hedge her bets, had taken out Daniel Jacobson's photograph and held it up within inches of Trish Fadden Castaway's face.

*

> *Got a wife and kids in Baltimore, Jack*
> *I went out for a ride and I never went back . . .*

Daniel Castaway hears Bruce Springsteen's "Hungry Heart" three times in one week. The first time, he is propped alongside his van, BRUNSWICK ARBORIST, filling up the gas tank. The car behind him has the windows down and its owner is blasting the radio, making his music everyone's music. The second time he's high atop a great oak tree, trimming its dead limbs and listening to music on the little transistor radio he has owned since his traveling days. He plays the radio to ward off the more aggressive birds and squirrels and owls that will occasionally perch in the light of day, if injured. When the song comes on the radio, the volume is so low, the lyrics barely register. The third time, he is on his way to treat a lemon tree for *Cameraria hamadryadella*, leafminer caterpillars. On the radio, the DJ says COVID's got folks looking back, nostalgic for old times and old music. Daniel recalls having seen Bruce Springsteen and the E Street Band once with his brother Roy in Asbury Park as a teenager. Jazz, then and now, has always been his music of choice, but he doesn't listen to jazz anymore to avoid a strange tightening in his chest.

Daniel Castaway lives in a two-bedroom stucco house, a modest dwelling with a garage that doubles as his workspace and man cave. The house is situated on a dead-end street in a rural area northeast of the neighborhood where twenty-five-year-old Ahmaud Arbery was hunted down and shot dead by two white men while on a leisurely jog. He has driven through the Satilla Shores neighborhood en route to nursing native trees back to good health on several occasions. He is an arborist, a profession that affords him time in the great outdoors, free from investment banking and the daily stresses of office life.

He cannot say what precisely caused him to leave his first wife and daughter to live off the grid for twelve years before putting down roots in Brunswick, Georgia, and marrying Trish Fadden. Only that in the spring of 2001, a keen restlessness overtook him. He began playing hooky from work, staying in the office late into evening, but calling his secretary early the next morning or dropping a written note on her desk the night before *not* to disturb him while he was in the office until after lunch, often leaving the lights on in his office and his blazer on his desk chair and his Newport cigarettes, lighters, and ashtray atop documents, evidence of work in progress. Sometimes he even left his cell phone. He was an investment banker and his father and father's father were investment bankers before him. Men who lost entire fortunes in the stock market crash of 1929 and a generation later recouped their money. But not without holding to the belief that always, always, money should be kept on hand, hidden, liquid. In the spring of 2001, Daniel picked up smoking again. He looked forward to the summer and time at the cottage with an intensity that bordered on impatient rage. Patience had always been his strongpoint. When the summer arrived, he hated leaving upstate once the weekend was over to return to work. The summer shot by fast. One Saturday evening, he and Maureen and Darla were lounging after dinner in the garden, their bodies digesting sweet corn on the cob grilled to perfection and salmon and a tomato and goat cheese salad, when he blurted out, "We should go to Niagara Falls."

"Now?" Maureen said.

"Right now." He stood up.

Darla and Maureen had thought he was joking, but within an hour, they were driving to Niagara Falls. Daniel wanted Darla to see the falls first thing in the morning. For some reason, he had never thought to take her or Maureen to Niagara, perhaps because of the commercialism or because he thought the falls would be anticlimactic for Maureen, who had spent her high school years upstate. But he had been several times as a boy. The sight of the untamed falls had blown him away. He wanted to give Darla that experience. And her reaction, teenage indifference overwhelmed by waters grand enough to humble Godzilla, had said it all. A day trip, hiking the falls and the caves, thrown together in the blink of an eye. You could do so much in the blink of an eye. The world could change in the blink of an eye.

He was on his way to work when the towers fell. Daniel had left his cell phone in the office the night before, along with a note for his secretary telling her not to disturb him. He stopped to get a Starbucks coffee. A middle-aged man in a nice suit, hat, and coat without a cell phone. He stood frozen on Church Street while the world melted around him and receded at the same time. Daniel heard himself say, "Dear God, I don't have to go home anymore." For his lies had rendered him at once dead and alive. A train to Long Island, the North Fork to Connecticut, and then up, up to

Nova Scotia. David Jakes became Daniel Johnson became Daniel Miller became Daniel Smith became Daniel Castaway, who has cast away so much. The ease with which he had been able to move through life unnoticed surprised him early on. He takes that ease for granted now. He is taking this same anonymity for granted when he returns home that evening to the smell of freshly percolating coffee. His wife, Trish, has high blood pressure, and one of the things she has cut back on is coffee. A small cup early in the morning, that's it. If Trish is brewing coffee in the evening, there's a problem, there's trouble.

"We have a guest," Trish says, mask off and normally smiling face gone sour sallow.

"Mr. Jacobson?" Detective Tender rises off the cushioned rocking chair in the living room. At the sound of that name, Daniel steps back and looks away.

"I think you have the wrong person," he says. "My name is Daniel Castaway."

"Perhaps at one point you were Daniel Jacobson?" Detective Tender has done this enough to know that it is best to plunge headfirst into deep water. What is happening now? What is urgent now?

"Mr. Castaway, your daughter, Darla Jacobson, has gone missing. I was hoping that she had found you first, but talking to your wife Trish here, I see she hasn't. And, well, there's no other way to put this. We're concerned for her well-being, that she might have been abducted or hurt or worse."

He repeats softly and slowly, his voice on the verge of cracking, "My name is Daniel Castaway."

Detective Tender persists. "Nineteen years ago, a woman lost her husband in the World Trade Center. Now she's lost her daughter. A double whammy if ever there was one. I'd like to give her a happy ending. Please tell me you're the missing link."

"Why did you let this stranger in our house?" Daniel Castaway says to his wife. Trish Fadden Castaway bursts out crying. Daniel Castaway is immediately sorry.

"This is a nice home," Detective Tender says. And she means this sincerely. She can feel the love and happiness, despite the fjords of new not knowing, the gaps Daniel Castaway will have to fill in for Trish later. "This is my card. I can't force you to come back to New York with me, but if Darla Jacobson is out there, you might be the best shot we have at getting her home. I will be staying at the Holiday Inn until Saturday morning."

"How did you find me?" he says, following Detective Tender to the front door, where her heart leaps with hope because the man has acknowledged something of who he was, though now he isn't.

Detective Tender does not tell him that she tracked phone numbers from three public payphones around Brunswick, including the one outside his wife's shop. She says instead, "We never leave the past behind completely. Everyone has been on the path of the living, but sometimes you find the living in the wake of the dead."

Two days later, Trish Fadden Castaway watches Daniel fold his clothes and roll them up in hard-shell luggage. He is a masterful packer. Past excursions—cities and towns that he called home for a week, a month, a day, sometimes one or two or three years, including but not limited to Yarmouth, Nova Scotia; Toronto, Ontario; Livingston, Texas; Long Beach, California; Boise, Idaho; Juneau, Anchorage, Alaska; and before his move to Brunswick, Georgia, Eufaula, Alabama—have taught him to always leave something behind. His wife, Trish, sits on the edge of their four-poster bed, her arms an X across her generous chest. She is on her fourth cup of coffee this morning, and when Daniel leaves home, Trish will drink a fifth. Holding the warm cup of coffee in her hands steadies Trish. And makes her feel close to Daniel. He is a good man, a warm man, who has in recent days collapsed them with a former life. A life that included a wife and a daughter. Perhaps if Trish drinks enough coffee, the dregs will function like tea leaves. And provide some glimpse into their future. She has never believed in leaving mad or sad or in between. Trish is counting on her husband to return home to south Georgia after he has made things right in New York City. And Daniel Jacobson has agreed to return to New York on the condition that he will not have to engage the press directly or field questions about the World Trade Center.

"You have my word, Mr. Castaway," Detective Tender assures him. "We will keep a short leash on this narrative."

KATSUMI IN NEW YORK

KATSUMI RENTED a suite with a kitchenette at the Beacon Hotel. The Upper West Side location was perfect—directly across the park from the East Side apartment of family friends who were hosting him for a monthlong stay. He had come to New York to dive into the restaurant scene and spend time interviewing Japanese restaurant owners and chefs, enjoying playing the tourist and eating his way along Eighth Street in Little Tokyo and the spattering of Japanese restaurants in Murray Hill and a personal list of gastronomical heavy hitters: Blue Hill, Nobu, Mary's Fish Camp, Craft, Per Se, Eleven Madison Park, and Café Boulud. His explorations took place mostly during the day; otherwise Katsumi enjoyed simple but lovely home-cooked meals with Akio and Gen Ito most evenings. The retirees taught conversational Japanese classes and aikido for seniors at their neighborhood Y and were also tasked by his family (Katsumi believed) with finding him a suitable Japanese wife while also keeping him well fed. The Itos' son Machiro and his longtime girlfriend, Himari, both worked in film distribution at Sony Pictures and would show up for dinner on Friday nights with pretty friends and coworkers.

"Why are you here in New York?" they would ask Katsumi.

"I'm here," Katsumi would say, thinking of Ruby, "to see if life is worth living. And I intend to eat my way through the city while I'm here."

The "see if life is worth living" statement brought conversation to a halt, and the Itos concluded that Katsumi was not in a mental state to partner with anyone. They thought he might be mildly depressed. The fall after Ruby left Kyoto, Katsumi sold his restaurant to Yuse and resigned from the family business. His sister, Chie, now ran the construction company with their younger brother. But Katsumi's secret plan was to return to Japan and open a hotel restaurant in a seaside town in Hokkaido and turn it into a major foodie destination.

As he approached the end of his stay, Katsumi decided he needed more time to explore the five boroughs. He had barely cracked the surface of the casual, family-run restaurants in Queens, which had the largest Asian population in the city. The Itos extended their home to Katsumi for as long as he needed, but he did not feel comfortable cooking in their kitchen. And cooking was what he longed to do. He also wanted to hold on to feeling like a tourist and thought the perfect compromise was to check into the Beacon Hotel, where he booked a room with a basic economy kitchen. He would dine at Jean-Georges, Masa, or Matsuri one night and the next day walk fifty blocks down Broadway to Sunrise Market in the East Village and load up on ingredients to experiment with variations on a recipe or dish he had sampled. Dishes that stomped his senses and made him want to fuck himself or weep: like the purple taro cake at a Filipino restaurant in Woodside that reminded Katsumi of the rice pudding his obaa-chan had spoon-fed him when he was small. After shopping at the H Mart, he always finds his way there.

The week before he was to return home, Katsumi overheard two hotel guests mention Jacob Lawrence's Hiroshima exhibition at an Upper West Side gallery. Katsumi had visited the Hiroshima Peace Memorial Museum earlier that spring with Chie. It had taken him months to forgive his sister for being a usurper. "Don't tell me you didn't sabotage my relationship with Ruby."

"It's eerie," Chie said, brushing past Katsumi's frost, "to walk through a room afraid you might see the face of a loved one on these walls." Brother and sister said nothing else, though they visited every room and every floor. Of course, each thought of their obaa-chan's family—distant cousins they seldom saw who had settled in British Columbia or Australia. And the ones who had stayed, fiercely protective of their Hiroshima.

Their obaa-chan had fattened them with food from her childhood, Onomichi ramen and momiji manju (red bean cakes in the shape of maple leaves) when she was homesick, but she never mentioned Hiroshima in the aftermath of the war. She only spoke of what the city had been like before the atomic bomb.

"You're a lot like her," Katsumi said to Chie. Their obaa-chan had been ahead of her time, studying civil engineering at Kyoto University in the 1950s, where she met Shiro Fujihara. She was two years Shiro's senior and worked as long as possible before agreeing to marriage. A marriage the Fujihara family could not discourage.

"What does it matter?" Chie said. "You were the firstborn grandson. So she always loved you more."

"Only because she lost her firstborn son," Katsumi said, accepting what he had not understood as a child. His grandparents' firstborn son had died in infancy. No one could tell his obaa-chan—or, for that matter, the Fujihara family—that his brief life had not been tainted by the atomic bomb. The second son, Takeo, whose name means "warrior," would grow into manhood and father Katsumi, Chie, and Nori.

"Yes," Chie said. "She watched you like you'd vanish before her eyes. Mom had to tell her, 'Katsumi is healthy. Look how he laughs and plays. Look how strong he is.'"

At the Upper West Side gallery, Katsumi heard a strange sound, not words but more a protracted moan or sudden, sharp intake of breath. He triangulated around the small crowd of viewers and took in the eight paintings from different angles. They were in the shades of candy and colorful sidewalk chalk, yellow and pink and brown and red and blue. Images inspired by the stories of eight Hiroshima survivors that Jacob Lawrence painted with tempera and gouache. Katsumi gazed at the faceless men, women, and children in panels marked one through eight; the artist had re-created them on the street, at work or play, holding black birds, trying to attend to the rituals of daily living in the aftermath of a man-made catastrophe. He was most famous for his 1940–41 series on the Great Migration, black Americans fleeing the Jim Crow South for northern cities, but these paintings evoked a migration of another kind— Japanese citizens living in the shadows of mushroom clouds. A docent slipped a small package of tissues into Katsumi's hand and this confused him. He touched his face to confirm that his eyes were dry. But from his mouth came a hoarse, aching sound that made him crumble the tissue into his jacket and exit the gallery. He didn't feel like going back to his hotel room. He continued walking south down Broadway. Before long, he was on his familiar route, cutting through the Union Square farmers' market on the way to Little Tokyo. And that's when he caught sight of Ruby Black bent over a small grill giving a cooking demonstration. Katsumi froze. Pride had not permitted him to look for Ruby, nor she for him. He crossed over to the table and picked up a Dixie cup and a miniature three-pronged wooden fork for tasting.

"Tabitha Ruby, we've got to stop meeting like this," he said, nibbling with approval the mélange of sautéed veggies she had prepared.

"Katsumi," she said, tossing peppers with a spatula. "I don't know why I say the things I do sometimes. Or leave the way I leave, but I have seriously missed you."

It was the summer of 2007. Ruby told him she had just finished a year at the Culinary Institute of America upstate and pointed to Republic restaurant across the street, where she was employed.

"What kind of food is it?"

"The trend right now is Asian fusion."

He shrugged. "I bet we could do better."

"I see you're still arrogant," she said, and smiled. "Maybe you should try the food before you knock it. It gets some things right in terms of ease that Fujihara Kitchen didn't under your management."

"Who told you?" Katsumi asked, and he realized Ruby had kept in touch with Nam-gil and Yuse.

"There I go," Ruby said. "That came out mean, but you can't diss where I work without dissing me."

"Hold that thought," Katsumi said, backing away from the table. "I'll be right back."

Katsumi returned forty minutes later with butcher paper, which he unrolled and sat on a bench and scribbled away on while Ruby worked. Katsumi presented the butcher paper to Ruby after he helped her break down the cooking display station. The paper contained a detailed blueprint for a restaurant.

"I've been thinking about this for some time," he said. "A boutique hotel with a first-class restaurant: simple, elegant, seating two dozen people at most."

Ruby could see his vision clearly: the setting, East meets West, high and low food, and a blank spot with the title menu that they would create together.

Now.

May 2020.

Mizu to Yama.

Katsumi's sleeves are rolled up above his tingling elbows as they were so many years ago in Fujihara Kitchen. Gone are the LPs and the American vibe, though Mizu to Yama is, by New York standards, intimate in scale and can accommodate twenty or so reservations at the most. The faces of the chefs have also changed over the years. But the kitchen staff is mixed and reflects Katsumi and Ruby's belief that diverse foods achieve harmony where diverse people often do not.

The masked staff has convened early to reinvent Mizu to Yama's lunch and dinner menus. Outside, a small crew of reporters awaits them, or more specifically, they await Ruby Black. Mizu to Yama is receiving the kind of exposure a lot of restaurants would kill for during COVID, but not the kind that Ruby or Katsumi desires. They have experienced a spike in DoorDash orders and takeout requests. They have been asked for profiles in local newspapers and magazines and on radio stations and on the news. There has been an increase in hotel reservations. They are booked for the summer, which feels like an embarrassment of riches. The @Save Darla Jacobson campaign has gone viral. This mystery of the pregnant woman who went missing while hiking and assumed the name of her African American childhood friend who happens to be partnered with an Asian man during a time when Asian bias runs high is a pleasant reminder about the nuance and complexity of life in New York City.

Reporters have rung the doorbell to Frida and Ulysses Black's brownstone, ambushing Ulysses on his way to work and Frida Black on her early-morning walks to the bookstore. Maureen Jacobson has been spared intrusions on her privacy because she's still in quarantine. And Theo Harper only ventures out after dark.

Who is the real Ruby Black?

Ruby sleeps in lately with the kind of bone-heavy fatigue that makes her think she just might have COVID. She does not. She is sad and a little perplexed that so many things are happening at once. The past is distant and closer somehow. The real Ruby Black is up in her feelings about her name being all over the news. The *real* Tabitha Ruby Black also knows that there are times when only one chef should address the kitchen staff, and when two speak, they should speak as a team.

"A restaurant that falls back continually on what it knows," Katsumi begins, "falls back. I used to think being a chef was only about creativity, but now I think it's about preparing creative food responsibly. And I know Tabitha Ruby is on the same page. We've always worked with an eye toward sustainability. But this pandemic is challenging us to embrace sustainability on a much higher level. We need a new relationship with our menu and what we prepare for our diners. How they will experience eating in and takeaway."

Katsumi looks at Ruby, who chooses her words carefully. "What Katsumi's saying is that we love you all, but we don't want most of you in our kitchen five years from now. We want you to go on and do bigger, better things. Open your own restaurants. I don't think any of us came into this profession expecting to run soup kitchens, but the streets of this city bring home the reality that food, like shelter, is in short supply. Restaurants are becoming more expensive to operate. One day you're going to open your refrigerator, if you haven't already, and see how little you've gotten for your money. And you're going to have to stretch that food into meals that are gratifying and nourishing and cost-effective. Challenge yourself to turn something mediocre into something great. This same truth will hold for your dream restaurants. Sometimes less is more, and to the degree that less is more, we all need to do more with less. That's a tongue twister. But I know you hear me and feel where we're both coming from. And I know you've got the skill and jobs to do this."

The kitchen staff claps. Ruby Black smiles and Katsumi Fujihara raises the blinds to their restaurant.

CHOPSTICKS, FORKS & KNIVES

ON TUESDAYS, Mizu to Yama is closed, but to peek is to spy is to see, between rectangular metal slates, contemporary moon lanterns casting long shadows on five people seated Western style around a cypress dinner table. Ruby is framed to her right by her man, Katsumi, and to her left by Maureen Jacobson. Maureen Jacobson is framed to her left by Theo and Alfred Harper. Katsumi and Ruby prepare to offer thanks for the source of the food when Maureen clasps her hand firmly over Ruby's.

"I want to thank Ruby and Katsumi for hosting us on such short notice." Maureen raises her sake glass for a toast. Theo and Alfred Harper join in.

At the dinner table, Ruby avoids Katsumi's gaze and gestures to an ice bucket. "There's chilled beer, shochu, and plum wine that pairs nicely with everything. Choose whatever tickles your fancy."

Mountain-shaped tofu floats in translucent broth with shiitake mushrooms cascading down their sides. One of seven dishes on a menu adjusted to accommodate the temperaments of each guest. A place setting of chopsticks, forks, soup spoons, and knives keeps poised, ready.

Theo grabs two beers and opens them for himself and his father.

"Maureen," Theo says, "is your private investigator coming tonight?"

"No, Detective Tender will not be joining us," Maureen says.

"How often do you speak with her?"

"Often enough to know that Darla's not here." Maureen does not share that she received a cryptic message from Detective Tender saying that she was off hunting. Or that the last invoice was the equivalent of Darla's first semester at college, or that something about this dinner already feels hopeless and futile. One glance at Ruby and Katsumi and she wonders how Ruby managed to travel to Japan and return home and later reunite with Katsumi. While her daughter ended up with a creep like Theo.

"I'm sorry," Theo says. "I didn't mean to pry."

"Pry as much as you like." Maureen picks up her knife. She twirls it in her hand. She does not need it to cut through the whipped mountain tofu. "But I might have to pry as well."

"Does she have any leads?" Theo presses Maureen.

"None likely that she would want me to discuss."

"Since Detective Tender isn't coming," Ruby suggests, "maybe we should drop the subject for now."

Katsumi rises. "I'll put on some music."

"Sure," Theo says. "But can we at least all agree that the @Save Darla Jacobson campaign has turned into a kind of freak show? And wasn't that your detective's idea?"

"This dinner was also Detective Tender's idea," Maureen says. "I would think you'd be delighted by the @Save Darla Jacobson campaign. It's gotten you off the hook for the time being because of purported sightings of my daughter. Play your cards right and you might even land a book deal: *How I Killed My Wife and Got Away with It.* Isn't that the way it typically goes?"

"A domestic spat is a long way from murder, Maureen," Theo says. "And it takes two to tango."

"But two didn't tango home," Maureen says. "One's still missing."

In the background, Prince's "Sign O' the Times" plays.

Katsumi tilts his head at Ruby. She reads his thoughts. *They have not even touched their food, and look at their aggression.* This was the reason Katsumi had suggested no fish, meat, onions, garlic, or leeks. But Ruby had insisted on one meat dish.

"Play nice, people," Ruby interjects, directing Maureen's and Theo's attention back to the dinner table. "This meal didn't come together by itself, you know. I hope that despite everything going on around us in this world right now, we're able to set aside personal grievances, even if just for an hour or so."

"Noted!' Maureen says. She is wearing Christian Dior's Red Rouge Forever Passionate lipstick. The lipstick brings back childhood memories for Ruby. When she and Darla were barely-there teenagers, after raiding Maureen's medicine cabinet for pills and ferreting pot from the Fishs Eddy cookie jar, they would apply lipstick, eye shadow, mascara, blush, contour powder at Maureen's makeup table.

Alfred picks up his chopsticks. "Everything looks so yummy."

Katsumi says, "This is our take on temple food. A tofu soup with rice to warm you up in all your cold places."

Maureen turns to Katsumi and asks, "Are you a Buddhist?"

"I'm not a practicing Buddhist. But I believe meals should be harmonious."

Alfred Harper inhales his tofu but lets the mushrooms float in the moat of broth, which he sips with great satisfaction. "There's no denying, I like to eat," he says. "Ruby, your broth is good and your man is smooth."

"So I've been told," Ruby says. Outside there's the distant *snap crackle pop* of firecrackers. Come June, they will become more prevalent, more intense. You will no longer need to take the subway to Coney Island on Fridays in July or Chelsea Piers in August or glimpse them from rooftop apartments along the East Side Highway. The clanging of pots and pans and the honking of horns will slowly fade, and the fireworks will steal their glory.

"Firecrackers? And it's not even Memorial Day weekend," Maureen says.

"I think they're for Breonna Taylor," Ruby says.

"Breonna Taylor?" Maureen has been abroad. So much of American news no longer registers. So much of news beyond the pandemic and beyond her daughter.

"A young woman shot by police in Louisiana," Ruby says.

"Well, that's not the most effective way to make a statement," Alfred says.

"Neither is having your apartment raided. I think she was shot six times?" Ruby says.

These are the events Ruby hears on podcasts or sees on the news when she is in bed and flipping the channels on the television or listening to NPR because deep down she is hoping to hear some good news about Darla. And because she needs to balance what she is experiencing personally. Yesterday, the *New York Post* ran an article with Darla and her high school graduation photos on the cover and the caption: DARLA JACOBSON OR RUBY BLACK? It's hard not to weigh this sensationalism against other world news she promised herself she wouldn't digest because lately everything is so toxic. And Ruby needs to do something about the toxicity. To make a difference somehow. So she takes out butcher paper and gets to work on a plan that includes statistics and numbers and measurements, much in the way she and Katsumi had done with their blueprint for Mizu to Yama. She proposes reserving two floors of their hotel for homeless residents to Katsumi. And Katsumi indulges Ruby. He follows her through the various rooms of the hotel and listens to her concept before rolling the butcher paper into a tight knot and securing it with a slender rubber band.

This is an excellent plan for the right hotel, but we'd be misrepresenting everything we've worked so hard to build, Katsumi says.

Even if we provide short-term housing during the pandemic?

It's too messy, Tabitha Ruby. Housing moratoriums always end up getting extended. And what happens when we get to know the homeless as people? When we become attached? It's not the same as walking by and dropping change in a cup.

You mean what if I become attached?

Maybe so. One of our jobs is to protect each other from our weaknesses. You're a businesswoman with a tendency toward idealism, especially when you're worried about something. Katsumi hesitates. I'm willing to use a portion of our loan to give back to the community and feed the homeless, he says. When Katsumi apprenticed with the monks, they would prepare a large meal once a year for the local village.

I don't like how you said that, Katsumi.

And I don't like how homelessness looks or feels. It's a permanent problem. We don't have this level of homelessness in Japan. The restaurant is yours and mine. The hotel is a conglomerate.

Are you speaking for yourself or your family?

There are times when I am my family. And this is one of them.

"I'll get the next course," Ruby says. Katsumi can tell from her body language that she's still angry with him for shooting down her idea. As she heads into the kitchen, she overhears Alfred say, "Maureen, I understand you being upset. If the shoe were on the other foot . . . I honestly don't know what I'd do or how I'd handle this."

He reminds Maureen Jacobson of Pierre, just a wee bit, this Alfred Harper. Not particularly handsome or distinguished. The good looks possessed by his son having skipped a generation. But a face that grows on you with time. Warm, soft eyes. "Thank you for saying that, Alfred. It means a great deal. It truly does. Tell me, I forget, what do you do for a living?"

"I'm an executive at a medical equipment distribution company in Iowa."

"And how does one end up selling medical equipment?"

"Well, my great-great paternal grandfather came to this country from Bavaria. He used to go door to door pulling teeth. That's how it worked back then. He'd pull your teeth and cut your hair. And the whole process was brutal."

Maureen smiles, bored to tears. "I didn't know that. My boyfriend Pierre is a dentist. I miss Paris." *Especially now*, she thought. It had been heartbreaking seeing the tourists the French loved to hate in Saint-Germain-des-Prés fade away or come upon her favorite restaurant for lunch with the handsome waiter who always asked would she like the salad Niçoise today and made Maureen think perhaps she was not too old to have some fun outside Pierre. When life was still normal, she would walk the streets of Paris in the early morning and delight in the city waking up to itself. The cafés and markets. Pierre's café of choice for baguettes and butter. How Pierre cored her green apples and uncapped the apricot jam. And when she felt like being an ugly American or just an American who was aware that she was homesick, Maureen would halfway tease: *Make me a sloppy joe.* And Pierre would say, *I don't have this sloppy joe.* And Maureen would say, *I'm not as nice as you think I am, Pierre.* And he would say, *Of course, my American, even better than nice, you take what you want and always want more.* And when Maureen saw the French children in the playground during her strolls through the Medieval Garden of Cluny, she'd always think of Darla—joy-filled, curious, stubborn, full of music.

"My forebear," Alfred prattles on, not noticing that Maureen's interest is elsewhere. "He never went to dental school. But he took over a farm later and sold dental and farming equipment."

Ruby brings in tempura misto and eggplant with small helpings of pickled vegetables.

"What did I miss?" Ruby asks.

"Theo's father was giving us his family history," Katsumi says, and attempts to help Ruby with the tray. Ruby brushes him off.

"There are some good hospitals in Iowa that draw doctors from around the world. Specialists who come to study techniques for club foot and ophthalmology."

"Theo, you're awfully quiet," Maureen says.

"You're wired to keep score. So I'm following Ruby's request to play nice."

"How am I keeping score?"

Theo turns to his father. "Dad, in New York, nine times out of ten, when people ask 'What do you do?' they mean 'How much are you worth? What do you own? What's your zip code? Where do your kids go to school? Who's in your social circle? What can you do for me?'"

"Son, people are like that everywhere," Alfred says.

"True," Katsumi says. "Snobbery is universal. It plays out covertly and overtly within and outside different cultures."

"Here it is heightened," Theo insists.

"Yes," Ruby agrees. "We look the other way and ignore this city's homeless."

"My point is, Dad, Darla's mom thinks you're a buffoon. She hasn't been listening to half of what you said."

"I don't care what she thinks of me. I only care what I think of me."

Maureen smiles mischievously. "I don't think your father's a buffoon. Maybe you're projecting."

Theo looks at his chopsticks. When he was younger, he would have poked her in the eye by now. "This is the same problem I had with Darla. You taught her to act as if she's superior to everyone. Like she's beyond bias or judgment or jealousy or spite. And then when those emotions come out, she doesn't know how to act."

"You never met Darla's father," Maureen says. "We both instilled in our daughter a desire to transcend bias or judgment."

"That's not possible," Theo says. "We're all biased. We're all prejudiced. Dad just spent ten minutes bragging about our Bavarian forebear and neglected to mention that same forebear married a Native American woman with a black father. A former slave whose farm and land enabled him to stop traveling from place to place and run his business."

"You have black ancestors?" Ruby scrutinizes Theo more closely.

"Not enough to matter now. Except it does matter, doesn't it?" Theo says.

Ruby looks at Katsumi and says, "Well, isn't this rich!"

Katsumi says, "It's something."

"No," said Alfred. "It is what is. And my son's take is rather lop-sided."

"Well," Maureen says, "in any case, I don't have a prejudiced bone in my body. And Ruby will back me up here."

Ruby keeps silent. Maureen looks at Ruby. Memories swim in the broth. Maureen and Daniel Jacobson always made a show of inviting her to their home and of letting Darla stay in Brooklyn, but she does not recall her parents' ever being invited to attend their dinner parties. And if they had been invited, they had never felt comfortable enough to accept the Jacobsons' invitations. Bonds that seem perfect in the past lose their glaze in the present. Ruby's eyes sweep around the room. Maureen has aged. Theo has aged. Surely she and Katsumi have aged. "I don't know your whole body," Ruby says. "Most days, I'm only moderately acquainted with my own body."

"Maureen, why don't you share with us what, specifically, your detective—" Theo says.

"Detective Tender. Drop the *your*. I find the *your* unbearably condescending."

"If we've come together to facilitate finding Darla—" Theo says.

"My daughter," Maureen corrects.

"My best friend," Ruby adds.

"My wife," Theo says finally. "Just tell us what we need to do, and then we can go our separate ways for the evening. No offense, Ruby. The food is fantastic, but we don't trust each other."

"I don't think it's that we distrust each other," Ruby says.

"Bullshit," Theo says, and throws down his napkin. "She hired a private investigator."

"I'm not ashamed of that," Maureen says.

"Theo," Ruby says, "Darla disappeared under mysterious circumstances. I think *hurt* is the better word. I think we're all hurt and have more questions than answers."

"When I'm hurt, I go to the doctor. I don't seek out a private detective," Theo says.

Maureen wants to pivot away from an argument. "The two women known to have last seen and spoken to Darla, one was a traveling plumber and the other was a doctor who paid house calls. What are the odds?"

"I don't know," Theo says after a beat.

"Well, I believe there are human angels out there. We run into them once in a while. And they help us. Maybe even come out on the other side of a concussion," Maureen says.

"Do you think *that's* why Darla used my name?" Ruby asks the question she keeps wrestling with.

Maureen looks at Ruby. "Darla loves you."

"And I love Darla, but I don't know . . . It feels—"

"Like an act of desperation," Maureen says, cutting Ruby off. "Assuming it's really Darla. Let's hope it's Darla."

"I was going to say a violation, but maybe that's too strong," Ruby says.

Alfred uses his fork and dives into his second dish. "Oh, this is eggplant. It's delicious."

"Marinated in yuba paste," Ruby says, delighted that someone's enjoying the meal.

"How did you and Darla become friends?" Alfred asks.

"A middle school trip. We just hit it off." The truth was Ruby had accidentally locked herself in the porta-potty and panicked because she was terrified of confined spaces and she would have peed her pants except that she was already in a porta-potty and it smelled but it didn't smell awful because at least it was a new one. Darla had come to use the porta-potty too and heard her screaming and freaking out. And it wasn't a big deal except that it was a big deal because she was the new girl and she was the new girl at a fancy

Manhattan school who came from Brooklyn and, even though she was not a scholarship kid, she was not yet one of them and girls can be so middle school mean, so cruel until you become one of them. And she heard herself pleading and crying, afraid more about what rumors might get spread around or blown out of proportion because everything in middle school is out of proportion. "I won't say anything," Darla had said. And she never did.

No one had to ask Theo how he and Darla met. They had told the story about the taxicab ride to Brooklyn on a rainy night many times, even at their rehearsal dinner. "We met," Theo said, "five blocks from my first apartment in New York—"

"From what I understand," Maureen says, "Detective Tender would like to put together a short fifteen-minute home video to counter any rumors of dysfunction."

"Haven't we had enough of the media?" Theo says.

"Do we have to commit right now?" Ruby asks.

"No, of course not," Maureen says. "Detective Tender will be reaching out to you all directly."

After a beat, Theo says, "I don't know. I guess I'm in."

Ruby nudges Katsumi as everyone digs into their fourth and fifth courses. She is relieved they're managing to be civil. Katsumi whispers to her, "Are you okay?"

"Long day in the kitchen," she whispers back.

Alfred Harper pauses between eating to permit himself to take everything in. Aware that he's eating faster than everyone else. "This is quite a restaurant," he says.

"Under normal circumstances, we'd give you a peek upstairs," says Ruby.

Alfred locks eyes with Katsumi. "You own this whole outfit? Hotel too?"

Katsumi nods and says, "It's a family affair. We're all in it together." He squeezes Ruby's hand under the table and notices for the first time she is quite warm.

"How many people does it take to run a place this size?" Alfred asks.

"Well, for the restaurant," Ruby says, "between lunch and dinner staff, we have about fourteen people, including ourselves. We're a pretty small operation, believe it or not."

"And the hotel," Katsumi says. "We have ten people in hospitality. Our rooms are Western with four ryokan-inspired rooms, which I'd highly recommend."

"That's impressive," Alfred says. "Did Theo here ever tell you that his mother's in the restaurant business too? She and her family. It's a different kind of family affair. Burgers and fries. Grilled chicken. Gyros. Not this swanky."

"How are they holding up during COVID?" Katsumi asks.

"Well, better than a lot of Asian restaurants. You know, with China. There's the whole Wuhan effect. The inevitable backlash."

"I'm sorry," Ruby says, putting down her chopsticks, "but where did that come from?"

"He didn't mean any harm," Theo says, but he looks at his father, who looks back at him. *Don't show your ass.* Theo glints. *Give it a rest.*

"No," Alfred says. "I honestly didn't. But . . . COVID started in China."

"Mr. Harper," Katsumi says. "You're aware that I am Japanese and we're eating in a Japanese restaurant, right?"

"Yes," Alfred continues. "I know you're from Nihon. I was just pointing out, for better or worse, mostly worse, that everyone gets a chance to be hated. And right now, it's your people's turn."

"For some people that turn never ends," Ruby says, glaring.

Maureen reaches for the bottle of sake. "I'm not going to touch this one. More sake for me!"

"I assure you," Katsumi says, "you don't have to expend energy worrying about Asian troubles as they pertain to our restaurant. We were recently awarded a business loan to keep us afloat."

"From the government?" Alfred says, scowling. "You seem to be floating pretty well to me."

"Yes," Katsumi says. "From the government. Along with several major restaurant chains that might surprise you."

It's clear this rattles Alfred. He shifts gears altogether. "Did Darla come to the restaurant a lot?"

"Not as much as she would've liked to," Ruby says. "Maybe every few months. But she worked six days a week on a Broadway show."

"Would you say she visited more during the months leading up to COVID?"

"Dad," Theo says. "Let it go."

"Why are you interrogating Ruby," Maureen interrupts, "about Darla coming to Mizu to Yama?"

"Maybe," Alfred says to Maureen, "she came in with friends?"

"I already supplied the cops with a list of contacts. Theo as well." Ruby sits back in her chair.

"Maybe there was a special friend she came in with?"

Maureen puts both elbows on the table. "How dare you."

"Goddammit, Dad. Stop it," Theo warns.

"Goddamn is right," Maureen says. "What is this fool implying?"

"Nothing. My dad isn't implying anything."

"I should hope not," Maureen says. "If anyone's going to imply anything, it *should* be me." Maureen squints at Alfred. "Do you know your son is a sex addict?"

"I think I'm going to be sick," Ruby says softly.

"Yes, Ruby dear, I feel the same way," Maureen says.

"No," Ruby says, standing up. "Sick as in nauseous." Katsumi stands up with Ruby. Ruby waves him off. "Let's just get through the final course."

Alfred turns to Theo. "What's Darla's mother talking about, son?"

"I'm not a sex addict," Theo says. "If *love* is an action verb, then *sex* is an action language. And what I do in my personal life is none of your business—especially if your daughter consents to my behavior."

"Darla would never," Maureen says.

"Maureen," Theo says, "you spend half the year in Paris. How would you know? Maybe you don't know your daughter so well at all?"

Ruby starts for the kitchen. Katsumi follows. In the background, Theo, Maureen, and Alfred continue to squabble, though now they reapply masks.

Maureen slaps the table. "Tell me what really happened up on that mountain with my child. Don't serve me the bullshit you served everyone else. I'm the only mother here."

In the kitchen, Ruby piles the final course—Kobe steak stuffed with shishito peppers—on trays. The dish is a staple on their menu. One that has not been modified because of its popularity. It is a variation on her uncle Freddie's steak.

"Please don't say I told you so," Ruby whispers to Katsumi. Katsumi nods and moves around Ruby, gathering the final course on trays as well. Maureen and Theo's argument flows into the kitchen mingled with Prince crooning "The Ballad of Dorothy Parker."

"Why do white people always think we want to hear them air their dirty laundry?" Ruby mumbles. Katsumi touches Ruby's forehead. She is fever hot.

It's hotter than a slave ship in here.

Now why would you want to cook in a kitchen when your ancestors slaved there?

Ruby, darling, haven't you ever heard the saying "It's hotter than a slave ship up in this motherfucka"? Nothing sexy about this motherfucking heat.

Just because you have an air conditioner or central air don't change the physics of the history or the psychology of the big house or big kitchen or institutions full of peculiarities that linger. Still.

When I see a black person in a restaurant kitchen—someone says, who says—Ruby says?—I sweat.

I don't want to work hard and go out to eat and be reminded how far I have come and how close I am to where I have been.

But I am head chef, Ruby says out loud to an invisible audience.

Head nigger in charge.

House nigger.

I have seen the view and the vista, Ruby mutters.

Still. Head. Nigga.

Have you never heard of Abby Fisher, Edna Lewis, Patrick Reynolds, Zephyr Wright, Leah Chase, Marcus Samuelsson?

Do you know how difficult it is to become a head chef at a Michelin restaurant?

There's only a handful of us.

Well, I've always had issues with educated people cooking for other people.

You love to cook. Ruby remembers saying to someone—who?

For me and my family. Behind closed doors. I will cook!

When I used to go to a potluck with white colleagues, her mother once said, I always took smoked salmon.

Mom, you don't even like smoked salmon.

That's why I took a smoked salmon platter, to spare myself the "Did you make this? Why, I have never had such good food in my life. I didn't know you were a good cook."

I tried to jump off a building at Yale.

But you landed in Japan.

Still, I tried.

Sweetheart, opening night at Mizu to Yama, after your mother and father eat their ramen and homemade soba noodles, after they savor the wasabi jerk chicken with such pride—they beam, this restaurant is everything, baby. And more.

Ruby promises them and herself, I'm going to turn this into one of the best restaurants in Manhattan.

What you've done so far is fabulous, her mother and father say.

Did you really engage the ledge at Yale? Frida Black asks.

Yes, in order to disengage from myself.

Ruby, Ulysses Black says, his train of thought losing him, I've made mistakes. No one is perfect.

Mom, Dad, stay upstairs in one of the ryokan-inspired rooms.

I slept on the floor in Kyoto when we went to meet Katsumi's family. We aren't so supple now. Your father has a bad back, and I can't get off the floor so readily. I'm not one of these petite Japanese women.

Mom, please don't say that in front of Katsumi.

Physically, I am not a small woman.

The room also has a Western bed if you don't want a tatami mattress.

I think Ruby wants us to enjoy the room, Frida.

Well, it's just one night, her mother agrees. And the food you prepared really was EVERYTHING.

It's just one night. Ruby nods, mopping beads of sweat from her head, remembering Mizu to Yama's grand opening.

"Tabitha Ruby," Katsumi says with growing concern and alarm. "Let's take your temperature. You're not well. You think it's COVID?"

"No," Ruby says, surrendering to the present moment. "Not COVID. But, Katsumi, I just might be pregnant."

Katsumi freezes. He and Ruby think the same thought at the same time. They raise the beautiful plates of food on the beautiful trays high above their heads and let them crash to the ground, leaving their guests with nothing else to eat and nothing more to say.

MAUREEN RECOGNIZES Detective Tender's car lulled in front of her limestone and feels her body jerk involuntarily. She had declined Theo and Alfred Harper's cold cool cordial offer to give her a lift uptown, letting her own two feet carry her there instead.

"I cannot stand any more bad news tonight," Maureen says aloud as Detective Tender ejects herself from the car and perambulates toward her.

"I have no Darla news," Detective Tender says. "But I need you to come to the car and take a spin around the block with me while we iron some things out."

Maureen studies Detective Tender's face, but Detective Tender turns away and motions for Maureen to follow her to the car. This is not a question, Maureen understands, but an imperative. Maureen climbs into the passenger seat.

"Is this about the press?" she confesses. "Perhaps I was misguided . . . reaching out to the press."

Detective Tender drums her fingers on the steering wheel. "Well, thank you for being forthcoming with me. But I need both of you to be very brave right now."

"Both of us?" Maureen says, peering over her shoulder into the back seat of the car as Detective Tender ignites the engine and waits for the inevitable stunned silence or scream from her client. When that scream comes, Detective Tender fastens Maureen's seatbelt with great care and drives off.

If you are Detective Tender, you are fine with the silence that fills the car. If you are Detective Tender, you count seatbelts as one of mankind's greatest inventions. Seatbelts protect drivers and passengers from the road and from themselves. They hold them in, lock them in place. Coupled with a child's security lock, they minimize hazards. If you are Detective Tender, you have seen men, women, children hurl themselves through a window or out of a car, use a red light to jump in the back seat and fight with the loved one they had imagined they would welcome back with open arms if God or the universe or whatever evil force that took them away sent them home again. You watch Mrs. Jacobson try the front passenger-seat door and steel for her reaction when she realizes the safety lock is on.

When you reconnect with a loved one long assumed dead, all the things you thought you would say fly out the window. When you sit in the front seat of your private detective's car while your presumed-dead husband sits in the back staring quietly out of the window, bashful almost, and old, so damn old, you crane your neck to its breaking point for a better view, trying to fathom the unfathomable, when you realize he will neither look at you nor respond in any human way.

"What is this?" if you are Maureen Jacobson, you ask repeatedly.

And Detective Tender answers in a sweet monotone. "This is your long-lost husband, Mrs. Jacobson. How was dinner tonight?"

"A fiasco," if you are Maureen, you manage to mutter. Screaming was your first impulse. But you now wish you could take that scream back. Your second impulse is to compose yourself. Somehow.

And Detective Tender says insincerely, for she knows that Daniel Castaway is a flight risk and she will need to keep him in her sight in the coming days, "What a shame Mr. Castaway couldn't stay at their hotel."

And Maureen concurs—for she must say *something*. "As good as we've been to Ruby over the years, I cannot believe she let Katsumi throw us out of their restaurant."

And this comment elicits the first response from Daniel. "Frida Black made it?" he asks.

"Yes," Maureen whispers. "Frida Black owns a bookstore in Brooklyn. She opened it the year after the towers fell."

Daniel grunts and trains his gaze on the city he hasn't seen in nineteen years. "Have you been?"

Maureen shakes her head no.

"Maybe I'll drop by . . . once I've done everything I need to do here," he says softly.

"To Mr. Castaway's credit, he flew in on his own accord," Detective Tender tells Maureen Jacobson, but Maureen's face is a river of confusion.

"*Who* is Mr. Castaway?"

"I haven't been Daniel Jacobson for a long time," Daniel says.

And Maureen, because she is unmoored and trying to find a safe shore to land on, repeats, "Where did my husband go?"

Daniel continues to stare out the window. He used to love the city. He was raised to love cities.

This time Maureen begins to cry. Silently. She will not give this Daniel Castaway the satisfaction of seeing her tears, so she turns around and faces the windshield instead.

Detective Tender drives the car around the block. She thinks they are both acquitting themselves quite well. Better than she had expected. "I can't tell you how many times I've had to fly to Barbados or St. John's or Hawaii. . . . I'm not going to lie, Hawaii was nice, because the mister and I went, and the Parkinson's hadn't yet reared its head. It's no fun hunting for people who don't want to be found, and legally, depending on the circumstances, I can't always force their hands or make them come back. But

Mr. Castaway has agreed to come back and help us with our search. I happen to believe your daughter is alive, though I can't say she's necessarily well. And Mr. Castaway is the bait we need to fish her out."

"This man is a criminal," Maureen snaps. "Living under an assumed name."

"I kept my own social security number," Daniel says, defending himself.

"How does that even happen?" Maureen asks.

"Tell me a little about Darla," Daniel says, turning his attention to the car's interior for the first time, sitting up in his seat. "Please fill me in on the details of our daughter's life, as best you can."

At this, Maureen attempts to put her foot on the brakes of Detective Tender's car. Detective Tender kicks her foot away.

"He can't stay at the house," Maureen says, spitting the words at Detective Tender first, then at Daniel. "Where is he going to stay? *You* can't stay at *my* house."

Daniel reaches forward and puts his hand on Maureen's. After all these years, after having the marriage voided, an order of absentia, out of respect for who her husband was and how he died, she still wears his wedding band.

"You've aged well, Maureen. You always were pretty."

Maureen's hand goes from limp to clammy and she lets her lost husband hold it for a few seconds.

"Mr. Castaway, would you have a problem staying with me in Pennsylvania for a night or two until we begin shooting? Or perhaps your brother Roy?"

Daniel says, "No siblings. No Roy. I'll stay with you."

Detective Tender nods. This means Daniel Jacobson or Castaway is planning on sticking around, at least for the time being. Run once, run twice. Land in the same place. It has been Detective Tender's experience, especially if they don't know what compelled them to run in the first place, that these men and women replicate the lives they leave behind without even realizing it.

"Now," Detective Tender says, parking on her final loop around Maureen's block in front of Maureen's limestone. "I want you two people to listen to me. Do you know what we humans want most in the world?"

Maureen and Daniel remain silent.

"We want things to work out differently or better than they did. And sometimes, Daniel, I don't know you, and it's not my place to say what made you choose flight, but it's often fight or flight in this life. Do you understand?"

"No," Daniel says flatly.

"Yes," Maureen says, done with Detective Tender. "You've overturned my life. For a shitload of money."

Detective Tender continues: "Children never grow up. They become adults. With adult-sized wounds. No matter how cynical or angry or belligerent or tuned out or radioactive, they're always ripe for fairy tales."

But this makes no sense, Maureen thinks.

She never read Darla fairy tales. She does not believe in fairy tales. Neither does Daniel. Fairy tales are dangerous. Maureen has worked since she was a teenager. When her much older father retired from the military and settled in the Finger Lakes, she spent the summer months as a tour guide at the Seneca Falls Convention Center acting out the roles of the suffragists: Elizabeth Cady Stanton and Susan B. Anthony and Lucretia Mott and once she even used Tropicana Tanning Lotion for an inspired interpretation of Sojourner Truth, a fact that she would never share with anyone today. She knows the "Declaration of Sentiments" by heart. And, of all the suffragists, her favorite has long been Lucretia Mott. Maureen's mother, a perfectly happy stay-at-home mom with little or no interest in the women's movement, once said, when she told her how it shocked her that visitors often commented on the suffragists' looks or lack thereof, how could Lucretia be anything but hideous? Coffin was her middle name. Maureen imagined their prettier selves and their clearer complexions. Beauty and youth have always opened the door a bit wider, if only temporarily. Maureen has trusted Detective Tender to find her daughter, but right now, Detective Tender seems hideous to Maureen. Who better to find a missing woman than another woman? Yet Detective Tender has gone and resurrected her dead husband instead.

"Will you be okay alone in the house tonight, Mrs. Jacobson?" Detective Tender asks with genuine concern.

"Why wouldn't I be okay alone? Darla and I lived alone in this house for years."

"Well, I suppose during COVID, it's not like there's someone you can call to come over."

Maureen climbs out of the car.

"Maybe," Detective Tender whispers to Daniel, "you want to just . . . I don't know, step out and say something to her."

"I don't live here anymore," he says. But Daniel steps onto the sidewalk anyway and catches up with Maureen.

"Maureen," he calls out. "I came back once. I saw you. The Christmas after the towers. You moved on without missing a beat."

"'Moved on,' you say?" Maureen still clings to her widowed lonely years. Years so full of missing Daniel no other man had been good enough. She had had to leave the country and find a foreigner. "How, 'moved on'?"

"You and Darla were ice skating in Bryant Park. I followed you. I had everything planned. What I would say and how I would say it, but then I watched you two, falling and getting up again. You seemed so . . . complete, like my being there would be an intrusion."

"The Daniel Jacobson I knew would never have done this." She puts Daniel's hand to her heart so he can feel it beating. "Or perhaps Daniel Jacobson was always Daniel Castaway. And never loved me."

*

Theo listened to the water running in the guestroom. Alfred Harper was preparing his nightly bath.

"I'm not sure it's good to take a bath every night," Theo said.

"Son," Alfred said, wearing one of the plush terrycloth bathrobes from the guest room and slippers, "dinner was a shit show on speed. I need a bath and a beer to relax. Grab yourself one while you're at it."

Theo went to the kitchen cabinet and took out cream of tartar. "Apply this to the bathtub when you're done."

Alfred shook the container. "What's this?"

"It's for the ring of dirt that settles if you don't wash the tub out right away."

"Is something on your mind, Theo?"

Theo reckoned that he had witnessed two for one tonight. Ruby Black and Katsumi Fujihara had destroyed their own dishes. What was that, if not their thirty percent? But then, hadn't Maureen shown her thirty percent as well? Hadn't he and his father behaved poorly too?

"Yes and no," Theo hesitated.

"Can you believe with an outfit like that those two have the nerve to accept money from the government?"

"Dad, they're in survival mode. Maybe we should apply for funding for Mom's restaurant as well. It might be a better use of your time than being here."

"If everyone seeks handouts from the government, son, we'll break it."

"As if it's not already broken. Look how we've mismanaged COVID."

"We didn't start this pandemic."

"It doesn't matter now who started it. Just like . . . it doesn't matter which one of us, Darla or me, started the fight on the mountain. It stopped mattering who started COVID when the first person died in America or China or Italy or France or England or Spain or Africa—"

"I don't want the water to overflow in the bathtub," Alfred said.

"This is my apartment. I will turn it off. You stay put," Theo said, moving quickly to the guest room and shutting off the bathtub faucet. When he returned, Alfred was standing with his hands deep in the pockets of the terrycloth bathrobe.

"Go ahead," Alfred said. "Say it."

"Dad, you've outstayed your welcome," Theo blurted out.

"But I came here to help you during this difficult time," Alfred reminded Theo.

"And you have. As much as you know how."

"I happen to think you still need me here."

"You have no idea how hard I've worked to leave certain things behind."

"By certain things," Alfred said as he leaned against one of Theo's end tables, "I assume you mean your family? You think I don't know we've never been good enough for you? Attractive enough?"

"What?" Theo wanted a beer. He had been knocking them back a lot lately.

"Maureen was right," Alfred said. "You treat us like we all have two left feet. Buffoons. Buffoonery."

"I'll ask you what Ruby asked you earlier when you did, in fact, make fools of us both. Where is this coming from?"

"My hollow soul," Alfred said, and shrugged.

"I love my family," Theo said. "And I don't take shit when people come at me the wrong way about where I was born."

"Theodore," Alfred said, shaking his head, mocking. "You're the stud. The good-looking one. The 'sun' we all look to. Our Apollo."

"Well," Theo said, stung, "it's nice to know how you really feel about me, Dad. Do my brothers and sisters share this opinion?"

"I cannot speak for them," Alfred answered honestly. "But I've been here for two weeks now and I see the problem with this country in a nutshell. Half of you are relaxing and sitting on your high chairs and preening and posing while the rest of us are working and holding on to our principles."

"I can assure you: I work hard."

"But you play harder. You play reckless. Do you think I needed Darla's mother to tell me you've no control of your wand? Waving it here and waving it there. In public and private places. Well, guess what, *I* have a wand, too."

"No one wants to hear about your wand."

"What if I went around acting like you? No, I don't. I wouldn't. I couldn't. Because I have responsibilities. A wife and kids. No matter how much you grow or how old you are, you'll always be our kids. And it just seems to me like your generation wants to have its cake and eat it too."

"I wouldn't call what I do eating cake," Theo said. "I choose not to be miserable."

"You *are* miserable. You're miserable as fuck," Alfred shouted.

"I'm distracted. There's a difference. I know you don't understand this, but I like sex and the possibility of sex the next time and the time after that, and I've never been dishonest with anyone about my proclivities, especially Darla, and it's taken a pandemic for me to realize life doesn't come down to percentage points or labels. I hate labels, Dad."

"No one said life comes down to percentage points."

"That's how I was raised. That's how you raised all of us." Theo looked toward the door. He wanted an exit but he went up to his father instead. He placed his hands on his father's shoulders. "Tonight, at dinner, you talked about your great-great-grandfather from Bavaria. You gave him value. That's something you've never given to my namesake. That other side of us, our family."

"I don't know where the jokes about our thirty percent started, but they didn't start with me," Alfred said defensively.

"It's all right. It's fine," Theo said.

"Clearly we're not fine."

"We'll be fine tomorrow," Theo said, "because you're going to take a nice hot bath tonight and get to bed early. I want you to be well rested for the drive home to Des Moines."

"You really want me to go home, son?"

Theo nodded. "The sooner the better. This should be about me and Darla."

"Okay," Alfred said. "But what happens when this city abandons you?"

"You and Mom raised me to be pretty self-sufficient," Theo said. "Anyway, cities don't abandon people. People abandon people."

DARLA EXERCISES her fingers to maintain their strength with daily practice of her bassoon. She disassembles and reassembles crook, bell, boot joint, butt joint, wing joint, and reed, reciting the pieces of her bassoon like a prayer. The postings of her image in local newspapers and around the country mean she can no longer risk playing the bassoon in public or near the falls. Gone too are her solo walks. She walks hand in hand with Greer now in Niagara Falls State Park, where to unseeing eyes they present as a normal, happy young couple. In many ways, they are a normal, happy young couple. Darla has resumed composing music and the routine provides a relaxing, healthy distraction from the @Save Darla Jacobson campaign. She gives Greer money to bring her a small digital recorder from Best Buy, and she sits at her hotel desk for hours at a time listening to the music of Debussy and Beethoven and Brahms and Hildegard von Bingen, composers who all also found solace and inspiration in nature. It will take four months for the bed of her pinky finger to grow back its nail, but Darla is teaching herself to play without using that finger. She practices the composers' moonlight sonatas and fugues and concertos and suites and orchestra pieces with Greer as her one-man audience when he isn't working. And she waits for Greer to expose her to the press. But to Greer's credit or gullibility, he does not. Instead, the two of them play musical floors and musical hotel rooms. Greer moves Darla around like a chess piece when guests check in so that Darla can practice her bassoon without worrying about noise complaints or being found out.

The nicest bassoon I ever held was on my senior trip to Russia. An ensemble of retired musicians performed Johann Christian Bach's Bassoon Concerto in B-flat Major in Ploshchad Iskusstv in St. Petersburg. The contrabassoon had belonged to the bassoonist's mother (Ukrainian) and her father before her and his father before him (Russian), so every note dripped with texture and history. To hold or attempt to play that bassoon was to hold something loyal only to its master. I understood then what my first bassoon teacher meant when he said an instrument will tell you everything you need to know. They have personalities like we do. And voices.

Greer rummaged through Darla's backpack for Tylenol when she was having one of her headaches. The headaches that caused Darla to splay herself across the bed like paint on a canvas. Darla told him that being pregnant was like possessing superpowers. She could hear a pen drop in a carpeted room two floors down. Everything echoed like she was in the forest. But when Greer opened Darla's wallet and saw her real name, Darla Jacobson, she confessed to her argument in the wood with Theo. And being picked up by Dr. Jennifer Klein on the road. And, of course, using Ruby Black's name.

"At least one person should know the truth about me right now," Darla said.

And Greer was glad Darla had leveled with him before @Save Darla Jacobson blew up.

"You could turn me in and pay for graduate school with the reward money," she teased, testing Greer. She often tested Greer.

"Why would I want to do that?"

"When an opportunity presents itself, it's for a reason. Take it."

"Does your husband play a musical instrument?" Greer began to test Darla in return.

"Theo is not musically inclined, no. But he does make beautiful bird calls. So I guess maybe he is a little musically inclined."

"What's he like?" Greer asked.

Greer, who had also lost his virginity at sixteen, had a string of girlfriends in college and after college. His most recent being a co-worker at Best Buy whom he had broken up with because he couldn't stand the smell of cigarettes and when they kissed he felt like there was a chimney in his throat. Greer reminded Darla of her younger self because in college she was never without a boyfriend. She lived alone but it wasn't until after college that she had learned how to be alone.

"I just told you Theo's bird calls are spectacular," Darla said. "I need two more Tylenol, Greer."

Sometimes Darla suffered mood swings and brief bouts of dizziness that she thought might also be linked to her concussion. She would vacillate then between wanting Greer within arm's reach and wanting him out of her hair, out of her sight. "Your questions make me glad we're wrapping things up."

"I was just wondering."

"Before you knew I had a husband it was just the two of us. And you never wondered. Shouldn't you enjoy these last few days with me?"

Greer no longer believed Darla was leaving. She said this mostly when the headaches came.

"Have you ever been in love?" He closes the curtains and the lights go out. Sometimes there's only the sound of the two of them breathing.

"Three or four times," Darla says, turning away from Greer to fend off encroaching attachment.

"Do you think you could fall in love again?"

"Greer, you are reliable. Who needs love when she has substance?"

When they shop for groceries together, Greer pauses in the aisle to ask after prenatal vitamins. He has begun to grow hair stubble. Darla marvels at the power of oxytocin.

"Darla," Daniel Jacobson says, removing his Miami Marlins baseball cap to reveal flattened silver-fox hair. "If you are out there, if you are out there, Darla, and can hear me, come home. I beseech you. And if there is someone out there who has my daughter, who is holding her against her wishes, please, please, let her go. She's so beautiful and kind and I . . . just let her go."

Detective Tender convinces the key players in Darla's life to co-habitate briefly under one roof, except Ruby Black. Miraculously, Theo Harper, Maureen Jacobson, and Daniel Castaway manage to put their best faces and voices forward with emotions strong enough to warm Old Man Winter, especially when the long-lost, stoic Daniel Jacobson stares into the camera. Detective Tender conducts interviews off-camera and intersperses them with home video footage of Darla's first toddle with her mother and father in the parlor of their limestone. Maureen and Daniel cooing, not unlike Detective Tender coos to her husband, Maureen and Daniel's home video on a shaky camera. *Come here, come to Mama and Daddy, Darla.* Darla in a romper with blue jays fills up the camera. There is the first pony ride and subsequent horseback lessons with her parents and her uncle Roy on a bridle path in New Jersey. She and Ruby and friends posing like figure skaters in Bryant Park. There are interviews with mentors and colleagues and excerpts from her early recitals and the final performance for the Broadway musical. There's Roland Paige hugging his Irish wolfhound and lamenting how Darla and her mother and father always treated him well when others did not. There's Darla and Theodore's wedding at Trinity Church. Darla's Vera Wang wedding gown, the flowers, the interior of the chapel. Darla and Theodore Harper kissing and ducking birdseed in front of Trinity Church. Then come the couple photos: Theo and Darla strolling in Prospect Park. Eating gyros at the Seventh Avenue Street Fair in Park Slope. Picnicking under the cherry blossoms in the Botanical Garden. A New Year's Eve party in 2019 at Ruby and Katsumi's restaurant. There's the couple in matching masks and then a cut to Darla's arts and crafts table. A close-up of the masks Darla made for her friends. And Theo sitting alone in their living room apartment, pointing at Darla's favorite spot on the sofa. And finally, Theo, Maureen, and Daniel Jacobson huddled together on the Jacobson living room sofa, each making a plea for Darla to be returned home.

The filming is hurried and harried and punctuated by fraternal disruptions. Roy Jacobson pays an impromptu visit to Maureen Jacobson's home, which is the set. Roy is a professional polo coach. An East Coast horseman. He owns a trio of Morgan horses and lets them roam free on his land, forgoing a barn for a shed that offers sufficient coverage when the weather veers rough. He kisses Maureen on the cheek and comes in shoving distance of his brother. Maureen, her vigilante heart stilled enough to get through the shoot, takes one look at Roy's fists and thinks, *At last, at last.* But Roy has come on their sister Birdy's behest. Birdy pleaded with Roy to confirm that Daniel's really their brother. Roy shakes Daniel's hand, face to face, nose to nose, pale eyelashes to pale eyelashes.

"I had to see you for myself," Roy says, visibly short of breath.

"Well, you've seen me," Daniel says.

"Birdy says hi."

"Tell Birdy I said hi back. Tell Birdy I wish her well."

"I hope you find Darla. She's a good kid." Roy backs away again. His nose exudes snot. He cups and uncups his hands reflexively. His pudgy eyelids are swollen in a way that hints at restrained tears. Roy wants to tell Daniel that he tried for a long time to be a father to Darla and his own five children, taking Darla on horseback rides, visiting her and Maureen on occasional weekends, but he was a poor stand-in for her biological father. "*You died.* That took Mom and Dad out within two years of each other. You fucking *died.* And now this? Who needs you, brother? I know horseshit when I smell horseshit. How do you live with yourself?"

"I live with myself," Daniel says, not without regret, "because I wasn't in the building. I wasn't there. I was playing hooky and enjoying my morning pour-over. It didn't go down so well, Roy. My morning pour-over. It doesn't go down so well now."

"Is that all?" Roy asks.

"That's all," Daniel says, nodding.

Roy Jacobson straightens out his blue blazer and gallops away.

In Niagara Falls in the same hotel in a different room on a different floor, Darla sits on the bed eating a bowl of shrimp fra diavolo. The shrimp fra diavolo drizzles down her chin because no one is around other than Greer. The dish is mediocre and Darla thinks if Ruby were there, she would pinpoint right away the missing ingredient. At the Blacks' house, dinners had been prepared according to a meal plan, shared between Ulysses and Frida Black, who were not inspired cooks and followed recipes to the letter. One of the highlights of sleeping over was the point when they would all sit down at the dinner table and inevitably Ruby would notice that the beef stew or the chicken parmesan or coconut rice was off.

"More pepper," Frida Black would say.

"More salt," Ulysses Black would counter.

And Ruby, even then, would taste the dish and move it around slowly in her mouth. "Mom, I think you used too much oregano."

Ruby didn't care about cooking then. And Darla wasn't in love with her bassoon then either, but things change. Just like her body keeps changing now. Her body has no shame, continues to astonish her with its metamorphosis. Body hair has never concerned Darla on or between her legs or under her armpits, but she is confounded by the little nipple hairs that have sprung up on her massive breasts. She often feels like a model in a Botticelli painting and is grateful that her parents, upon buying the summer cottage, kept for reasons not known to her the old *Vanity Fair* magazine with the picture of a very pregnant Demi Moore on the cover. She tries on gray days when she wonders if she will ever have complete control of her body again to embrace a modern take on pregnancy, right down to how each orgasm strengthens the pelvic muscles for labor.

"Holy shit," Greer says, eating from a second container of shrimp fra diavolo. Greer will eat just enough and be sure to leave extra for Darla. "That's your dad. And he sounds like he's trying to appeal to the humanity of a serial killer."

But Darla is not listening. It takes a long, hot minute before it registers that the man on the screen is her father. This man who says he is Daniel Jacobson looks nothing like the "dad" in Darla's memory. Darla's brain.

She had applied herself to the bassoon after his death and revived herself with the bassoon because of his death and mastered the bassoon in college, receiving a scholarship though she did not need the money, but on the merit of her persuasion of the instrument. She grew with the bassoon in the way one grows with a child and loved the instrument like a parent. It is a difficult instrument to play and she has been in some ways a taxing master.

As the images flash across the television screen like a Kodak ad with the jingle "Times of Your Life," Darla thinks, *These are the times of my life.*

Darla bolts away from the bed and makes her way to the flat-screen television. Her shrimp fra diavolo lands on the comforter and carpet. And on Greer.

"Dad?" Darla says, touching the TV. Blinking as the credits begin to roll and Darla, sensing that the days of their lives have played out in some sneaky way, rubs her face against the flat-screen television.

Greer rises, unsure of how best to approach Darla. This is beyond his life experience and pay grade.

"I can't be here, Greer," Darla says softly. "I have to go home right now."

If Darla could, she would hug the TV. She would pull it off the wall. Instead, Darla steps away and begins rummaging through drawers, pacing, grabbing her coat, backpack, water, Tylenol, and bassoon.

"We'll get you home," Greer says, automatically ferreting into his pockets for his car keys while also trying to slow Darla down.

Darla shakes her head. "It might already be too late. What if it's too late, Greer?"

They decide that Greer will drive Darla as far as Albany and that Darla will drop him off at the train station and then drive the rest of the way in his father's Chevy pickup truck. But the closer they get to Albany, the more Darla speeds and Greer thinks, *This is a great big mistake.*

"Darla," Greer says firmly. "You are one bad-ass pregnant lady, but you won't make it to New York alone."

AFTER WE shared the results of the pregnancy test—positive—and
the COVID test—negative, Mom and Dad arrived masked up and
giddy and bearing fresh fruit. "If you're pregnant, you need to test
often for COVID. You can't risk a false negative."

Mom eases a pillow I don't need behind my back and points to
the screen. "There's not many images of you in their video."

"That was my request. And I'm glad to see that Maureen honored it." How easily I have been edited down and cut around. My
choice, yes. But disturbing nevertheless.

"Do you think Daniel Jacobson embezzled money?" Frida Black
asks.

It is Sunday and my father is downstairs in Mizu to Yama with
Katsumi and the staff preparing bento boxes for the homeless.
There is a longer line than any of us could have imagined and I am
certain we will run out of food and be forced to turn people away.
It seems fitting somehow that our restaurant is in the Bowery,
which is no stranger to human traffic and hunger. My attention is
torn between the thirty-minute video and the line beneath my
window.

"No," I say to my mother. "I don't think embezzling is his style."

"One can never really say with investment bankers." My mother
shrugs. And I laugh. It is the understatement of the century.

Dad had said something similar. "Lord, the burdens our secrets
bring."

Like Katsumi, my father saw no need to watch the @Save Darla Jacobson video, even when I tried to explain to him that this video was down-to-earth and effective.

"When I was pregnant with you, they put me on bed rest my first trimester," Mom says.

Tomorrow I will see the ob-gyn. And there will be an ultrasound. I am trying to remain calm and not get overly excited. It is enough to let Katsumi and my parents be thrilled for me. When I try to make sense of Theo and Darla, I wonder if perhaps COVID hasn't permanently altered our emotions and brains. I wonder is it right or even selfish to bring a newborn into a world like this. From the starting gate, there are structural components to who fails and succeeds. When does selfishness become hope or faith? Does every new parent imagine their baby will tip the scale, open a door, and land us in a better place?

Mom came to our penthouse with a revised funding application for her bookstore for me to review and contact numbers for Monty and my old friends from Yale.

"You know after the funeral and after you ran off to Japan—" she begins.

"It's the other way around. I didn't run off to Japan. I ran back home."

Mom says, "Monty and Jacintha and Candy would call and check in on us. They would say, 'Mrs. Black, you let us know if you need anything.' Whatever happened to your college chums, Ruby? I bet they would be happy to hear from you. COVID gives us permission to reach out again."

"I see what you're doing, Frida Black."

"What am I doing?"

"Trying to keep me off my feet and out of the kitchen."

"Just for the time being. Until we know all is well," she says. "I also want to see you have more black-girl joy. More black girl-friends . . ."

This throws me a minute. I laugh. "Where's *your* black-girl joy, Mom?"

"How do you think I got through 9/11? Or this mess with my skin? I joined a black women's support group shortly after."

"You never told me that."

"Or Ulysses. Or Freddie."

We return our attention to the video and I try to process what Mom has just said. Theo and Darla swirl around on the dance floor at Tavern on the Green. I'm the maid of honor. I am in there. Somewhere. Seeing Daniel Jacobson stare into the camera brings up complicated memories.

On 9/11, my uncle Freddie showed up at the Jacobson household. He rang the doorbell then banged on the door. "Anyone in there? Open up!"

And when Mrs. Gonzalez opened the parlor door, he said, "Is Ruby here?"

Mrs. Gonzalez was from East Harlem. She had four children of her own. She had relatives and neighbors, who, like my parents and their neighbors, were six or one degree removed from loved ones in their lives.

"Yes," Mrs. Gonzalez said. "Ruby is here."

I don't know if she would have let Uncle Freddie in the house if he hadn't picked me up on so many occasions before. I came down the stairs and there he was in a dirty Knicks T-shirt and jeans that were too big for his narrow frame, rolled up to reveal his sneakers. He used rubber bands to keep the jeans from falling below his ankles. Uncle Freddie was on somebody's old racer bike with Spokey Dokeys and silver masking tape on the seats. He smelled wretched.

"Ruby, your dad is down at the World Trade Center looking for your mom. Come on." He held out his hand. Before Mrs. Gonzalez could say anything, I said goodbye to Darla and grabbed my backpack. We climbed on the racer bike, me gripping Uncle Freddie tight and Uncle Freddie riding standing while I sat on the seat.

Sometimes you just want your family in whatever shape size and form they come in. You want the comfort of their link to you, their DNA. If the world is going to end as you know it, you want a voice, a face who knew you when language was little more than a rattle.

"Big-headed Ruby," Uncle Freddie said, "it's crazy today. Hold on. Don't let go."

He cycled south down Central Park West zigzagging between streets: Columbus and Amsterdam, making his way to Broadway and Columbus Circle.

"Look at all these people. Too many damn people," he muttered. From Columbus Circle, he looped to Eighth Avenue and Ninth Avenue, stopping and starting in fits to catch his breath.

"Let's take turns, Uncle Freddie." I could feel his rib cage. I was five-six and growing and wouldn't have been surprised if I weighed more than Uncle Freddie. He let me cycle up Ninth Avenue for a few blocks until we swerved onto the curb as I maneuvered between cars and people who had abandoned the C and E and A trains. Uncle Freddie took charge again. Then all the way down to Fourteenth Street, where he turned east away from the Hudson and toward the East River as smoke made pillows over the city. Uncle Freddie pumped. Over the Brooklyn Bridge with hordes of cyclists to Tillary, Flatbush, Myrtle, right on DeKalb, home, home. Soaking wet in his funk. Now both of us. Panting. We both knocked on the door. And Mom and Dad came out. Uncle Freddie hugged Mom. Mom and Dad hugged me. Dad even hugged Uncle Freddie, which was a first.

"Thank you, man," Dad said to Uncle Freddie. Slapping him on his back repeatedly. "Man, thank you."

"Safe," Uncle Freddie said. "I got her home safe."

"Come on in, Freddie," Mom said. She reached out to her brother, but Uncle Freddie shook his head, sniffed his shirt and pulled away.

"This one needs a bath," he said, nodding in my direction.

"So do you," Mom said. "You can borrow some of Ulysses's clothes."

An expression came over Uncle Freddie's face then. It was always there but it took center stage. "Water rusts iron. And sinks battleships."

"Freddie," Mom said as he started toward the racer bike. "Wait, I didn't mean it that way. Why don't you stay awhile and eat dinner with us? All that cycling, you don't have to go right now. You're tired, Freddie."

He blew her a kiss. "I got people to see and places to be. Catch you later . . . sis. Ulysses. Big-headed Ruby."

When the video is over, I take the remote and turn the TV off. Mom says, after a beat, as if reading my thoughts, "Sometimes, I just don't know. Maybe I could have done better by Freddie. Whatever better is."

*

In the Jacobson household, the camera crew has left for the evening, but the A and B and C cameras, the lighting and sound equipment and screens remain in the living room, which resembles a sleek set on a soundstage in a movie studio. The video cameras, the tech equipment, are a constant reminder that life is being staged and a story being told that Daniel Castaway was once a part of, but not anymore. He can leave when their mission has been accomplished. Detective Tender is determined that he will not leave a second before. As soon as the day's filming wraps, Daniel Castaway announces that he is going for a walk in Central Park. Detective Tender volunteers to join him.

"Am I the leash or the dog?"

"Neither," Detective Tender says. "You're doing so well, Daniel. Please don't go anywhere I wouldn't go."

Left to his own devices, Daniel Castaway strolls to Zabar's and

Fairway and he orders General Tso's chicken from Ollie's on Forty-second Street and he walks around Central Park and studies the trees and then walks to Riverside Park to feed the birds near Grant's Tomb and, from there, he stands in front of the Beacon Hotel, where he had stayed that December he returned to New York briefly and nearly revealed himself. Outside of the interviews, he says little or does little to make himself emotionally available to Maureen, including but not limited to asking questions about her life, their old friends, what Maureen has done in the intervening years, or who she is partnered with. Daniel returns late in the evening and sequesters in his room with the door slightly ajar. And Detective Tender notices that when given a choice of rooms to sleep in, Daniel chooses the room farthest away, on the very top floor with enough boxes to double as a storage closet. This behavior is in keeping with patterns she has witnessed in estranged adults and children who shuttered themselves away, a cold calmness in their voices like automatons flat-lining. "Please leave me alone. Don't you understand? I can't stand to be here."

Sleeping in Darla's family home is stimulating for Theo. It is a beautiful limestone that reminds him of Chris Beam's house in Chelsea. Theo had never spent much time at the Jacobsons' when he and Darla first started dating because Darla already had her own place, but now he could roam up and down the stairs and admire the details. The emergence of Daniel Jacobson has left Maureen Jacobson aloft, like a cat who doesn't know if it should hiss or claw or retreat to a scratching post. Theo can't help but think just a wee tad bit little, *Goody-goody, that's what you get,* but he doesn't quite know what to make of Daniel Jacobson himself. Their one conversation, the first day on set, he was prepared for Daniel Jacobson to at least try to beat him up. "Mr. Jacobson," Theo had said. "I feel awful about Darla."

"Daniel is fine," Darla's father had said. "Let me ask you something: coming down the mountain, did you hear the rooster crow three times?"

"What?" Theo asked.

"I heard Bruce Springsteen's song 'Hungry Heart' three times in three days. And thought: something's coming."

Theo decided to end the conversation quickly. "The blueberry handprints are still there on the stone wall you built with Darla at the cottage."

"It's good to know some things can't be washed off," Daniel said.

Theo was glad to be actively at work again. He had a brownstone in Fort Greene to see tomorrow. Theo had come across so well on the video, though not nearly as well as Mr. Jacobson. He kept busy with phone calls or on his laptop or Zooms. The real estate agency that had fired him now wanted a rehire. His voicemail was full of referrals and inquiries for his aesthetic advisor services. So much so, Theo called Simon Pratt to see if he could poach him away from his former employers.

Simon Pratt had already signed up for Zoom sessions with his old therapist. He knew she would tell him to get more exercise. He had begun doing brisk walks around Sunset Park and in Green-Wood Cemetery. Some people found cemeteries discomfiting, but when Simon looked at the mausoleums and tombstones, they made him want to live better and make wiser choices. Something he wasn't sure he was capable of yet.

"Really?" Simon said. "You want me to do you a favor? What about the little issue of your missing, possibly dead wife? How could you . . . *you know*, with her being missing?"

Theo adjusted his cell phone. "Simon, if you really believed I hurt my wife, you wouldn't be talking to me."

"You're the devil in training, so I honestly don't know. . . ."

"Yes you do. And this devil needs an aid."

"A devil's helper?"

"I won't beg. But I will text you the details."

Simon hedged. "It's not a good time, Theo. I'm sleeping in the bedroom and my partner is on the couch. Felix Ramirez is my husband, by the way."

"Well, that explains a lot," Theo said. "Detective Ramirez was up my ass like a colonoscopy with his probing fucking questions. That's a serious conflict of interests."

"Oh please. None of us are innocent," Simon said. "Especially you."

"Can I count on you or not?" Theo said.

"I think not."

Maureen Jacobson had never thought she would have Daniel Jacobson in her home again because he had a plot in Trinity Cemetery. She never thought she would have Theo in her home again because he had abandoned her only daughter in the woods. And yet here they both were: the ex upstairs on the top floor of their limestone, and her son-in-law making himself good and comfortable in her basement. After the first day of shooting, Maureen said to Detective Tender, "Daniel does not get to stroll in here like a knight in shining armor on his white horse."

"I thought he flew in on a plane."

"You know what I mean."

"I really do not."

"Sarcasm doesn't suit you."

"Let me do my job, Mrs. Jacobson. I'd advise you not to let a fragile ego derail our investigation. We are doing so well."

For her sanity, Detective Tender spent a fair amount of time in the Jacobsons' garden. May was the season for roses and the roses were spectacular. They seemed to peek out at Detective Tender from every corner and descend the trellis and burst into red yellow orange pink white life. She took pictures and sent them to the nurse to show to Ollie. She herself did not have a green thumb. She killed flowers.

"I'll give you the name of my landscaper," Maureen said.

"Is your landscaper budget-friendly?"

"With all the money I am paying you, what's a budget?"

"Mrs. Jacobson, while you're at it, pour me a cocktail, please."

Detective Tender encouraged Maureen to enjoy aperitifs as well as digestifs when they were done shooting. We all need something. With the unwanted and unexpected guests in the house, Maureen didn't want to take the last joint out of the cookie jar.

Every night, Daniel Jacobson faced a barrage of questions from Trish Fadden Castaway. "Is your first wife really that attractive in person? Where does she buy her lipstick? I never knew you came from so much money, Danny. Are we rich? If your daughter wants to visit us, when she's found, if she's found, we could always redecorate the spare room."

"It's fine just the way it is."

"This whole thing makes me feel so naked," Trish said. "Does she have a nice figure?"

"Trish, if I compliment Maureen, you might mistake that as my still being attracted to her. If I insult her appearance, after what I have done, I'd be a heel and not worthy of you."

"You're not—worthy of anyone." Maureen had come up the stairs to eavesdrop in the hallway.

"You're trespassing," Daniel said.

"In my own house."

"This house belonged to both of us once upon a time."

"Not anymore."

"Honey," Daniel said, "I'll call you right back."

" 'Honey'? Is she round? Is she shaped like a honeycomb?" Maureen said.

Downstairs, the doorbell rang as Detective Tender was taking a photograph of a species of rose called Nostalgia. She left the patio and moved through the parlor to the front door.

"Is the coast clear?" Greer asked. A slim man of twenty-three or so stood with his hands in his jeans pockets and a coat that zipped up the front. His face was scarred with acne.

"So clear you can see the sea," Detective Tender said.

Darla appeared behind Greer. She wore Big & Tall men's clothes. Darla looked nothing like the photos in the videos. The heart-shaped face had turned full-moon round. The blond eyelashes mascara dark. The eyes the same blue, but everything about Darla was a bit too shiny. She carried her bassoon. Detective Tender, who normally kept her cool, raised her hands in the air like she had scored a touchdown. Darla pushed past Detective Tender.

"Where is he?" Darla asked, halting for a second, momentarily thrown by the equipment. A film set can look like prehistoric monsters of a lesser kind with the space they take up. Darla did not like stepping over the equipment. She did not like it one bit. Neither did Greer, who leaned against the front door and tried to make himself inconspicuous.

Maureen came to see who had rung the doorbell. When she saw her daughter, she ran into Darla's arms, ignoring the advice Detective Tender had given her to keep emotions in check and steady. Advice Detective Tender had not been quite able to keep herself.

"Mom," Darla said, hugging her tightly.

"Oh, thank God. Oh, Darla . . ." Maureen said.

"Mom, where is *he*?" Darla asked.

"In the spare guest room."

As Darla moved for the stairs, Theo came out of the basement. Darla locked eyes with her husband and faltered. She held out her arms to keep Theo at bay. She was remembering their first kiss in his apartment. The broken umbrella on the rainy night he climbed into the taxi after her show. The day she told him she was pregnant and the boyish grin on his face. "Something good has to come out of COVID," Theo had said. And she had loved him so much. She still loved him but . . .

"You left me in the wood," she said.

"I looked for you."

"Not hard enough," she said, flinching. "Theo, did you hit me with the rock, too?"

"*No*, Darla."

"Just admit it, please?" Darla said. "So, I don't feel—so crazy."

"Maybe we're both crazy."

She shook her head. "I threw hot tea in your face. If I can admit that, *admit* you threw the fucking rock."

"I *didn't* throw a rock."

"Well, I don't know if I will ever trust you again. I don't know if I even want to."

"I'm sorry, Darla," Theo said. Theo wanted to take Darla home. He wanted to make things right between them. "You're my wife and this is not a conversation I think we should have in front of everyone."

"Where should we have it? The wood didn't work out so well for us."

Theo is momentarily stumped. "And our baby?"

"She's in me," Darla said. "She's mine. We're growing."

Daniel Jacobson appeared at the top of the landing then. Darla squinted. She watched him proceed slowly down the stairs. He had the strong features of someone who had lived a life that had included bartering, but what this Daniel had bartered, Darla could not say. When he came within arm's reach on the last stair, she met him there and touched his hands and his face. She counted his fingers. She tugged at the silver-fox hair. She poked at him in his old man's pajamas. Pajamas the father she remembered would never wear. Darla studied her father.

"Where have you been, Darla?" Daniel Jacobson asked. He hadn't seen her in over twenty years. Now she was a woman. There could be no connection because he could no longer connect the dots.

"Niagara Falls," Darla said and smiled.

"Everyone's been looking for you, Darla!" Theo shouted.

Detective Tender went over and put a hand on Theo's.

"What Theo means is that we've all been worried about you," Maureen said soothingly to her daughter.

"I've been worried about me too," Darla said.

Darla covered her ears. Detective Tender put a finger to her mouth. *Silence.* She sensed that Darla was tired of the questions, but Darla could feel a headache hovering. Darla turned to her father again.

"Dad?" Darla said, hands still covering her ears.

"Yes, Darla?"

"You loved us?"

"Yes . . . Darla."

"But not enough to stay?"

Daniel Jacobson sat on the bottom stair. And said nothing.

"Is something wrong with me, with us?" Darla stood over him.

"Wrong, no. I wouldn't say wrong."

"Tell me, you are here for good?"

Daniel was quiet.

"Darla," Detective Tender said, wishing Daniel would say something comforting. "I'm Detective Tender. I've been helping your mother and father. And young lady, I just want to say it's a pleasure to finally meet you in person."

Darla turned to Detective Tender as if seeing her for the first time. "Fuck off. This is a family moment," Darla said. "Tell me you're going to stay, Dad."

"I'm glad you came back, Darla. Home," Daniel said. "But I couldn't if I wanted to. And I don't want to."

"What are you, Dad?" Darla asked.

"I'm an arborist," Daniel said.

Darla smiled sadly. "You still love nature?"

"Nature still loves me."

"Do they have nice trees where you live?"

"Well, I'd say oak trees are most prevalent. You have your scarlet and your pine and red, white, water oaks. There's sweetgums and maples and hickories. And, of course, there are the trees that flower. . . ."

Darla shut her eyes. "I have a headache."

Darla knelt beside her father. She opened the bassoon case. She assembled and disassembled her instrument, saying the parts out loud. She fumbled through the intro to Hildegard von Bingen's "Canticles of Ecstasy," but the music did not ring right in her ears. So she stopped. Darla remembered Dexter Gordon's music playing when she was a little girl and her parents listening to jazz and going to Lincoln Center and jazz concerts. She picked up the bassoon again and played her own rendition of Dexter Gordon's "Scared to Be Alone," which was flawed and imperfect and the only answer she had right now for everything that had happened. Everything in her heart.

JUST AS easily as Nadine had dropped into unconsciousness, she opened her eyes during a brain imaging test and knew the worst was over. She had been in the hospital five weeks. More than thirty-five days. Half that time spent in a coma that lingered after they took her off the ventilator and sedatives. Two days later she was responding to stimuli, moving her fingers and toes, and turning her head. Three days later she said in a voice as hoarse as a frog's, "Xavier? Irvin?" That same afternoon, they put the phone to her ear for a three-way. And she repeated, "Xavier? Irvin?" These were the only two words she said. Four days later, she spoke in complete sentences. "When can I go home?" Five days later, she sat up in bed and asked them to remove the catheter. With the nurse's help, she walked to the bathroom and sat down on the toilet. Six days later, she was on a Zoom with her husband and son. She could not wait to be released. She remembered that she was preparing to be sent home the first time and then she had begun having trouble breathing.

"Are you keeping up your grades?" Nadine said.

Xavier was thrown for a minute. He was thinking that his mother's skin looked gray. That the liquid diet had resulted in a drastic loss of weight.

"Son," Irvin said to Xavier from their apartment. This was one day Irvin would not go to work. "Your mother's talking to you. Answer your mother."

"Yes, Mom. . . . My grades are dope."

Nadine touched the screen and blew Xavier and Irvin kisses. She moved in close, so close she blurred the screen, took up all the space. She wanted to see how life had altered Xavier in her absence. "Did you grow?"

"No."

"He grew," Irvin confirmed.

"Maybe a little," Xavier said.

"Something's different," Nadine said.

"We're in COVID, Mama," Xavier said. "Everything's different."

Irvin looked at his son. He knew Kimi was going over to Julian's apartment. And hanging out with Xavier. "The important thing, Nadine, is that you're back with us. And coming home soon."

Nadine reclined in the hospital chair. She never talked about her previous life as a professional dancer to Xavier. She could not stand the sight of her limber dancing self. Though she snuck off pre-COVID to see Misty Copeland's performances at the American Ballet Theatre, eschewing Julian's invite to join him and members of their old Harlem School of Dance troupe, not wanting to reckon with the complex mixture of joy and sorrow and pride and disbelief and envy and what-if-it-ness in the presence of loved ones or friends. Nadine had a family, but she shouldered her disappointments and regrets alone. But those regrets made her human.

"And your dreams?" Nadine said, looking at her only son. "What about them? Have they grown?"

The Five Amigos see one another for the first time in living color since COVID put them in lockdown and ended school as they knew it. Xavier's mother is home, released from the hospital, and Diji Tersoo, father to Bayo Tersoo, Xavier's best friend, drives the amigos to Fort Greene in his yellow taxi cab. The friends arrive bearing the universal gift of food as a homecoming, a welcoming. Nadine Curtis has been to the brink and now she is back. Now it is time to heal and eat well.

Ifeoma, Bayo's mother, has prepared ogbono soup with fish and pounded yams. After California, Georgia has the second-largest Nigerian population in America. Her youngest sister attends Spelman College in Atlanta. Sometimes you can taste Nigeria in Georgia and Georgia in Nigeria. It is Ifeoma's hope that her Igbo meal will give Nadine loving spoonfuls of coastal Georgia and southwest Nigeria, where Ifeoma was born.

Lian Ming's parents send scallion noodles and shrimp and pork dumplings to eat or freeze later and special sticky rice in lotus leaves. Tian and Yuechen Ming own a laundromat and dry-cleaning business where Ridgewood abuts Bushwick. Their dry-cleaning business has come to a standstill. The laundry business is open until nine because there are not enough machines in the nearby rentals and co-ops to meet demand.

Selim's parents, Fatima and Ziki Habib, professors at Long Island University, have sent an assortment of Middle Eastern dishes from their biweekly visits to Atlantic Avenue: kibbeh, falafel, hummus, baba ghanoush, spinach, chickpea and walnut salad, tabouleh, lamb pizza, grapes, olives, pita and honey cakes from Bedouin Tent, Damascus Bakery, and Sahadi's, respectively.

Veer Mehra's parents send kale pagodas, Tandoori ghost chicken, vegetable and jackfruit biryani, butter naan bread, and gulab jamun for dessert. They have added paneer Nizami, a cottage cheese with nuts, for they remembered that at Parents' Night the previous autumn, Nadine and Irvin ate several helpings of this dish.

Now that the sun is out and the days are long, the parents of the Five Amigos have agreed that their children should pod during the summer. Time outdoors, weather permitting, is better than losing their minds. It is Sunday and the Five Amigos will go to Fort Greene

Park for an afternoon picnic. Irvin has assumed responsibility for delivering Xavier's friends to their respective neighborhoods, Morningside Heights, Upper East Side, Ridgewood, and Bay Ridge, between seven and nine P.M. For a moment, when Xavier sees the generous trays of food, which he helps his father carry into their apartment building—no one is comfortable letting people enter their homes just yet—Xavier thinks of *A Raisin in the Sun* and Ruth always trying to convince her family to finish their eggs. He received an A− on his paper, and in the weeks since, the play has stayed with him. He wishes he had been able to discuss *A Raisin in the Sun* at the dinner table with Nadine and Irvin Curtis. He might have said some things differently. Been kinder in his analysis.

Despite all the homemade food, Xavier and his friends put in a special picnic request for Chick-fil-A, though none of them are down with the politics. They order on the Chick-fil-A app and Xavier convinces Irvin that it's cool to let them pick up the food at the Chick-fil-A on Atlantic Avenue. They are ambling down the street with Irvin waiting for them to get out of sight when Pinkeye pulls up in a car with a group of boys and climbs out. For a moment, Irvin, who is still on the curb, thinks, *Oh shit.* But Pinkeye holds up a bag of Katz's pastrami. "For your moms," Pinkeye says. And then he's back in the car and on his way. Xavier and Pinkeye are moving now, perhaps always, in different directions, though in a few days, they will move in the same direction at Barclays Center. Kimi joins the Five Amigos in Fort Greene Park, and Veer, Bayo, and Selim all turn to Xavier.

"She's your cousin?" Veer asks.

"No," Xavier says, taking Kimi's hand.

Kimi sits down and joins them on the grass. She does her best not to give Lian the stink-eye. The boys have wolfed down their Chick-fil-A, but Lian has an untouched order of waffle fries, which she slides Kimi's way.

"Like some?"

"Sure," Kimi says, pulling out her chemistry book and placing it on top of her knapsack. "Deliver me from chemistry!"

The Five Amigos all lean in.

*

We have the same gynecologist, so of course we will see each other. Our doctor has known us since we were teenagers headed to college and we came in for our first Pap smears. It is the following morning after we returned home and Ruby doesn't know that we're in the city. It is the morning after we said goodbye to Greer and gave Greer the remainder of the money from our bassoon case. And acne medication. Our return has not been announced to the press. Now we are in the waiting room sitting talking to Mom while Dad picks up different magazines and puts them down again. And we are off-balance anyway, but when Ruby comes out of the examination room into the waiting area, for a moment we think Ruby's come for our exam, don't we, baby? We think this, but we see Katsumi and he is grinning ear to ear and he is so proud and he is talking to his parents in Japanese on the phone. And we understand enough to know the moment is multifaceted. And we cheat time, Darla and Ruby. We embrace and cry out like we did when we were childhood friends at the end of summer, when we'd grown and wanted to compare our heights and our adventures and we were returning new people, the same but new. Older, wiser, all those things. We see Ruby taking in our father. And we think, for a moment, this is like it once was when our worlds were intact. No death. No loss. A nurse appears and reminds us that we are next and that a maximum of four patients are allowed in the waiting room at one time (not including the receptionist). We notice Mom glide over to the receptionist's desk and grab her cell phone because she is sneaking photos of us on the sly.

And then Dad, or the man who once was Dad, puts down the

National Geographic magazine with Great Places to Get Lost and comes over and takes Ruby by both shoulders.

"Ruby," Dad says, "Maureen tells me your mother made it?"

Ruby hesitates. "She did."

"All in one piece?"

"You would have to ask her that for yourself," Ruby says and shifts. Dad was once her favorite of our parents. Now it is like seeing a ghost. And we don't believe in ghosts, do we, Ruby? We know this. We feel this. Just like we know that when we were girls, we never thought we'd be twenty or thirty or forty. We preferred men to women but the road is shorter.

"My mom," Ruby says, "started losing pigment shortly after the towers fell. But I think the bookstore helps. Every time she gets a spot, she finds a rare book."

Daniel smiles, deeply satisfied by Ruby's answer. "We mend by any means necessary."

"The doctor is ready for you, Mrs. Jacobson," the nurse says.

But we don't go in because Ruby holds up a finger.

"Explain yourself."

"I can't," we say.

"Try. Darla."

"Come by the house," we say. But we feel the icicles building a wall between Ruby and us. A glacier.

"I'm afraid that's not feasible right now," Ruby says.

"Aren't you happy to see me?" we ask Ruby.

"Happy to see you?" Ruby says. "Darla, I'm relieved you're not dead. That's the first thing you think when something like this happens. You think it and then you try to put it out of your mind. *Of course I'm happy to see you.*"

Maureen comes over and takes Ruby aside. "Go easy on Darla, all things considered."

"I'm not coming at Darla hard, Maureen. I'm just trying to make sense of everything while we're all here."

"Yes," Maureen says. "But now is not the time."

"I know you're the mother lioness. But you are not the only mother in this room now. We're both going to be mothers and we're not going to get everything right, but something about this feels so wrong."

"Ruby, I shouldn't have used your name," we blurt out.

"Were you hurt?" Ruby asks.

"A head injury." We nod.

"So it's true. You had a concussion?"

"Yes, I think I did. I was scared and I couldn't remember if Theo had hit me in the head with a rock and I wasn't sure . . . if I wanted to come home."

"Jesus," Ruby says.

"Theo will never admit it, Ruby. I'll never know. And that's the worst part of this."

"That's shitty. That's horrible. You should press charges."

"I'm considering it," we say with conviction. "I will."

"So, help me out here. When did my name come into this, Darla?"

"On the spur of the moment. Your name came to mind."

"And you took it. Just like that?"

"I didn't think you would mind." We can never tell Ruby that we have tried her name on for size before. When we were young. And it fit us well.

"Why not some *made-up* name? It took a long time to get comfortable in my own skin, with who I am—with my *whole* name."

"I get that," we assure Ruby.

"Then why would you go and appropriate half of it?"

Katsumi finishes his phone call. He's ecstatic. Darla hugs him before he can speak. "Congratulations, Katsumi."

Katsumi looks at Ruby over Darla's shoulder and says, "Did you know?"

Ruby shakes her head. "I had no idea."

Maureen says, "Well, you might have known if you hadn't kicked us out of the restaurant."

"Are you okay?" Katsumi asks Darla. "Where have you been?"

"I don't want to talk about it," we say finally. "Ruby can explain everything."

"Not everything."

Katsumi whistles. "I'd love to hear your father-in-law's response if the state's picking up the search and rescue expense."

"You can't put a price on a human life," Maureen says.

"Depends on the human life," Ruby says.

"I don't like the implication," Maureen says. "Our family has been very good to you."

"Wait a minute now," Ruby says, bristling. "How were you so good to me? I wasn't exactly a pauper coming for handouts to your house."

Maureen rubs her hands down the side of her dress, like she is pressing something away. Her hands an iron. "I hired black and Latina dermatologists in my practice because of *you*. I looked at those women and I saw you. My daughter's best friend, whom I have loved like my own flesh and blood. I hired minority doctors because of what your friendship meant."

"I don't think that's the right tack, Mom," we say miserably.

"Did those women attend medical school?" Ruby says, looking at Maureen now.

"Of course."

"Did they get good grades and pass their medical exams?"

"With flying colors. I wouldn't have considered them other-wise."

"Then you didn't do it for me. They earned the right to be in your fucking practice."

We don't like the arguing and we don't want Ruby talking about our mother. "Ruby, don't cuss my mother."

"Oh please. You cussed your mother all the time when we were growing up."

"Maureen," Daniel interrupts. "Let the girls handle this."

"The girls?" Maureen says and laughs. "Daniel, they haven't been girls since the early two-thousands at least."

Ruby agrees. "That's the first honest thing someone has said since I stepped into this waiting room."

The nurse insists, though both she and the receptionist are enjoying the show, "Appointments are timed, Mrs. Jacobson."

Maureen says, "Come, they are calling us."

"This is where I get off, ladies. I won't go back there," Daniel Castaway says.

Maureen looks at Dad with contempt and relief. "By 'get off,' I assume you mean abandon us again?"

Dad hugs Mom and kisses us. "Please send me pictures when the baby is born."

We look down at our belly. "There is you and there is me."

"Do. Not. Go. After. Him," Maureen says. Dad disappears through the glass doors.

We turn to Ruby and Katsumi. "I tend to love men who don't love me back and I don't want to be that girl. I won't be that girl."

"None of us want to be that girl, Darla. Sometimes it's just a rite of passage. That we, I don't know, passage out of, if we're lucky or smart enough, fast."

"Please tell me how to make it right. Please accept my apology. If you're in your first trimester our babies will be godsiblings."

"No, not necessarily," Ruby says, and covers her stomach instinctively.

This makes us sad. We grab Ruby's arm. "What do you mean?"

"Darla, if I had disappeared like you did, I don't know that the police or the media or anyone would have exerted the same amount of energy looking for me."

"That's *not* my fault."

"No, but it's your privilege."

"You're privileged too, Ruby," we say, turning to Katsumi. "We all are."

"My uncle used to say I was a member of the landed gentry. But it's not the gentry that matters. I won't have my baby living in your baby's shadow. Even now, our babies don't have the same odds. And they haven't even come into this world yet. I go into a delivery room and there's a chance me or my baby might not make it out. So our privilege is real but different."

"Ruby—"

"I love you, Darla," Ruby cuts us off with a brisk hug. "And I'm glad you made it home safely. Please take care of yourself. And I'll try to do the same here. Timeout."

For exercise and so she can cool down, Ruby and Katsumi walk from their doctor's appointment and stroll through Union Square Park. It is Monday and the greenmarket, with its spring and summer produce and vendors, is a welcome sight. A reminder that New York is a city that keeps going, despite all the odds. They walk hand in hand, stopping to admire the assorted greens and apples and vegetables. Ruby eyes a young cook putting together a food demonstration. "Look," she whispers to Katsumi, her hands resting on purple beets, the Gandhi statue her backdrop. "That was me once."

That same morning, before Darla's appointment with the ob-gyn, there is a final video, short and sweet, of Darla's face freshly cleaned and scrubbed, making eye contact with the camera. She wears old maternity clothes that Maureen has salvaged. "It's too much," Darla says, sitting awkwardly on the sofa between her mother and father, with Theo on the armchair next to them. "It's too much," Darla repeats. And she means it. Coming home has not been what she had hoped for or expected.

"Cut!" Detective Tender calls. "Check the gate."

"Checking the gate," the camera assistant says.

"We're done here. That's a wrap." Detective Tender motions for the efficient two-person crew to begin breaking down the set.

Theo, Maureen, and Daniel looked stunned. Maureen rises. "Wait. That's it?"

"You heard your daughter, Mrs. Jacobson. "If she says it's too much, we must take her at her word."

"But what do we do now?" Maureen says, half stepping in Darla's direction as Darla retreats to a bathroom.

Detective Tender checks her watch. "Doesn't she have an ob-gyn appointment at noon? A late breakfast? An early lunch? You've got options now."

"I'll look in on Darla," Theo volunteers.

"Mr. Harper, I don't think she'd appreciate the gesture, though, truly, I understand the sentiment. Your work, like mine, is done here," Detective Tender says. "How about I give you a ride to Brooklyn?"

Theo shrugs and says, "I know the way home."

Daniel stands up. "I could use a lift."

Detective Tender smiles. "It might be a nice gesture, considering that Mr. Harper won't be joining Darla for her appointment, if Mom and Dad took her there together?"

Detective Tender doesn't wait for Daniel to respond. She finds her purse, her packed luggage. She fights the temptation to rap on the bathroom door and say goodbye to Darla Jacobson, whom she has not spoken more than a sentence to since Darla walked in last night. Detective Tender holds her breath as Daniel goes over and raps on the bathroom door.

"Are you okay, Darla?" Daniel asks.

"Well," Maureen says, considering her long-lost husband. "That's something."

"He'll be in a different state by nightfall."

"How do we proceed from here?"

"Very slowly," Detective Tender says.

Daniel Jacobson climbs into a yellow cab on Fifth Avenue. He tells the taxi driver he's going to LaGuardia or JFK or Newark Airport. He's not sure of his destination because he plans to take the first flight he can get. But he would like to make a detour to Bedford Avenue to check out a bookstore called the Duke of Bedford. He will not step out of the car. It is enough to lower the window and see that the bookstore exists. That one person in those Twin Towers he knew firsthand still lives. And there she is: Frida Black ascending a ladder in the Duke of Bedford bookstore, adding a new book to the shelf. Daniel sees her stop and look through the bookstore window. Later Ruby will tell Frida Black about the waiting room encounter with Daniel Jacobson and that Daniel Jacobson asked after her. "I had a feeling, Ruby, that it was him. You can't tell me that man didn't embezzle money or something. Skulking around in his guilt."

"I surrender where the Jacobsons are concerned, Mom," Ruby says. "There's just no telling with them."

After her examination, Darla Jacobson is admitted to Columbia Presbyterian for further observation. Her blood pressure and sugar are sky high and she is diagnosed with acute temporary delirium brought on by exhaustion and dehydration and a head injury. The family releases a statement to the press asking that their privacy be respected and thanking everyone who has aided in their daughter's safe return home.

Theo, freshly showered and eye-dropped, arrives at his new client's brownstone and is pleasantly surprised to find Simon Pratt has beaten him there. He watches Simon offer the new client a box of bing cherries and Hungry Ghost coffee.

"How's Simon treating you?" Theo asks, half-jokingly, noting that the woman does not seem to fit with the décor of the house.

"Well, he was asking me about the house's life," the woman says.

Simon mouthed behind the client's back, *How are you? How are you really?*

"My wife's alive," Theo said aloud.

The client was not *the* client, but a neighbor showing the house for her neighbors who were waiting out COVID in Pacifica, California, and wondering how much their brownstone might fetch if they decided to stay out west.

The neighbor said, "I'm told this was once an SRO before the owners bought it and renovated. A boarding house for women."

"Well," Theo said, smiling, "we'd love a tour."

Immediately Theo could envision the house being updated with little touches here and there that he had admired in the Jacobsons' house. Everything seemed to fall into place for Theo as they moved through the parlor, the music room, the dining room, the kitchen, and up the spiral stairs. He felt his cell phone buzz and reached into his pocket to answer it. He was feeling relieved, not necessarily happy, but not rock-bottom down, either. More in his element. Theo wasn't sure he was up for a text from his dad, but when he stared at his cell phone, an image peered through him.

This is your forebear: The First Theo.
On the drive home, son, I had time to think about what you
     said.
During COVID, all things are forgiven? Love, Dad

Of course, Theo knows that all things can't be forgiven and it unnerves him to stare at this stranger that he has never known. He wishes his father had shown him this picture a long time ago, because the face looks nothing like the face of the old man he imagined in the woods. Theo thinks that he must have been hallucinating, for sure. If the tall, refined man in this picture could talk, what would he say? If he could tell Theo, his descendant, though now he cannot, would he say the body endures but so much, the body endures all measures of pain that the soul registers and resists? If he could, this First Theo, would he say how a body loves and aches and laughs and strains itself against the tide of all the things that would hurt it, how a body that's been hurt sometimes wants to hurt itself or someone who would dare to love it after it's been hurt, put a poultice or a heating pad on a festering sore, pulling out the infection burrowed deep within man woman original sin against a body? If he, the First Theo, could talk, *oh God now,* Theo thinks he might say one body isn't so different from another until it is, until someone decides or renders a body more or less, head shoulders knees and toes and fingers too and eyes and shin bone and neck and back and wrists and arms and elbows and hamstrings, examine them and they fetch a whole price though the price be made of parts of the body his body her body our body somebody now body why body whose body old body young body— no bodies.

Nadine Curtis has missed the routine and her students' affection. A speedy review will reveal if the substitute teacher was up to her standards. She cries when, via Zoom, students in her morning and afternoon chemistry classes hold up pictures of yellow roses. They were not allowed to send flowers or get well cards or treats during Nadine's hospital stay. For the first half of 2020, many people will continue to believe COVID is transmissible through surfaces. Nadine is moved by the images of roses, the synchronicity of her welcoming back. It is a good day, a long day. She will finish teaching at four-thirty but will work well into the evening, grading papers, checking in with families. Irvin has taken vacation days to keep an eye on Nadine.

"What do you want for dinner tonight, baby?" Irvin asks.

"I think I'll go with the biryani rice if you and Xayxay didn't eat all of it."

That evening after dinner, around eight, while putting a load of clothes in the wash, Nadine asks Xavier if he wants to retire the Cardi B T-shirt. Xavier has worn the T-shirt so much it is beginning to fray around the neck and arms. Xavier nods and tells Nadine that he probably should toss the T-shirt in the waste bin. In the hospital with nothing on her hands but time, Nadine had googled Cardi B and Nicki Minaj and Megan Thee Stallion. She thought these women were reincarnations of singers from her parents' era: Millie Jackson, Betty Davis, Tina Turner, Patti LaBelle and the Bluebelles. . . . She started to tell her son as much but caught herself. *We lose them when we lecture. We lose them when we judge.*

An hour later, after coming into his bedroom and finding Cornhusk curled up on his bed (Nadine and Irvin have agreed that while Julian is away, the tabby cat can stay with them), Xavier goes back into the laundry room and retrieves the Cardi B T-shirt. He doesn't have to wear the T-shirt every day, but it has gotten him this far through COVID. Xavier lays the T-shirt over the back of his desk chair, and when he looks at Cardi B's face, for a second he sees Kimi smiling back at him. Kimi, who will wake him up at three something the next morning when his phone blows up with texts from his other family, his amigos: Bayo, Selim, Lian Ming, and Veer:

Xavier, did you see it?
Bro, this is so evil.
What?
Minneapolis.
Did you see it?
Tell me this isn't happening?
Yeah, bro. Xavier will say:
I see it.

Acknowledgments

IN MARCH 2020, I had the pleasure of meeting Tom Stoppard in person for the first time. He asked me, "Are you working on another book?" Neither of us knew in the days and weeks to follow that a pandemic would take over the world. This novel was not the one I had planned to write but the one that forced itself upon me with characters who took on lives of their own. Stoppard's question gave me the impetus needed to engage a new work during a time of great uncertainty. Margot Livesey, Monica West, and Deshawn Winslow were early readers of the short story "Daily Cleanse," which *Esquire* magazine went on to publish. I will be forever thankful to Alexis Washam for seeing the potential of the short story as a novel and to my editor, Parisa Ebrahimi, for picking up the baton and guiding me to the finish line with patience, skill, and grace. I extend my honest gratitude to David Ebershoff, who grasps my sense of humor on a gut level, and the entire Random House team. They are first-rate. My agent, Ellen Levine, had a fierce commitment to this novel from the first page on and worked steadfastly to see its vision fulfilled. I extend thanks to Audrey Crooks, Martha Wydysh, Nicole Robson, Michael Pintauro, and Trident Media Group. The Ernest Hemingway Foundation and the Pen/ Hemingway Awards Committee gave me time via a stipend to work on the novel as a 2022 Ucross fellow. I read "We Cook at Night" aloud there, which is always the beginning of a short story's real life. A nod to Tracey Kikut, Ben, Vickie, Melissa, Cindy, and all the staff who worked in front and behind the scenes to support the

Ucross fellows. A special shout-out to fellows Eric Glover, Guillermo Galindo (who sent a detailed list of musical compositions suited to the bassoon and hipped me to Hildegard von Bingen), David Ulin, Vesna Jovanic, Florrie Marshall, Meghan Kenny, Mikayla Patton, and Jane Schiffhauer. I still remember visiting the Brinton Museum with Jane and Mikayla.

Evelyn Porter, my mother, has always supported my writing and creativity. I love her and thank her along with my siblings: Ronald, Michael, and Jackie. And my daughters, Gabriela and Nuala Mernin. We couldn't always look forward during COVID, so we often peeked back, and I am especially fortunate to have good childhood friends: Michelle Owens, Bridget Battle, Gale Mitchell, Tony Osborne, and Evan Smith. I hope another childhood friend, Stephanie Brown, and my niece Tammy Middleton will smile when they see the homage to Prince, for I do not know two fans who loved him more. I would like to thank my Iowa family, Deshawn Winslow, who cheered me on when I wanted to stop, Mia Bailey, and Monica West. Will Shih, Claire Lombardo, Magogodi Makhene, JM Holmes, Sasha Khmelnik, Garth Greenwell, Dawnie Walton, and Paul Harding (with whom it's always a pleasure to riff) and Robin and Kim Christianson. Thank you, my dear friend Drew Reed, Heather Gillespie, Carolann Spence, Chris Llewyn, Cass Medley, Charlie Schneider, Mateo Askaripour, Caoilinn Hughes, Tim Cockey, Matt Nemeth, Emily Ragsdale, Jimmy Ma, Allen Steinberg, Elisa Seeger, Shari Axelrod, Kelli Souder, Ruth Wyatt , Jonathan and Mari Wagg, Teresa Zak and Jeremy Pace, Dave Darraugh, Jo Duer, and beloved friend and foodie Crystal Beauchamp, with whom I enjoyed meals in Japan Village in Industrial City and Little Tokyo in the East Village and shared recipes during much of COVID.

I have been to Japan but could not travel there during the pandemic and would like to thank Sensei Rika Kobayashi, Flavio Shigeru Yamashita, Beatrice Bailey, Charles Fontana, Michael Fox,

Andrew Mason, Sensei Ty Heineken, Bridget Battle, Tony Osborne, and Liz Lazarus for answering my questions and enriching my research.

I would like to thank chefs Jessica Mullice, Joe Brancaccio, Gregory Tetaud, Louis B., and the waiters who put up with annoying questions or shared their knowledge of cooking and working in restaurants and let me sit at the bar or table without interruption to take notes, write, people watch, and learn. Thank you to the staff at Kuraichi Brooklyn and Windsor Liquors in Windsor Terrace for answering my queries about sake and wine.

I would like to thank Ann Caplan for fielding my questions about high school curricula. And Alice Kaplan whom I met after the novel was written but respect much. I had the good fortune to study with playwright Adrienne Kennedy as an undergrad at NYU for a semester. Indeed, everything comes full circle. She took great care to show us the brilliance of *A Raisin in the Sun*. Stefanie, Nick, and Patrick at Windsor Terrace Books; Maryse Duvalsaint; Ron Carpenter; Jeff Klein; Giacomo Noto; Rita Taryan; Ed Kelley; Doug Proscia; Maria Sandomenico; and, because no one can underestimate the value of pets during COVID, my dog, Douglas.

Last but not least, thank you to Marty Molitoris of Alpine Adventures for tips on upstate hiking. Tom Fontana fielded countless questions and gave great answers. Detective Wendell Stradford was equally generous with his knowledge about police investigations.

List of Illustrations

Page 24: Greenaway, Andrew, *Teenager in the Cardi B T-Shirt*, commissioned painting, 2023.

Page 43: Richbourg, Gailliard, *Demonstrates the use of a Bell Rack, used by Slave Owners to guard a Runaway Slave, originally topped by a bell, which rang when the runaway would attempt to leave*, Mobile, Alabama, 1936, Universal History Collection/ Getty Images.

Page 47: laroslav_Brylov, *Turntable playing vinyl close up with needle with gray background*, 2015, iStock by Getty Images.

Page 73: Retrieved from Walter A. Dyer's "The Great Hound of Ireland," Mr. McAleenan's son in the costume of an Ancient Irish master of the hunt, with the wolfhound Finn McCumhal, *Country Life*, February 1920, Hathitrust Digital Collection, University of Pennsylvania.

Page 86: Dance Theatre of Harlem in Carre, rehearsal date July 24, 1971, BNA Photographic, Alamy Stock Photo.

Page 93: Brigitte Bardot (1934–). French film actress. With Jean-Louis Trintignant in *And God Created Woman*, directed by Roger Vadim, 1956, Granger Historical Picture Archive.

Page 125: MCHE Lee, *White Table with Black Chairs*, October 2020, Unsplash.

Page 143: Pattison, Hugh Lee, daguerreotype, *Oldest Known Photo of Niagara Falls*, 1840, Robin Library Special Collections, Newcastle University.

Page 146: Weems, Carrie Mae, photograph, Kitchen Sink Series, 1990, John Shaiman Gallery, New York.

Page 158: Hood, Sam, *Two Different men, one bearing the compulsory mask, brought in to combat the epidemic of flu of 1919*, State Library of New South Wales.

Page 197: Mirrorpix, *Gambling in the Launderette*, 1969, Getty Images.

Page 209: *Black Brazilian Bride and Japanese Husband*, circa 1920, the Historical Museum of Japanese Immigration in Brazil.

Page 250: *African American Children Playing on the Sidewalk in Chicago*, 1941, Everett Historical Collection/Alamy Stock Photo.

Page 257: Library of Congress, Prints & Photographs Division, Winold Reiss Collection [Reproduction number e.g., LC-USZ62-123456].

Page 299: Russian Bassoon (Bass Horn) MET Mus453A5 Russian Bassoon (Bass Horn) MET Mus453A5 /504920 Cultural Archive/Alamy Stock Photo.

Page 331: Harper, Alvan S., 1847–1911. *Man in a satin-faced coat, holding a cane.* 1890 (circa), State Archives of Florida, Florida Memory.

About the Author

REGINA PORTER is an award-winning playwright and author of *The Travelers,* which was a finalist for the PEN/Hemingway Award for Debut Novel and longlisted for the Orwell Prize for political fiction. A graduate of the MFA fiction program at the Iowa Writers' Workshop, she has been published in the *Harvard Review, Tin House, The Virginia Quarterly Review,* and the *Oxford American.*